# Readers love the Vigilante series by TERE MICHAELS

## *Who Knows the Storm*

"A really fun start to a series with two smoking hot guys and a teenage son that I adored."

—Love Bytes

"This book is 5 stars all the way. That ending was seriously nail biting! It was a bit of a cliffhanger and I cannot wait to read the next book in the Vigilante series."

—The TBR Pile

"*Who Knows the Storm* is a great, fast-paced action/thriller with a strong focus on family. Of the sacrifices we make for those we love. Of finding love ourselves."

—The Boys in Our Books

## *Who Knows the Dark*

"I love the world the author created in this series. We get the familiarity of places we know well, like New York City. Everything is so vastly different, but still recognizable. The dystopian setting is amazing to read. The author's descriptions of the destruction caused by the storms are so clear you can actually see ruins in your head."

—The Novel Approach

By TERE MICHAELS

Groomzilla
Groomzilla & Groomzilla Does Vegas Anthology
The Heir Apparent
One Holiday Ever After
One Night Ever After

FAITH, LOVE, & DEVOTION
Faith & Fidelity
Love & Loyalty
Duty & Devotion
Cherish & Blessed
Truth & Tenderness
Forever & Ever

THE VIGILANTE
Who Knows the Storm
Who Knows the Dark
Who Knows the Moonlight

Published by DREAMSPINNER PRESS
www.dreamspinnerpress.com

# WHO KNOWS THE MOONLIGHT

## TERE MICHAELS

Published by
DREAMSPINNER PRESS

5032 Capital Circle SW, Suite 2, PMB# 279, Tallahassee, FL 32305-7886  USA
www.dreamspinnerpress.com

Who Knows the Moonlight
© 2021 Tere Michaels

Cover Art
© 2021 L.C. Chase
http://www.lcchase.com
Cover content is for illustrative purposes only and any person depicted on the cover is a model.

Digital ISBN: 978-1-63216-786-6
Trade Paperback ISBN: 978-1-63216-785-9
Trade Paperback published February 2021
v. 1.0

Printed in the United States of America
∞
This paper meets the requirements of
ANSI/NISO Z39.48-1992 (Permanence of Paper).

# DEDICATION

To all the readers who have waited patiently for the next installment of the Vigilante—thank you. Every time you asked, you pushed me closer to finishing. And here we are! Couldn't have done it without you!

"A dreamer is one who can only find his way by moonlight, and his punishment is that he sees the dawn before the rest of the world."

—Oscar Wilde

"Revenge is an act of passion; vengeance of justice. Injuries are revenged; crimes are avenged."

—Samuel Johnson

"Love is our true destiny. We do not find the meaning of life by ourselves alone— we find it with another."

—Thomas Merton

# PROLOGUE

*Before*

"THE STORMS happened, Nox. I had nothing to do with that," Carson said, his slick, used-car-salesman tone at odds with his expensive suit and haircut. "Things were moving so quickly...."

Nox laughed, bitter and cold. "Moving so—I realize it was seventeen years ago, but I remember it very fucking clearly. You were away for months. You left Mom in that disgusting asylum. You left me at the house." His gaze narrowed as the memories of those days and the sheer, unadulterated terror of meeting Jenny and the men trying to kill them washed over him. "You sent Jenny to kill Mom and me. Don't you try to deny it."

It was a calculated move. His trust of Rachel was tenuous, but the stark reality resonated inside him—he trusted her a thousand times more than his father.

Carson's eyes widened, and his body stiffened at the accusation.

"Jenny? My assistant wouldn't do anything like that," he said, recovering quickly. "She died on the ferry, Nox. Poor girl."

"Really? You didn't know?" Nox tipped his head to one side, ignoring his vulnerable position, pinned to the bed by his injuries and at the mercy of a man who hadn't told him a lick of truth in possibly his entire damn life. "She came to Morningside to kill Mom, but she was already dead." His heart fluttered, but his voice stayed calm. "Then she tried to kill me, but I managed to buy her off to leave me there." Nox watched his father with as much focus as he could muster, very aware of every bead of sweat creeping along Carson's hairline. "This was all before her tragic death."

When he finished speaking, the room was utterly silent. He felt every breath controlled in his lungs, the sparks of pain from his wounds a flicker compared to the growing rage.

"She—I mean, I'm shocked," Carson said faintly. Finally. "Jenny was such a sweet young girl...."

"Who did your dirty work, compiling blackmail material on government officials." Nox finished Carson's sentence and watched him go pale. "I assume she killed for you as well. I saw her in action—getting rid of whatever henchmen were sent along. At least four." In a conversational tone, the words fell out of Nox's mouth. "Did you send them as well? Roy Grimes, the guys at the rendezvous point... I'm just curious, Dad."

"So you think you know everything," Carson Boyet said, leaning his hands on the small table at the end of the bed. "You think you have all the answers."

Nox shrugged and a twinge of pain shot down his spine. He didn't even flinch. "I know enough."

His father's fingers tightened on the edge of the table, going white with tension.

"You don't know anything."

"Is this where you tell me the whole sinister plan? I assume it'll be quite justified, after which you'll blow my head off or dump me in a pit of alligators."

With every poke, Carson's expression grew angrier.

"I kept you and your little brother alive, all this time," Carson exploded. "I let you play fucking superhero on the streets. I let you interrupt my business. You should be dead about a thousand times over, and don't you ever forget that."

Nox couldn't hide his derision. "Fuck you. You should have killed me," he snapped, rage coursing through him.

"Oh really? I should have? Then what would have happened to the kid, huh? You think I was going to waltz in and raise Natalie's bastard?"

Jerking his torso off the bed, Nox reached for his father with both hands, fingers itching to close around his throat, to snap his neck like he had Mr. White's. He bit his tongue as the anger waged war with the ravages of his weakened state.

"I protected you," Carson spat, not even flinching as Nox wrenched his body in a vain attempt to get at him. "I'm protecting you now. The Vigilante is dead, your friends are free, and I scraped you off the fucking pavement. You don't want to be grateful? Fine. I'll dump you on the street and let the District cops throw you in jail. I'm thinking some of the inmates might be interested in learning who you are."

With that, Carson shoved the table to the floor. The clatter echoed as he stormed to the door, wrenched it open, and left. In the space of the door going from open to closed, Nox caught sight of Antonio laughing.

Nox fell back against the pillows and twisted furiously against the tangle of the bedclothes.

No one came to check on him—not Kyle, not Antonio or the doctor. His IV dried up, and his head began to pound with the withdrawal from whatever they had been injecting into his line. The pain, exacerbated by his encounter with his father—Jesus, his father—wrecked his ability to think about or deal with what had transpired. Time seemed to drag on until he felt the burning pain of fever, the swollen tongue filling his dry mouth.

In the twilight of his pain and delirium, he sank into his too few memories of Cade and tried to catch and hold on to them as they slipped through his fingers. He felt Cade in his arms, the pressure of his head against Nox's shoulder, the simple peace Nox gained from touching him. Maybe that was the dream and this was purgatory, an endless wheel of paranoia and darkness where respite came in the form of a tease and a man with blue eyes.

Nox couldn't quite grasp what was going on—the rattle of the metal, and then he was moving, the bed was moving, released from its mooring and banging against doorjambs and walls he could see as his eyes flickered open. In his hazy vision, he could make out Dr. Khanna at his side. When he tried to speak, nothing came out.

"You're being moved," Dr. Khanna said, and that was when Nox became aware of a thudding noise, a growling whine filling the air. Something—machinery perhaps.

Then the smell overwhelmed him.

The white walls and lighting gave way to darkness. The dank smell of rot and decay hit his nose and irritated his gag reflex.

"Turn on a flashlight," the doctor snapped. Nox heard fumbling, cursing, and then a bright flash of light trained over his head revealed crumbling pink plaster and peeling walls.

Another nightmare. He knew this place.

The wheels of the bed ground through something, their forward movement slowed as the men pushing tried to get it free. The sounds grew louder, forming into a memory for Nox.

Construction equipment.

A shove and the bed came free, and they started moving down the hallway again. At the corner, they pivoted, sending Nox into inky darkness.

He waited for lights, for Dr. Khanna to issue another terse order, but nothing came. The light moved—away from him, away from the bed. No voices save for the whispered words before the door slammed shut.

"Don't bother screaming."

THE OFFICERS in the room ranged in age from twenty-five to fifty, judging by the oldest man's military-cut gray hair. They were all wearing the same expression of neutral authority, including the only one allowed a seat.

It was Detective Francis, the man who had arrested Sam and charged him with being the bomber.

The man's smirky grin confused Cade, even as his body rejected any attempts to move it from the doorway. Francis tipped back his chair and gestured with aplomb at the empty seat. He couldn't have looked more out of place if he'd been wearing full Joker makeup.

"How are you doing, Mr. Creel?" he asked.

Someone pushed Cade from behind, and he stumbled into the room.

"I...."

"Maybe some coffee would help. How about a blanket?" He snapped his fingers at the youngest of the officers, and the flicker of a snarl alerted Cade to what had been apparent when last they'd met— everyone thought Detective Francis was a piece of shit.

Cade dropped into the chair closest to LJ and shivered a little as the cool air of the room mixed uncomfortably with his wet, dirty clothing.

"Agent Allard was telling me about your adventures," Francis said, rubbing two fingers on the table in ever-widening circles. "And what you're trying to do."

This didn't sound like the plan—LJ was grinning, Rachel sitting there with her lips pursed, and Cade had no idea what to say or do. The only things he had at this moment were a host of acting skills and a desperate need to stay alive.

"How lucky you're the person we met today," Cade said coolly. He glanced around, judgment plain on his face. "Interesting promotion."

Francis's smug face fell at that. "Change in leadership at the precinct—you know how it is. Politics."

Someone coughed, another person cleared his throat, and the snarl came back to the policeman's mouth.

"Of course," Cade said graciously as the young officer returned with a large cup of coffee and a blanket that matched Rachel's. "Maybe this is an even more fortuitous event than I thought."

Detective Francis opened his mouth to speak, then glanced over his shoulder at the silent assemblage.

"Get out, all of you," he snapped. None of the officers refused his order, though the pure contempt thrown his way was impossible to miss.

When the room was cleared and quiet, Cade tucked himself into the blanket and toyed with the steaming cup in his hand.

Rachel made a little gesture, her arm peeking out from behind the blanket, fingertips together as she tipped her head toward Francis.

"You think you can do something with our information, then?" Cade wrapped his hands around the coffee cup.

Francis laughed—a ha-ha-ha sound, fake and disingenuous. "I think I can turn you all over to the District police and get my job back. Orrrrr… I can turn you over to some friends and make a fucking fortune. Maybe enough to retire."

"Or we can arrange a third option—perhaps give everyone what they want in order to get what we want," Cade said casually.

LJ pointed to Cade. "Good idea, good idea."

Detective Francis let his gaze linger on each of them, as if trying to determine if they were telling him the truth. Cade suspected that, even if he'd once been an actual cop, those skills were long deteriorated, fallen to ruin and overrun by his selfish motivations. Satisfied they were going to help him get what he wanted, Francis nodded.

"So I bring you to the city, but maybe you get lost before you hit Central Booking," he said finally.

Cade tried to control his expression.

"Then we go to the house, we get the money," LJ added, drawing Francis's eyes to him. Dollar signs glowed over Francis's head.

"I want proof it's as much as you say."

LJ lit up like fucking Christmas.

"Bring me my laptop."


"LET'S GO," Francis said about two hours later, startling Cade out of the daydream where he wasn't cold and afraid and unable to breathe properly. He blinked himself back to full consciousness to find Rachel curled up in LJ's lap and Francis grinning maniacally from the doorway.

"Okay, sure." Cade got out of the chair with creaky legs and shaking hands, and his gaze met LJ's.

LJ smiled, a half grin that was probably 40 percent bullshit. Cade matched it with one of his own.

They could both pretend they felt secure about getting on a boat with a crooked cop.

As they walked through the building, the officers who bothered to glance up gave them nasty looks—and a few pitying, which didn't sit well in Cade's stomach. The cops clearly all expected the three of them to be floating in the waves before they touched the shore of the District.

"We're going to the house," Francis muttered when they reached the back door. His beady eyes alighted on Cade, greed dripping from his pores. "I get the money, and then I let you go. If you try anything...." The gun in view on his waist punctuated the threat.

Cade nodded slowly. "We don't have anything to gain by crossing you," he said, allowing his voice to take on a shaky timbre. The sound made Francis grin. "We need you."

Francis opened the door and waved them through. The wind rattled Cade as he stepped into the darkness.

THE TINY boat bobbing at the dock had clearly seen better days.

LJ—Rachel tucked tightly at his side—went first. The floodlights picked them up as they stumbled down some concrete stairs toward the dock. The cold bit into Cade's face as he watched LJ's broad back a few steps ahead.

Francis came up next to him, shoulder to shoulder in a weird intimacy that made Cade uncomfortable.

"You're a pretty boy," Francis muttered, his voice cutting through the wind. "Maybe you need a daddy when this is over...."

Cade swallowed down a rise of bile.

But he was an actor, a professional whore, and a man who could seduce open the wallet of anyone with a working dick.

"Maybe I do," Cade said, flashing Francis a sideways look with flirty eyes.

He didn't flinch when Francis licked his lips.

He could do this. He could do whatever it took to get to Nox.

# CHAPTER ONE

THE RAIN and wind rattled the small NYPD boat as they battled the waves toward the city. Cade held on to the railing with a death grip and struggled to stay in his seat, as the canopy and windshield did nothing to protect them from the elements. Water splattered through the open sides, and behind him, LJ and Rachel huddled down between the seats, more secure on the floor than trying to keep their balance. They'd been forced to leave their backpacks behind, which meant no weapons, none of Rachel's box cutters, and no laptop—all things they'd have to waste precious time replacing. He thought of LJ's fancy gizmo phone—their only way to contact Sam and the others—in the back of the Denali, which was who knew where.

All their plans and supplies, gone.

Francis piloted the boat through the waves with maniacal glee, and every bounce and violent shimmy delivered Cade's courage another blow.

Rushing him now wouldn't do much good—they still needed to get to the dock and get past the security that ruthlessly guarded the shores. With the raid coming soon and the city officials aware, he assumed it would be even harder to get through on their own. Once safely on the island, they'd lead him to Nox's house, disarm him, and....

And.

Somewhere in the city was Nox—or at least an answer to where Nox was—and he needed their help—all of them. The certainty that he was alive fired so deeply inside Cade he never questioned it for a moment.

If this was the madness of love, so be it.

"Fuck," Francis crowed, uselessly wiping at his eyes with his sleeve. Cade hated him with the intensity of a thousand suns. They hit a particularly hard wave, were airborne briefly, and then hit the water with the force of an explosion. For a second, Cade felt his body rise from the boat, and the force nearly threw him over the side.

Rage and fear rocked Cade as the boat skipped across the surface like an out-of-control stone. Only a little farther—maybe. Hopefully. He couldn't make out much in the swirl of the water and darkness, but the bright lights of the city blurred and flickered through the mist like a teasing beacon. Surely they must be close. It felt like they'd been hurtling through the wet darkness forever.

A horn sounded over the chaos of the storm, and Cade took a wet gulp of air. Another horn. Then another.

*Thank God.*

Francis brought the boat in close to the dock, and it banged slightly against the pylons as he threw a rope up to an orange-suited dockworker. Cade took a deep breath as best he could while his teeth rattled with fear and cold. Then he looked over at his brother and Rachel. They were slowly rising from the floor of the boat, clutching each other.

"Let's go," Francis said roughly. When Cade turned his head, he saw the gun pointed in his direction once again. "Up the ladder and don't try anything."

Cade nodded. On rubbery legs, he stumbled to the rope ladder thrown down to the boat's surface. Not exactly a normal docking experience, he thought absently as he grabbed the rough handholds with numb fingers.

He struggled to the top, his lungs protesting the cold air and wind, the icy water droplets and the exertion. By the time Cade made it to the top, the lack of oxygen made him light-headed.

Strong hands yanked him up the last few inches and tossed him to the side. Bright floodlights blinded him, and he brought one arm up to shield his eyes. There was no mistaking the barbed wire and shadows of men with automatic weapons crossing his field of vision.

No. They would not have made it here without Francis.

Behind him, he heard Francis cursing and bitching as he came up over the side.

"Get up," he snapped as he walked by and kicked Cade in the leg.

Cade struggled to his feet, then found LJ and Rachel behind him. They exchanged glances and resolute expressions, and Cade tried not to appear terrified. He hoped it was working.

As an almost military level of security surrounded them, Francis didn't seem concerned they'd make a break for it. He disappeared into a guard shack for a few minutes as Cade discreetly checked out the situation.

The dock seemed to be makeshift, erected for deliveries, not visitors. They didn't seem to be protecting anything—he could make out no buildings beyond the shack next to the fencing. He estimated they were closer to downtown than the District, which meant mobsters and shitty casinos and drugs, not just Dead Bolt.

Francis seemed very familiar with the scene; he exited the guard shack whistling, throwing a set of car keys into the air with the hand not holding the gun.

"We got ourselves a ride, kids."


SOAKED TO the bone, Cade, LJ, and Rachel squeezed into the back of the borrowed patrol car, and they sped through the city at a breakneck pace, as Francis drove the car the way he drove the boat.

Like a maniac.

Francis ran lights with the sirens blaring and blew past various roadblocks and checkpoints set up in the center of the district, flipping off the slicker-clad officers as he went by. Cade could see the increased police presence on the street, the lack of civilian cars or limos. The lights from the airport blinked in the distance, but Cade saw no planes land or take off in the entire time they wound their way uptown.

In fact, Cade didn't see a single person who wasn't a uniformed cop or private security walking or standing on the street. For a Saturday night, that was unheard of in the district, even during the harshest weather or one of the frequent bomb threats.

A sense of foreboding stabbed him in the gut.

Shivering, Rachel curled a little closer to Cade, still wrapped tightly in the wet blanket.

"I'm going to kill that fucking prick," she rasped, just loud enough for Cade to hear.

Cade shook his head.

"He stays alive," he muttered back. "We can use him for information."

She responded with a sneer and then turned back to LJ, who gave Cade a questioning look over the top of her head.

Cade's attention was pulled to outside the window. How did he end up in charge? This was Rachel's forte, not his. Maybe he drove the rescue train, but thinking on his feet and formulating plans of attack were so far outside his comfort zone it was an out of body experience.

They were almost to the house. His plan to use Francis to find Nox was 5 percent prayer and 95 percent making shit up as he went along. Subdue Francis, extract information. Rachel would calm down once he let her loose on the detective—she had a lot of pent-up rage, and he would probably wish he were dead soon enough.

Was that a plan?

Because the rub, the part that Cade tried to ignore as they sped through the city, was that there was no guarantee Francis knew anything about Nox.

*No. It's a sign, running into Francis at the port*. This self-talk, Cade knew, was a drop of fuel to add to his sparsely burning fire of hope.

Nox was alive, he repeated to himself, lips moving in the reflection of his face in the raindrop-stained window. *He's alive.* The Feds hadn't found a body. No body proved he was alive.

Clearing his throat, Cade called out directions to the Boyet house, which earned him a curious look from the detective in the rearview mirror. They'd fed him some bullshit about a safe house—hopefully it was just normal curiosity that they'd be so far uptown. No comment, however, just more reckless driving that set Cade's teeth on edge. Eventually the patrol car pulled into the large empty space at the opening of the block, as far as they could get before they had to go on foot.

Francis turned to face them through the bulletproof glass.

"Okay, pretty boy, you and me are taking a little walk," he said, part menacing and part oily predator.

Cade used every trick he'd ever learned at the Butterfly when dealing with a dangerous client—he let his body relax and tucked his blossoming fear away behind an implacable smile. "Sounds good. What about my companions, here?" Terror flickered through Cade's body. What if Francis decided LJ and Rachel weren't worth keeping alive?

"Oh, they're going to wait here for my partner to pick them up." Francis didn't provide more information than that bombshell. He unlocked the door and got out of the car.

"Fuck," Rachel muttered.

LJ managed to say, "What are we...?" before Francis and his ever-present gun opened the door on Cade's side.

"Out." He waved the piece at Cade. "Nice and slow, hands where I can seem them. Anyone makes a move I consider unnecessary and I will shoot you in the face."

Cade slid out of the police car, hands aloft. He moved slowly, deliberately, until he was standing. With his free hand, Francis yanked him away from the open door and slammed it with his foot.

"Later," he called to the car's remaining occupants as he shoved Cade toward Nox's house.


CADE FORCED himself to breathe through the growing panic, keeping the façade up as he took his first step forward. A flash of the night of the explosion at the Iron Butterfly caught him off-guard—the scent of blood, Billy dead on the floor, and Cade... not. He'd killed Billy in self-defense, but if the opportunity came now, could he do it again?

Every step over the torn-up and puddled street brought him closer to the house. To calm himself, he imagined Rachel freeing herself and LJ, them skulking in the shadows, tailing them to the front door.

It helped.

"Oh hey, one more thing," Francis said from behind him, his voice soft and casual. "I know exactly who you are."

Cade froze for a split second, then forced himself to relax. "We established that already. You recognized me, from the police station."

"When you got that kid released." Francis's tone was so light, so... friendly that Cade began to shake. "That judge you fucked called my boss, and my chance to break the bomber case went up in smoke."

"He didn't do it," he croaked out as Francis grabbed his shoulder and spun him around. "I was just helping a friend."

"Like Rachel Moon? Like your brother? The fucking Vigilante?" The last word was a whisper. "You really think I'm that stupid? I haven't kept myself alive this long without being attached to the right people, you stupid whore. I know exactly what's going on. There's some shit coming down on a federal level any day now, and I need to get the hell out of here with my pockets lined." He laughed, a nasty and oily sound that made Cade feel dirty. "You're not the only good actor around here, Cade."

Terror enveloped Cade. His brain started throwing out plans of attacking Francis, overriding the chances of disarming an asshole cop with a murderous bent. Chances of success—horribly slim. A stutter step back and Francis didn't move. He didn't see Cade as a threat.

"So, what happens now is we continue on our little walk. You tell me what you know, I decide if it's useful, and then...." Francis shrugged. "Then I make a decision. Either you take a ride with me to the station or I drop you off with some people I know who aren't as, uh... polite as I am."

The station sounded like a far better idea, given Francis's tone.

"We can still," Cade choked out, but Francis shook his head. "The money...."

"No. Sorry. You think I bought that little melodrama about accounts and hidden money? What? Like there was an ATM at this place you were taking me? You and your hayseed brother are full of shit." He waved the gun in Cade's face. "Move."

Mournful grief pushed down on Cade's shoulders. All for nothing—everything they'd done to find Nox would end with them in cells. Or worse. The Feds would be next, and if they knew what they'd done to Alec....

All for nothing.

This block—he remembered walking down it that first day, letter in his pocket from Mr. White. Just an errand, a simple task for a well-liked client. He didn't have any idea how his life was going to change. He didn't know he was walking into Nox's life and the turmoil that would follow.

It felt fitting it was going to end right here.

# CHAPTER TWO

NOX WALKED with halting steps down the pitch-black corridor of Morningside, barely illuminated with emergency lights dim on the walls, listening to the echo of his footsteps break up the silence. He knew there was something he had to do, someone he had to find, but every room he passed was empty.

A scent caught his attention. It was metallic and sharp and burned the inside of his nose—smoke and blood, twined together in a disgusting duet, drawing him closer even as he struggled to turn and run away.

But no. He kept walking, alert for any sound, for any indication of who he was looking for.

The walls crumbled as he walked by, his footsteps as triggering as an earthquake. Chunks of rotting plaster fell around him, increasing in size until the air was filled with choking dust.

He coughed the garbage out of his lungs, but every breath brought the stink of death at higher and higher concentrations, until his stomach rebelled violently.

Then he heard a baby cry.

Just a short, sharp scream, echoing against the walls and ceiling. But Nox knew that sound; it had haunted his sleep for so many years.

"Sam!" he choked out, the air thickening into a snowstorm of toxic debris. His boy was somewhere in the middle of this, lost and alone....

Nox's arms flailed against the mess, reaching out for something solid to hold onto. One, two, three swipes and he felt a grab at his wrist. He flexed his hand, but the fleeting touch didn't come back.

"Nox!" A shriek of pain ran through his brain. A woman's voice. No—a man's. No, no. A child. All of them, shrieking out his name in terror. "Nox!"

The mounting debris cemented Nox's legs. He struggled to move a step and then another, but no... no. He was trapped in quicksand as the plaster storm buried him alive. Air squeezed out of his lungs—a last breath, a choking sensation of a thousand tiny particles blocking air and light and life.

The last thing he heard was people screaming his name.

A FLICKER of light, just a tiny trickle. Heaven? Hellfire? Hallucination?

Somewhere between dream and death, Nox felt a needle pierce his bicep. The first blip of pain quickly became fire, raging painful fire, rushing through his blood in a heart-stopping wave. He went hot, then cold, muscles paralyzed as they revolted against the intrusion of whatever was now replacing every cell. Everything was so loud. He could taste the temperature of the air, feel the molecules making up the walls.

Nox had never felt so alive, even as his life force blinked closer and closer to nothing.

THE NEXT time Nox opened his eyes, he wanted to tear a hole in the ceiling and fly into the sky.

The second injection reduced him to a growling fury—hot, hard, trapped, angry.

*Escape.*

*Kill.*

*Consume.*

Every drop of blood Nox had ever spilled on the street bathed him as he lay there, He felt the heat and life force of every one of them, their screams and their fury. He swelled to be ten feet tall, then shrank down to a tiny speck, a molecule racing around the room. He would burst free, fly through the city, kill them all—the dealers and the rapists and the murderers. He would lay them all down, cut their throats, and clean the city of their filth once and for all.

Rachel came to him, smug smile and calculating gaze. Next to her stood Jenny, young but hard and dangerous in a way that made him back against the wall. A third person, shadowed in the corner, remained unclear in features, but the malevolence couldn't be ignored. Of his silent observers, that was the one to fear the most.

"Who are you?" he called, his voice barely a sound. "Do I know you?"

He tried to be brave, but as the figure moved closer, he shrank back, his heart beating as though it were a bomb, ready to explode.

Before the darkness consumed him again, he caught a glimpse of clever eyes and red hair.

EYELIDS FLICKERING, Nox stared into the darkness. Horrified, he realized it wasn't the absence of light. No, it was blood and it was moving. Reforming. Growing faces.

The people he didn't save.

The people still crushed beneath the wreckage of the Iron Butterfly.

His mother.

They stepped closer and closer to his bed, squelching footsteps and fetid breath. He struggled to get up, to run away from them, even as apologies fell from his lips.

"Ssssorry, sorry," he muttered, lips and tongue desert dry. He moved his head to one side and slid his body a few inches. The wave of pain knocked him out before he could fully appreciate that he wasn't tied down anymore.

SOMETIMES HE dreamed of happier things.

Sometimes he lay in Cade's arms, without the taint of danger or anger, listening to peaceful waves and feeling a rare breath of contentment. No place to go, no place to be, no sword of Damocles swaying over his head and whispering threats in his ear.

He felt a deep sense of relief, knowing Sam was safe—everyone was safe.

Those dreams didn't last long. They were ripped away without warning when another needle plunged into his arm.

SOMETIMES HE imagined his body made up of millions of pixilated bits, vibrating. He saw the tiny pieces shift and move, knitting together spots that were weak or missing. His wounds, his brain, his muscles, his skin. Moving and changing and growing and evolving.

AT SOME point—a day, a week, a thousand years—Nox woke up. Truly woke up, conscious of the dank floor beneath him and the cold rotting wall at his back. He was naked; he could feel the layers of filth and god-knows-what caked on his skin. His throat and tongue swelled with dry disuse.

He blinked until enough funk cleared from his eyes and he could see a figure standing in the doorway.

Carson.

His father, gaze full of manic attention, a hanky-covered hand against his nose.

He took the protective covering away for a second.

"Thank you," he said, weirdly pleased. "This was quite a helpful demonstration."

Nox's weakened hand shook with a desire to grab at him. No, don't leave me, he thought wildly. Don't leave me here.

Carson turned to go. "He's learned his lesson. Get him out of here, and for God's sake, clean him up."

The pronouncement was the last thing Nox heard before the door slammed again.

He hung his head and cried.

TWO MIDDLE-AGED men built like linebackers and wearing modified hazmat suits dragged Nox out of the room he'd been held in a few minutes later. Flashes of white hallways confused him; this wasn't Morningside.

They were quick and efficient. Nox was thrown into a white-tiled shower and scrubbed impersonally with long brushes—quite thoroughly. He spit out the faintly rusty water that soaked into his mouth, and he winced when they were rough on his genitals and face.

He shook the droplets out of his eyes as the water stopped. One of the men poked him with the tip of his boot.

"Can you walk?" the man asked, throwing a heavy towel at Nox's head.

Nox struggled to his feet, the edges of his vision going black as he swayed.

He wrapped the towel around himself as best he could, and his two jailers shoved him out the shower door.

The next hallway Nox walked down—still dripping wet, cold—looked nothing like where he'd been last. Neatly painted hospital white, overhead lights. Disorientation wracked his brain. Flashes of the degraded wing, the tiny room. The pain and anger rushed back.

Fear.

His legs stopped working suddenly, and his knees buckled.

Before he could hit the floor, two sets of hands grabbed him. They dragged Nox the rest of the way as he slowly lost consciousness.

WHEN HE opened his eyes again, a light assaulted him. He was naked, lying on a gurney that was metal, cold under his body.

"Welcome back, Mr. Boyet," an accented voice said. Dr. Khanna.

Blinking, Nox came back to himself. Dr. Khanna's cheerful and bearded face greeted him when his vision stopped swimming.

"Fuck you," he said weakly.

Dr. Khanna patted his shoulder. "I'm going to give you an injection that will help."

Nox's entire body reacted before his brain caught up. He threw himself to one side and hit the floor with a force that knocked the air from his lungs.

No needles, no more of the fire, no more....

He was frog-crawling across the floor, desperate to reach the door.

"Ah no, none of that."

A shoe came down hard against the small of his back.

Nox moaned.

"Don't worry, Mr. Boyet. I'm not giving you more of, uh... your father's injections. Just something to clear your head."

He couldn't fight back as the foot released him. Dr. Khanna rolled him over like he was a doll. Nox gasped and tried to catch his breath as the doctor stooped and knelt on his chest.

Nox struggled, but the needle pressed into his skin. He waited for the fire to start to consume him as he passed out.

THE RATTLING of wheels filled Nox's ears as he slowly woke up. He felt warm and realized he was dressed in soft clothing and swaddled under blankets. On a gurney, moving down the brightly lit hallway, he confirmed as his eyes flickered open.

Dr. Khanna walked at his side, calling out orders to someone. Nox turned his head slightly and found Antonio, grinning as always, on the other side.

A bump and Nox was pushed through two swinging doors and into the bright sunlight. The sting of cold made him shiver as the gurney came to a halt.

"He should be fine for the trip," Dr. Khanna said, patting Nox's shoulder. "He's sedated. If he gives you any trouble…."

"I'll make sure he doesn't," Antonio interrupted slickly. He moved past Nox, who registered an ambulance waiting at the end of the small ramp he was on.

Dr. Khanna frowned but nodded to the orderlies to move Nox down to the ambulance.

Nox breathed through a moment of panic and shook his head. The edges of his consciousness felt like a heavy fog, as if he couldn't quite see everything around him. He tried to identify where he was, how many people were in the ambulance, but everything shifted too fast, and it was too blurry for him to pinpoint anything.

At the bottom of the ramp, Nox bit his lip in frustration. The orderlies manhandled him onto a different gurney. Straps draped over his chest, then were pulled tightly until it was clear he wouldn't be able to move, even if he could convince his body to try.

"That's not really necessary," Dr. Khanna said, but no one appeared to be listening. "He's sedated."

"Thanks, doc, you've been real helpful." Antonio reappeared as Nox—trussed up and strapped down—was moved into the ambulance with a thump and then rolled to the back. Antonio followed, hefting his bulk to thud down on the small bench to Nox's right. "The boss appreciates your discretion."

Nox knew a threat when he heard it.

He stared at the ceiling, breathing shallowly as he tried to formulate a plan, a thought.

When the ambulance door finally slammed, Nox let out a shaky sigh.

"Let's get you home," Antonio said with a nasty chuckle. "Daddy's waiting."

# CHAPTER THREE

THE CABIN was beautiful, nestled on twenty private acres not too far from Phenix City, Alabama, and accessible only through one dirt road, which could be seen from the front porch of the house. The back of the property dropped off a literal cliff into the river below—all that was missing was a moat. There were pathways utilized by family friends and friends of friends that weren't as easily controlled, so Mr. Creel spent most of the day sitting out front, watching the road with his shotgun across his lap.

He wasn't taking any chances.

Sam divided his time between helping Amelia in the kitchen, soaking up her cooking tips like a sponge, and spending time with Mason. He figured it would eventually make this feel like home, or at least give him some quiet time so his brain might stop chattering like an angry monkey.

Two weeks. They'd been here for two weeks without any messages from anyone.

The restlessness plagued him, thoughts of the last conversation he had with his fa—

With Nox.

And that's usually where he got tied up, conflicted to the point of nightmares.

The question that had haunted him for so long—who were his natural parents? What happened to them?—was answered. That secret wish, that somehow the names would be enough, the reassurance that maybe he was wanted and desired and cherished, even for the briefest time. Then he would be at peace.

He had always suspected they were dead.

He had secretly hoped they weren't.

Now he knew.

Natalie and Carson Boyet were his parents. And if he'd never known them, if they were both dead, at least he had a brother, right?

More than he ever dreamed of finding, and not just a brother introduced into his adult life. No.

His beloved father, his adored hero, the man who would do anything for him.

That was his brother.

Sam should feel better than he did.

"Come on, come for a walk with me," Mason cajoled as Sam sat tucked in a dusty-rose-covered easy chair in the corner of the living room. He'd taken to sitting there after washing the breakfast dishes, an open book in his lap, unread for days. It was so easy to let the dark wash over him and drag him into an endless cycle of negative thoughts. His entire world had been upended so many times in the past few months—who wouldn't feel adrift?

But Mason refused to let him sink into despair.

"I...." Sam started to protest, but Mason's sweet smile and proffered hand were impossible to say no to. Sam hauled himself out of the chair and grabbed the oversized black hoodie off the back. "You're right. It's a good idea. I can try to work off breakfast."

Amelia Creel was a stress cooker on top of her nurturing nature, which meant every meal seemed like something out of a cookbook titled, *A Feast Fit for Royalty*. Somehow she'd transported enough food during their exodus from the farm to keep them well-fed, in addition to the fresh game Mr. Creel delivered every few days.

Sam made the appropriate thank-you and "mmmm" sounds at every meal, but he didn't think he would get used to the sights and smells of Mr. Creel butchering animals in the shed.

"We're city boys," Mason murmured whenever Sam mentioned it. "Meat comes shrink-wrapped in a Styrofoam tray."

Sam thought about that as he and Mason walked outside the cabin and to the area that Mr. Creel designated as safe for them to move around. It wasn't a long path or much of a walk, but fresh air and a sense of normalcy—or as close as they could manage—were in rare supply these days.

Hand in hand they strolled into the woods, following the narrow pathway that wound through Aunt Belinda's "backyard." Overgrown beds of flowers and vegetables, a remnant of times past, filled openings between the tree canopy every few yards. They'd found some vegetables growing wild and reckless despite the lack of care—a welcome addition to dinners.

"It's beautiful out here," Sam said as they moved down a slight slope. A rare warm streak in the weather was coaxing wildflowers out between the rocks and fallen trees. "I keep thinking it wouldn't be the worst place to live."

Mason made a noncommittal noise. "I guess. Are we living with the Creels forever? Because I am not a trained hunter, and the closest thing I've ever been to growing something is a Christmas cactus I kept alive for two years."

Sam kicked a rock down the path and watched it skip and jump before it came to rest in a pile of fallen leaves. "I didn't say I was being practical." He kept his tone light lest Mason think he was being argumentative. "I guess I'm trying on all sorts of different ideas. To figure out the next step."

Tugging Sam a little closer, Mason rewarded him with a bright grin. "That's a good idea. We should be making decisions about our future."

Heart going pitter-patter, Sam tried to control what he assumed were cartoonish heart eyes. Mason's hand in his, the idea of "them" and a future—these were the only things keeping him from falling into a thousand pieces.

"We talked about Boston. Going to stay with your parents for a while." That was before, when Sam was too angry with Nox to think straight. Now, in the light of day, he tried to imagine them showing up at Mason's family home with no money, no jobs, no prospects, and oh right, holding hands.

"Yeah," Mason said, but there wasn't a lot of enthusiasm there.

"Could be complicated, though," Sam plowed on, avoiding scraggly tree roots exposed by receding topsoil. "Lots to explain, like a… uh…."

"Boyfriend," Mason supplied smoothly, not hesitating as he squeezed Sam's hand. "Yeah, that's going to be a fun chat."

Sam swallowed. "We could, you know, just say I'm a friend."

But Mason was already shaking his head. "No. I'm not ashamed of you, Sam. Or us. And we already told Nox we'd meet him in Boston, so we kind of have to go."

Nodding, Sam fell silent. Nox remained a difficult subject to navigate between them. Mason had already expressed his anger that Nox would keep such a secret, but that had banked into just the occasional glare when the topic came up. Sam didn't want to make it a battle, because he knew in his heart that when they were reunited, his forgiveness would be complete.

"Yeah. I guess it's just a matter of deciding when," Sam said eventually as the path rounded through a flat area where a small brick patio peeked out from a wild assortment of weeds. He imagined Aunt Belinda and her guests relaxing in the sun, drinking iced tea and absorbing the shafts of sunlight spearing through the trees.

"Mr. Creel wants us to wait a few more weeks before we split up," Mason said, slowing their progress. "He seems a little paranoid, though." He drew Sam closer, their bodies fitting together in an easy embrace.

Sam sighed with contentment.

"He reminds me of…." He trailed off, resting his forehead against the cool surface of Mason's down coat. "We'll sit down with him and Mrs. Creel, make a plan," he murmured. "Maybe… maybe we can call them, see how things are going."

Mason tightened his arms around Sam's shoulders. It was a matter of contention in the group, as Mason and Mr. Creel thought radio silence made the most sense, but Mrs. Creel and Sam just wanted proof of life at this point.

"Maybe," Mason said diplomatically. "We should start heading back."

"Right." Sam let go reluctantly and tipped his head back to smile up at Mason.

"No fair," Mason whispered as he leaned down and slotted their lips together in a tender kiss.

RED-FACED AND breathless, they finally made their way back to the house. Sam was grateful for long coats and oversized clothing as they dodged Mr. Creel—ever present on the front porch—and Amelia vacuuming the parlor as they hurried upstairs to "change out of their sweaty clothing."

It was getting tougher and tougher to stop when things got… heated. The lack of true privacy kept them solidly at second base, but every day, Sam felt the incredible pull for more.

He ducked into the bathroom and threw cold water on his face until he felt a semblance of dignity. In their room he could hear the sounds of drawers opening and closing. He waited until he was sure he had full control before opening the bathroom door.

Mason had changed into a camo jacket and pants, his blond hair a flyaway mess as he sat on the edge of the bed pulling boots on over heavy socks. His beard was coming in slowly as shaving every day quickly became a "why bother" scenario.

"Time to head out with Mr. Creel," he said, his cheeks reddening as he looked at Sam.

That look…. Sam exhaled and laughed under his breath. Yeah, he wasn't the only one who felt pulled toward more.

"Be careful," Sam said, trying not to let longing seep into his tone.

He wasn't very successful.

Mason cast him another adoring glance and then stood and shook his hair out of his eyes. "I'd kiss you good-bye but…," he said reluctantly, a quick eye dart down to the front of his pants.

Sam laughed and felt the blush burn on his cheeks.

"Go."


NOT WANTING to be alone, Sam sat at the table, shucking corn, listening to the pretty sounds of Gospel music over the satellite radio.

Amelia sang along, and Sam was amazed she knew every word to every song, her voice strong and sure. He'd noticed her praying more since they came to the cabin, head bowed in many quiet moments through the day.

"Do you think they're all right?" Sam asked suddenly, breaking into Amelia's song. He flushed at the rudeness, but before he could apologize, she turned around from her place at the stove.

"I don't know. That's why I keep asking God to keep an eye on them," she said, her voice soft. "I'm pretty sure he's gotten the message, but can't hurt to remind him." She smiled tremulously.

"I'm sure he's doing his best," Sam said politely.

Amelia regarded him with a curious gaze. "You don't believe in God?"

"Um—I've never really thought about it, to be honest. I studied world religions in high school, but my d—Nox never pushed it or anything. Not a lot of churches in the city anymore, at least being used as churches."

"Mmm—that's truly a shame. I've seen pictures of some beautiful places of worship before the storms. St. Patrick's Cathedral, of course." She went back to her frying pan to stir the wild onions and mushrooms she'd picked from the woods—under shotgun supervision—earlier in the day.

"St. Patrick's is a dance club," he said, going back to the methodical task of pulling all the silky bits off the corn. "It's by the Hellfire Hotel." He made a face when Amelia's jaw dropped. "I know, right? It's dumb. But super popular."

"Mercy. I'm glad you're not going back there," Amelia said, returning to her cooking duties.

Sam concentrated on the corn. "Yeah. Me and Mason have been talking."

"Oh."

Looking up, Sam saw Amelia's back taut with tension.

"Not right now, of course," he hurried to say, to make that sharp line of her spine go away. "We won't go until it's safe."

Amelia turned off the burner and wiped her hands. She turned slowly.

"I understand you boys are gonna have to move on," she said sadly, her sweet face sagging under the weight of her fears. "Doesn't mean I'm happy about it."

"Me neither," Sam said gently. "I'm really going to miss you."

He felt himself unfolding toward her like a flower toward the sun, a motherless kid toward a woman whose own children were out in the world, away from her protection.

Amelia didn't hesitate to hurry over, her arms already open for a hug.

# INTERLUDE

*Before*

SAM IS *fourteen years old.*

*He's technically a sophomore at his online high school, but most of his classes are advanced, junior or senior, a few college. He's smart and he knows it, interested in tons of different things–math and science especially. He thinks about the future, what he might do. A doctor or an engineer, building complex machines or curing diseases. He has high hopes for his future.*

*Then he leaves his room and goes downstairs.*

*His father has been depressed for a while. The initial moods come without much warning, but the pattern is always the same. A lot of late nights and early morning returns from patrol. Melancholy drawing his father into the library or his room to look at pictures of his mother or just stare out the window.*

*The angry outbursts come next. Sam is on his best behavior during those times, keeping his nose in a book or his brain focused on daydreams of life outside these walls. They're never directed toward him, and Sam never feels afraid of his father. If anything, he can see the desperation and worry that tinges those moods, as if his father is afraid of what will happen next.*

*He knows his father loves him. Sam knows it isn't his fault when he disappears down a dark path. He's done research on this, pretending it was for a paper and asking his English teacher for assistance. Depression is brain chemistry, not a way for Sam's father to make him feel bad.*

*It always cycles away, though. After days of darkness and stifling silence, Nox will start exercising, doing reps of sit-ups and push-ups and weights until the tension dies down and the amount of time he sleeps rights itself into something normal for a man who works a full-time job and then patrols the streets with an iron fist.*

*Sometimes Sam imagines inventing a medicine to make his father happy all the time—a pill to turn all that angry darkness into something quietly positive. Because sometimes Sam lies in bed while his father is out in the streets, and he fears never seeing him again, that the black, soul-crushing quiet will dull his skills and slow his hand and Sam will be once again left alone. Not able to survive.*

*Abandoned.*

# CHAPTER FOUR

EVERY STEP Cade took—with Francis impatiently poking a gun into his back like he'd gotten his tough-guy training from old B movies—drew him closer to Nox's house and the end of the line. His mind raced for a way to talk his way out of this. Maybe his best bet was the police station—a chance to get to relative safety, break out....

His heart sank even as he tried to reframe it into something positive.

Much as he didn't want to face it, miracles were all they had left, and Cade, despite his mother's best efforts, put zero faith in those.

He did a quick calculation of scuffling with Francis—maybe he'd at least be able to yell out a warning to Rachel and LJ, and they could get away before the partner showed up and continue the plan to find Nox. They were smart and capable, and Rachel enjoyed killing people. They didn't need him.

Memories flashed again and again—Nox saving him from the thugs and being unmasked. Frantically standing on the other side of the door the night Sam went missing. In a better story, another life, Nox would come to his rescue, Sig in hand, and Francis would be dead before he hit the ground. A shudder of shame overwhelmed Cade as he stepped up to the door.

All of these scenarios involved him either being dead or saved. Some hero. Some fool for love.

"Hurry up," Francis snapped, jamming the gun into Cade's spine.

"Why?" Cade tried to ask as he stumbled over the uneven concrete of the long-neglected sidewalk.

"I know you're bullshitting me about the big payday," Francis answered, "but there might be something in the house I want." He leaned in closer. "Even if it's just a little privacy."

Cade's stomach roiled.

"So, you want information, or do you want to fuck me? Make up your mind." The words flew out of his mouth, and he regretted them immediately, as Francis shoved him to the ground.

On his hands and knees on the cold broken pavement, Cade felt his anger rising.

"Fuck!" Rolling over, he glared up at Francis. "Jesus Christ—can you just stop and think this through? We're both running out of time! You know the Feds are coming? Great. Me too." The shaking fury of Cade's voice wasn't acting. "They're going to roll through this island and grab everyone they can. The rich guys will head out on their private fucking jets, and people like you and me are screwed." Shivering, Cade pressed his scraped hands against his knees. "We have to get the fuck out before anything goes down or it's all over—and we don't have a lot of time."

A flicker of panic crossed Francis's expression. No one knew better, Cade supposed, how crooked everyone on this freaking island was.

"I turn you and the other two in, I get money," Francis snapped, but Cade could see him wavering. "Mr. Smith is going to pay big, bigger than anything you could...." He cut himself off, his gaze tightening.

Cade filed that information away like a sticky note on the fridge.

"Or maybe you turn us in and this Mr. Smith blows your brains out. That seems like a better deal," Cade said, defiant as he could manage. "Not like anyone in this town is going to give a fuck if you end up floating in the East River."

Francis tilted his head to one side and scrutinized Cade's expression. His nostrils flared, and he muttered a curse as he glanced up and down the street. "You know what's worth even more? Tell me where your boyfriend is. The bounty on him could make me a millionaire."

His breath caught in his throat, and Cade shook his head. "We split up. Too much heat, you know? I just wanted to get some money to disappear. I earned it."

Francis laughed in his face. "So you escaped from federal custody in New Jersey to come back here, to what? Get money? Jesus Christ, you're stupid. Or a terrible liar." The detective motioned with his gun. "Tell me where your boyfriend is. And make it fast. My partner should be here any minute."

Questions raced through Cade's mind. He wanted to ask the right ones, get information, but his heart rabbited in his chest. He needed more time.

"I tell you where he is, you let me go?" Cade asked, his voice trembling.

"No. You tell me where he is, I get him and collect the bounty. Then I drop your ass off at the police station," Francis said coolly.

Cade shook his head. "No."

"This isn't a fucking negotiation," he snapped back.

"I tell you where he is, you let me and my brother go. I'm done with this shit." Cade pushed himself up off the ground, eyes wary on Francis's gun. "I'm fucking done with it."

"What about your dear friend Rachel?" Francis's anger seemed to cool, replaced with curiosity.

"I just want to save my ass and my brother's. Everyone else can fucking kill each other for all I care." Cade struggled to his knees.

Francis nodded slowly. "You give me the Vigilante and Rachel Moon, I'll have enough to get the hell off this piece-of-shit island." He waved his gun. "Talk."

Cade swallowed repeatedly until he felt steadied enough to speak. "We're supposed to meet here. Tomorrow night."

The detective made a sound of impatience. "Fuck."

Cade took a deep breath and pushed himself halfway off the ground, moving slowly as his gaze never broke from Francis's. "In the meantime, we can pass the time, right? You get what you want—all of it. Just... let me and my brother go." His teeth chattered; his voice hitched. None of it was an act. "You and your partner can split the money."

Francis shook his head, his expression shifting into something mean and greedy. "My partner... maybe they don't need to know about this little development," he murmured.

After an interminable wait, Francis nodded. "Let's go."

Cade followed instructions as quickly as he could, immune at this point to the endless wet and cold. He turned, his strides long and purposeful as he made for the familiar front steps. Behind him, he heard Francis talking to someone on his phone.

"Yeah, I got them. But things are hot right now. We gotta lay low. I'll call you, let you know where to pick up the woman," he said, disingenuously casual.

There was a long pause, and when Francis spoke again, he wasn't nearly as friendly.

"The brothers don't know shit. But they're good enough bait for now. Just sit tight."

The conversation clearly ended, Francis caught up with Cade and pressed him against the gate.

"We got some time, baby. Let's have a little party."


OKAY, HE had Francis off-balance. Fan dance the idiot into the house, make for the safe, knock him out. Cade scrambled up the stairs, Francis at his heels.

"Blow the lock off the door," he murmured, wiping a hand uselessly over his mouth.

"I don't want some fucking busybody neighbors...."

"You could literally set a bomb off and no one would open a window. They know better."

Roughly shoved aside, Cade winced as he watched Francis fire expertly at the lock, and he heard metal break and bend. With a show of strength that set Cade's teeth on edge, Francis kicked open the door.

The house was dark and still. A waft of mildew and the whistle of wind told Cade there was a broken window somewhere. Shapes of furniture meant it hadn't been entirely pillaged, but the shadows indicated the place had been tossed.

Cade took a deep breath and detached from his body. Whatever it took to get Rachel and LJ here, whatever it took to at least give them a chance to get out of this alive.

"Where's the closest bedroom?" Francis asked, pushing Cade into the nearest wall. He hit it hard, but pushing back did no good—Francis had him pinned. "I wanna make good use of our time."

"Down the hall," Cade murmured, indicating it with a tilt of his head. "Third door."

Francis breathed a low chuckle into the back of Cade's neck.

"Can we turn on the heat and lights, at least? We're going to be here for a while." Cade took a chance, hitching a hint of a whine in his voice. "This place is a pit."

Silence. Francis didn't respond at first, but then Cade felt the telltale hardness against his ass and Francis began to rub against him in earnest.

"This ain't the Butterfly," Francis mumbled, but he didn't say no. Cade held his breath as Francis continued to move, fumbling figure eights against him until he stopped suddenly and pulled away.

"Take off the jacket."

Without protest, Cade stripped down to the jeans and shirt he'd stolen from the trailers—which felt like it happened a hundred years ago.

"That too," Francis said, tugging at the next layer of clothing clinging to Cade's body.

Grateful to be staring at the wall, Cade did as he was told. "I'd kill for a shower," he muttered as the sweatshirt cleared his head. "A change of clothes."

Francis snickered in the darkness. "After I get what I want, maybe I'll reward all this cooperation."

In just a long-sleeved T-shirt, jeans, and his boots, Cade tried to relax his body. Over the years there had been customers who tripped his danger switch—men who had unhealthy appetites for dark acts, women with anger they needed to unleash in a safe space. He'd gotten a reputation for handling people like that, and right now every trick he'd ever utilized to stay alive and whole came back in a rush.

He could hear Francis breathing, feel his heat—and he was well aware of the gun pointed in his direction. With a calculated swagger, Cade turned slowly and swiveled a few steps toward the detective.

"Well? Are we going to have this party or not? We got all this time on our hands before your partner shows up and crashes it. Maybe I can see if there's any booze left…." Cade let his voice flow silky smooth.

Francis's gaze didn't waver. "I thought you said this place was a pit."

"It is. I'm just saying, a little light, a little warmth, some drinks. Maybe you and me pass the time until we get what we both want." Cade's eyes went to the gun, ever pointed in his direction. "You gonna put that down?"

The detective smiled. "Not yet."

After an agonizingly long pause, Francis glanced quickly right and left. He spied the light switch on the wall and leaned over to flick it. Nothing.

Cade almost fainted. Finally, an opportunity.

"Fuse box is in the basement," he said casually, as if this weren't a fucking miracle.

Francis narrowed his gaze. "Great. Let's take a little tour. You can show me the bar."

Shrugging, Cade turned and headed toward the kitchen. In the moonlight he could see the place, and nothing seemed to be missing. Less looters or squatters, then, more someone looking for something.

He moved slowly, kicking aside knocked-over furniture and belongings. The kitchen beckoned, deep shadows at the end of the hallway. He remembered Sam cooking for him. He remembered being on his knees…. "I'm glad my guy fucked up," Francis said suddenly, and Cade stumbled.

"What guy?"

"The moron on the boat."

The information took a second. Cade's brain caught up slowly with what Francis was saying.

He had something to do with the crewmember who tried to kill them during their escape.

"How… how did you know where we were?" Cade asked as a shiver ran through his body.

"Like I told you, I have my own ways of getting information," Francis sneered.

Then a sound from outside—something faint and scratchy—startled him, causing him to pause involuntarily.

A heavily breathing Francis didn't seem to notice and pressed the gun deeply into his spine.

"The door is right—" Cade started, but he got no further. There was a whistling sound and then a violent crack. Francis's oppressive presence disappeared as Cade tripped one way and the detective's body went the other. A clattering identified the gun falling then skittering across the floor.

"Get his gun," Cade yelled as he hit the wall, twisting his body to see what was going on.

LJ loomed over Francis's prone form with a kitchen stool in his hands while Rachel emerged from the shadows with a gun in her hand.

"Jesus Christ," he said, straightening up, one hand clutching the counter as he tried to regain his balance and breathing. "I was afraid you weren't going to get loose."

"It wasn't that hard." Rachel kept the gun trained on Francis as she stood over him. "He's an idiot."

Cade wiped his face with both hands, tremors still wracking his body. "I convinced him Nox was meeting me here tomorrow night. He called his partner, told him to hold off. So we've got some time."

"Did he say who the partner was?" LJ asked as Cade shook his head.

"No. He mentioned a Mr. Smith, but more like he was working for him. The interesting tidbit of information, though—Francis claimed responsibility for the near hit on the boat."

"Jesus," LJ said, leaning against the counter. "Well, at least we're gettin' some questions answered."

"That sounds like bullshit," Rachel snapped, raspy and pissed. She kicked Francis in the side. "He's just a dirty cop. He doesn't have that kind of power."

"How would he know otherwise?" Cade asked, but Rachel didn't answer. She was staring down at Francis's limp form. He moaned weakly, then quieted. "Maybe it's his partner who has the information."

"Shit. You don't think that guy Damian is his partner, do you?" LJ asked.

"No," Rachel said quickly. "No way." She waved him off.

Cade wanted to argue the point, but he was tired and shaking and just not in the mood. They were all on edge.

"We need to tie him up," he said, pushing off the conversation until they all came down from the adrenaline rush.

"Go get the power on. Maybe there's some rope in the basement." Rachel gestured at him with the gun. "I got him covered."

"Right." Cade felt his way to the basement door and looked into the yawning abyss of blackness with trepidation. Given the way things were going, he expected a host of evil monsters to swarm up and tear him apart.

"Just in case," he called back over his shoulder, "if he does have a partner, and said partner is the same level of double-crossing lowlife, I'd rather be safe than sorry. If Francis was my partner, there'd be a trace on every call. Block the front door with furniture. The lock's blown out."

"Right," LJ responded. "Good idea."

He heard LJ and Rachel's voices as he descended, clutching at the walls and feeling out each step with the toe of his boot. He finally hit the bottom and stepped onto the concrete floor. Okay, feel against the walls until he found what he was looking for.

It took seemingly forever, but Cade's questing fingers finally hit the cold metal of the electrical box. He fumbled the door open and touched each switch to flip them back to the other side. The hum and rumble of the house coming to life filled him with gratitude. Finally, something went right.

The basement filled with light, and Cade gave a quick glance around. Empty shelves and boxes, spilled-over bags of clothing and tools, a few unidentifiable chests. Nothing out of the ordinary. No monsters.

Halfway up the stairs, Cade let himself exhale.

Then he heard the gunshots.

# Chapter Five

Nox felt every bump and shake of the ambulance as it bounced over the worn streets of the city. They weren't in the District yet, he surmised, still woozy from the sedation but slowly gaining some clarity. Eyes tightly closed to avoid Antonio's smug grin, he considered their direction. When they stopped, he heard a loud exchange between the ambulance drivers and someone else—presumably a checkpoint into the District.

His guess was confirmed by the smooth ride as they continued on.

Antonio said they were going to see his father—his father, alive, and the one who threw him into a cell, injected him with God only knew what, and then pulled him out for....

What?

Carson Boyet had stayed hidden from him for seventeen years. Stayed hidden from the world, actually, although Nox couldn't really fault him for that. He'd done the same thing.

Shifting on the gurney, Nox turned his head away from Antonio. Between the creaks and groans of the ambulance, he heard his guard grumbling about how uncomfortable he was, how this assignment was shit.

He wished he were at full strength. The frustration made Nox want to move again. He could easily overpower Antonio, take his weapon, get out of the ambulance, and be gone.

Nox paused his train of thought. Where was he going to go? Last he knew, Cade, Rachel, and LJ were at the abandoned school in West New York, back across the river. He hadn't seen them, and in their brief conversation, Carson hadn't mentioned them specifically. So maybe he didn't grab them as well. Maybe they escaped.

A ton of brutal reality rained down on Nox. He didn't know who the men surrounding the building were, with their massive display of firepower. Didn't know who shot him. What were the chances Cade and the others made it out alive?

The grief strangled him.

He pictured Cade, who granted him the brief experience of… feeling. To care for someone so deeply, to consider a future where he wasn't alone with his inner darkness. Cade, who just had the misfortune of delivering a letter that swept him into this insanity. Cade, who didn't deserve to die because he chose to stick with Nox out of loyalty.

Love.

He spared a moment of sadness for enthusiastic and good-natured LJ, who wanted to protect his brother. Even a second for Rachel, who remained an enigma he never truly trusted.

For a moment the inky black of despair shoved him completely under.

The ambulance ground to a halt with a screech of tires. A loud bang then a groan of metal indicated garage doors opening. Nox barely registered the sound or the forward motion of the ambulance as it dipped down a winding path.

An underground garage, he thought vaguely.

Antonio waited for the ambulance to come to a complete halt. Then he banged on the panel between them and the drivers.

"Let's go," he shouted and kicked the gurney under Nox. "Wake up, sleeping beauty. You have a meeting to get to."

INSTINCT, IN the end, overrode grief. Nox opened his eyes to watch as they moved him from the ambulance, across a full parking garage, and into a large elevator. He blinked up at the lights, breathing slowly.

If Cade was dead… he wanted to know who killed him.

The elevator jolted to a stop, the doors opened, and the two uniformed drivers pushed him into an elegant hallway. Nox registered the opulence, the pristine condition of the flocked gold wallpaper and elegant sconces. They traveled past at least ten doors before they arrived at their destination.

Antonio, who'd remained out of sight, could be heard speaking to someone above Nox's head. He turned slightly, just enough to catch a large suited guard holding a machine gun to his left.

A flash of memory nearly knocked the breath out of him.

The Iron Butterfly. The men who took over before the bomb went off. The men who had Sam.

The realization that Sam was still out there brought Nox back into himself with a slam. He shoved the grief down into the deepest corner of his heart, where he held his mother's loss and his fears of not protecting his son. That left him with anger and a need to move that blew the fog of sedation out like a furious storm.

A door opened and Nox was on the move again. He registered a double-doored entry and then a level of wealth that made the hallway seem like a tenement.

Chandeliers dripped crystals down from the soaring ceiling of the entryway, and the smell of fresh flowers hit Nox as he took a deep breath. Everywhere he looked was white—walls, ceiling, flowers. Pristine and perfect. They took a left down a small hallway where he glimpsed artwork of a caliber usually seen only in the Museum of Modern Art.

"In here. Get him into the bed," Antonio barked as another set of double doors led to an enormous bedroom.

Nox didn't even hide being awake and curious, neck craning to see the gold embossed wallpaper, heavy wood furniture, and peacock-blue bedding and curtains.

"Definitely an upgrade from your last accommodations." Antonio stood guard as the ambulance drivers helped Nox sit up and swing his legs over the side of the gurney. Any ideas he had of making a break for it ended as he swayed weakly at the move from the gurney to the bed.

When he was finally tucked under the covers, Nox felt like he'd been running for an hour.

The last thing he saw as his eyes flickered shut was Antonio, standing over him with a smirk.

THE NEXT time Nox opened his eyes, he was alone. The shift in the patterns of sunlight streaming from the windows told him it was at least six hours later. He felt himself again, lucid and clear. For a moment, he luxuriated in feeling warm and clean and comfortable.

Nox took a few deep breaths. His body began to respond as he gave it commands—sit up slowly, push the covers off, swing his legs over the side, press his bare feet against the plush rug. A moment of dizziness, then he was fine.

For the first time in what seemed a hundred years, Nox wanted food and water and to run around the block a few dozen times. The bullet wounds inflicted on his body seemed a distant memory. Slight spots of tenderness dotted his flesh, but he felt healed. He flexed his leg. His knee was bandaged but moved with only a twinge.

Miracle or hallucination, he couldn't tell.

He took in the accommodations—a king-size bed in the center, a looming wardrobe and long dresser still not taking up all the floor space. A seating area with a club chair and small sofa was tucked against the far wall. Everything was perfectly coordinated, with dark antique finishes and gold and peacock in various combinations on all the soft surfaces. Nox felt an itch of memory, not of the room but of the colors, the furniture. From childhood? He certainly hadn't been anywhere this beautiful outside a casino since....

Everything slammed back in one brutal punch.

His father was alive.

Cade might be dead.

A jumble of information shifted and tumbled, like a room full of gold coins disturbed. Every time he latched on to something, it would clink away.

The door and its shiny gold knob caught his attention. He stood on shaky legs, aligning his body in its direction. Every halting step—concentrating on not falling, staying on track—kept him hyperfocused. The nightmare of being in the cell flared, but Nox shook his head. No, no. He wasn't getting sucked into that spiral. He was out of that prison. This was real.

He touched the knob with tentative fingers and prayed the illusion didn't shatter.

The coldness of the metal made him gasp.

Not a hallucination.

He tried to turn the knob, but that's where his excitement ended.

Locked.

Still a prisoner.

Think, think, Nox told himself, hands in tight fists at his sides. He had to get out of here, protect Sam….

Find out exactly who killed Cade and the others and rip their hearts out.

Oh right, and deal with the fact that his father was, in fact, alive.

A shock of pain went through Nox's skull, and the reality of his weakened condition fueled another pang of anger. Better did not mean full capacity, and time was the one thing he didn't have—he couldn't wait in this room, letting God-only-knows-what happen to his son.

Blinking back the anger, Nox noticed another door. He made his way across the room, ignoring the twinges and shaking of his muscles. This one wasn't locked, but it only led to a bathroom.

Nox flicked on the light. It was as opulently rendered as the bedroom—gold and white, with a toilet, rainfall shower, soaking tub, and double-sink vanity. He held his head under the faucet to gulp down water, suddenly aware of his own thirst and hunger. His head a bit clearer, he did a thorough search of the space, hoping to find something to use as a weapon. But it quickly became clear there was nothing glass or plastic or easily removable that could be useful.

Someone knew him entirely too well.

So he had to improvise, use his wits until his body came back on track, break the plan down into smaller pieces.

Nox took a deep cleansing breath. His resolve didn't weaken, but his strength trembled. Damn it, he thought as he went back into the bedroom and lay down on the bed.

The room warm and toasty, the mattress soft and welcoming. Nox felt his entire body shutting down from the stress, the exertion. A quick nap and then he'd be ready for his next move.

His dream wasn't anything like the Dead Bolt hallucinations—no blood, no anger. Just Cade, smirking, teasing. Tempting. Cade lying against the covers in Nox's guest room.

Cade standing at his door, angry and defiant.

Cade facedown on the bed at the Iron Butterfly, handcuffed to the headboard.

Cade on his knees in the kitchen.

Cade sitting on the corner of a bed, somewhere quiet and simple, smiling that smirky grin, hand outstretched.

"Come here. I'm tired of chasing after you," he said in the dream, inside Nox's head. And Nox went because he was powerless against Cade, bewitched and bewildered, and oh, how good it felt to sink into his arms, to lie down and feel himself be held and touched and stroked and soothed.

"You should stay here with me," dream Cade whispered, his breath hot against Nox's ear. "You can't save the world, but you can save me. You can have me."

Their mouths touched, and Nox fell into the sensation of peace.

His eyes flickered open for a brief moment before he submitted to his exhaustion again.


IT WAS dark when he woke up again. The dream of Cade lingered, choking his throat with grief. He sat with it for a while, tormenting himself with the guilt. Then he moved slowly, sat up, and rested his face in his hands.

The rattle of the door startled him. He lay back down and pulled the covers up to his chin. If there weren't cameras tracking his every move, he might be able to use his mobility to his advantage.

When the door opened, the ever-present Antonio and his gun entered first. He scanned the room. Then his gaze settled on Nox, and he seemed pleased to see him in bed.

A freckled young woman in a maid's uniform came in at the snap of his fingers. She pushed a silver cart, as if delivering room service. As she drew closer, Nox could see a wicker basket sitting on the lower shelf of the trolley.

"This is Greta," Antonio announced. "She doesn't speak English, and she isn't going to help you escape," he continued, that ever-present smug smile on his face.

Greta avoided landing her big gray eyes on Nox entirely. She pushed the cart near the bed and then ducked away as if he might reach out and grab her.

"Dinner is served. Basket on the bottom has some toiletries and unmentionables." Another snap of his fingers and Greta turned and ran out the door like her hair was on fire. "Greta's bringing you a suit. You need to be ready in an hour."

Nox weighed the pros and cons of silence versus normal curiosity. A suit?

"Where am I going?" he asked, startled by the rusty grate of his voice.

"Nowhere. But you need to not look and smell like a homeless piece of shit."

Greta reentered, holding a bag on a hanger. It was nearly taller than she was. She hung the garment bag on the wardrobe door and then shot a look at Antonio.

He cocked his head to one side, and Greta didn't hesitate to flee without a glance back at Nox.

"Shoes are in the bottom of the bag. You got an hour." Antonio didn't wait for questions or conversation. With a final glance, he backed out, shutting the doors as he went.

The lock clicked back into place.

Left alone, Nox sat up. He uncovered the meal left for him—a gold-rimmed mug of tomato soup, a grilled ham-and-cheese sandwich, and a bottle of water. Linen napkin, no silverware.

Hunger gnawed at Nox's stomach. The worry over the food being spiked held him back for a moment, but the fragrant smells drove him to pull the cart closer. He had no recollection of the last time he ate, and every mouthful, every swallow was heaven.

The food helped move him from the bed to the bathroom. Armed with the wicker basket, he showered and brushed his teeth under the heavy spray of the rainfall showerhead.

The catalog of bruises, wounds, and scars had increased exponentially in the past few months. But even his scraped and scratched torso and limbs felt better than they should. He remembered the bullets tearing into his body, the blood and pain. How long was he out after being shot?

Nox's hands shook as he soaped his hair. He was clean-shaven in South Carolina, right before they left. He smoothed his hands over his face to feel the regrowth. It was enough to confuse him further. Could it have been weeks? A month?

But that didn't feel right either. How had he healed so quickly in so short a time?

A wave of nausea sent Nox clutching at the pale-golden tiled wall. Water splashed, forming a soapy swirl around his ankles.

Maybe Sam thought he was dead. If no one had contacted them, if they called and no one answered....

Would they still go to Boston?

His heart pounded. Okay, okay. That was okay. Boston with Mason's family. He'd escape, get off the island, and make his way to the cabin. He could do this. He could.

But his previous resolve eluded him as he struggled to calm his racing pulse.

Nox let the water pound his face until he couldn't breathe. Before spots appeared, he looked away. He'd been alone for most of his life. If there was one person he could depend on, it was himself.

Determined, Nox turned the elegant levers to shut off the shower, shook the hair out of his eyes, and pulled back the fogged-up door.

He closed his fingers around the towel and then methodically dried himself off. A host of grooming products provided him distraction—shave with a flimsy disposable razor, shape out-of-control hair into something manageable with damp hands and a tiny squeeze of gel from a sample container. Thinking about Cade in the bathroom back in the farmhouse, thinking of him close and tempting and inviting, and God, if it was just sex between them, maybe the pain wouldn't be a knife in his heart.

Nox tore his gaze away from the mirror and then limped back into the bedroom to get dressed, the static of his thoughts distracting him from everything else around him.

For so long he'd slogged through his life with a fatalistic ticking clock over his head. He was tired of it. Tired of the games, the fear, the hiding. The reality of his father being alive had collapsed the past seventeen years of his life to rubble. Imagining himself a puppet of Carson's whims humiliated him to his core.

The only things keeping him going for so long were his anger and Sam.

For a brief moment, he had imagined his life having more....

Now?

Now he'd push aside his grief and be exactly who he was meant to be.

He was the Vigilante, and people were going to pay.

HE'D JUST finished the last button on his shirt when the doorknob rattled. Breath catching, Nox stepped back, suddenly forced to decide on a plan of action.

The door swung open.

His father—groomed and pressed for a day at the office—entered the room.

"Nox," he said, as if he weren't a murderous monster. "Good to see you up. We have a meeting to get to."

# CHAPTER SIX

CADE RACED up the basement stairs and into the kitchen, almost tripping as he went. The smell of gunpowder lingered, as did that of blood.

"Rachel!" he yelled as he ran to the opposite side of the island.

Rachel was on her knees, gun still in hand. A few feet away, Francis lay on his back, dead, half his face blown away.

"Fucker tried to grab the gun. He was faking it," she rasped, struggling to her feet. Cade was propelled out of his shock and reached to grab her arm. "Goddammit."

A second later, LJ tore through the door, calling Rachel's name.

"She's fine, she's fine," Cade said, releasing her arm as she dropped the gun on the counter and LJ swept her up into an embrace.

Cade stared at Francis's body, registering the blood and gore. After everything, all of it, the danger and the detours and the fear, Francis was dead and they'd gotten no new information that could help them formulate a next step.

One step forward, a hundred miles back.

A wave of grief and then anger rolled through his body. Rachel couldn't have shot him in the fucking arm? The leg? *Jesus.* As his brother comforted Rachel behind him, he heard their murmurs, and his irritation grew.

"We should put the body downstairs," he said, his voice hollow. "Then, fuck, figure out our next move."

The blood seeped onto the kitchen floor and pooled under Francis's head.

"Search the body," Rachel said briskly, as if coming back online. She moved to stand next to Cade. "We got a gun out of it. Maybe he has some money too."

"His phone is goin' be locked," LJ said from behind them. "But maybe once we get back online, I can hack into it."

"Sure." Cade moved away from Rachel with a jerk of his limbs. He just wanted to be somewhere she wasn't for a moment.

He knelt down, vaguely aware how the past few months had changed him. Tossing a dead guy for money and weapons? Sure, why not. Maybe he'd steal his shoes while he was at it.

"Knife, ammo clip," Cade recited, passing things up to his brother. "Another knife, Jesus Christ." Both looked like something out of a slasher movie. After emptying his jacket pockets, Cade checked his pants next. "Phone." Before handing it off, Cade checked to see if there were any missed calls or texts on the home screen, but apparently Francis wasn't a fan of notifications. Unhelpful dick.

"You think you can break into it?" Cade leaned over to empty the other pocket.

"Yeah," LJ said, deep in thought. "Soon as we get a laptop."

"I'll add it to the list." Rachel was still standing over Cade, who rolled Francis slightly to get at his back pockets. A thick wallet was his prize. He let the body drop, then stood, opening it as he went.

"Christ, a thousand bucks at least," he said, flicking through the money. "His detective shield, two key cards. I think one is for a casino VIP lounge. The Flamingo, looks like. Not sure about the other." Cade let his fingers slide around the edge of the second key card, examining it for a moment before Rachel yanked it—and the wallet—out of his hand.

"Good. Bribe money. I'll head out to the District, see what I can find. Get us our supplies." She concentrated fully on the wallet. Cade watched her take out the money and the two key cards and then toss the billfold on the counter.

Cade felt a weird tremor of cold lick through his body.

"We'll go together," Cade said. "All three of us. No need to stay behind now with Francis dead."

Rachel gave him a sharp look, eyes narrowing. She clearly read his tone and didn't like it.

"I need to go by myself. The people I know aren't going to welcome a crowd," she said evenly.

"There's a price on our heads. Francis knew exactly who you two were, even with the fake fed ID." He cast his gaze at LJ, who looked shocked. "They got a bounty on Nox, and we're all back on the radar."

"The Feds in South Carolina—" LJ began.

"Are not on the same page as law enforcement in the District," Cade finished. The smell of blood and death was starting to sink into Cade's nose; a fissure of nausea began to form in his stomach. "Let's just get him downstairs, and then we'll shower, find some clothes, and head out."

Rachel opened her mouth to protest but instead turned on her heel. She walked out of the kitchen purposefully, leaving Cade and LJ to clean up her mess.

"I guess she's real upset she had to shoot him," LJ said as he reached for Francis's feet.

Cade said nothing. Holding his breath, he grabbed Francis's arms to pull him toward the basement steps.


BODY DISPOSED of for the moment, Cade checked his brother's handiwork at the front door. Living room furniture provided a barricade. At the very least they'd hear someone trying to get in.

Cade shut off the lights and then directed his brother upstairs. "The water should be working. We'll get cleaned up, and I'll find us some clothes."

They passed the bathroom nearest Sam's room, and Cade heard the shower going. Rachel, clearly.

In Nox's room, Cade shut down the cascade of memories and focused on finding things for them to wear as he methodically went through the chest of drawers. He tossed things onto the bed, items that would be warm and sturdy as they ventured into the world—jeans, thermal underwear, some hooded sweatshirts, wool socks. The urge to linger over everything—faintly scented if he concentrated enough— he managed to push down.

He turned to find his brother watching him curiously. "I know you're mad about Francis," LJ said gently. "But I haven't given up hope, and neither should you."

Emotion clogged Cade's throat. "Thanks. I just wish we had a starting point, at least."

LJ nodded, and Cade tried not to cry at his brother's clear attempt to keep his spirits up, even if it wasn't backed by anything but love.

"Rachel'll find somethin'. Soon as I get online, we'll be back in business." LJ smiled, sweet and unconvincing.

"Right." Cade clapped his hands together. "You go shower. I'll see if Rachel's almost done."

A BUNDLE of clothes at his side, Cade settled down on the bed in Sam's room, facing the bathroom door. He knew this was a jerk move, knew that Rachel would come out and her back would go up like an angry cat, but he didn't give a shit.

She'd blown their one chance to get some information, then made decisions without consulting him or LJ.

No. Just… no.

The water shut off, and Cade waited, tapping his foot against the floor. Remnants of Sam were a painful reminder of how far away the young man was, which led to a clutch of worry about his parents. Yeah—Rachel didn't get to make the rules. Not now. No one had more at stake than Cade.

Eventually the door opened, and Rachel emerged in what were undoubtedly purloined items of Sam's clothing—a pair of heavy jeans, work boots, and a white thermal top. No bra. Her damp red hair fell in two plaits, draped over her shoulders. She looked like a fresh-faced teenager, and suddenly he knew exactly how Jenny/Rachel survived all this time.

"That's a different look for you," Cade said, finding himself pinned to the bed by Rachel's glare.

"They're looking for Rachel Moon. I'm giving them Jenny," she said, her voice gentle and soft.

"Wasn't Jenny some kind of teenaged hit woman?" Cade watched the barb fly and fall, as Rachel's expression grew shuttered.

"Executive assistant," she said, her tone belying the flash in her eyes. "Were you here to ask me something, Caden?"

A thousand questions and accusations crept to the tip of Cade's tongue, but he just shook his head. "No. Just waiting to use the shower. LJ's getting ready in Nox's bathroom. We should be ready to go soon."

Rachel's face grew harder—and older—in a split second.

"It's easier if I go," she said, her voice back to normal. Far less raspy and damaged, Cade realized, adding it to the growing list of Rachel's strange behavior.

"And LJ and I wait here for Francis's partner to show up? Too risky."

"He was probably lying about having a partner."

"I heard him on the phone…"

"You heard one side of a conversation." There was a smugness to her tone that heightened his irritation.

"You can't know that for sure." Cade watched Rachel's expression morph into bland acceptance.

"Maybe," she said finally, eyes glittering. "Hurry up and shower. I'd like to sneak into the District before daylight."

She stepped away from the door and walked slowly toward Cade. Her gaze never left him, not when he got up, not when he walked into the steamy bathroom. Not even a blink until he shut the door between them.

IN THE bathroom, Cade ran the water hot as he could stand. Steam filled the tiny room as he shed the disgusting clothes he'd been wearing for so long he couldn't remember putting them on. He stuffed everything in the tiny wastebasket and reminded himself to find an incinerator.

He stayed in the shower until the water ran cold, repeatedly soaping and rinsing every square inch of himself. The towels were just as soft as he imagined, and the sudden vision of his mother folding laundry nearly brought him to his knees.

Where was she? Were she and his father okay?

"Stay focused." Although Cade couldn't quite land on a thing to focus on. Get dressed—start there. He dried off and then layered on clean clothing. Underwear, socks. Jeans and a sweater—both slightly too big and hanging on his ever-shrinking frame. He found a toothbrush and shaving supplies behind the medicine cabinet mirror and then busied himself with that.

The hair was too long to do anything with, so he pushed it out of his face and confronted the result in his reflection.

Up until this point in this life, had he ever looked so... hard? Worn down? Nothing pretty, everything functional, existing in a place of survival? His skin was chapped in places, broken out in others. He'd lost weight, his cheekbones prominent, and not in a sexy way.

When this was over, provided he wasn't dead, Cade promised himself he'd sleep for at least a year.

"If I'm not dead," he said to his mirror self. "So... goals."

The bathroom, once warm and cozy, was fast becoming oppressive. Cade took a deep breath of tepid air and opened the door.

His brother stood in the center of the room, his face a conflict of worry and confusion.

"What?" Cade asked, although he already knew the answer.

"Rachel's gone."

# CHAPTER SEVEN

DURING THE second of their twice-daily patrols, Mason and Mr. Creel spotted a man in the woods. Dressed like a hunter—but a little too clean for their liking—he did more walking than shooting. They followed him back to his vehicle—a rental—and watched him drive away. When they reported it to Sam and Amelia during lunch, it cast a pall over the group and killed everyone's appetite.

Sam had been lulled into a sense of safety—it was stressful enough to worry about Nox and the others without thinking of someone lurking in the woods.

"Didn't act like a hunter," was all Mr. Creel would say. Mason frowned and picked at his food. Sam wanted to reach out and reassure him, but he sat frozen in his seat. Walking the property took on a more tactical feel. They worked out signals and hand gestures before the two men went out again, leaving a silent Sam and Amelia at the table.

"Maybe we should call them," Sam said that night, deep in a nest of blankets as Mason walked toward the bathroom. They were pushing a month since they'd separated from the rest of the group, and no call had come through on the special phone LJ had given them.

"They specifically told us—"

"Not to, unless it was an emergency. And I think not hearing from them for so long, plus this… this… guy." Sam trembled, fisting his hands in the covers. "I have a terrible feeling about this, Mason. I swear. It's like I can't shake the feeling something happened."

Mason pursed his lips and raked his hands through his unruly hair. "Let's talk to Mr. and Mrs. Creel in the morning," he said diplomatically. Sam could read him well enough—he thought it was the wrong idea.

"Fine." Sam turned over, leaving his back to Mason for the rest of the night.

AND A sleepless night was had by all; that much was evident as they sat down to breakfast. Sam could see his own anxiety reflected back on everyone's faces.

"I'm thinkin' maybe we need to move on," Mr. Creel said, his breakfast untouched in front of him. He cast a side-glance toward Amelia. "I don't like anyone bein' this close to us."

Mason nodded.

A flame of anger grew in Sam's chest. "Or we could call my dad. We haven't heard from anyone in a month."

"That's a different matter, son." Mr. Creel reached for his coffee cup but didn't bring it to his lips. "We knew they might not be in touch right away."

"A month." The table rattled as Sam jerked in his chair. "Are we just going to drive around, hiding, forever? Don't you want to know if they're okay?"

A dark pall fell over Mr. Creel's normally inscrutable face. "Both my boys are up there, young man. Both of 'em."

Amelia sniffled into her napkin, making Sam feel like shit.

"Sorry," Sam muttered, his face hot with shame. Caught up in his own anxious fear, he had forgotten just how much the Creels had on the line.

"Me and Mason are gonna take another walk around. Amelia, you and Sam start packing up. Stay away from the windows—I don't want them to see what we're doin'." With that, Mr. Creel and his coffee cup left the table, headed for the front porch.

Mason didn't say a word, but he touched Sam's shoulder as he stood—just a tender squeeze that let his boyfriend know he wasn't angry. Then he was gone, following Mr. Creel into the morning.

Amelia's sigh spoke to Sam. It said, "I'm running out of hope," and he understood perfectly.


IN SILENCE he and Amelia packed up whatever they could fit in the SUV. Nonperishable food, a replenished first aid kit, weapons and ammo. Anything that could hold water was filled. They stacked everything in the dining room, at the far end, away from the windows. Comforters, linens.

"Pack up yours and Mason's things," Amelia said finally as she emptied the refrigerator of fresh food they wouldn't be taking with them. "Bring your pillows." Her voice was steady, but Sam could see the line of tension along her back as she moved methodically. Lean into refrigerator, straighten, throw item into trash bag. Repeat and repeat. "Unplug everything. Lock the windows."

"Yes, ma'am," Sam murmured, turning to do her bidding as quickly as possible. Sam's hearing keyed into the world behind the house. Did he hear gunshots? Approaching vehicles? A creak on the porch?

There were guns—he knew how to fire them, and so did Amelia. If someone tried to get into the house, they'd defend themselves. Long before this moment, his father had... Nox had taught him how to hide, how to run, how to make a stand if it was his last resort. Raised on paranoia, Sam thought as he quickly filled his and Mason's duffel bags. How handy was that?

The phone, though—he couldn't shake the need to have it close. While Amelia ducked into the cellar for some canned goods, Sam snuck to the unlocked safe in the living room. With frequent glances over his shoulder, he moved the painting of trees and fall leaves that concealed it, then gently pulled the door open.

No one seemed to be nearby. Sam grabbed the phone, then put everything back where it belonged. Treasure deep in his pocket, he ran to his and Mason's room to get their bags.

What next? Did he make a quick call? Send a text? Hands shaking, Sam took a deep breath and powered the phone on. When the screen lit up, he typed in their code word and waited. Phone, text, and little else—this was pure function. He hovered, then clicked on the text box.

Leaving current location. Confirm receipt.

Sam heard the sounds of their exodus coming from downstairs. He only had a second to decide. Praying it was the right move, he clicked Send, then shut the phone down. LJ's phone and Nox's phone would receive the message, and hopefully the next time he turned the phone on, he would have a response.

In the lining of his backpack, Sam wrapped the phone in some socks and tucked it between the layers of material. The furious knot of tension in his stomach lessened somewhat. He grabbed the rest of the gear and headed out.

"WE NEED to get movin'," Mr. Creel announced as he and Mason entered the kitchen just before sunset. "Right now."

Amelia and Sam were in the process of filling a few more water jugs. His terse words set them into a flash of motion. Sam ran into the dining room and started grabbing things, even as his heart thumped in triple time.

Mr. Creel interrupted. "We got company."

Mason, damp with perspiration, kept his gun as he walked through the house, checking windows as he went.

"Way too much going on in the area," he said as Sam began to trail behind him. "It feels like the woods are moving."

Amelia gasped. "Can we get out of here?" she asked, her hand at her throat.

"Soon as it gets dark. We're gonna head down the mountain, take the fire road," Mr. Creel said. "Load everything into the pickup. Maybe takin' a different truck'll buy us some time."

IN QUIET shock, Sam dressed warmly, then gathered his bag and followed Mason through the side door and out to the garage. Everything was packed into the enormous gray Ridgeline sitting idle in the garage. They'd be leaving their own vehicles behind.

"That everything?" From his perch at the side door, Mr. Creel watched the inky darkness like a hawk. He'd taken up that spot within minutes of announcing their departure; it gave him the best view of anyone coming up to the house from the road. Motion sensor lights would alert them around the perimeter.

Mason grunted a yes even as he cast a sidelong look at Sam, who pretended to be rearranging things in his backpack. Mason would have gone for the phone, and with it missing, he'd know exactly who had it.

They scurried then, the final items tucked into the back of the cab, and slid into their seats, all in a state of quiet hurriedness.

Mason was the last one into the truck. Having disabled the automatic garage-door opener, he pushed it open to let them out. Quietly.

Sam sat in the back with Amelia, who took his hand as gravel kicked up beneath the wheels. Then they pulled down the driveway and toward the fire road, and he bid silent farewell to the sweet little house that had been so comforting.

Mason drove, and Mr. Creel rode shotgun.

Literally.

Sam leaned his head against the window and stared unseeing as the trees flew by.

AFTER HOURS of pure breath-holding terror—expecting at any moment to be set upon by black SUVs—Sam watched the city pull into view.

After Savannah was nearly wiped off the map, most folks had moved inland. And kept moving, since no one trusted being anywhere near the water. The area around Rossville, Georgia, had gone from a tiny town whose main selling point was "close to Chattanooga" to a booming metropolis, while cities near water limped back from the brink.

Mr. Creel wasn't too happy about the choice, but Mason rightly pointed out they needed resources and anonymity—and a big city would provide both.

Every city had an unsavory section. Mason directed Lee Sr. to a motel hovering just within city limits, surrounded by pawnshops, gun stores, and tattoo parlors.

"Perfect," he said grimly as he got out to secure them two rooms.

Sam pulled his hood down low, ignoring the pointed looks from Amelia, who sat beside him in the back seat.

"How are you feelin'?" she asked gently, as she had every few hours since they fled the cabin.

He responded as he always did—"Fine, thank you."—even as a dark cloud established over his head. The phone LJ had left them consumed his thoughts. He wanted to use it, desperately wanted to hear his father's voice. How could the Creels not want to know that Cade and LJ were okay? At this point, if Sam could talk to Rachel, he'd probably cry like a baby.

Self-recrimination roared back with hurricane force. Like the letter that had arrived at the door a lifetime ago, Sam was the catalyst for everything falling apart. He took the letter. He pushed the issue. He wanted to know about who he was and where he came from. And now? Now look where he was.

Out the window, he watched dusk fall on the dirty and derelict concrete jungle. People shuffled about, pushing shopping carts into narrow alleyways. Others waited blank-faced at a bus stop, staring straight ahead as if disconnected from their surroundings.

Sam could relate.

The door opened again, and Mason slid into the passenger seat. He turned to face Sam and Amelia in the back seat.

"Got us two rooms around back—can't see the truck from the street," he said, looking pleased. "Booked us for a week."

"We're gonna be here that long?" Amelia didn't sound pleased, and Sam's stomach convulsed. She should be home in her kitchen, singing and making food and not afraid for her life.

"Best let them think that, regardless," Mr. Creel answered in his usual gruff tone. He put the truck in reverse, waited until Mason slammed the door shut, and then drove around to the other side of the motel.

They unloaded what little they had immediate need for out of the truck and settled into two rooms side by side. Mason was brisk with energy, hustling people along, locking the truck, and getting the Creels into their room with the admonishment to rest while he went to find food.

"Come with me," Mason said as he closed the door behind him.

Sam laid on the bed, smelling mildew and bleach as they struggled to cover up the odors of everything that had gone on in these rooms since the place opened. The beige walls and green floral-print bedspreads were faded with time and use. His backpack remained resolutely at his side. He wasn't letting it out of his sight for the rest of his life.

"Tired," Sam responded. Maybe if Mason left, he could check the phone, see if they got a response.

"You need to move around a little—you didn't even get out during the rest stops."

"Tired," he repeated. If Mason went out for food, maybe he could make a call—hear someone's voice to know everything was okay....

"Sam." Mason's usually gentle tone took on something a little sharper. "I know you're worried and upset, but I... I can't take care of you. I need you to... to pull your weight."

Sam didn't say anything. He sat up slowly, feeling the gravity of depression yanking him back down.

"What do you need me to do?"

Mason sighed and then walked the few feet to sit down next to Sam on the bed.

"I just need you to keep your chin up. I know this is hard—I'm scared too."

Sam scoffed and tangled his hands together in his lap.

"Much as I enjoy being your, uh... knight in shining armor...." Mason knocked their shoulders together. "The truth is I'm just a dumb rookie kid in waaaay over his head. Like so over his head. I wish your, uh... I wish Nox was here. Sorry."

"Don't be. I wish that too. Heck, I wish Cade and Rachel were here. I'd feel safer." Sam gave his boyfriend a sideways glance. "Sorry."

"Oh my God, I'd give my left kidney for Rachel to be in charge." Mason's smile helped. A little. "But they're not here, and we're like... it. For this group anyway. And what we're supposed to be doing is staying safe, keeping Mr. and Mrs. Creel safe."

"I wish we could do more," Sam whispered. He wanted to thrust the phone into Mason's hands and insist they call, but something held him back. If Mason knew he had the phone but didn't want to use it, if he got angry with Sam for sending the message—the fear of making another mistake, of putting them in further danger stayed Sam's hand.

Mason reached over and slid his hand around Sam's wrist. "Hey. We made it off the mountain, right? That's good. That's step one. Now we have some time to come up with our next move."

Mason's positivity—oh God. Sam would probably be totally lost without it.

"Okay. And we have to get some food."

"Yeah, 'cause jerky and peanut butter crackers are not going to cut it after all that good stuff Mrs. Creel cooked us." Mason pressed a gentle kiss to the corner of Sam's frown. "You'll feel better after a hot dinner and a shower. Promise."

*I'll feel better when I hear my dad's voice*, he thought, but Sam nodded, feigning a smile to make Mason happy.

BACK IN the room, Sam and Mason ate chicken and waffles out of paper boxes at the tiny table under the window.

The fresh air had done Sam some good, and while the food wasn't anywhere near Amelia's—something he mentioned when they dropped off food for the Creels—it was still hot and filling.

They shared a giant orange soda, and Sam savored the artificial goodness on his tongue.

"Not a lot of soda machines in my part of the city," he said offhandedly when Mason mocked his pleasure.

"Not a lot of anything." Mason wiped his hands and face with the convenient wet nap.

Sam shrugged. "Honestly, I liked it better than when I was in the District. It was quiet."

"Not a fan of flashing billboards and way too much neon?"

"Or traffic or noise or drugs or people acting like idiots. Even when I dreamed of leaving, I'd always end up dreaming of a quiet place." Sam started gathering up the garbage. Maybe there was a dumpster outside to drop the trash, because God, old grease would not complement the staleness in here.

"And now? Where do you want to end up? I mean, when all of this is over."

Mason's voice was gentle, and it did things to Sam's gut. He dared a peek and then went back to straightening up. "I don't know. So far, I've been in the city and to a farm in South Carolina. Is there a middle option?"

"My family is in the suburbs—houses and lawns and backyards and giant superstores just down the road."

"That could work." Sam snuck another glance. "Is that what you want?"

"I…." Mason stopped, seemingly almost surprised by his lack of an answer. "I don't know. I guess I assumed that I'd settle into the same life as my parents and siblings, but… I don't know. Depends."

"On?"

Mason's head ticked to one side. "You."

"Oh."

"You can't be entirely surprised. I mean, going on the run with somebody is really not a casual-dating scenario."

Delight fanned through Sam's body. So okay, maybe he was a terrible person and everything was shit, but also? Mason's smile made him so freaking happy he wanted to jump on that lumpy awful bed.

"So, we're officially going steady?" he asked, in his best teasing voice.

Warmth flickered through Mason's expression as he leaned over. "You could say that."

When their lips met for a kiss, Sam let the clouds part for a few minutes and let himself believe in happy endings.


SAM WOKE with a start and fumbled to get his glasses from the nightstand onto his face so he could see.

The red numbers on the clock said 3:47, and Sam was alone in bed.

A panicked squall rose inside his head as he sat up and frantically looked around. Had someone broken in? Did Mason leave? He felt around for the backpack on the floor next to the bed.

The silence felt unnatural—he couldn't hear traffic or people in the parking lot or even the ice machine. A second stretched and twisted into a full minute as Sam watched the clock tick to 3:48. Then all hell broke loose.

In the space of a breath, the door to the motel room splintered into pieces as men wielding guns burst inside. Sam instinctively rolled toward the wall, his body instantly realizing the need to get down low. Fast.

"Hands up!" Someone was screaming as two black-clad men grabbed Sam and yanked him to the dank carpet, knee to his back.

"Federal Agents," a voice sounded over the din. "No one move."

# CHAPTER EIGHT

CARSON WAITED impatiently as Nox pulled on the suit jacket and ran nervous hands through his hair. His father—Jesus, his father—watched him carefully, assessing his appearance through familiar eyes. He felt as though he were thirteen again, waiting for his father to point out what he was doing wrong.

It had been a while, but the quality of the suit—and the way it fit him almost perfectly—was not lost on Nox.

"Given the circumstances," Carson said finally, a critical look on his face, "this is the best we can do." He checked the thick gold watch on his wrist, then stepped back through the doorway, gesturing for Nox to follow.

*Surreal*, Nox thought as he followed Carson out of the room and down the hallway. They reentered the enormous entryway and then continued through the apartment.

The trip gave Nox a better look at the place. A quick glance out the floor-to-ceiling windows of the formal living room told him they were in the penthouse. Familiar landmarks placed them in the heart of the District, nearly dead center. His mind raced. There was only one building this could be—the Regency.

A trickle of hope wormed its way into his heart. He was well acquainted with this high-rise. He'd been on the crew that renovated it.

They passed through another hallway, and Cade refocused on the layout and his father's casual air, as though this were an everyday occurrence. As though his father hadn't been presumed dead for seventeen years. As though he hadn't, quite recently, locked Nox in a cell and pumped him full of drugs.

No sign of Antonio, Nox realized as they arrived at a closed door. Carson stopped, hand on the knob, then turned to Nox, who waited a few feet away.

"Keep your mouth shut. Nod and smile. If you do anything to create a disturbance, Nox, I will kill that whore of yours. Is that clear?"

Nox rocked back, his knees weak as he realized what Carson was saying in his bland and polite tone.

Cade was alive.

That thought distracted him enough to nod his agreement to Carson. The door opened and Carson stepped through. Nox followed blindly.

The size of the office rivaled that of the living room. The walls were wood paneled, the furniture masculine and dark, everywhere an accentuation of wealth. On the matching facing leather sofas sat six men, three on each side, each a replica of his father's wealth and neatly dignified age. Their heads turned as one when Carson moved aside to reveal Nox.

"Gentlemen," he said. "Let's get things started."

NOX SANK into a leather club chair, catty-cornered to the sofas and tucked between two built-in bookshelves. There was a second door to his left, and the door they came from to his right. His mind raced as he tried to gather his thoughts, focus on the task at hand.

Cade was alive.

He shook his head. Two doors, no guards, though no telling what was on the other side. If he had oriented himself correctly, they were on the opposite side of the building from the elevator. Nox struggled to remember where the fire exit had been located.

His father stood in front of a large desk, forcing the men to twist and turn in his direction. Carson let them sit for a dramatic moment as the sound of a clock ticking filled the quiet.

"Thank you all for coming today. I realize the past few weeks have been very difficult for all of us, with the bombing of the Iron Butterfly bringing scrutiny upon us from Albany."

A low murmur went up among the men. Nox looked at their faces, searching for clues to who they were. Did he recognize any of them from the limited news in the District or his dealings at the casinos?

They were a mix of ethnicities, but each bore the carriage of someone accustomed to being catered to. The stench of multi-generational wealth permeated the room. Nox had grown up around these people, and every one of them was clearly a longtime resident of his father's world.

"To that end, we are going to need to move up our timetable." Carson cast his gaze over to Nox, a small smile playing on his lips. "We have five days, possibly seven, but no more than that."

The murmur grew louder. Two of the older men exchanged heated whispers. Another threw himself back against the sofa, muttering a curse.

"I understand, I do." Carson held up his hand. "But in the end, the profits will far outweigh the risk."

Nox watched his father carefully, dragged into the undertow of memory. Long ago he realized his father had a tell, an uncontrollable clue to when he was lying. It made its appearance when he said he'd be home for dinner or back by the weekend or in attendance for a sporting event or awards banquet. Even as a child, Nox learned to read his father's trustworthiness when it came to being an active part of his and his mother's life.

The little pulse caught his attention as his father spoke—the left side of Carson's jaw jumped as he issued his platitudes to the men.

Nothing he was saying was true.

Forcing himself to relax, Nox crossed his arms over his chest, one leg over the other. He lifted his chin and met his father's occasional look with an implacable face.

He could feel that Carson was ramping up to something.

Carson didn't disappoint.

"In forty-eight hours, I will disperse the product to the drop-off points. You should have your transportation ironed out. Once the trucks are parked, I am no longer responsible for the merchandise, gentlemen. I suggest you make your travel plans now."

The man who'd been so angry leaned forward again and gave his fellow attendees a sharp glance. "Will no one ask?" he questioned, then huffed in annoyance.

"Fine." He stood and drew up to his full height, pressing his shoulders back as if physically psyching himself to confront Carson.

"This will cost us more money," he said, a slight quiver in his voice. "Increase our risk of being found out. Will the price be adjusted appropriately?"

Carson blinked, then tilted his head. It was such a benign move, the silently sarcastic gesture of a man who wasn't interested in your thoughts or opinions. But the palpable fear in the room as the other men stared in quiet horror—and curiosity—kept Nox riveted.

"That seems a little greedy on your part, Gerald," Carson said quietly.

Absolute silence reigned.

Gerald, it seemed, was not about to give up.

"Given the risk," he said, weak chin quivering but raised. "Given the risk I would say it's entirely rational."

Carson nodded and then folded his arms across his body. He bobbed his head and let out a gentle sigh. "All right, Gerald. I will contact my employers—" There was no mistaking the gasp that filled the room. "—and speak to them," Carson continued as though he hadn't heard the reaction. "I will say, Gerald Forsky no longer believes he is being treated fairly."

Gerald Forsky began shaking his head. "No, no. That's not what I'm saying."

The two men on the couch with Gerald began making gestures to him—sit down, sit down and be quiet.

"That's precisely what you *are* saying, Gerald. And *I* am saying that I can bring up your dissatisfaction."

Another man, considerably younger and taller than Gerald, stood up quickly.

"Mr. Smith, please. Gerald is just anxious about the date being pushed up. We're fine with the original deal." Nox couldn't place his faint accent, but the pleading cadence of his voice suggested someone with courtroom experience. "It's perfectly all right. No need to bother anyone."

His couch companions had succeeded in getting Gerald Forsky to sit down, and he slumped back, sweat dotting his face as he pushed away the concerned whispers from the other men.

Nox watched his father, heard the echo of "Mr. Smith" in his head.

"Thank you for clearing that up, Andre." Carson unfolded his arms and gestured to Nox. On alert, Nox sat up straighter.

"Before we move to the dining room for some refreshments, I wanted to introduce you to my son. He will be taking over for me upon my retirement in a few weeks, so I thought you should get to know him."

The floor dropped out from beneath Nox as every head in the room swiveled in his direction.

# CHAPTER NINE

CADE FELT his paper-thin control tear as LJ gave him the news that Rachel had left without them. With all they'd been through together, he'd let himself be fooled that she wasn't a liar and a thief and could not be trusted. Worse, he'd exposed her to his brother.

"Goddammit," he swore, slamming his fist into the wall as he left the bedroom. "She took the gun, I'm sure. And the money." Cade took the stairs two at a time, navigating by pure rage as he stormed into the kitchen. The knives sat on the island, but everything else—the things most useful—were gone. Including the phone.

"Fuck." Cade leaned his hands against the cold steel of the stove and tried to rein in his temper.

He heard his brother walk in.

"Maybe she just wanted to keep us safe," LJ said awkwardly. "She's so take-charge, and—"

Cade put his hand up. "No. She left us behind for a reason, LJ, and I'm sorry. There is no fucking way it's altruistic." He took a deep breath and pushed himself into a standing position. He turned to LJ, glad the shadows hid his sorrowful expression. "We're on our own now."

"Cade…."

"I'm sorry."

"Listen, I know you think I'm some dumb farmer who got taken in by a con, but I know Rachel. I do. We've… she's told things to me, okay? She's told me things she's done. But Rachel has changed. And I know in my heart the only reason she'd leave is for a good one." LJ sounded so sincere it broke Cade's heart in half.

Cade rubbed his palms over his eyes, trying to rub the tears and ache away. "What do you want to do? Sit here and wait? Pray she comes back?"

"Why not? It's warm. We got food and water."

Cade shook his head. "No. I still don't know if Francis was lying about the partner."

"Rachel said—"

He put his hand up. "We're going to figure out where Rachel went. She can't have much of a head start. There's only one semi-safe route to the District, where I have to assume she's going."

LJ shifted from foot to foot, silently expressing his disapproval of the plan, but finally he sighed loudly.

"Fine. Let's go."


THEY BUNDLED up with winter wear found in the downstairs coat closet. Francis's knives were divided between them, pocketed for protection. Out the back door and into the predawn night they went, with Cade leading the way.

His brother met Cade's long strides. They stuck to a path closer to the water, parallel to the street that ran downtown. In the distance, Cade could see patrol boats, more than usual, running up and down the river. It seemed the city was gearing up for a battle, and he prayed they were gone before it all went down.

LJ didn't speak during the entire trip. Cade's every sidelong glance was met with a resolute expression of determination. LJ wanted to be right about Rachel, and Cade hated how positive he was that his brother was wrong.

And Nox—Nox had been right from the beginning.

Cade had advocated for Rachel to come along, insisted she'd changed, but her shooting of Francis seemed to trigger something slightly hysterical in his gut.

Why was she so insistent he didn't have a partner? How could she be sure?

The shot to the face, so precise, seemed to bely her story of him trying to get the gun.

He knew she was a killer. His mistake was believing she only killed for the right reasons.

Cade stumbled. He stopped to catch his breath and get a better handle on where they were, and as he tried to decide which direction to head in, LJ grabbed his arm.

"Up there," he murmured.

As the roughness of the former Upper East Side gave way to the District, streetlamps began to illuminate the darkness. Ahead Cade could make out a small figure walking quickly between the puddles of light.

Rachel.

They jogged as quietly, avoiding the streets until the last possible second. Cade's anxiety began to bubble in his gut as they ducked and weaved through warehouses and supply companies.

"Thank God there are no cabs running," he muttered to himself as they watched Rachel bypass the street leading to the heart of the District and instead veer off to the right.

"Downtown," Cade said to his brother, pulling him to the parallel street. The seedier casinos and hotels—unsurprising. And also very helpful, as the police presence was generally slim and the private security stayed close to home.

A cruiser sped by, lights off, and didn't seem to notice them crouched in the doorway of a closed restaurant. The momentary pause let some cold seep between Cade's face and the scarf wrapped tightly around him.

When this was over, he thought as they took off again, I just want to be warm.

Finally the downtown area came into view, with all its gaudy neon signs and dimly lit alleys, perfectly suited for a drug deal or a blowjob, depending on your poison. Cade slowed LJ down as they settled in a narrow opening between a cleaner's and a small coffee shop, both closed this early in the morning. It gave them an excellent vantage point to see where Rachel went next.

The Flamingo sat squarely on the edge of downtown and whatever came next—half demolished buildings where squatters were neighbors to drug dens and entire fields of overgrown debris served as graveyards for those who died when buildings collapsed into the water-soaked tip of Manhattan. The patrons of this particular casino didn't come for the view—no one did down here—but rather for low-bet tables, sparkly slot machines, bartenders with a heavy pour, and whores without limits.

Cade had heard stories. Stories that made him grateful for the Butterfly.

Now he watched as Rachel, tucked into a huge down coat and black skullcap, hurried to the side employee entrance of the Flamingo, one last anxious glance over her shoulder before she paused at the key card reader and then disappeared into the darkness.

"See," LJ whispered from their hiding place. "She's just findin' information, like she said."

Cade shook his head. "Side entrance?" he asked. That's where the real security was. She'd used Francis's key card, the one they couldn't identify right away. And even with the card, the guards wouldn't let her by with a flirty smile or even a bribe. A thousand wasn't getting her in through the back. He didn't elaborate, though; he just slipped from the shadows, putting a hand up for LJ to stay put. "Wait for me," he said. Then he slid down the block, doorway to doorway, to get a better vantage point to see where Rachel had gone.

He was almost in position, cursing the first rays of morning beginning to cut through the darkness. The lightening sky meant he didn't have much more time.

Cade heard the shout before he registered the giant mass of a man in a black velvet tracksuit coming toward him. He was calling out in a language Cade's brain quickly identified as Georgian. *Thank you, Iron Butterfly international clientele, for an interesting set of skills to take into the world.*

Hands up, a smile on his face, Cade stumbled forward as if he were just a happy drunk going on his merry way.

"Hey, man, hey, sorry, sorry!" he called out in his best slurry, overserved voice. "I'm a little, uh… lost. What street is this?"

The man walked right up to Cade, dwarfing him so completely that Cade had to tip his head back to look into his scowl.

"Whoa, shit." Cade laughed nervously. "You're a big… hey, I'm sorry. I'm just… I'm lost, okay?"

"Shut the fuck up," he said, his accent thick. With one massive hand, he pushed Cade back against the building, holding him there as the other hand began to search his pockets.

Shit.

"What the fuck is this?" the man asked, dangling one of Francis's knives from his fingers. "What the fuck?"

Everything else from that point on was in the man's native tongue. He pocketed the knife and grabbed Cade's arm. It was fairly easy to discern that, first, his drunken act hadn't worked, and second, they were headed for the Flamingo.

He prayed LJ would stay hidden. With every skidding step toward the massive building, he waited for his brother to try to save him, or for LJ to be found. But nothing happened, and he was grateful.

Less so when his captor shoved him into the arms of two men wearing red jackets and holding machine guns.


THE BACK end of the Flamingo was as far from the Butterfly as one could get. Dust and grime coated every surface, and piles of building materials lined the hallway Cade was being marched up. He was cuffed, arms behind his back, and his silent sentries didn't seem interested in telling him where he was going.

They pushed through a scarred metal swinging double door, into a wider and brighter hallway. A gaggle of bleary-eyed women in Uggs and thick pink terrycloth robes sat smoking in an empty delivery stall, watching him without interest as he went by.

One of the women seemed to recognize him. She leaned over to whisper in the ear of the person closest to her.

"No autographs, please," he muttered.

Another set of doors and then into an elevator. Cade began to shake in anticipation. He assumed he was being brought to see Rachel and whoever her contact was. He didn't know what to expect when the car stopped at the tenth floor and the doors jerked open.

The elevator opened directly into a suite, as garishly pink as the neon sign outside—leather on the walls, fur on every surface, a sectional in pink velvet so bright it hurt his eyes. An enormous chandelier, dripping with diamond crystals, presided over the room.

Pink, pink. Everywhere, everything… pink.

His guards shoved him into the suite, and Cade caught himself before he fell. It took a second, but he registered Rachel walking toward him, her coat and cap discarded.

She had a crystal tumbler in her hand.

"You couldn't just trust me, could you?" she asked, bemused.

"Clearly no," he snapped, turning slightly. "Seriously?"

"Not my call. The Flamingo takes its security very seriously." She gestured toward the two men. He felt the cuffs release a second later. "Drink?"

"Rachel," he said, warning in his tone. "I'm not playing around here."

"Neither am I, Cade." Rachel turned, walked into the suite, and settled on the corner of the pink couch. She looked over as a side door opened, and Cade followed her line of sight.

Damian Oh walked in, a sheepish expression on his face.

"Hey, Cade."

Of all the people Cade expected to see, Damian—wearing glasses and dressed in a pair of jeans and a black cashmere sweater—was the last. He looked apologetic, shooting glances at Rachel, whose expression didn't change.

"What the holy fuck," Cade finally managed to spit out. He took a step back and then forward toward Damian.

The click of safeties being released stopped him from moving another inch.

"It's fine. Go," another voice said. Cade didn't dare turn his head.

The woman in question came into his view with a sweep of floral pink silk kimono and wild white hair chopped close to her head. She dropped down on the sofa next to Rachel, right up against her, and then draped her arm over Rachel's shoulders.

"Galina, your friend is very tense," she said, watching him with pale blue eyes, the remnants of makeup caked on her face. Her accent was very faint, but Cade surmised her to be Russian.

Rachel took a sip of her drink. "Sit down, Caden. Then we can have a conversation."

Cade shot a look at Damian, who'd skirted over to the bar in the corner.

"A conversation about you and Damian working together? About you killing Francis so he couldn't talk?" Cade shouted. A small voice in his mind told him to keep it together, but his anger bubbled out, fueled by fear and shame at having trusted these people for a second.

Sitting up straighter, Rachel didn't answer, but her complexion went slightly pale. Cade refused to fall for it.

"Sit down or Mitzie will be forced to call her guards back, Caden." He recognized that steel tone from a thousand or so staff meetings at the Iron Butterfly.

"They are not very nice people," Mitzie offered lazily, playing with Rachel's braids in a way that spoke of intimacy. "I hire them for that very reason."

"Cade," Damian said, hands wrapped nervously around a bottle of water, "please sit down."

His blood still buzzing with anger, Cade sat down with a thump in a pink leather chair across from Rachel and Mitzie.

"Just waiting for one more person," Mitzie said, leaning over to press a wet kiss on Rachel's cheek. She nuzzled her, then stood up, her hand lingering in Rachel's hair.

Cade felt a vein ticking in his jaw. Rachel and LJ, just another part of the act.

The elevator dinged again, and Rachel's demeanor shifted. She tensed as she stood up and walked away from Mitzie's grasping hands.

"Stop," she hissed as she walked toward the elevator.

It wasn't a surprise when the doors opened and LJ walked into the suite, his eyes wide.

"What the hell, Rachel?"

# Chapter Ten

Nox sat frozen in the chair as his father announced him as the next boss of the family business. Every head in the room turned in his direction, and penetrating stares pinned him in place. He could see curiosity, animosity, fear. Blinking, he kept still, his face bland even as he managed to look over at Carson.

His father smiled—an insincere and calculating curve of his lips—and then loudly cleared his throat. Everyone swiveled back to attention.

"As we finish up here and begin our move to greener pastures, he will be transitioning into a more hands-on role." He paused for effect, then continued, "Coordinating further deliveries, handling payments. Were there any questions?"

Not a hand went up, though a few allowed their eyes to dart in Gerald's direction.

"Marvelous. When you return to your offices, you'll find updated documentation, everything you'll need."

Nox watched as every complexion in the room paled a few shades.

Clever, he thought. Let all of them know Carson's people were in their offices. They had no secrets from him.

Nox wondered whether he did either.

"There are refreshments in the dining room. Please help yourself."

As if on prearranged cue, the doors farthest from Nox opened, and he glimpsed the heavily armed guards who had been waiting outside. The men got up, slowly and awkwardly, and then filed out dutifully like schoolchildren on their way to class. No one looked back at Carson.

"Gerald," Carson called at the last second. "Can you give me a private moment?"

A chill ran through Nox and, it seemed, the entire room.

Gerald broke into a sweat. Nox could see it glistening on his neck and forehead. He stepped out of line, helplessly throwing out wordless pleas, but the others picked up their pace, almost as one, and disappeared through the doors.

Antonio stepped in and then closed the doors behind him.

Nox felt a panicked-rabbit heartbeat nearly blow his chest out. He made a move to stand, but Carson, his gaze never leaving Gerald, held his hand up.

"I...," Gerald began, a begging note to his voice. "I'm sorry...."

Carson never said a word. He simply nodded, then turned to move behind his desk.

Gerald seemed to think this was a cue to continue talking, and he opened his mouth, but that was as far as he got. Behind him, Antonio pulled out a pistol, aimed it at the back of Gerald's head, and pulled the trigger.

Blood and brain matter sprayed violently across the leather sofa and antique rug, reaching the edge of Carson's sprawling desk.

Carson didn't flinch.

"Thank you, Antonio. Wait five minutes and then send the maid in."

This wasn't the first time Nox had watched someone die. He'd pulled the trigger himself more than a few times. In all those occasions, he'd been angry and fearful and fighting—this execution stunned him momentarily.

The click of the door refocused him on Carson, who was regarding him from across the room. Gerald lay facedown on the rug between them.

"He was an idiot," Carson said conversationally. "Identifying chinks in the armor of an operation, Nox, that is a crucial part of business."

Nox opened his mouth but closed it. His brain stumbled over itself as he tried to figure out where to start.

"You're confused, of course. I understand." He leaned back in his chair, and the leather creaked.

"You threw me in a cell and pumped me full of drugs," Nox said, a rumble of anger in his tone.

Carson shrugged. "You were rude. And I needed some... information."

"Information? I'm not telling you anything," he snapped, finally released from his paralyzed state. Nox leaned forward and pointed at his father. "Believe me."

"You," Carson said slowly, his face alight with something close to amusement, "Have literally no information I could possibly need. In fact, what you think you know is rubbish." He rubbed his chin with two fingers. "Those men, the ones who seem to hang on my every word and, uh, poor Gerald here, they are... worker bees on my payroll. They're rich but stupid and easily manipulated. I needed them to believe... some things... and you provided me with an opportunity to perform a little... let's say necessary theater."

Nox pushed himself to the edge of the chair. "I will not work for you."

With a barking laugh, Carson pushed his chair back even farther. If anything, Nox's anger seemed to delight him.

"God, Nox, please. You would do something stupid like liquidate my assets and feed poor hookers or something." Carson leaned forward, elbows on the edge of his desk. "Your usefulness to me was playing boogeyman on the streets. Compensation was me keeping you and Sam alive."

The foundation under Nox's feet quaked and crumbled a bit.

"You said that before. I don't believe it. I raised Sam, I protected him, and I shut down the drugs," Nox said, frustration rising.

"No, you dealt with the trash trying to steal from me," Carson interrupted. "Street deals and tourists looking for a quick fix outside proper channels don't add to my bottom line, Nox."

Illumination beamed down into Nox's brain. "You control the Dead Bolt."

The man who warned him off, the man with his boot in Nox's side.

"Every last ounce of it." Carson ducked his head as if bowing. "It was created in my lab, manufactured here, and distributed. Helped me bring the more... organized businesses into the city, if you get my meaning. Invest, then get a piece of the worldwide distribution when the time came."

Nox shook his head. "No. That doesn't make sense. It's been around for more than ten years...."

"Yes, it certainly has. And in that time, it's gotten quite the reputation. People smuggling it home to share with friends and loved ones—the most toxic of souvenirs. Bringing them to the District to get more. Revenues up. At the same time, some very well-paid scientists were coming up with other uses for it. Medicinal uses." He gestured toward Nox. "Uses that will make me an even richer man. And now... now it's time."

A timid knock interrupted Carson.

"Come in," he called. The doors opened tentatively as three young men in white overalls peeked their heads in.

"Oh yes." Carson indicated Gerald's body as though he'd forgotten it was there. "Nox, come with me. Let the boys do their job."


ON STIFF legs, Nox followed Carson through the penthouse. Two guards trailed them, keeping a respectable distance, though close enough that Nox dared not try anything.

Carson led him into a second office, this one much smaller. It was clearly used for actual work, with multiple computer monitors and stacks of black boxes that Nox supposed were backup drives. Not a single piece of paper was apparent, not even a calendar.

"Wait outside," Carson said to the guards as he shut the door behind him.

Once they were locked in the small room, Nox glanced around, seeking a way out. Window, door....

"You can't get out of here, except through that door," Carson said mildly, settling in behind the L-shaped desk. He looked weirdly out of place, his expensive suit and regal bearing at odds with the blinking screens around them.

Nox refused to acknowledge Carson's words, even as he inwardly cursed them. Instead he focused on the codes rolling by on the monitors.

God, he wished LJ were here.

"Nothing you'd understand," Carson said, but he turned the screens so they faced away from the visitor's chair across from him. "Sit. Please."

Reluctantly Nox dropped into the chair, his attention still crawling around the room. So many black boxes, stacked neatly on shelves.

"I imagine you have questions." His father tapped on the desk with his knuckles, like an irritated headmaster. "You have ten minutes of my time, and then...." Carson made a gesture toward his watch. "Then I have something of importance to deal with."

A red stain filtered Nox's vision. Anger, confusion—the urge to end this now by simply reaching over the desk and killing his father the way he did Mr. White....

Mr. White.

"Did you point Mr. White in our direction?" he asked finally, earning a genuinely surprised expression from Carson.

"Oddly enough, no. I was fine with the way things were—you skulking about the city, your brother tucked away like a fair maiden in a tower." He chuckled at his own joke. "You getting involved in matters forced me to speed up a few things, spend a little extra money. Bothersome until the end, Nox."

Nox didn't see the telltale throb of the vein in his father's jaw, so he accepted that answer for now. Reluctantly.

"You know him, though." He paused. "Knew him."

"Ah, that was your handiwork. Unsurprising. Thank you for taking care of him." Carson shrugged. "I suppose he told you he was Sam's... biological father."

Swallowing down the stomach acid bubbling up in his throat, Nox dipped his chin once in confirmation.

"No one will connect you, so there's nothing to worry about there." Carson leaned back in the chair and steepled his fingers together. "Honestly, Nox, why aren't you asking the million-dollar question? It has to be eating away at you."

Gaze narrowing, Nox stared directly into Carson's face.

"How the fuck are you still alive?"

# INTERLUDE

WHEN HIS *private line rings, Carson tenses, pauses before accepting the call. Not even Jenny has access to this number. Only one man does.*

*Mr. Smith, his contact from South America, begins to speak as soon as the call connects.*

*"They're coming for me," he says, his voice frantic. "I've burned everything but...."*

*"I understand," Carson responds, his voice monotone even as his heart jackrabbits in his chest. He's already got his fingers on the keyboard of his computer, calling up files buried deep within the system, only to be accessed in an emergency.*

*Like his business partner being taken out.*

*Carson doesn't ask if Mr. Smith is referring to their Columbian associates or the DEA or a rival organization. This part of Carson's life is officially over, and he—quite frankly—isn't sad about it.*

*"Good luck," he says as the line goes dead.*

*Money laundering—the family business, as it were—was profitable and boring. Carson allowed Mr. Smith to do whatever he needed to while Carson enjoyed building a real estate empire with his share of the profits. On the back of the company he received for marrying crazy Natalie, Carson has reaped infinite rewards—like a deal to build affordable high-rise housing on the southernmost tip of the island. Carefully orchestrated partnerships with some international connections helped raise profitability and kept building costs low. Carson is about to make more money this year from his growing empire than he is from the cartel's business.*

*He's a fucking genius.*

*But he hates being tied down to the city—to Natalie, to fatherhood and generational expectations. He thought erasing his father from the equation would set him free, but no. He's trapped.*

*Has been trapped.*

*Oh, he's managed a few luxurious "bachelor pads" where he meets women around the city. Natalie is in the hands of Mr. White at Morningside—the epitome of "out of sight, out of mind." Jenny pays his bills and deals with any of Nox's school issues that require a payment or his signature.*

*Still.*

*Responsibilities that don't interest him hang over his head.*

*Carson begins to run a program that will destroy the records of his association with Mr. Smith—the benign "seems clean to the IRS" versions as well as the heavily coded ones that track their real business. As lines of code scroll by, he sits back in his chair.*

*If Mr. Smith goes down, it's very likely Carson will be next. Destroyed records or not, the cartel will be looking for their money. Looking for Carson. He has no desire to be a casualty of this venture.*

*Unless he could do it on his own terms?*

*Outside, the seemingly endless storm continues to rage. It's been raining for weeks, months. He's lost count and he's sick of it. All pretense of family life is gone. Thanks to Mr. White, Natalie is turning into a vegetable at the sanitarium. And his son Nox is practically an adult. He's fine without Carson. Will be fine.*

*A plan begins to come together.*

*If everyone believes him dead—his business associates, the DEA, his building project partners, and his family—then Carson is free to start over again. New name, new city. Maybe a new face.*

*His office intercom beeps once. Jenny only uses the intercom when one of his legitimate contacts is there, when she's pretending to be his executive assistant instead of the world's most innocent-looking muscle.*

*"Who is it?" he asks, picking up the phone. His excitement at imagining a different life is too delicious. He doesn't want to be interrupted.*

*"Gerrity," she says, her tone indicating just how irritating she finds the mayor's right-hand man and Carson's main cohort in the high-rise scheme.*

*Carson swallows a sigh. "Send him in."*

TWO HOURS *later—Gerrity long gone, his news that the city is being evacuated as more and more buildings collapse, several with their names attached to them, ringing in Carson's ears—he packs up his briefcase, grabs his umbrella and overcoat, and heads out the door.*

*"I'm going to Gracie Mansion," he says sharply. "Anyone calls, I'm in a meeting." How to soothe the mayor's panic about the unstable buildings until he can get away....*

*"All right." Jenny stands, and his last image is her sharp gaze and the calculating tilt of her head, her simple—and tight—black sheath, hair piled on top of her head making her seem older than she is. She'd gone through a period of wearing serious suits, and he hated it. She'd also put a stop to their office assignations.*

*They'd reached the end of so many roads traveled together.*

*He finds her to be invaluable. Her ability to present whatever mask someone needs to see supersedes even her skill with a gun or her talent for digging up dirt on his associates. They have that in common, which is why he's leaving her behind. She sees through him in a way he's become wary of. And now he'll use her opportunistic and murderously practical ways as his ticket out of here.*

*He doesn't say good-bye and lets the door slam behind him as he heads for the elevator.*

*THE MAYOR is hysterical. As they leave the office and fall into a swarm of city and state officials frantically running around the mansion, Gerrity tells him that they need to leave. Immediately. Destroy as many records as possible on the way out.*

*Which is ridiculous. The paper trail to who built the affordable housing ranges from permits to a fucking two-year nonstop splash on the front of every New York City paper and magazine, with the mayor taking full credit for everything.*

*Carson has kept to the shadows, citing "family reasons" for his dislike of photos and articles. He keeps his comments brief.*

*But there is nothing that will stop the truth from coming out with so many of those involved still breathing.*

*IN A shitty building up near Morningside Sanitarium, he has rented an apartment under a series of shell corporations. He's placed the call to Jenny, voice disguised, and is unsurprised when she confirms—without substantiation—that he is skimming profits from the cartel. Carson has a moment of concern that the girl knows exactly who killed her parents and hungers for revenge, but he dismisses it. It doesn't matter. In a few hours, policemen will bring her to the morgue to identify the body of Carson Boyet, and his death will set him free.*

*He has one thing to do before that.*

*The haircut and dye and glasses alter his appearance enough so he can casually stroll into the Morningside Sanitarium and ask for Natalie Boyet's suite. Lifts and padding under the suit have rendered him slower, but with even his body posture changed, Carson already feels like he's walking to his new life.*

*There's an urgency pulsing through the hallways as he heads for her room. In just the ten hours since he spoke to the mayor and Gerrity, the weather has pushed the island to full crisis, with thousands fleeing in a panic, clogging the bridges out of the city, with others left behind for lack of resources. The National Guard is preparing to descend, and Albany is taking control. A perfect storm of chaos, as it were, and Carson plans to take full advantage.*

*He pushes open the door to Natalie's room and is greeted with his blank-faced wife and—much more surprisingly—Mr. Smith petting the rounded mound of her pregnant stomach under the covers.*

*"Congratulations," his business associate says, no longer sounding panicked.*

*Carson plucks his courage and stomach from somewhere around his feet, and his hand tenses on the doorknob.*

*"Not mine," he says breathlessly.*

*Mr. Smith turns around and gestures for Carson to come in.*

*"I see you've already begun your transformation."*

*Carson's eyes dart from Mr. Smith and his smug smile to Natalie. She doesn't appear to hear them, but Carson knows from experience that guarantees nothing.*

*"She's fine. A nurse gave her her—"Mr. Smith smiles widely. "—medicine?" He ends the word with a questioning lilt. "She'll be quiet right up until the end."*

*Carson has no practical use for Natalie. Their marriage was a business arrangement, and dealing with her paranoid delusions has muted any vague affection he'd occasionally had for her over the years. But Mr. Smith's words are chilling.*

*"Until she gives birth," Carson says, gauging Mr. Smith's reaction.*

*"Of course," Mr. Smith responds, smooth as ever. He gestures for Carson to sit down on the edge of Natalie's bed.*

*The close proximity to his wife keeps Carson off-guard, which is clearly the point. Mr. Smith watches him closely for a long uncomfortable moment before he speaks.*

*"I know you're confused, Carson. It's quite understandable. As it is quite understandable that you're making plans to leave the city." He pauses dramatically. "As a new man."*

*"It seemed the wisest thing to do," Carson says, his tongue thick as his mouth goes dry. "I thought... I thought you were...."*

*"Dead? In jail? Both good guesses. But no, I am, as you can see, perfectly fine and in good health." Mr. Smith reaches his hand out again to touch Natalie and lightly stroke her arm. "Your idea about becoming someone new—a rebirth—that was quite smart, Carson. Because you see, I've done the same thing. Yesterday, my body was pulled from the wreckage of a plane crash." The stroking turns to a caress. "Very sad, yes?"*

*"So you're...." Carson flounders. "So they won't... find you."*

*Mr. Smith ducks his head with a faux boyish grin. "Oh, Carson, there is no... they. There is only me."*


*AN HOUR later, Carson sits sweat-soaked on Natalie's bed, his throat constricted in shock.*

*Mr. Smith has taken his leave, clapping Carson on the back before departing in a cloud of expensive cologne and amusement.*

*Carson's worldview is lying in a crumpled heap, tossed in the corner.*

*All this time, Carson has not been laundering money for a ruthless cartel—thereby securing his loyalty and fear and unquestioning participation—but rather for one man, a man who has emptied their accounts, reducing Carson's empire to barely enough to keep the lights on in one of his buildings.*

*While his ego insists this could not possibly be true, the tide of reality cannot be deterred.*

*His only contact—Mr. Smith.*

*The person who handled "cartel" business—Mr. Smith.*

*And now Carson has destroyed all records, so that even if he wanted to go to the DEA, make a deal, he has no proof. He has nothing.*

*But Mr. Smith has the knowledge that Carson hired him to kill his father. Wire transfers. Recorded conversations.*

*"Oh God," he chokes. In a few hours, Carson Boyet will be "dead," if all goes according to plan. And the money that was his ticket off this island and into a new life is gone.*

*Frantic, Carson spares a look at Natalie. Then he stands, his mind racing. He has to find money that Mr. Smith doesn't have access to…. Nox's trust fund. Natalie's assets. Not enough. The thought thunders into his brain.*

*Life insurance.*

*Carson begins to laugh.*

*Perfect.*

*He will be dead. His insurance company will pay survivor benefits to Natalie and Nox. They'll collect, and he'll reveal himself— tell a story about drug dealers and faking his death. He'll take them with him—who cares? Natalie will end up in another hospital, and Nox will go off to school.*

*Perfect.*

*"You're still worth something," he says as he turns to Natalie.*

*Only to find her staring right at him, eyes weirdly lucid.*

*He jumps in surprise.*

*"Carson?" she murmurs, "I had the strangest dream…."*

*Carson sits at Natalie's bedside after her initial pronouncement, eager and fearful to know what she heard. She drifts in and out, lucid and then paranoid, her eyes frantic as she looks around the room for danger in every corner.*

*She has always been a burden to him, and Carson would never categorize her as someone he loved. Their marriage was arranged. His reward was her family's real-estate empire. She is… a line on a spreadsheet, an income source. But that tiny sliver of him that biology demands he recognize as "the mother of his child" cannot be entirely smothered.*

*But this pregnancy? Not his. He hasn't touched her in five, seven, ten years? He can't even remember. It's not a surprise, though—Mr. White has always seemed a bit... possessive of her.*

*While he's musing, Carson gets the sense he's being watched. When he looks at Natalie, her gaze is direct and curious.*

*"Why are you here? Where's Nox?"*

*Carson is taken aback but adopts his standard soothing tone, the one he's always used with her. "Home, Natalie. He's home. Safe," he adds, though he cannot possibly know that's true. "We're going to be leaving here...."*

*Natalie shakes her head and sinks back into the bed, as if deflating. "I want to see Nox."*

*Carson resists the urge to press the button for the nurse. He might not want Natalie harmed, but he also doesn't want to have to deal with her. And he can't call his son, ask him to come here.*

*Can't call Jenny either.*

*His master plan is evaporating, and Carson struggles to come up with a new direction to take himself in. Natalie is just too unstable to deal with, so it seems like Nox will be the lucky inheritor of both his parents' money. At least until Carson can get to him. In the meantime, Mr. White's services will be called upon.*

*"Just relax, Natalie. Nox'll be here soon," Carson says absently, patting her hand.*

*"That man," Natalie mumbles. "He said...."*

*Carson's attention snaps back to his wife. "What?"*

*Natalie's head rolls back and forth, her distress growing. "You're... not here. You're dead. You're going to be dead."*

*"Going to be?" Carson leans closer. "Going to be?"*

*Natalie begins to cry, fat tears rolling down her face as she sniffles and screws her eyes shut. "I want Nox."*

*Carson does press the button for the nurse then. Then he hurries off the bed to stand near the window, where shadows have gathered.*

*The door opens, and an attendant pokes her head in.*

*She looks around, confused until she registers the man near the window.*

*"Um… yes?"*

*"I'm Mrs. Boyet's cousin, Daniel Van Zeldt. Who was that man here before? I didn't recognize him, and he… he upset my cousin," Carson says, affecting a faint Southern accent. He keeps away from the spill of light from Natalie's bedside lamps.*

*"Um… I don't know. I can check the visitor logs," she answers, clearly reluctant to do that work.*

*"I don't want anyone who isn't family near her," Carson huffs. "I will be speaking to Mr. White about this."*

*That gets the woman's attention. She steps fully into the room.*

*"I'll make sure the desk knows," she says politely. "Was there anything else?"*

*"She's very upset. Perhaps you can give her something…."*

*The woman casts an eye at the still silently crying Natalie, then at the bump unconcealed by the blankets.*

*"Um… in her condition…."*

*Carson makes an annoyed noise. "There must be something."*

*"I'll see what I can do. Let me speak to a doctor." The woman waits for Carson's response, to know she can leave without another threat of a complaint to the sanitarium's administrator.*

*"Fine," Carson snaps, eager to get her out of the room. To get Natalie settled down. To get himself the hell out of here.*

*The woman takes her leave, finally, and the door clicks closed behind her. Carson goes to Natalie's bedside and leans over to look at her, realizing it will be the very last time.*

*"Good luck, Natalie," he says. He leans over, pats her hand, then drops an impulsive kiss on her damp forehead.*

*She doesn't open her eyes, just keep crying. It's the last thing he sees when he walks out of the room.*


CARSON STARED at Nox, so much so that he felt his face grow hot as Nox twisted in his chair.

"Well?"

"Faking my death was the only way to keep you and your mother safe," he said finally.

Nox watched the pulse in his father's jaw begin again.

# CHAPTER ELEVEN

SOMEWHERE BETWEEN the motel door flying open and being dragged out of the room between two federal agents, Sam went into shock. They let him get dressed with shaking hands, their guns trained on his every move. "My backpack," he muttered, pointing to it dumbly. "I... I need it... my inhaler and stuff."

One of the agents did a cursory search and tossed it to him. He clutched it to his chest and followed. Dimly he wondered if Mr. Creel and Amelia were nearby and if Mason had come quietly. He'd heard no screams or shots—or any sounds, for that matter. He did hear his heart thudding and his teeth chattering.

Outside, a nondescript van sat idling. An agent opened the back and pushed Sam inside. The cold van floor didn't help as he lay down and rested his forehead against the chill.

The sound of crying caught his attention.

Walking past the back of the van were the Creels, Amelia weeping as Mr. Creel kept an arm around her shoulders. Sam wanted to call out, but a broad-shouldered agent stepped into his view, blocking the sight of his friends and the thin light from the parking lot.

"Step aside," a hoarse voice said, and the man disappeared. In his place, framed by the van's back door, stood a dark-haired man in a windbreaker, his mouth drawn in a thin line.

"Sam Boyet?" the man asked as Sam struggled to sit up.

"Sam Mullens," he responded automatically as he brushed his hair from his eyes and straightened his glasses. "I don't understand what's going on. Where are my friends?" Even in the face of fear, he remembered what his father had driven into his brain for years—stick with your story, sound confused, keep it simple.

"I'm not in the mood, Mr. Boyet," he sighed, his voice scratchy, as if he were recovering from a serious cold. A scarf was wound tightly around his neck. "I'm Agent Allard, and you are being taken into custody on suspicion of aiding and abetting a federal fugitive."

Before Sam could protest, Agent Allard stepped back and slammed the doors of the van, leaving him in darkness.

The ride to wherever they were going didn't take long. Sam breathed through a panic attack and even, in desperation, said a prayer like Amelia would have. He prayed the Creels were safe and Mason... God, that Mason didn't decide to be a hero.

His fingers itched to dig out the phone, but he didn't want to take the chance, not yet. If they found it before he could make a call, he'd lose any chance of reaching his father.

Deep breath, he thought as he heard doors slam.

But no one came for him.

A few minutes turned into an uncomfortable length of time. Sam pressed his ear against the door to catch some sound, something that would tell him where he was. Maybe he'd try tears and plead ignorance—anything to get him some information about Mason and the Creels. If they were thrown in jail....

The handle rattled, and Sam scurried back to the other side, knees up, backpack clutched to his chest and his expression wide-eyed and terrified. It wasn't a stretch.

Agent Allard was once again on the other side of the door. Behind him, Sam could make out the bright lights of a parking lot, neon just beyond the Fed's shoulder.

"Thought you could use some company." He turned to his left and gave a wave. The broad-shouldered agent reappeared with a large black gun trained on Mason and the Creels.

Sam couldn't hide his relief.

He crawled over to help Amelia into the van. She was still in her nightclothes, a blanket wrapped around her shoulders. Mr. Creel followed and settled down next to her against the far wall of the van. Mason got in last, and even in the faint light, Sam could see he hadn't gone along without a fight—a story told in bruises and a split lip.

"You should see the other guys," he murmured in the face of Sam's horror as he sat down beside him. "I'm fine."

"Great. I love reunions," Allard said. "We're going to go on a little ride now. Hold tight."

The door slammed with dramatic finality.


THEY WHISPERED in case the agents were listening.

"Aiding and abetting a fugitive," Mr. Creel said quietly, repeating what Sam had been told. "Not what those Feds back home said."

"Started with three vehicles. Then they combined to two, then one," Mason added. "Less agents each time."

"No handcuffs," Sam said, thinking out loud. "That's weird, right?"

Amelia shifted under her blanket. "No one showed a badge. Just guns," she said with a shiver.

Mason slid his hand into Sam's, allowing Sam to take a breath. "If they separate us again, tell them you want a lawyer. That you're not saying a word without a lawyer," Mason whispered urgently. "Your name and then ask for a lawyer. Nothing else."

They exchanged nods, regarding each other gravely as the van shifted to the right, then the left, and began to traverse seriously bumpy terrain.

"Left the highway," Mason said. They stopped talking after that.


AGAINST MASON'S shoulder, Sam drifted into uneasy sleep. He dreamed of the house he shared with his father, the locked doors and windows, the safety he felt when Nox was there. He dreamed of seeing Mason walking out of the shadows at the construction site when Detective Francis arrested him.

When he opened his eyes, he felt the phantom vibrations of the journey rumbling through him, then… the realization they'd stopped yet again. Not a sliver of light reached Sam. He felt Mason's tense body shoulder to shoulder, hip to hip, and he heard the rapid breathing of Mr. Creel and Amelia on the other side of the van.

"How long?" he murmured against Mason's ear.

"About ten minutes" was the terse answer. "I don't hear anything."

Mr. Creel rumbled in the dark. "You gonna make a move?" he asked, and he didn't need to specify that was for Mason.

"I don't think it's worth it. We ask for lawyers and see how they respond." Sam rubbed Mason's thigh gently in support. The chill seeped up through the walls and floor of the van, and Sam was the only one at all warmly dressed.

"Shit."

Fifteen minutes later, the van's back door handle rattled.

AGENT ALLARD and the large man guided them from the van, through the darkness, toward a looming shape—a dilapidated farmhouse perched in the middle of a dead field.

Sam stumbled up the stairs, and the warped, unused wood too long in the path of storms and disuse creaked and groaned under his sneakers. If the agents had guns drawn, Sam couldn't see them, but there was no mistaking the air of menace.

This wasn't a government facility. This wasn't a police station. What looked like a raid by federal agents had devolved into two men, a van, and a place in the middle of nowhere.

"Change of plans." Mason's voice was barely a whisper, more a breath against the back of Sam's head.

Sam swallowed hard, his nod imperceptible.

They crossed the porch, and the beam of a flashlight suddenly lit up the front door and Agent Allard, his gun indeed drawn.

"Sam? Why don't you go in and have a seat," he said pleasantly. The door creaked open next to him. "Your friends are going to wait out here."

"No!" Mason yelled, but Agent Allard didn't even blink.

"He's the most valuable person here, Mr. Todd. I suggest you keep your mouth shut for the moment."

Deep breath. Sam reached back and put a gentling hand on his boyfriend's arm. "It's okay. Let me do this," he said, all bravado with absolutely nothing to back it up. "He probably just wants to talk about my dad," he added boldly.

"Smart kid." Agent Allard waved his gun again. "Go ahead. Everyone here will still be alive when we're done." His smile oozed across his face.

Mason made a sound of distress and anger as Sam pulled away and walked up the last few steps and through the doorway, his heart trying to escape his chest.

"Thank you for your cooperation."

Sam stepped over the threshold.

The main room of the house was devoid of furniture except for a small table and two chairs. A hunting lantern, dimly lit, sat in the center of the table, casting a circle. Behind him, the door shut with a slam. Sam felt himself nudged forward with an oddly gentle hand.

"I apologize for the serial-killer setting," Agent Allard began, guiding Sam to one of the chairs. "I felt we needed a quiet place to talk."

Sam kept his face as neutral as possible. Agent Allard sat down across from him and rested the gun on the table, completely in Sam's reach. He wiped a hand over his face, then sat forward, forearms on his knees.

"I'm a friend of Cade's," he said gently. "When I was undercover at the Iron Butterfly, we were…." He paused, flickering his gaze to the table, then up again. Even sheltered as he was, Sam could read that calculated look perfectly. "Close."

"Oh," was all Sam could manage.

"I'm worried about him. I tried to get him to come in, get some protection, but he's determined to continue this vendetta—"

"It's not a vendetta," Sam butted in. "I mean…."

"This is very serious, okay? You and your boyfriend and those nice people from South Carolina are in a lot of trouble." Agent Allard sighed. "Sam? Listen to me. Whatever you think you're doing, whatever side of goodness you think you're on, you need to leave it to the authorities. Interfering with an investigation of this magnitude is going to get you killed."

Sam squirmed in the chair. The dusty buildup, the mildew infesting the place made his throat hurt, and the agent's words made his chest ache. A thousand arguments that all boiled down to "Well, they started it!" welled up inside him. But he tamped them down, all of them, because a gentle voice and kind eyes didn't mean jack in the world. He was sheltered, but he wasn't stupid.

"The other agents said everything was fine." Sam crossed his arms over his chest. "They came to the farm and said it was all fine. We…." He gestured to himself and then toward the door. "We're just trying to stay out of it. You grabbed *us*." His voice rose with emotion and anger. Petulance, ignorance, stubbornness.

Allard's gaze narrowed. "You're interfering—"

"We were sleeping," Sam said snappishly. "Like, just sleeping in the motel."

"You left the cabin in a hurry."

"It was a temporary place to stay. Jeez. My father and Cade left a few weeks ago. We have no contact with them." He let his stress and annoyance punctuate the words. "I don't know what you're expecting me to do."

An irritated breath was all the reaction he got from Agent Allard, who suddenly stood up. He paced a circle around the room, just outside the fall of light from the lantern.

The gun sat on the table.

A thousand scenarios rushed through Sam's brain. Grab the gun, shoot the agent, shoot the second agent, save the day.

No. He couldn't take the chance. What if the agent outside heard the gunshot and did something to Mason and the Creels? It wasn't a good strategy.

"Was there a rendezvous point, Sam? A way to reach them?" The agent came up behind Sam, startling him.

"No." Sam pressed his bottom and thighs into the chair to keep himself still. "We all went our separate ways. Me and Mason—we just want to settle somewhere quiet."

"Bullshit." Agent Allard's voice vibrated off the walls.

"Me and my dad had a fight," Sam maintained calmly. "I told him I was done with this crap, and he left. You talked to Cade; why didn't you just get my dad then?" The casual question at the end squeezed out of Sam's throat. It dawned on him that, if the agent had really spoken to Cade, there was more to this story.

Underestimate me, he thought. Go ahead.

Silence greeted his query, but Agent Allard recovered quickly.

"They also split up, apparently. Lot of people seem to be sick of your father lately."

"So Cade is done with my dad?" Sam asked with as youthful and stupid a voice as he could muster. "But he wouldn't turn him in if they broke up? That's weird." He shrugged, an exaggerated movement. "Whatever, I don't care."

"Sam...." The warning was clear.

"I don't have a way to reach him! I don't even have a phone anymore." The second he said it, Sam felt a tremor through both hands. Shit. He said *a* phone, not *the* phone. Please don't look in the backpack, please.

In the middle of his panic, Agent Allard threw himself into the chair across from him again.

"You have to give me something," he said, quiet now but no less dangerous.

Sam swallowed the fluid filling his mouth as nausea overtook him. "I don't know *anything*," he responded, emphasizing the last word. "We haven't been in touch. I don't know how to reach him."

Agent Allard sighed, and his hand went to the gun. He stroked it with one finger, then tapped the barrel.

"Okay, Sam. I believe you. You don't know how to reach your father." His gaze glittered with a different sort of emotion. Sam frowned as he tried to read the Fed's tone and body language.

"So you'll let us go?" he asked hopefully, a hitch in his voice.

A laugh broke the tension as Agent Allard stood up, replacing the gun in his shoulder holster as he stood. "No. Because we're moving your status from informant to bait."


SAM HATED him with a fury that choked his breath. He felt strangled as he stumbled down the stairs, wanting nothing more than to wheel around and break this asshole's nose with his fist.

"Sam!" He heard Mason call, but he just shook his head, fighting back tears and curses.

"Where… where are they going?" he asked, his voice trembling. "Are you bringing them?"

"Oh, they're coming with us, Sam," Agent Allard said smoothly. "But you are the most important part of this little trap. Daddy is going to drop everything and run to stand in front of every bullet we might throw in your direction."

Sam's heart sank.

"He's going to kill you," Sam muttered.

"I'm a federal agent," Agent Allard said, though there was something in his tone that prickled Sam's skin. "I'm going to serve him to my boss on a silver platter with a fucking apple in his mouth."

They reached the open back door of the van.

"And then," he finished, shoving Sam into the darkness, "I'm going to get paid."

*Then*

*"COME ON, " Alec cajoles, trying to get Cade to drop the towel and come to bed. Sometimes they do this—fuck and hang out when work is slow or they have a rare evening off. He's not in love with Cade, but those pale eyes and that wicked smirk take his mind off everything else.*

*Deep cover is exhausting, and being the guy who agrees to fuck and be fucked makes him useful and... weird. They've tried depositing other agents into the casinos, but the longest operation lasted four months before the guy ended up in the East River.*

*Alec has... skills. He's everything to everyone, a changeling who can project Alpha Male and submissive without ever seeming out of character. It's easy to believe a big, polite, good-looking guy who stands out just enough to be memorable but not threatening.*

*He'd have made a hell of an actor.*

*But for now, at his father's insistence and his mother's disinterest, he's making a career for himself as a federal agent in a dangerous assignment no one else wants.*

*Three years, and just when he thought he was going to get pulled, he's been given additional orders.*

*Soul-crushing additional orders.*

*"Cade, seriously. We have ten blissful hours of not needing to be anywhere,"* Alec murmurs, pushing the silk sheets down low on his hips. *"No one staring over our shoulders...."*

*"Eh, you know there are cameras everywhere."* Cade's towel hits the floor, and his grin sets off a thousand different ideas in Alec's head. Why shouldn't he take some pleasure in this sewer? Everyone else got what they wanted from Alec—his clients, his bureau bosses. His father. Why can't he take what he wants? A small secret part of him was envious of the criminals in this city who took what they wanted without shame and without worrying about the consequences.

*"True. Maybe we can get a copy of last Tuesday night."* Alec sits up slowly, flexing and turning toward Cade, who still hovers just out of his reach. *"I think I did some good work,"* he purrs.

Cade shrugs in that maddening, standoffish way. Everything is jokes and deflection. Even after a year, Alec knows Cade's body and his background and his mother's social security number, but he doesn't know Cade.

Frustrating. Intriguing.

*"I still make more money than you do."* Cade smirks, taking a step closer to Alec's outstretched hand. *"Maybe you can watch the tape, recognize your flaws, and try to improve."*

It's their game, a running joke about prowess and pay, but beyond Alec's flirty smile is a sense of irritation. He wants to tell Cade who he really is, impress him.

Shut him up.

*"Stop playing hard to get."* Alec lays back among the tumble of pillows on his bed. *"It's boring and a lie."*

*"Even whores have standards."* Cade laughs and walks over to Alec's wooden butler, where his clothes are neatly laid out.

*"Where are you going?"* He works to keep the snap out of his voice.

*"This was fun. Thank you for the use of your shower. And now I'm going to bed."* Cade pauses as he slides his briefs up over his slim hips. *"Alone."*

*"But...."*

*"Spending the night is never on the agenda," Cade says gently but firmly. There is no mistaking the set of his lips. "I kick, you snore. It's a whole big thing."*

*Alec says nothing. He just stews among the pillows and the silk sheets in a bedroom decorated in early masculine sex den. He hates it, hates this assignment with a rush of anger. This isn't his life.*

*"Stop with the pouty face." Rolling his eyes, Cade buckles his belt and grabs his watch to slide it on his wrist. "Let's have breakfast, okay? Or meet me earlier. I'll be at the gym."*

*Alec breathes, controls himself. He has a job. He will succeed.*

*"Sure. Six?" he asks, his voice perfectly modulated.*

*"Yeah. I'll even pay," Cade says, clearly trying to make amends.*

*Alec pulls the biggest smile he can manage. "Oh, in that case, we're going to the French place."*

*Cade makes a face as he steps into his loafers.*

*"What? You make more money than I do." Alec winks as he pulls the covers back up to his chest.*

*"Ha-ha." Cade gives him a look, and for a second, Alec believes he might climb back into bed. But Cade shakes his head, blows him a kiss, and has his hand on the doorknob before Alec has a moment to dream. "See you at six."*

*"Later," Alec says, and then Cade is gone.*

*He turns out the light, stares at the expensive light fixture overhead, and burns.*

*Tomorrow he'll deliver another report to his superiors—about organized crime and low-level drug dealing, about corruption and casinos, about a tiny hotbed of nothing that seems more a quaint throwback cronyism than anything else.*

*And then he'll make a decision about what happens next.*

SAM WASN'T tied up or cuffed. He sat on the van floor and waited until Agent Allard returned with a heavy jacket, two blankets, water bottles, and a canvas bag of sandwiches and small packets of cookies. He pushed everything toward Sam without a word, took a step back, and slammed the door.

Listening carefully, Sam heard people talking in normal voices and then more doors being opened and closed.

"He's fine. You want him to stay that way, cooperate." Agent Allard was right by the driver's side door, his voice unmistakable. "I'll meet you at the next spot," he said in a less strident voice. Sam heard more doors open and close, and a few minutes later, they were driving off into the night.

# CHAPTER TWELVE

RACHEL STOOD her ground as LJ strode up to her. It hurt Cade to see the look on his brother's face—desperate, devastated, and pleading at once.

"Tell me you're doin' this to help," he said quietly. "Tell me Cade's wrong."

Cade winced. Did he want to be wrong? For his brother's sake? For his sake—because the reality was that Rachel, of all of them, had the best skills to help them find Nox and get the hell out of here alive.

He needed her, but he didn't want to be wrong.

"LJ," she said gently, laying her hand on his chest. "Honey, I know this all seems crazy right now, but you have to trust me."

LJ didn't touch her, didn't respond to her touch.

"Tell me. That Cade is wrong. That you've been sayin' the truth this whole time."

When Rachel's breath caught, Cade watched his brother deflate like a pricked balloon. He sagged and then stepped away from her silent form. He turned as if to leave but only got a few steps before Mitzie, in all her hazy-eyed, half-naked glory, stood in his way.

"No," she said. "You do not leave."

"Rachel." LJ didn't turn around, just stood face-to-face with Mitzie.

As if woken up, Rachel started, eyes darting between LJ and Mitzie.

"Mitzie," she said warningly, but the other woman just laughed. In LJ's face.

"Galina," she replied, her voice singsong. "Maybe your handsome friend will come sleep with us in our bed? He looks like he could be some fun," she purred, running a finger across LJ's face.

Cade moved quickly and pulled his brother back before he could do something that would end with Mitzie's goons popping back in and lighting the place up.

"Come on, come sit down," Cade murmured, maneuvering his brother back to the sofa. It was like moving a sack of bricks.

"Enough of this," Rachel snapped. "Just... enough."

CADE AND LJ sat side by side on the giant pink sofa. Mitzie, laconic and amused, draped herself on the other end, her robe open enough for Cade to see she wasn't wearing anything underneath. She seemed to find the entire tableau hilarious, occasionally calling things out to Rachel in Russian—things that made Rachel's expression harden.

"Shut up," Rachel muttered, standing in front of Cade and LJ.

"I didn't say anything," Cade sassed back, still a seething ball of rage. He wanted to shake Rachel until she told him everything, then lock her in a closet somewhere so he never had to see her face again. The betrayal he felt....

He couldn't imagine what LJ was going through.

His brother, who never took his eyes off Rachel.

"Cade...." Rachel took a deep breath and held a hand up as if to stop them both from proceeding. "I need you to shut up, resist the urge to push me right now."

Cade felt his face burn. "Let us go, then." He lifted his chin, defiant. "We'll find Nox ourselves."

Mitzie barked out a laugh.

"You have no equipment, no leads, no weapons, and no money. How exactly are you going to do that?" Rachel looked imploringly at Cade and then LJ, who said nothing. "I know what I'm doing, okay?"

"No." Cade shrugged. "No. I should have trusted Nox when he told me to leave you behind."

"We wouldn't have gone anywhere without Rachel," Damian chimed in, timidly joining them, but then stayed out of their immediate reach, hands in his pockets. "I wouldn't have gotten you the boat...."

Cade snapped his attention to Damian. "So you two have been working together the whole time."

Rachel and Damian exchanged glances.

"Yes," Rachel said, taking a few steps back. She sat on the pink leather ottoman nearest to the sofa. "There was no text to Damian, no mysterious person directing us to find you. Mitzie's people have had a tail on your for...." She paused and seemed to deflate a little. "For months. They followed you up to Nox's house, to deliver the note to Sam."

The cold sense of dread crawling up the back of Cade's neck was like a spider. His body broke into goose bumps as Rachel watched him carefully.

"Why?" Beside him, he felt LJ tense up.

"Because I was sending the messages to Mr. White," she said, sitting up a little straighter. "I told him to send you with the notes for Sam."

The room spun, a wicked ride that left Cade swallowing repeatedly until he could erase the nausea building. He vaguely felt LJ's hand on his arm, as if steadying him.

"You... you were behind all of it," Cade managed, but Rachel was already shaking her head.

"No. I had nothing to do with Sam's kidnapping or the bombing," she insisted. "I just needed to get Nox to stop fucking hiding and get involved in the big picture. He wanted to knock off the little fish while the big one was causing all the damage."

Damian came to her side. "She's telling the truth. We didn't get involved... heck, we had no idea what was going on until...."

He stopped, his jaw locking, and Cade felt the click clack click of the roller coaster as it went up the tracks. The next dip was going to hurt. He could feel it.

"Until Zed told us Carson Boyet was alive."

# INTERLUDE

*RACHEL IS finishing up her day's reports, scowling at her pad as she plugs in numbers. Only three incident reports on this shift—she might actually get some sleep before it's time for the staff meeting.*

*Preparation for the Anniversary Weekend has started to creep into her daily checklist, which adds another brick of work to her life. And she knows she shouldn't complain. Zed hiring her away from Mitzie's whorehouse was the best thing that has happened to her since the storms hit. Running strippers and managing Mitzie exhausted her. Her ex-lover remains an ally, but at least Rachel doesn't have to deal with her every damn day. Now she lives a life of luxury under Zed's protection, and if she has to fuck him occasionally, so be it. She's done worse.*

*A knock on her office door riles her mood further into blackness. She barks out something that sounds like "Come in."*

*Damian peers his head in as the door slowly opens.*

*The seriousness of his expression is several degrees more intense than usual, and Rachel hits Save and places the tablet on her desk.*

*"Zed needs you in his suite."*

*Generally when Zed wants her in his bed, he texts her. They've known each other for too long to stand on ceremony. Zed conducts business by phone while he does everything from sit on the toilet to get a blowjob. She's heard it all. But sending Damian to fetch her—that's Defcon five or above, something that can't be shared electronically or trusted to one of the assistants.*

*She and Damian head silently for Zed's suite. Rachel knows not to ask questions until they're somewhere secure.*

*THEY ARE five feet from Zed's suite when she hears the furious screams coming from inside.*

*"Motherfucker," Zed spits out as Rachel enters the suite. When he sees her, he snaps his fingers and points to the large walk-in closet near his bedroom.*

*She and Damian tuck themselves in among the suits and shiny shoes and wait for Zed to join them. The door slams behind with a vicious rattle.*

*His dark eyes, deep and probing, zoom onto Rachel's face. She realizes suddenly that her back is to the wall, literally. She cannot get out of here if things go badly.*

*"Did ya know?" he hisses, leaning down until they are inches apart.*

*Rachel's quick mind zips around the club, her staff, money, anything she can imagine Zed is talking about, but nothing comes to mind. She knows better to bullshit him, though; very few people on this island know her secrets, and Zed is on that short list.*

*"You have to give me more than that," Rachel says bravely, meeting his anger with her own cool façade. "I know a lot of things."*

*"Rachel," Damian whispers, a warning.*

*"I got a visit from my boy, who's been doin' some diggin' on my behalf," Zed says, leaning back slightly. "I wanna know who's trying to bring Dead Bolt into my club and not compensatin' me fully."*

*It's been a source of tension for Zed over the past few months. They pay protection to the cops, bribes to city officials, even some money to the organized business that "owns" the land under the Iron Butterfly. Now the Dead Bolt people want Zed to exclusively run the drug through his casino, pushing out everyone else supplying pill and powder "entertainment" to his customers.*

*He pushed back.*

*He wanted more money than they were offering and refused to back down. Since then, they'd had to deal with an escalating series of headaches and issues that made it harder to do business. When the bomb threats started, Zed was done.*

*Zed was pissed.*

*Rachel nods through Zed's word spew. A sense of relief rolls through her—she has nothing to do with any of this. She doesn't know who runs Dead Bolt and doesn't actually care. Mitzie—sometime lover, longtime friend, and another person who knows her secrets—*

has no tangible information on it either. It's a cartel, it's dangerous, and only fools fuck with it.

"What did he find out?" Rachel asks.

Zed's eyes go hard. Her relaxed demeanor seems to trigger something in him. She feels his rage building again.

"If you knew...."

"Knew what? You know I don't fuck with the drug people," she snapped. "And you know why."

Her boss pauses, then says the name she has been hiding from for seventeen years.

"Carson Boyet."

Rachel feels the blood drain from her face.

"He's alive. And it's his organization runnin' the Dead Bolt in this city."

She shakes her head, voice stuck in her throat.

"He's dead. I identified the body. They killed him," she babbles out. "It's... maybe it's the cartel...," she says, even as it sounds wrong in her head. "They're using his name."

"They're not usin' his name. My boy got on the payroll, doin' surveillance of some electrician and his kid livin' on the Upper West Side. They're followin' him, keepin' an eye on the place. Turns out he's the son of a bitch killing drug dealers in the city. My boy says the boss doesn't care, lets him do what he wants."

"So they're... they're keeping an eye on his son...."

"Rachel."

Her head begins to throb. She puts her palms against her temples, as if to keep her brain in place. "He's dead."

"My boy saw him."

"He's...." Rachel, to her horror, feels tears gathering in her eyes. Carson Boyet is alive, running drugs through the city and muscling her boss to get his way. She can barely process it—worse, he knows about Nox and Sam. "Fuck."

"How is he still doin' business after rippin' off the cartel? How is he still runnin' their shit?" Zed's bulk sets the suits shifting and turning as he begins to pace in the tiny space. "Makes no sense."

"Forget about that for now." Rachel attempts to get a handle on herself. She needs to think. If Carson has his sights on Zed and the Butterfly, does he know about her? "Can we use this to get him to back off?"

"Blackmail?" Damian squeaks. "Are you crazy?"

Zed stops moving and turns slowly. "Maybe. Maybe I let the fucker know… or…." He rocks back on his heels. "Maybe I go over his head."

"Oh my God." Damian leans against the wall of shoes, rubbing his hands over his face. He's a moneyman, damn good at it, trained and educated. Another one of the unemployed and starving masses left behind on the island that Mitzie scooped up to help build her casino from the money her whorehouse sucked in. And while he works for a gangster—has worked for them for years—he doesn't have the stomach for violence.

"Dangerous," Rachel says.

"He's gonna push me till he gets what he wants or he's gonna kill me. Maybe I make a better deal with his bosses, yeah?" A manic gleam lit up Zed's eyes. "Maybe I convince them I can do a better job of it. Take their little operation to a wider audience."

Rachel nods absently, but she's thinking of other things. Like Nox, who is apparently the vigilante fucking up the drug trade in the dead of night. Like Nox, who might want to know that his father is alive.

But she knows it can't come from her.

Resolution and a plan click into place. Rachel feels back in control—afraid, but sure in the knowledge that she's a cat with nine lives and she can maneuver her way out of any situation.

"You find a way to get to the cartel, let them know the man who stole their money is still alive," she says to Zed. "I'm going to see what I can do on my end." She flips through a rolodex of people locked inside her memory. There are very few people from her old life still alive, let alone still on this rock. Then a creepy old face comes to mind, one that she sees every week on the casino floor.

Old, feeble-minded, and easily manipulated. She hasn't had reason to make contact with Mr. White over these years, but maybe… just maybe he can be useful.

MR. WHITE isn't happy to see her. In fact, he refuses to speak to her. Apparently as Rachel she has displeased him, and he can't seem to remember she's Jenny.

*Irritated, she paces her office until a plan solidifies.*

*She walks down the hallway toward Damian's office. Cade passes her. With a quick wink and a gentle jibe, he's gone around the corner, Alec at his heels. She stops, stares.*

*"I need Mr. White's private cell number," she tells Damian. "I have an idea."*

# CHAPTER THIRTEEN

NOX SAT patiently through his father's speech, only taking in about half the word nonsense as he watched the lie detector in his father's jaw translate it all.

The family business was laundering drug money. His father attempted to get out. Faked his death. Planned to flee. Got caught in the storms. Natalie was dead, and he stayed away from Nox to protect him.

A dozen tractor-trailer-sized holes turned that story into tatters, but Nox said nothing.

Not a word.

Heroic backstory provided, Carson attempted to look sad and contrite as he watched Nox. "Those were the men who came to kill you. I can only assume that Jenny was working for the cartel...."

Nox nodded.

"She must've told them she killed me, which is why they never came after me, you know, since I was living in the house I grew up in," Nox said smoothly, dropping a bit of bait for his father. "I remember, she texted someone."

"That must be it." Carson feigned a smile, then discreetly checked his watch. "I really must be going to this next meeting—"

"What happens now?" Nox interrupted. "To me, to my friends. Sam. I don't want to work for you."

Carson was halfway out of his chair, but he settled back in. "I require your presence here for about a week. Maybe ten days. After that time, you are free to go. I'll even throw a little cash your way."

"I just have to live here. For a week."

"Yes."

"I want to see Cade and my son," Nox said, his voice dropping into a dangerous tone. "I want to know they're all right." Did his father know where they were? Did he have them here? Nox wouldn't make a break for it until he was sure.

The calculated flare in Carson's eyes was unmistakable. What answer would give him the best cooperation from Nox? He shifted in the chair. "They're fine. I collected them when I scraped you up from that stairwell. They're being well cared for."

Nox schooled his features at the massive lie. Because Sam wasn't with them in West New York. "And the others?"

"Sent on their way. I had no need for them." Carson rocked out of the chair and pushed his way toward the door with a sudden sense of urgency.

How easily his father stepped into it. Confirmation that he didn't have them—and didn't know where they were. Clearly he hadn't seen Rachel.

A stray thought wandered in.

Which meant he wasn't following them all this time. The man on the boat, South Carolina....

"A week, Nox. Then you'll be free to do whatever it is you want," his father said as he paused, his hand on the doorknob. "Antonio will take you back to your suite. If you need anything, just let him know."

Carson turned the knob, and Nox felt a flare of panic. He wanted more information, wanted more answers from his father.

"You haven't told me everything," Nox blurted out.

Regarding him with a bland expression, Carson nodded as he opened the door. "No, I haven't."

And with that, Carson was gone.

ANTONIO POKED his head in a second later and gestured for Nox to get up. "Let's go. Back to your room."

Nox slowly got out of the chair, calculating how to play this. Did he feign weakness? Pain? His knee acting up? The latter thought forced a split-second decision. As he put weight on his injured knee, Nox let out a groan and grabbed the edge of the desk.

"What?" Antonio snapped.

"My knee," Nox said, leaning heavily. "I think something popped."

Antonio rolled his eyes and made no move toward Nox. "Let's go, I said."

"I can't walk!"

"Then fucking crawl." Antonio matched Nox's tone and volume, impatience dripping from each word. "I am not your fucking nursemaid. Move."

"My father…," Nox attempted.

"I give you the chance, you gut him like a fish." Antonio refused to be fooled, clearly. "Don't make like suddenly you're part of the family." He aimed the gun at Nox's chest. "Move. Now."

Nox's face twisted into a grimace. "He needs me alive, apparently. You're not allowed to kill me."

A smile flooded Antonio's face. "Only for the next week. After that? I'm going to enjoy dicing you up into little pieces."

Nox kept up the pretense. He limped dramatically through the penthouse, back to the suite of rooms that were apparently his during his stay. With Antonio on his heels, he did a quick but thorough recon of the apartment. Maybe his best bet was the front door.

He stopped a few seconds too long, head turned toward the entryway. Antonio prodded him once, then twice. Then he shoved Nox hard—hard enough to slam him into the wall, knees first.

Then it was no longer a ruse.

Nox cursed as he hit the ground. The pain radiating from his knee almost took his breath away, and he writhed around until he could get a handle on the flood of agony.

"Shit," Antonio muttered over his head. A second later Nox felt his body being lifted off the floor and dragged into the room.

The pain ebbed away, but Nox continued to play it up, choking and grabbing his knee as Antonio threw him unceremoniously on the bed. He buried his face in the pillow as Antonio continued to curse.

"Shut up," the man said. "Just… shut the fuck up."

Nox heard the fear in Antonio's voice and moaned louder.

"I'll get you a doctor, okay? Just shut up," he whispered. Then Nox listened to heavy footsteps, followed by a door slam and the tumble of the lock.

Nox laid there for a few moments more, tossing out the occasional sigh and muted cry. Then he rolled onto his back.

Okay. A doctor. Would it be Dr. Khanna from the clinic or someone new? Either way, it was the best shot for him to create an opportunity to escape.

Lying there in the bed, waiting, Nox's thoughts careened and crashed into each other. He gripped the bedcovers, his arms constricted by the suit jacket. In his mind's eye, he saw himself as a teenager, clutching newborn Sam to his chest as his mother lay dead in a pool of blood. He saw Rachel—Jenny—flicking between saving him and killing him, her eyes wary and calculating. He saw the bodies of Roy Grimes and the other man on the floor of his bedroom.

He heard the policeman telling him his father was dead—the moment that kicked everything else into gear.

Everything, Nox thought, a pang of helplessness washing over him, everything he knew was a lie.

Nox let himself feel sorry and sad for a moment and then shook his head as if to scatter those thoughts. This would do him no good. It wouldn't help him get back to Sam or to find Cade. His father was a monster, and the revised version of him that Nox had clung to these years didn't matter anymore. His family, the one that counted, was out there, and he wouldn't rest until they were safe.

The temptation to go down in a blaze of glory, killing his father and ending his filthy enterprise, still sang a seductive song to him. But he refused to give in.

Sam. Cade. The others who'd risked their lives to help him. They were all that mattered.

Wiping a coating of sweat from his forehead, Nox tentatively sat up. He removed his jacket and tossed it on the end of the bed, then unbuttoned the cuffs and loosened his tie. He flexed his knee once, twice. He accepted the faint twinge and returned to pressing matters.

Without a weapon, he wasn't getting out of this room, and he sure as hell wasn't making it past the guarded front door. At best, Nox would find his chance in the middle of chaos, when he could create a diversion, take out a guard, and snag himself a gun.

The door rattled, and Nox threw himself back on the bed, arms and legs akimbo as he resumed a low-level moan. Antonio ducked into the room, followed by two people. The first was Greta, the terrified maid, and the other was a man Nox had not seen yet. He was middle-aged and slight, with a dramatically receding hairline and a thin mustache. A doctor's bag swung from his arm.

"Take care of him quick, Felix," Antonio muttered, quietly closing the door behind them. "Give him a shot or whatever. Just—he needs to be quiet."

Nox gave a louder, more theatrical moan.

"Are you sure—" Felix started to ask, but Antonio cut him off. "Now."

Felix hurried to the side of the bed and gave Nox an appraising stare.

"All right, young man, let's see what the problem is." He set the bag down next to Nox's arm and opened it. "Can you sit up a bit?"

Nox let the smaller man grunt and shove him up and back against the pillows. He fell limply, adjusting his arms a little higher. The position gave him the ability to look into the doctor's bag, his eyes quick to find a potential weapon.

"He pushed me," Nox ground out, clenching his jaw. "I hit my bad knee. The left one. Something… something popped."

"Such a fucking whiner," Antonio snapped, but he resumed his hurried pacing. Greta stood frozen in place by the door, hands clenched at her sides. "He'll give you some painkillers and you'll be fine."

Felix made a face as he leaned over Nox's knee. His hands were gentle as he prodded the kneecap, then gently pushed it into a bent position.

Nox howled. Loudly.

Antonio kicked the side of the small sofa in the seating area and walked back to the door. Voices could be heard on the other side.

"Shut up," Antonio hissed. Then he shooed Greta out of the way and pressed against the door, ear at the seam, as if trying to hear what they were saying.

Nox's brain signaled "now or never."

The voices got closer. He groaned as Felix slowly straightened his leg out.

"You should probably have an MRI," Felix said. He dipped into his bag, rooted around for a moment, and produced a small bottle and a packaged needle. "There doesn't seem to be swelling, but something else might be going on inside," he continued conversationally as he opened the package and loaded the syringe.

Nox looked at Antonio, who was distracted by the people outside. He looked at Greta, whose gaze narrowed on Nox's face.

Did she know he was faking it? Would she sound an alarm?

He felt the sweat trickling down the back of his neck and under his arms.

Now or never. Now or never.

The syringe full, Felix motioned for him to roll up his sleeve. "I'll just give you this—"

He didn't get to finish because Nox grabbed him around the neck and covered his face so he couldn't call out. They struggled for a moment as Nox pushed off the bed to stand, still holding Felix immobile. The syringe shook and spurted in Felix's hand before he flung it aside.

The silence went on a beat too long. Nox watched Antonio's back go up. As he began to turn, Nox had to make a split-second decision. He threw Felix as hard as he could, an adrenaline-fueled move of desperation. The older man slammed into Antonio's back, momentarily knocking him off balance. Nox ran desperately, his only chance to reach Antonio before he got a grip on the gun slung over his back.

Felix flailed and kicked his feet and arms in a panicked attempt to get up. Cursing and shoving, Antonio pushed him away. He reached for the gun as Nox jumped, catching him in the chest.

They struggled. Nox pressed his elbow into Antonio's throat in an attempt to keep him quiet. The position—his body pushing Antonio into the door and immobilizing one arm—made the scramble for the gun impossible for either man to gain the upper hand.

Nox panted as he used every ounce of his energy to keep Antonio still. He waited to hear Felix call out or Greta scream, but he heard nothing—nothing outside of Antonio's rasped breathing as he struggled to get free.

Needing to break the stalemate, Nox put his weight on his good leg, rammed his knee into Antonio's testicles, and ground up until Antonio began to choke.

The gun clattered to the floor.

With the upper hand, finally, Nox felt Antonio go limp with pain. He moved to put him into a chokehold and then dragged him down to the floor as he increased the pressure.

Antonio's pain was forgotten as Nox cut off his air. He fought back and tried to use his bulk to throw Nox off. This was for survival, and Nox fought just as hard, straining his muscles as he bore down and squeezed everything he had left into the crush against Antonio's windpipe.

His death wheezes seemed like amplified screams to Nox, who grunted as he flexed his arms, trying to stem the sound lest someone hear the commotion.

Finally. Finally. The fight began to go out of Antonio. Nox gave another jerking squeeze and felt the dead weight of the man start to crush him. He rolled him to one side and dropped his face down on the rug.

Panting, Nox scrambled for the gun and jumped to his feet as he turned his attention to the room's other occupants.

Felix lay on the floor, his face covered with a pillow. His arms and legs were spread out, and he wasn't moving. Nox blinked in surprise. Standing above him was Greta, white and shaking.

She said nothing, just stepped over Felix's body and ran toward the bathroom. A gesture toward the knob and then she shut the door behind her.

Nox didn't waste time. He hurried to lock the door, even lifting a chair and putting it against the knob to sell the story even more convincingly.

Back at the doors, he listened for anyone in the hallway. Nothing. He took a moment to search both men. He grabbed Felix's wallet and keys and the same from Antonio's pockets, as well as a white key card. Hurrying, he slipped the jacket back on. With a silent prayer it would get him out of there, Nox stuffed everything else in his pockets and readied his gun.

Time to go.

# Chapter Fourteen

Sam woke up from a dream that he was back on the boat when they escaped the island.

He sat up, suddenly aware of the sounds of water outside—boat engines and waves and wind. Not a dream at all.

The van lurched, and the movement made his backpack slide closer. Sam clutched it, then resolutely opened the top zipper. The phone—he could use the phone and call his father, call Cade, tell them he was....

Somewhere. With a federal agent who referred to him as bait, as something that would get the man paid. Oh God.

Sam swallowed his bubbling hysteria. Okay, he had to think. While he didn't know exactly where they were going, it was clear they were heading back to the city. He would let his father and the others know that, and maybe....

Sam felt his brain turn on like an actual light bulb.

"Turn it back on, leave it on, and they can track it," he muttered, frantically pulling the backpack apart to reach the phone wrapped and tucked into the lining. With shaking hands he turned the phone back on and prayed he'd find a message.

Nothing. The message he'd sent said, "Read," but there was no response.

Sam's heart fell. With shaky fingers he typed out:

*On the move. Track the phone.*

And hit Send. Then he wrapped it all over again and hid it back in the bottom of the bag, between the outer layer and the lining. When Sam closed the zipper, his palms were slick and his heart raced, but he felt the smallest bit of control.

If he used his brains, he just might make it out of this mess.

A few minutes later, there was a thudding noise, and the van shook violently. Someone started the engine again, and the van lurched forward. Sam scurried back into a fetal position, head resting on the backpack as he feigned sleep. Grinding noises and shouting went on for a while as Sam surmised they'd been loaded onto a ferry to get to the island.

Then they were driving.

THE DRIVE felt endless. Sam fretted about where Mason and the Creels were, and he listened carefully to make sure the phone didn't make any noise—though at this point, everything was a canon boom. When the van finally stopped, Sam screwed his eyes shut, buried his face in the backpack, and prayed.

A slam rocked the van. Then the back doors opened and light poured in.

Agent Allard stood, framed by sunlight, regarding Sam with curious eyes.

"Time for a little chat." He gestured for Sam to come out.

"We already did that," Sam grumbled, clutching the backpack close.

"This isn't about your…." The agent smiled thinly as he wrapped his arm around Sam's shoulders. "Well, I guess technically it is."

Sam blinked in the bright light and looked around in confusion. They were definitely back in the city but outside the District. Farther north than his house….

Agent Allard led him through a copse of trees that opened into the remains of an enormous building. One wing had collapsed, its roof crumbled into the top floor. The other side of the building was still standing but looked terrible—crumbling brick with ivy nearly overrunning the structure and half the windows shattered.

"What is this?" Sam asked, utterly confused. He assumed they'd be back at the police station or somewhere official, not this wrecked building.

"Morningside Sanitarium," Agent Allard said, leading Sam around to a back door.

SAM SNEEZED violently as they walked through the disgusting mess that was the stairwell. He hadn't reacted when the agent identified where they were, because he refused to give him the satisfaction. But he knew where they were.

This was where he was born. This was where his mother died.

Agent Allard didn't say anything else as they walked through the debris. He also didn't let go of Sam. They wound their way up another decrepit stairwell, thick with bird shit and moldy plaster. At the top of the steps, Agent Allard pushed open the emergency door, and suddenly there was air.

Fresh air and light.

Sam bit the inside of his cheek. He wanted to know why they were there.

He wanted to know what the agent was going to do to him.

A flare of panic faltered Sam's steps. Would the man bring him here just to kill him? That didn't make any sense.

At the end of the hallway, Sam realized there were two men with automatic weapons standing outside a doorway. Agent Allard raised his hand in greeting.

"Gentlemen. Is he here?"

The taller of the two men nodded and tilted his head toward the door on the right.

"Thank you. I'll keep an eye out here. You go get our other guests."

Sam's heart leaped. Other guests? Mason and the Creels—it had to be!

The men ambled off as Agent Allard knocked twice. He gave Sam a strange look and patted his head like a small child until someone in the room called out for them to come in.

Sam shivered as the door opened and the agent pushed him inside.


IT WAS like he popped through a magic doorway. The run-down, disgusting building disappeared, and Sam stepped into another world—a nice apartment with old-looking furniture and oil paintings of horses and lakes. It smelled like bleach and coffee.

A man sat in profile on the couch, wearing a neatly pressed suit and holding a china cup. He was middle-aged, okay-looking, with artificially brown hair artfully styled. Not that scary, Sam thought, inching closer. The door closed behind him with a definitive click.

Sam shuffled closer, and his sneakers caught on the Persian rug under his feet.

There was something familiar.... Sam cleared his throat, hoping the man would say something, identify himself.

"I'm...." Sam coughed, inching closer to the man.

"Sam Boyet," the man finished, and Sam jumped.

"Mullens," he said automatically, but the man laughed.

"It's all right, Sam." The man stood up and faced him. "I know exactly who you are."

Sam gasped. He knew the pictures; he'd seen them growing up. Nox had them in his room—not many, but enough so that Sam knew the man standing in front of him was Carson Boyet.

His father.

"Well, well," Carson said, setting the cup down on the coffee table. "You look exactly like your mother, don't you?"

Sam's mouth dropped open as though his jaw had suddenly unhinged. He couldn't wrap his mind around this man—his father—who was dead but not. He stepped back, shaking his head.

"It's all right," Carson said soothingly. He reached his hand out to Sam. "I know this must be a terrible shock. I know your brother didn't tell you I was alive."

Sam froze.

He tried to make his mouth work, but nothing happened. It seemed like he was nailed to the floor, his lips sewn shut.

Blinking, Sam refocused his gaze to the floor. He counted backward and pushed the panic down.

For a brief, terrible moment, Sam wondered if Nox could lie to him like that, and oh right, he had lied for the entirety of Sam's life. Could this be one more untruth stacked on top?

"N... no," Sam finally stuttered out, still not looking up. "He s... said you died. Before I was born."

"Ahhh."

Sam heard Carson getting closer and flinched when the man touched his arm.

"Come, sit down," he said soothingly. "Are you hungry? I can get you whatever you want."

Sam let himself be led to the couch and settled down. When Carson touched his backpack, Sam wrenched it away and tucked it behind him.

"My apologies," Carson murmured. "I just want you to be comfortable, let us get to know each other a little better."

"Where's Mason and Mr. and Mrs. Creel?" Sam asked, eyes boring in on his sneakers. "I'd like to know, please."

"They're being taken care of quite nicely," Carson said. "Food, drink, a place to rest. A chance to change into their own clothing. It was a long trip up here."

"I'd like to see them, please."

"Later. After we spend some family time together."

Sam finally turned his head and stared directly into Carson's face. "They *are* my family."

Carson didn't even blink. He smiled benevolently and nodded. "Of course. Can you at least give me fifteen minutes? Then I'll have them join us."

Weighing this bargain, Sam regarded Carson from behind his smudged and streaked glasses. He could do fifteen minutes, maybe enough time to find out why he was here.

"Okay."

"Wonderful, thank you." Carson patted Sam on the shoulder in an awkward gesture of pleasure. "I've been waiting for this moment for a very long time, Sam. A very long time."

# LATER

CARSON BOYET *has his plan in place.*

*He hides in the run-down apartment, pacing and compulsively checking his burner phone. Making his own murder seem like a drug-cartel hit disguised as a mugging? Genius. Every so often he thinks about Mr. Smith, and he panics but manages to push it down.*

*Mr. Smith has all his goddamn money, he thinks bitterly. He doesn't need Carson anymore. And once he's "dead"? Well, no sense in retribution, right?*

*Right?*

*His plan about the insurance has to work. It's the only chance he has now.*

*It will be easier, he reasons, looking out the window again, aware of the sweeps of light as the National Guard moves through the city methodically knocking on doors. Easier because Nox will soon be notified of his death and then aided in escaping the danger of the city thanks to Roy Grimes, who is on his payroll. Once Nox is safely at the house upstate, he will wait patiently until the insurance money comes through, then pay his son a visit. Surprise, Daddy is back from the dead, and he needs that money.*

*What happens after that, he hasn't decided.*

*Natalie, bless her crazy little heart, is no longer a viable part of the plan. Mr. White, that fucking pervert, went against his directions and changed her medication, leaving her lucid for the sake of the baby.*

*Making Carson vulnerable because of it.*

*Mr. White is under strict orders, orders that he accepted after a prolonged negotiation. He will induce labor, take the baby, and then make sure Natalie is one of the tragic fatalities of this crazy weather—a footnote. And because he can't entirely trust Mr. White....*

*Jenny will have her orders from "the cartel." And then Jenny will be taken care of.*

*The child is of no real consequence to him. It isn't his. He doesn't care if it lives or dies. He just needs Mr. White's cooperation and silence.*

*Everything is hanging by the slimmest of threads. Everything can be derailed by the slightest mistake.*

*Not knowing where Mr. Smith is makes his skin crawl right off his body.*

*His phone buzzes.*

*It's Roy Grimes.*

*Carson Boyet, for all intents and purposes, is dead.*

*His jubilance doesn't last long.*

*The check-in calls from his people never come. The building he's hiding in evacuates entirely as the National Guard repeatedly pounds on his door. Jenny has gone rogue, it seems, as no one can seem to find her.*

*He gets ready to flee the island. Fake identification, money....*

*A polite knock at the door.*

*Carson ignores it until he hears Mr. Smith's pleading tones through the wood.*

*"Carson?"*

*He flings the door open. On the other side, Mr. Smith and two of his men stand, water streaming from their rain slickers.*

*Carson bites back a sharp retort and gestures for them to enter.*

*"Sorry to bother you, Carson, but we seem to have run into some issues," Mr. Smith says politely, removing his coat. "It seems your assistant, Jenny, has decided to take matters into her own hands."*

*Oh shit, he thinks.*

*"I have no idea what she's up to," he lies. "I'm dead as far as the law is concerned, and I'm leaving. Now."*

*Mr. Smith's smile is terrifying. "Carson, I am more than willing to allow you to go, to start your new life. But first I need to know what she might want from the safe in your house."*

*Carson wracks his brains. He keeps everything in his office, and everything of real value is electronic anyway. Family papers? Birth certificates?*

*Or else Jenny put something there on her own.*

"*I don't have anything of value in that house anymore,*" *he says defiantly.*

"*Just your son.*"

*Mr. Smith sits down on the edge of Carson's bed. His men stay close to the door. Carson wonders if he's going to have a heart attack right on the spot.*

"*I thought we were done,*" *Carson snaps.* "*You have all my money, and everyone thinks you're dead. Why can't I just leave?*"

*Mr. Smith waits, crosses his legs.* "*I don't like loose ends, Carson.*"

*The silence is deafening. Suffocating. Carson's throat closes up. He claws at the top button of his shirt to get some air.*

"*Send them to kill her,*" *he croaks, pointing at the bland-faced guards.* "*You know where she is, right? Doesn't matter what she has.*"

"*I could do that,*" *Mr. Smith seems to agree.* "*Or perhaps she and I could have a little chat about what happened to Vera and Marat.*"

*Carson is sure he's dying. He chokes on his own spit and staggers back to lean against the wall.*

"*For a real estate mogul, you seem to have a lot of people killed, Carson.*" *Mr. Smith smiles, showing all his teeth.*

"*They were... they were stealing from me,*" *Carson says, thinking wildly as he puts dots together. If there was no cartel....*

"*Oh, don't get me wrong. I'm not sorry. Vera had some very deep contacts back home, and they were interested in getting in on my business. I didn't want that to happen.*"

*Carson's vision narrows.* "*You said there were no drugs.*"

"*No, I said there was no cartel. That word, and I have to thank Hollywood for its help, brings about terrifying visions of swarthy types with guns and machetes, coming for your family should you cross them.*" *He gestures toward his face.* "*I just used that fear to keep people in line.*"

*Like me, Carson thinks. Fool.*

"*And while business has been quite good, there are too many players these days, too many greedy people. A new product only I have the formula for.*" *Mr. Smith stands slowly.* "*I'm looking for a fresh start. Like you.*"

*Carson, still breathing heavily, is beginning to think there is no fresh start, that he isn't getting out of this room alive.*

*"I don't know what Jenny has," he says.*

*Mr. Smith turns to his guards. "Send Roy and John to the house. I want her dead."*

*The door opens and closes, and they are alone.*

*Carson shivers. Roy's been working for Mr. Smith. No one is loyal to him. He's alone. He's going to die in this room.*

*And then it wells up in him.*

*It's not fair.*

*None of this is fucking fair.*

*He's lost everything he counted on—his money, his grandfather's trust fund, and his freedom. The chance to enjoy his life. All because of this... this... lying son of a bitch....*

*The red haze that falls over Carson's eyes blocks out everything but Mr. Smith. His body moves before his mind catches up. He throws himself at Mr. Smith, catching him off guard. They slam to the ground, narrowly missing the corner of the dresser. Mr. Smith struggles to reach inside his jacket, but Carson punches him in the throat, then the face. Stunned, Mr. Smith lays on his back, looking up at Carson.*

*He reaches out, grabs the lamp tottering on the edge of the nightstand. There's no hesitation as he brings the base down repeatedly onto Mr. Smith's face.*

*His hands are slick with blood when he stops. Some is his, as the lamp has broken into shards. Most is Mr. Smith's, unrecognizable and dead on the floor.*

*Operating in survival mode, Carson gets the gun from Mr. Smith's inside pocket. He takes his wallet and everything else he can find, stuffs it all into his bag, and sweeps Mr. Smith's rain jacket around him.*

# CHAPTER FIFTEEN

CADE FELT like all the energy had drained out of his body as Rachel recounted her story—every lie she told, every confused look, every single thing. She'd put this mess in motion, dragged Nox and Sam into danger, pulled in LJ and him as well.

He'd been wrong about her, and it broke his heart.

Rachel must have recognized the look on his face, because her voice kicked up an octave, the words rushing quickly.

"I know you don't understand, Cade, but it had to be done."

He looked up at her incredulously. "No, it didn't. Not this way. You could have just gone to Nox, told him about his father. Saved all this… bullshit and chaos!" Cade's temper rose dangerously. "They killed Zed! They almost killed Sam! I…." He thought of Billy's dead body back in the Iron Butterfly. "You ruined people's lives!"

"Nox wouldn't have believed me," she snapped, spots of color high on her cheeks.

"With good reason!" Cade yelled back. He stood, and Rachel, shockingly, took a step back.

"I needed for him to follow the trail himself." Rachel took a steadying breath. "When they grabbed Sam, I got worried. After all these years of hiding in the shadows, all of a sudden, he got bold. Out of the blue. And now we know why."

"The Feds," Damian offered helpfully. "Apparently some people in Albany have decided enough is enough. The lawlessness of the District is outweighing the economic benefits."

"I swear, Cade," Rachel said, but she was looking at LJ. "I swear, if I thought they were going to hurt the kid, I would've stopped it. Zed got all panicked and told me to leave. Told us to leave. Then those fucking goons showed up with Sam." The tinge of emotion in her voice almost swayed him, but Cade viciously pushed it down.

"At any point since then, since you showed up at the printing place, you could have told us the truth."

Rachel didn't respond.

"We were afraid of what Nox might do." Damian stepped closer to Cade. "And we needed to get out of the city."

"That guy on the boat," Cade asked, ignoring Rachel. Maybe Damian would be more inclined to tell him everything. "You know who he was?"

"No. But it made things even more nerve-wracking for us. We decided to keep quiet…." Damian shot a look at Rachel, who stiffened, then turned to walk away, back toward the bar. "And ah… well, when you all started investigating things, Rachel nudged you in the right direction. Mitzie let us know how badly things were deteriorating in the city, so I headed back to help her…."

Cade let his gaze drift to Mitzie, who smiled back placidly.

"You work for her?"

"I used to." Damian gestured toward Rachel, a blush staining his cheeks. "And since the Butterfly was destroyed and I didn't have a job…."

"He does things for me," Mitzie said, rolling up off the couch with a catlike stretch. "To move my money so I can leave without issue."

"We don't have much time," said Damian. "When the Feds hit the island—"

"Where are they hittin'?" LJ's voice cutting through the conversation took Cade off guard. "This place is too big, too many hotels and casinos and offices to raid at one time. No way the Feds got that much manpower for one operation."

Cade looked at his brother, the red-tinged eyes and pale face, but his words rang true.

"They're not gonna waste time with small-potatoes operations." LJ shot Mitzie a sharp glance. "No offense."

Mitzie shrugged. "You are right. That is why the panic. Why people are paying huge sums to get out."

"Do they want drug dealers? Hookers? The mob? Crooked politicians and cops?" Cade ran both hands through his hair. God, he needed a drink. Food. Forty hours of sleep and a fucking clue to how to find Nox and get the hell out of the city in about thirty-five hours. "Where do they start?"

Silence sat heavily in the room for an unbearable amount of time.

"We need to find Nox and get the hell out of here," Cade said finally. "Everything else the law can figure out on their own."

"Rachel and I have been talking," Damian said tentatively as Rachel returned to the group with a silver tray of tumblers, each with a healthy serving of vodka. "We were thinking maybe… maybe Carson has Nox."

Cade's knees gave out and he sat down hard on the couch.

Dark spots filled his vision. He felt LJ's arm around his shoulders, then a cool crystal tumbler pushed into his hand.

"Drink," Rachel said, seemingly far away and through a narrow tunnel.

Cade downed the entire glass, ignoring the serious burn flaring in his throat. It hit his empty stomach with a searing jolt.

Carson Boyet was alive. Carson Boyet was running drugs in the city.

Cade parsed through the information they'd painstakingly added to the wall in LJ's office back in South Carolina. Through the throbbing haze of too much stress, not enough food, and a punch of vodka, Cade turned to his brother, a hint of desperation in his voice.

"We need a laptop."


MITZIE PROVED to be helpful in two ways—backed up by Rachel, in Russian—she provided a gleaming laptop of the highest military grade and plunked it down on a marble table near the bar as she gestured to LJ with a flourish.

A few minutes later, several women in honest-to-God French-maid outfits entered, each pushing a gleaming silver cart. The scent of hot food hit Cade's taste buds hard.

Rachel and Damian herded the brothers to the table, where ornate high-backed pink velvet chairs provided a place to sit. LJ opened the laptop, and some light and color came back to his face.

"We need the pictures you took of our notes," Cade said, unashamedly filling two plates with fragrant lemon chicken, roasted potatoes, and a forest of broccoli spears.

Damian plopped down across from Cade, and Rachel hovered around the table, as if unsure where to go.

Cade ignored her.

"I need a password," LJ said, "and silverware."

Silently Rachel slid a piece of paper onto the table next to him. Then she darted away and returned with a fork and knife.

LJ didn't acknowledge her, but Cade saw the furtive look his brother gave Rachel when she walked away.

"We talked about whoever was running Dead Bolt and how it was only here," Cade said, reluctantly including Rachel in their conversation. "He has trucks and seemingly no distribution outside the city. And no international drug cartel would bother with a small operation like that."

"No, they wouldn't," Rachel murmured, standing next to Damian. "Given how much businesses here pay for protection and bribes."

"But why, after all this time, would he want the hotels and casinos to supply only Dead Bolt?"

"On the surface, to make more money." Damian rested his elbows on the table, frowning as he used to do over his tablet. "But it's still a finite market."

"So he works on his own," LJ said. He turned the laptop around so they could see. Their multicolored notes, pictures of the walls from back at the house in South Carolina filled the screen.

"Some questions answered." Cade leveled a glare at Rachel. "We know who sent Mr. White the notes—Roy Grimes and Jennifer," he said. "Clever."

Rachel set her shoulders back, chin up. Cade watched her walls snap back into place, that ruthless and determined fire come back into her eyes. "It worked."

"No, it really didn't," he snapped and turned his attention back to the laptop.

"Carson Boyet... let's say he fakes his death, goes underground, and reemerges in the middle of the birth of the District, starts running Dead Bolt on the island." Cade toyed with his food, then stuck a forkful into his mouth and almost moaned from the pleasure.

"Runs his drugs, stays in the shadows," Rachel picked up, her hand tight on the back of Damian's chair. "Then, for whatever reason, decides to expand into the casinos."

"Did he come here? Ask your friend to make it exclusive?"

Rachel glanced over her shoulder. Mitzie had grown bored and disappeared when the French-maid parade did.

"Yes. She called me the day after Zed told us what was going on," Rachel admitted. "All the casinos down here got the same offer."

"Did anyone say no?"

"A few. Mitzie agreed because she doesn't run heroin here like some of the other establishments."

Cade ate a few more bites, his stomach warming. "The places that said no… any retribution?"

Rachel shook her head. "Nothing overt—no bomb threats or fires. Nothing like that."

"But Zed," Cade mused. "Zed takes it a step further. He tries to find out who's the bigger group behind Dead Bolt and finds…."

"Just a guy behind a curtain, pretending he's big and powerful."

Cade nodded at Rachel's assessment. "He kills Zed. Shouldn't that be the end of it? Kill the people who know his secret, stay hidden. Instead he blows up the Iron Butterfly, making things ten times worse."

"It was a terrible miscalculation," Damian said with a sigh. "Albany couldn't ignore something that big, not with the whispers of terrorism."

Cade chewed slowly and felt his brother's eyes on him.

"Maybe that was the point."

Cade reached for his refilled tumbler of vodka. "He wants the government to fuck up his little goldmine? How does that make sense?"

Damian leaned back and tapped his fingers against the table, his expression thoughtful. "What happens when your business isn't profitable anymore and you can't sell it?"

"Burn down your barn or your warehouse," LJ offered. "Poison your animals. Insurance money is better than nothing…. Sabotage— but you gotta make it look like an accident."

Rachel made a quiet gasping sound, then went into a flurry of action. She leaned over LJ's shoulder, frantically pulled the laptop closer, and scrolled down.

"What?" Cade stood up and walked over to see what she was looking for.

"We said that killing people during the storm was a brilliant idea because who's checking? Who's sorting out bodies to see what was an accident and what was murder?" Rachel breathlessly pointed at the screen. "Flooding Morningside. Sinking the ferry. Who knows what else? Clean the slate and then—"

"Collect your money and move on," Cade said slowly. "But how does a fed raid equal the damage of the storms?"

"There must be more to it. A distraction. Obfuscation." Her voice trailed off as a look of horror crept across her face. "Feds show up, eyes on Dead Bolt, and then… what gets rid of evidence as handily as floods?"

Cade thought of the Butterfly collapsing into a rubble, smoke, and death.

"Fire. Explosions."

"Jesus." Damian grabbed the table.

The need to find Nox ratcheted up. Cade pushed away from the table, unable to stay seated another second.

"We need to figure out where this guy is set up. Where he would take Nox." Cade snapped his fingers toward the elevators. "Your friend. She's got contacts? Enough guys with guns?"

Rachel straightened up, her face unreadable for a brief moment. "The Dead Bolt operation has guys with guns too, Cade. This isn't just… kicking in a door."

"No shit, Rachel. But we're pretty much at zero options beyond that right now. We need to find out where Carson Boyet is, kick down a door or two, get Nox, and leave."

"We don't even know for sure…."

"Rachel, listen to me very closely. You're the reason we're in this fucking mess, you and your lies and your machinations," Cade said, his voice deadly as he trapped her in his glare. "Help me get Nox, help us get off this island, and maybe I won't let him know what you did."

It was a lie; he wouldn't let that hang between them. But Rachel didn't need to know that. He couldn't do this without her and that freak Mitzie's firepower.

Her lips a tight line, Rachel nodded. Then she turned and walked to the elevators without a backward glance.

Cade watched her go and sat back down with a sigh. He reached for the vodka and emptied the glass in two swallows.

"Trusting her to help us seems like a mistake," LJ said, his tone belying his words. "She might be the one who has Nox tied up somewhere right now."

"She doesn't," Damian said timidly. "When Sam got kidnapped, Rachel went nuts. She threatened me, told me either I helped save you all or…." He shrugged. "Or else. She didn't get specific, but I knew she meant it."

"I don't care." Cade turned to his brother. "We don't have a lot of choices at the moment, LJ. I'm sorry, so sorry I brought her into your life."

LJ held up his hand. "Stop. That's not important right now."

"Right." Cade leaned back in the chair. The once delicious scent of the food turned his stomach. So much ground to cover and every tick of the clock another second until everything exploded. Maybe literally.

Footsteps caught his attention as Rachel returned, her face inscrutable.

"Whatever we need," she said, walking to the end of the table opposite LJ. "Whatever we need to find Nox and get the hell out of here."

# CHAPTER SIXTEEN

NOX EASED open the door, anticipating gunfire as he moved. Furtive glances up and down the hallway revealed no one in the immediate area. Still as a statue, he listened for movement beyond and heard nothing. Saw nothing.

There were still guards at the entrance to get past, and he had no idea how many other people—armed people—were in the apartment. Nox considered his two options—attempt to get out the guarded front door or move through the apartment to the fire exit without knowing what he was up against.

A rush of thoughts, soaked in adrenaline and the sheer will to live, propelled Nox a few steps out the door. The fire escape gave him a sure shot all the way down to the back exit, which was less likely to be heavily guarded.

*What have I got to lose?* he thought darkly as he stepped fully into the hall and shut the door behind him with a quiet click.

Focused on his previous trip through the penthouse, Nox practiced his most silent and deliberate movements—long perfected on the streets—to recreate his path from earlier in the day. He heard a vacuum in the distance, but muffled as if behind a closed door. Noise from the kitchen caught his attention. He'd have to navigate past it to reach his destination.

The brightly lit living room, open and exposed, was his biggest obstacle. He skulked around the pristine furniture. Antiques and gilt-edged tables formed a complex pathway toward the next hall. When the vacuuming stopped, Nox hurried his steps and ducked into the shadows of the hallway near Carson's second office just before he heard the rattle of a doorknob.

Conversation—Russian, he quickly registered—filtered through from the kitchen. He got down low, almost crawling past the wide arch that led to what looked like a dishwashing area. Beyond that, he could see several women chatting as they packed dishes away in large padded bags.

Given their lightheartedness, Nox dared to hope the penthouse had been cleared of most of the armed guards. And his father.

At Carson's second office door, Nox paused. Should he risk a detour? Grab a few of the ominous black drives as leverage? He slid into a pocket of shadows and gently touched the knob. It turned, and he took it as a sign.

Keeping the lights off, Nox closed the door behind him, then quickly got to work. He randomly chose two drives off the desk—small enough to carry and not weigh him down, and stuffed them into the waistband of his pants, at the small of his back. The lack of discovery emboldened him. He gently eased open a few of the drawers of the desk, straining to see the contents before moving onto the next. In the bottom drawer, he found rolled-up blueprints, clearly old and well used. On a whim, Nox yanked them out and secured them under his shirt.

Not wanting to press his luck, Nox closed the drawers and walked around the desk to the shelves of black drives. He chose two from a low shelf, then moved them to the desk.

At first glance, no one would notice anything missing.

At the door, Nox paused to listen and wipe the sweat from his jaw and hairline. He was ignoring the growing fatigue and aches from his knee, pushing them from his mind for the moment. Nothing mattered unless he got out of here.

Again, the hallway seemed quiet. He opened the door and winced at the creak it made. Still nothing. No one.

If his memory was correct, the fire exit sat fifty or so feet around the next corner.

Nox took a deep breath and slipped out the door.

Every step felt like a clanging bell, and the drives and blueprints weighed him down even as he logically knew they were barely an additional two pounds. Thirty steps. Twenty. Ten. This part of the penthouse seemed to be the back of the house—nothing ostentatious or overly decorated, just dimly lit and institutional-white walls.

Nox spotted the fire exit, half blocked by a stack of ornate chairs and a vacuum. He stopped dead, alert for anyone in the vicinity. The voices from the kitchen had died away, and only the faintest hum of the central heating system registered. Taking a deep breath, Nox pressed ahead and wedged himself awkwardly around the chairs, the fit tight. Stuck, he shoved the chairs slightly, then froze as the upright vacuum wobbled and fell over with a crash.

Now or never, Nox thought frantically. He used the tiny breath of space to give one more push and then hit the metal bar on the door. It opened, and Nox nearly fell through to the other side.

The stale air of the stairwell was the best thing he'd breathed in ages.

Once they found Antonio and Felix, they'd search the penthouse and quickly guess how he got out, so he didn't wait to see if anyone had heard him.

His feet slapped the concrete as he raced down the endless flights of stairs, cursing his ridiculous expensive shoes with each step. He wanted his boots and his jacket. The echoes of his escape sounded like gunfire, his panting breath like shouts. He estimated the chances of anyone coming into the stairwell, and then just how loud a gunshot might be—would that bring people running?

Nox had no clue how much of the building his father controlled, and he didn't want to find out.

With shades of the night the Iron Butterfly blew up, Nox felt the sweat dripping off his body by the time he registered the numbers on the walls. Ten. Nine. Eight.

By the time he reached five, Nox allowed himself a flicker of hope.

At lobby level, Nox reached the end of the line. He searched for another door, but clearly access to the garage or service entrance was elsewhere.

"Fuck," he muttered, wiping his face on his jacket sleeve. He hastily fixed his hair and smoothed out his shirt. No hiding the sweat, nor the wrinkles. Thinking quickly, Nox pulled out the blueprints, put the gun in the inside pocket of his jacket, stuck the roll of papers under his arm, and took in a calming stream of air.

He yanked open the access door, head down and talking to himself as soon as his feet hit the pristine white marble of the lobby.

"Goddammit," he said, just loud enough to be heard. He surreptitiously checked his surroundings to see just how many people would be witness to his little performance—a man and a woman behind the ornate front desk, two young men tending to the various plants and flowers that formed a tropically themed lobby. No one had looked up yet.

Nox patted his pockets as if searching for his keys. He muttered under his breath, scanning for the entrance to the parking garage. A blinking box sat next to the door handle.

Praying to every deity he could think of, Nox quickened his pace toward the front door. But a spin of the revolving door brought an alert-looking security guard, hand on his hip. And his gun.

On a pivot, Nox changed directions toward the door. Okay, so maybe this was going to end in a shootout in the lobby of a tony apartment building that he helped build.

The white key card he'd lifted from Antonio came to mind. Still muttering, still clutching the blueprints, Nox reached into his pocket to grab it. A few feet to the door, to the blinking box. He heard the security guard speaking to the people at the front desk, but quietly enough for him to be unable to parse out words.

*Shit.*

The white card in hand, Nox closed the distance. The blinking slot taunted him with red as Nox swiped, estimating the time it would take between it rejecting his card and him getting his gun out....

It turned green, and the door unlocked with a loud click.

Nox heard, "Excuse me, sir?" behind him but yanked open the door and slipped through, head down as he made his escape.

In the cool darkness of the parking garage, Nox hurried down the steps to the main level. The musty smell of flooding still hung in the air, or maybe he could just always sniff it out. When the door didn't open behind him—and the security guard didn't appear, gun blazing—Nox slowed his walk and took in his surroundings. He considered stealing a car, but all the resident spots were taken up by an array of new models that he knew would be armed to the teeth with security protocols.

He had ducked around some cars, searching for natural light—and an exit—when he spotted a sign—Employee Parking—in bright red letters.

Bingo, he thought. It only took five minutes to find a piece-of-shit smart car, so old it belonged in a museum.

"Apologies," Nox said to the car, barely breaking a sweat to get the door open. Inside, the faint scent of pot greeted him, along with a pile of candy wrappers and empty soda bottles.

Nox dropped the blueprints onto the seat next to him but kept the gun in his lap, just covered by his jacket. Getting the car started took a few extra minutes, and the sound it made when the engine turned over made him wince. So much for getting out unnoticed.

Slowly, Nox backed out of the spot and then rumbled through the parking garage toward the neon-signed exit. No attendant, but the automated box was yet another blinking slot, awaiting his compliance. And pass.

"Let's hope these lazy motherfuckers get one card for everything," Nox said aloud as he slowly lowered the window.

Nox tasted freedom… mixed with the disgusting smell of the car's interior. It sat on his tongue, and he swallowed repeatedly as he rolled up to the blinking machine.

This time a swipe of the card didn't produce the instant relief of that green light. Nox cursed as he swiped again, and again, and the red light responded with a "No." His gaze darted around—to the right, the left, behind him—and no one seemed to be coming to investigate. Then the roar of an engine announced another car in the queue.

Nox swiped again. Then again. The BMW—he checked in the rearview mirror—didn't extend much patience. After a frantic heartbeat, Nox heard the squall of a horn. Twice.

Another swipe and the machine began to squawk. Nox could see the sidewalk, and he leaned down to grab the blueprints, make his escape on foot, when a voice called out to him.

"Sorry!" The parking attendant, swathed in a winter uniform and cap, gave him a wave. He walked up to the machine, smacked it hard twice, his bundled-up form leaning nearly into Nox's driver's side window. "Gimme your card. Let me try…."

Nox almost said "No, it's fine," but that would be ridiculous. He offered up Antonio's stolen card, and the man took it with an odd expression, but he swiped it.

The green light seemed miraculous.

The attendant handed back the key card with agonizing slowness. He moved away, his gaze taking in the details before him—Nox, the car he was driving, the card.

"Thank you," Nox said hurriedly, snatching back the card. The automatic arm shuddered up, and Nox held his breath as the man remained far too close to the car for him to move. He let his foot off the gas ever so slightly. The car vibrated, which seemed to distract the man long enough. The guard stepped back slightly, and Nox gave up all pretense of not wanting to get the fuck away.

He hit the gas, bounced over the speed bump and sidewalk, and sped out into the District streets.

For a few blocks, Nox just sucked in air and freedom, letting the windows down and the cold in as celebration at being out and away from captivity. He checked the rearview mirror frequently and was aware of the District police and security rolling their cars down the streets—and aware of the lack of people and taxis.

Once the pulsing of his heart and brain slowed down, Nox faced his next question—where was he going?

The house was out of the question. He assumed his father would look there first. He needed a secure phone line, some way to contact the others. He needed information—about Carson and his operation and exactly what was coming down the pike. And then? He needed someone to tell him what was on those hard drives.

The only answer he could come up with was Brownigan, his go-to for electronic free passes, who was afraid of him just enough to skip the part where he turned Nox in. To anyone.

So Nox got his bearings and navigated toward the seedier, less-patrolled downtown area. The tension dissipated as he reached the lower tip of Manhattan, where once high finance and history shared tiny cobblestone streets and extraordinary views. Post 9/11, it became a neighborhood to live in and a tourism destination. The housing they built seemed a brilliant flourish—another space in the city to attract retail and restaurants.

Those housing complexes were among the first victims of the storms. The buildings sank and collapsed in the onslaught, killing too many people to count. Much of the debris had been washed away, but the ragged landscape hadn't yielded much progress since.

In the distance, visible between buildings, Nox could make out the shoreline. People who frequented places like the Flamingo weren't here for the view, which worked out. The car rattled down another empty street, though Nox could make out people lurking in the shadows. Drug dealers and seekers, prostitutes who weren't attractive or healthy enough for the casinos, others who'd washed out of one business or another and now tried to make enough money to survive.

Nox pulled into a side street where he puttered along until he found a space both legal and tiny enough for him to wedge into.

Brownigan's building—a place that would once have attracted hip squatters—sat a few blocks down.

Windows up, Nox collected his blueprints and turned off the car. It wheezed, and Nox sat in the silence for a few moments, centering himself. Brownigan, information, then....

Cade? Sam? Provided he could reach one or both of them, the next decision was critical. Did he then do everything he could to get off the island and be reunited with his family? Or did it point him back to Carson, back to his father and taking him down?

Nox wiped his face with his sleeve and shook off the pall of doom that dropped over him. No time for that, no time for anything but the part where Nox was armed with more than just a gun.

Clutching his blueprints, and with the gun in his pocket, he left the little car in the middle of the street. The streets seemed to whisper with a dark energy; Nox could hear the desperate people in the shadows. He focused on Brownigan's dilapidated tenement, overgrown with ivy, its stoop a crumble of concrete.

Nothing had changed since last he visited; the entrance was through the basement apartment. He walked through the rusted iron gate and took a last look around to make sure he wasn't being followed. Down three steps, then a warped white door to be pushed open. No visible security at this point, but Nox knew there were hidden cameras catching his every movement and angle of his face.

In the mold-filled basement apartment, a weak light spilled down from an overhead fixture. Nox moved through the darkness, toward the second door he knew was ahead.

Before he even reached it, he heard the lock disengage.

A sliver of light lit the rest of the way, and he hurried through. The hallway and wooden staircase were familiar, so he took the stairs two at a time. Another door, another lock disengaged, and Nox pushed his way into Brownigan's lair.

Computers lined every wall of the main living space, on shelves stacked nearly to the ceiling. Cords and wires crisscrossed like a mass of snakes wriggling along the floor. Nox put his hand in his pocket and closed it around the gun, just in case. Then he turned the corner into the kitchen, where Brownigan had his desk.

And stopped short.

Gym bags sat on the counter, stuffed with computer equipment. Brownigan, soft, round, and frantic, was struggling under the weight of a stack of hard drives.

"What the fuck are you doing here?" he asked, his eyes wide behind his glasses. He didn't stop packing as Nox walked cautiously into the room. "I thought you were dead."

"No." Nox didn't give more information as he looked around curiously.

"You need to get out. Now. I got a guy waiting for me down by the waterfront." Brownigan dumped the hard drives into a half-full bag.

"I need your help." Nox put the gun away.

"No." Brownigan breathed heavily, leaning against the kitchen counter. "I gotta get out of here."

"This house?"

"This fuckin' city. The Feds are comin'. People like us...." He indicated Nox, then himself. "You know we're gonna take the blame. Not the rich folks. The ones that've been leavin' like rats off a sinkin' ship. Us. We're gonna go down for everything." He was winding himself up for a rant, so Nox raised his hand.

"I need your particular expertise. Then I'll help you leave," Nox said smoothly. "I'll make sure you get out in plenty of time."

Brownigan gave him a wary look, his jaw working frantically. "You need money? Security pass? What?"

"Information."

Reaching behind him, he pulled one of the black drives from the small of his back. "I got this from the guy who controls all the Dead Bolt in the city. And I want to know what's on it."

Brownigan's beady little eyes tripled in size. He sucked in a dramatic breath and nodded. Nox didn't know what he held in his hand; that much was clear from the expression on the other man's face.

"You got me for forty-five minutes," Brownigan said, almost breathless. He reached out his hand for the drive. "And it's gonna cost you."

# CHAPTER SEVENTEEN

SAM DIDN'T know why Carson Boyet just sat there, staring at him. He let his attention wander around the room, a weirdly civilized and refined existence in the middle of the destroyed chaos.

"You were born here," Carson said eventually, his eyes glittering. "Here at the sanitarium."

Twisting in his seat, Sam nodded. "My mother died while I was being born."

A strange expression settled over Carson's face—distaste and regret at once. "I wish I had been there to help her. To help you."

"My dad…." Sam felt his face burn. "I mean Nox… Nox delivered me. Saved me from the storm. All by himself." That seemed the right thing to add, to make sure this man knew… understood what Nox did.

"No help at all?" Carson asked, leaning forward slightly. "That's quite impressive."

Sam's brain provided a picture of Rachel, her smug smile and the way his father snapped at her. The story written on the wall… *Jenny.* But Sam had been trained by his father on what to do when someone asked you questions. He let his expression go blank and blinked idly at Carson.

"He didn't have a choice," Sam said, holding Carson's gaze with his own until he thought he might explode.

"Hmmm." Carson crossed his legs. "Very brave," he murmured. "Do you have any questions for me, Sam? Anything you want to know?"

The trap lay in front of him, neatly set up.

Letting his youth be his cover for the moment, Sam shrugged. "I mean, I think you know the obvious one," he said, defiance creeping into his tone. Petulance. He slid down in the chair a bit.

Carson regarded him for a long, uncomfortable moment. "Of course. My being… here. It's quite a surprise."

"Understatement," Sam mumbled, crossing his arms over his chest.

"As I told your brother, I was involved with some… unsavory people and needed to make them think I was no longer a threat. In order to keep your mother and Nox safe," he added, almost as an afterthought.

Everything in Sam wanted to scream, "When did you speak to my father?" But he let himself nod, eyes darting around the room. "Okay. Except…."

"Except?" Carson prompted.

"I don't know. Why didn't you tell us you were alive? Help us?" He let a distasteful, offended sneer come to his lips. Sam looked at his father, gaze flicking over his expensive suit, the beautifully furnished room they sat in. "Seems like you were doing okay for a guy with such scary enemies."

Carson pursed his lips. "True. I have been fortunate to recoup some of my standing, albeit under another name. But I never was far away, Sam. I kept an eye on you and your brother, made sure you were all right."

"You didn't help me out of jail," Sam snapped. "Or when I got grabbed by some goons and almost got blown up at the Iron Butterfly." The momentary flare of anger surprised Sam. He bit back any other words and pressed his back into the chair.

Carson's jaw pulsed for a moment, so much like a tic his father had that a wave of sadness pulled at Sam's heart. Tears threatened as he swallowed again and again, staving off the darkness.

"I'm sorry for that, Sam. There are many unsavory people in this city, and they aren't afraid to use violence to get what they want," Carson said gently. "You can't trust the police or the local government either."

"Can't trust anyone."

"No, that's not quite true. You can trust me," Carson said.

Sam swallowed a nasty laugh.

"I don't think so. Some federal agent grabs me out of bed and brings me here, not to his bosses? Unless you're the head of the FBI, I don't think this is on the up and up." Sam lifted his chin. *When did you see my father, when?* he thought frantically. *Tell me.*

Carson's smile never faltered.

"I am a businessman, Sam. I work with many people." A rapid knock on the door interrupted Carson, clearly much to his displeasure, as his expression turned dark.

A second later the door opened wide, bringing Agent Allard into the room.

"We have a situation at the house," he said, his voice hard.

Carson looked at the agent and then Sam and got to his feet.

"Keep him here," Carson said, his tone entirely different than the soothing tones he used with Sam.

Without another word to Sam or a look back, Carson Boyet stormed out the room, shoving past the agent into the hallway.

Sam spared Agent Allard a nasty look and then concentrated on his feet.

Leave me alone. Just go out and leave me alone.

Agent Allard stepped fully into the room. He locked it behind him, and Sam's heart fell.

"Listen, Sam, you need to stay calm and helpful, and everything will be fine," Agent Allard said, walking slowly toward Sam. His gaze flickered to the backpack, and Sam drew it closer, like he could hide it entirely.

"You're crooked," Sam said. "If you were doing your job, I'd be somewhere…." He glanced around him. "Official."

"This is official as we can get for the moment." The agent came closer. "I thought you'd be happier to meet your father."

"He's not my father." Sam's face grew hot.

"Back from the dead," Agent Allard continued, as if Sam hadn't said anything. "You're not curious?"

Sam shrugged. "I don't trust him." The other man was just a few feet away, fixated on Sam's backpack.

That made Agent Allard laugh. He tipped his head back and let out a loud snort.

"Smart kid. You're very smart." Agent Allard stepped right up against Sam's knees. "What's in the bag?"

Sam lifted his chin in defiance. "Clothes and stuff. You people already searched it."

"You seem pretty protective of it." The agent leaned over and reached for the backpack with a slow movement.

Sam kept it away from him as best he could.

"It's mine."

"You going to fight me for some sweatpants and clean underwear? I don't think so."

Sam thought about fighting back when Agent Allard grabbed the backpack, thought about kicking and punching, but as the man pulled back the zipper, he knew there was nothing he could do.

The tears that threatened before came roaring back.

Agent Allard unzipped the top of the pack, then turned it over, allowing everything to fall out. He didn't even stop to search through the crumpled clothes; he began to feel inside the back, much to Sam's distress.

"Ahhh," he said finally, pulling his hand from the bag.

The gizmo phone sat in his palm.

Sam kicked the leg of the chair in frustration.

The agent inspected the phone for an agonizing long moment before dropping it into his pocket. Then he grabbed the clothes and shoved them inside.

"Here," he said casually when he was done. He threw the bag into Sam's lap.

"I...."

Agent Allard shook his head. "Nice and calm and cooperative," the man said. "Be a good boy, okay?"

Then he, like Carson, walked out the door without a backward glance.

# CHAPTER EIGHTEEN

AN UNEASY truce settled into Cade's heart. He would use Rachel and Damian and Mitzie for whatever he could get out of them—information, guns, shelter, technology—anything and everything to find Nox and get the fuck off the island. Like it or not, he and LJ couldn't do it on their own.

Mitzie remained out of sight, which was a relief. Various maids and staff walked in and out, carrying more laptops, phones, and large pads of paper, pens and refreshments. Rachel directed them as Cade bit his tongue. Truce. They had a truce.

Damian had ants in his pants. He couldn't sit still for long, jumping up and pacing around until Rachel pushed a cell phone into his hand and said, "Start making calls." He didn't ask her to elaborate, just huffed a yes and left the room.

LJ continued on the laptop, mumbling to himself as he talked to his various hacker/anti-government friends. He was sending out calls for help far and wide—whatever information could be gleaned from those hacking the police department mainframe or the mayor's personal communications or even a survey of the grid. Cade watched him watch Rachel as she darted around the room speaking rapid-fire Russian on a small black cell phone.

He thought of the gizmo phones that LJ had passed out before they left South Carolina. Two, he knew, were locked up somewhere in the Feds' evidence lockers, the third with Sam, Mason, and their parents, hopefully safe at the cabin. When Cade wasn't consumed with worry and stress over Nox and everything else, he remembered his parents. If they made it out of all this alive, he would have to spend a thousand years apologizing to LJ, Momma, and Daddy for bringing them into this nightmare.

Rachel's voice rose and fell with anger as she argued with someone—a fight that ended when she threw the phone across the room and it shattered against the slim strip of pink wall between the windows.

"Problem?" Cade asked snidely.

Rachel shot him a look that could incinerate the moon. "No."

"You going to tell me why you killed Francis?" Cade stared at Rachel as she whirled around and walked away from him. "Were you his partner?"

Rachel ground out a rude laugh as she went to the bar. "That piece of shit? No. He came after me, so I killed him."

Cade's gut warred. Was she lying yet again?

"He knew we were going to the boat. Who else had that information?" Cade wondered out loud. He could feel his brother's attention directed to him. Even Damian was watching the conversation. "Damian? You his partner?"

Damian looked confused. Genuinely confused.

"Who?"

"I'm thinking it's not Mason or Sam or me or Nox." Cade felt dangerous. He felt weirdly powerful as he watched Rachel's back muscles contract, her shoulders up around her ears. "That leaves you."

Rachel didn't speak. She poured herself a full glass of clear liquid from a crystal decanter.

Then she took her time turning around, letting the air swell with tension.

"I wasn't his partner," she enunciated slowly. "Believe me or not. I don't care."

Something plagued her, though. Cade thought that obvious. But she shut down, refusing to speak any more on the subject.


CADE HAD been tasked with trolling through the various social media tagged with District-focused words—people complaining about the shutdown and their vacations being cut short, travel bookers lamenting their drop in profits and the uncertainty of the future. Here and there, someone spoke up about corruption and cover-ups or the victimization of sex workers, the latter of which seemed to spark "Choices were made! It's not like they're hookers!" arguments that confused and nauseated Cade.

He closed that tab and started over.

Conspiracy theorists were having a field day, still, over the Iron Butterfly bombing. Terrorism, a government false-flag operation, the assassination of a Saudi businessman—Cade recognized the man's picture—all got thousands of hits and comments, a tangled web of mistrusts and coincidences that might have made him laugh a few months ago. But as he was currently living it....

"These are the people LJ is trusting," Cade mumbled to himself, scrolling down a bit further.

The story about "the Vigilante" being the culprit got only a few hundred up votes, and very few comments. "Sounds made up" was the most popular theme of response and "convenient" with a dozen eye-roll emojis when a poster shared a news report that the Vigilante had been killed in a shootout.

A new discussion thread by someone called BackInBlack claimed to have survived the bombing. They laid out how the evening went—a different point of view than Cade's.

Different, but spot on.

Cade read all their posts with interest. The explosions, the frantic push to escape. He mentioned "two guys who dragged an injured kid out and got the door opened," which sent a chill down his back.

*It wasn't one guy. There were a bunch of dudes HEAVILY ARMED, all over the place before the first explosion. This was a mafia thing.*

*Drug-running mob bullshit and people DIED. Why isn't the government doing anything about it? PAYOFFS!!!! BRIBES!!! CORRUPTION!*

*Albany needs to step in.*

"Right on," Cade said out loud.

He read the comments eagerly, then came across another poster who seemed to also be living on the island.

*If u live here, get out now. Right now. Today. Shit's going down. Rich people already gone. Just like last time. Swim if you have to. No one getting out alive.*

The poster's name was GonAgin.

Continuing his scroll, Cade finished the thread, then looked up to find Rachel on yet another phone, texting rapidly.

"Anything on your end, Rachel?" he asked, unable to keep the nastiness out of his tone.

Rachel didn't answer or acknowledge him.

Damian returned from who knew where, looking upbeat. "I may have found something."

Everyone's attention turned to him.

"I called someone I know who works for the power company. I thought maybe we could track down some locations supplied with electricity that were... unusual." Damian sat down at the table and began to fidget over a piece of paper. "Like places that were abandoned but still pulling a large load of power."

LJ snapped his fingers and then rapid-fire typed on his laptop. "You got addresses?"

Damian recited half a dozen spots, slowly and clearly. When he said an address in Inwood, Rachel stopped dead.

"What was the last one?" she asked.

Damian repeated it.

"Let me get these checked out, got some people on it," LJ said, the clatter of keys nonstop. "Good call with the power."

Flushing with pleasure, Damian waved the paper. "I mean, they have to be manufacturing the drugs somewhere, right?"

Nodding, Cade typed in the hashtag deadbolt and hit Enter. "Nox said there were white trucks working out of the abandoned hospital up near his house."

"Lennox Hill?"

"Yeah."

Damian read over the list again. "No, not on the list. Doesn't mean they aren't up to something there, just that they aren't pullin' a ton of power."

"We'll check it out anyway." LJ motioned for Damian to come over to look at his screen. They began to talk about utilities and crosschecking, which Cade shut out. He wanted to know more about the drug that tethered Carson to the city.

Cade focused on reading the posts regarding Dead Bolt—mostly sad stories of death, injury, and addiction from those unfortunate enough to start up, with a few singing the praises of the drug and its "magical powers."

"Rachel, when did Dead Bolt hit the city?" he asked.

When she didn't respond, he looked up, only to find her gone.

"Where'd Rachel go?" he asked. LJ and Damian glanced around.

No one answered because no one knew, so Cade stood up, a rumble of anxiety and suspicion burning his stomach.

"Maybe she went to the bathroom," Damian offered halfheartedly. "Or to go to talk to Mitzie."

The hair stood up on the back of Cade's neck. Could be something innocuous, could be more.

"Damian, can you just...." Cade waved toward the door that had gotten most use during their time there. "It would make me feel better if I knew where the hell she was at all times."

Lips in a tight line, Damian nodded and cast an apologetic look at LJ. He hurried out of the room, Cade's eyes on him the entire time.

"Maybe we should pack up and take the party elsewhere," Cade said, unable to shake the goose bumps.

"You said we needed these people and their resources... and you were not wrong," LJ countered. He gestured over the laptops and phones, then to the cords and, above them, the lights. "We don't have shit if we leave here."

"I don't trust her," Cade said, but he winced when LJ's face tightened into a painful rictus.

"I...."

LJ held up his hand. "Let Damian see if he can't find her. She doesn't come back, we get the hell out of here. Okay?"

"Yeah." Cade dropped back into his chair but only lasted a second before he jumped back up. "Yeah. I'm just gonna...." He stuck his hands in his pockets and began a slow circuit around the room.

Cade wove through the myriad of furniture, the tiny glass tables and awkward placement of "art." The entire suite was a salute to decadence and indulgence, bought and paid for by a soup of excess, corruption, and exploitation.

His own role in this awful ecosystem couldn't be pushed aside. For all his "fuck the world, I'm doing me" attitude, he'd also willfully overlooked those who weren't him, those whom this place ate up and spit out. How many times had he barely spared a moment to wonder about a new hire who disappeared after just a few weeks? Or an old-timer who'd slowed down being packed up and shipped off? As long as the money ended up in his account, did he care?

A burn of shame paused Cade as he stopped by one of the tall windows. He looked down on a city cold and silent, all the pretty sparkle of the District absent down here. Before he delivered the letter from Mr. White, before he met Sam and Nox, did he ever think about the people who struggled to survive in this place?

When—and he had to think when, not if—when he found Nox and they got out of here, what were they leaving behind? Who?

Cade pressed his hands against the window, absorbing the chill. He wished he could pretend the raid would work, that the bad guys would be dragged off, and the good guys....

How were they going to tell?

Everyone, from the mayor's office down to the drug dealers skulking around in the shadows below, had a piece of the dirty pie. Even if they succeeded in finding Carson, alerting the Feds, and stopping the bombs, what was going to happen to the city? There was no way for them to root out all the corruption in one day. It would take years. Not to mention all the rebuilding, the restoration.

A wave of hopelessness ran over Cade.

"Hey." His brother's voice reached him, filtering through the rustle of anxiety in Cade's head.

He turned around slowly.

"C'mere. Let's look at what I got so far," LJ said gently. He gestured toward the empty chair next to him. "We got a lot of stuff to get through here."

Cade forced himself away from the window and back across the room. He felt encased in concrete, each step a chore. When he fell into the chair next to his brother, the sigh he let out was barely audible.

"We got this." LJ reached over and squeezed Cade's shoulder with one strong hand. "You and me. Okay?"

Struggling against a wave of unbidden tears, Cade just nodded. He leaned forward so he could see the screen.

"From what Damian found out, these are three spots that also have water and gas being used on the regular. One of 'em seems to be a squatter's paradise. Bunch of people living in a fancy apartment building in an abandoned neighborhood all the way on the East Side. Seems on the up and up."

Cade nodded. His brother's screen flashed with a dozen open chat windows, with code running in a line across the top of the screen and search-result hits on the bottom. It hurt his eyes.

"But the other two...." LJ clicked a few windows, and a schematic of the city filled the screen. "That place in Inwood?" LJ said the name cautiously. "They're runnin' up some serious bills there. Have been for a while, which is surprisin', since that building hasn't been open since the floods. And then there's a spot...."

Cade stared at the map of Manhattan, the bright red spot indicating the place Rachel asked about. "What was it? Before the floods?" Cade asked.

"Uh...." LJ clicked a few buttons, and the results made Cade sit up with surprise.

"Morningside Sanitarium," Cade whispered. A long-ago website proclaimed it the premier accommodation for patients and showed a picture of a large, bright building sprawling into two wings and luxurious green grounds.

He knew because it had been on the wall at the house in South Carolina—Morningside Sanitarium, where Nox found his mother giving birth, where he rescued Sam....

Where he met Rachel... Jenny.

"That's it. That's the place," Cade sputtered out. "That's where Carson is."

"Maybe. Could be more squatters," LJ said, tapping out a response in one of the chat windows. "The other place ain't too far from here...."

"LJ, listen to me. That place... there's a reason Rachel freaked out." Worry propelled Cade back to his feet. "We should leave."

"Cade...."

"That's where Nox's mother died." Cade began to close the laptops on the table, then hurriedly gathered up everything Rachel had given them into a hasty pile. "I need a bag."

LJ's face lost all color.

"I refuse to believe in coincidences right now." Cade looked around frantically. "Help me look for something to carry this all in."

Morningside Sanitarium. If that's where Carson Boyet was, could it be where Nox was as well?

# Chapter Nineteen

In Brownigan's living room, Nox watched him settle at a wide industrial desk and pull a wireless keyboard into his lap. He fiddled around under the desk and emerged with a mess of cords and a dirty wireless mouse that seemed to be held together with duct tape.

"Forty-five minutes," he repeated, not looking up at Nox. Brownigan attached the black drive to the cord and the other end into a massive tower sitting precariously on a small table.

Nox stepped over the wires lining the floor. There was nowhere to sit, so he let his hand rest in his pocket, over the gun, and used the other to unroll the stolen blueprints.

The dim light didn't help much. Nox leaned close to get a sense of what they were for.

The Iron Butterfly.

Nox squinted at the corner of the blueprints. They were old—the first plan for the Butterfly, according to the date and numbering system. No surprise why his father had it. He must've used it to set the bombs to destroy it.

He pushed that print aside and scanned the second. The old Port Authority Building, which now housed the majority of the police force.

"Shit."

Nox pulled it up and quickly checked the one below. It wasn't even a surprise to see Morningside's name on the third sheet. The final sheet, as Nox shifted to see it, wasn't a building. It was an old subway map, or at least the part that ran under midtown.

The District.

Could this be his father's hit list? Locations to be destroyed to disrupt the city as his father took his leave? What did they have to do with the men at the penthouse?

Nox looked over at Brownigan, hoping to get some information. The man sat transfixed by whatever he saw on the trio of screens surrounding him.

"What did you find?" Nox asked, and Brownigan jumped as if he'd forgotten Nox was there.

The wash of calculation was unmistakable, even in the dim light. Brownigan glanced at the screen, then back to Nox, gaze narrowing.

Nox was not in the mood. He pulled the gun from his pocket as he walked over to where Brownigan worked.

"What did you find?" he repeated slowly.

The gun changed Brownigan's expression and his demeanor.

"It's a carrier drive. A way to move large sums of money. Like… a portable bank, but no one can trace it." Brownigan gestured at the screen. "Someone paid this company a shit-ton of money for, uh…." He squinted. "Doesn't say exactly what. But the only people who use this shit are moving drugs or guns or like… bioweapons. Big time villain motherfuckers." The man nervously wiped his mouth. "You kill whoever you lifted this from?"

Nox shook his head.

"That was maybe a bad idea." Brownigan began to jiggle his knees. The movement rattled the entire setup of computers in front of him.

"So, if someone had… multiples of this drive, that meant they were all worth…."

Brownigan's eyes almost burst out of his head. "This one's for half a million."

"Can you access it?"

"Like… can I get the money out?" Brownigan's tower of equipment swayed as his nervous tic increased. "Uh… yeah. Take some time, but yeah."

Nox considered the drive still concealed under his jacket. He considered the pile of drives in Carson's office and nodded. "Consider it a parting gift in exchange for you forgetting you ever knew me."

Brownigan nearly choked on his own tongue. "Are you shittin' me?"

"No." Nox pocketed the gun again, then gestured to the blueprints. "Tell me what you know. Why are you leaving?"

Brownigan began to disconnect the drive, as if afraid Nox would change his mind. "It's been tricklin' down since the Butterfly got blown up. People sayin' how it's time to move on. Those assholes in Albany just remembered we still exist." He wrapped the cords around the drive and clutched it to his chest. "A few days ago, one of my regulars from the Flamingo said to pack up and get the fuck out. They're going to slam the hammer down, and that means everybody who can't afford to take their private fuckin' jet to Switzerland is goin' to prison."

He stood up, still holding the drive tight. "I got a call this mornin'. My friend tells me to pack what you fuckin' can and go. Now. They got me a boat."

"What do you know about the Dead Bolt operations?"

Brownigan squinted in his direction. "I don't know. Same as always. Pumping it into the casinos and every available arm on the island."

"You hear anything about them expanding the operation?"

That seemed to take the man aback. "I been out of that life for a long time. You know that," Brownigan warned. "You know that."

"Not saying you're dealing or using. Just asking a simple question," Nox said patiently. "You're into everything, Brownigan. You know people's business—their private business. None of your customers got anything going on with Dead Bolt?" He gestured toward his wrist. "How much time you got for some in-depth conversation?" He took a menacing step in Brownigan's direction.

The man leaned back in fear.

"I don't deal with that shit, man. My customers… maybe a few of them got money for me to, uh… discreetly move to an offshore location. But none of them are…." Brownigan made a furtive gesture. "You know, high on the food chain. "They clean some money for people, take their cut."

Nox frowned. Unhelpful. "And no one's said anything about the operation leaving the island?"

"No. In the past, maybe a few people thought it would be good business. Bring it to the mainland. Make serious dollars." He drew his finger across his neck in a slitting motion. "They're no longer with us."

A con then, Nox thought. His father takes the money from a select few businessmen, promising them a cut of wide distribution, then takes the money and disappears.

"When did your contact say shit was going down?" Nox asked suddenly, the question almost subconscious.

"A day at the most. Maybe thirty-six hours." The recitation of time seemed to ignite Brownigan's nerves.

Nox considered everything and added it to what he already knew from interacting with his father. In the meeting he made it sound like they had a few days, almost a week. If he knew about the raid.... "Who's your contact?"

Brownigan squirmed. He looked at Nox, then glanced toward the kitchen, where his belongings were, as if to gauge his chances of running past Nox.

"Her name is Mitzie. She runs the Flamingo. Russian girl," he said finally.

"Recent import?"

Brownigan scoffed. "Fuck no. She's original like me. Her parents came here when she was a kid—Brighton Beach, running numbers, I think they were. She's a fuckin' monster. Survived everything. Ran hookers before the water receded."

"Why is she helping you leave?"

He shrugged. "I been doin' work for her for a long time. We go way back. She's got… let's call 'em arrangements, with everybody— city officials, the mobsters, the cops."

Nox let his fingers dance at his side. An original—like Brownigan and like him. She might know something that could help him. She certainly seemed to be sharing quite a bit with Brownigan.

"She leave yet?"

"No. She's got something to finish…." Brownigan trailed off, as if realizing he was getting chatty with the wrong person. "Said she'd look me up when we got to… Chicago."

Clearly a lie, but Nox didn't care. Let Brownigan and his dirty money flourish somewhere else.

"Thank you."

Silence filled the room as Brownigan tentatively began to move. "So... okay," he said finally. "I'm gonna...."

"Go. Just remember our deal."

"I ain't never seen you before," Brownigan said breezily. "Don't know, don't care. Found this box on the street."

Nox gestured toward the kitchen, and Brownigan didn't hesitate another second. He darted around Nox and disappeared into the next room.

Mitzie. Russian. Brighton Beach. Nothing out of the ordinary. Running hookers and that shithole, the Flamingo? Sat her in the middle of a hotbed of loose lips and drunken blathering. Being an original? She'd seen it all, from the center of the action.

Nox gathered up the blueprints and tucked them behind some of the computers. Brownigan taking off meant his place would be available to hide out in—something useful at least. He checked his gun out of routine and then used the reflection of a monitor to smooth his hair.

"Hey, I need an ID card," he called out, and Brownigan answered him with a frustrated groan.

BROWNIGAN GOT out fifty minutes after he made the deal with Nox. Lugging bags in both hands, an enormous backpack strapped on, the man struggled to get up the stairs to the street level. With dispassion, Nox watched him go. He wasn't going to hurt the guy, but he also wasn't going to help.

"You gonna make it?" he called, having followed Brownigan back down to the basement.

"I hope I never fuckin' see you again," Brownigan huffed back.

"You're welcome." Nox watched the struggle a bit longer and went back upstairs.

Off the kitchen was a back door Brownigan apparently used for regular comings and goings. Nox left it open enough so he could get back in, then squeezed through the stacked-up junk metal—old appliances, broken computers, furniture—that formed a fake wall to hide movement. He jumped over a half-eroded retaining wall that divided two barren "backyards." The buildings along this small street all appeared to be empty, but Nox couldn't be entirely sure. He moved quickly.

Weaving through the yards, Nox reached the end of the block and squeezed through the narrow alley to the street. He'd come at the Flamingo from the other direction, as if stumbling in from the District.

The stillness of the street felt unnatural. Beyond the strict adherence to the curfew, beyond people just feeling safer with walls and locked doors between them and the outside world, the city felt... empty, in a way Nox hadn't felt since after the National Guard gave up and left all those years ago.

Curfew and lockdown or not, the garish pink lights of the Flamingo called to him. He adopted a slightly drunk, relaxed air as he came into view of the front door, where a doorman and two security guards waited. He'd go onto the floor, maybe gamble a little, then find this Mitzie....

Then a man walked out of the front door, and Nox froze in place.

Damian Oh, his face twisted into worry, exited and frantically looked up and down the street before talking to each of the men in turn. Nox didn't know how to proceed. The surprise of seeing the no-longer-missing man at the place of Brownigan's friend robbed him of his previous plan.

Russian. Brighton Beach. Running hookers.

Mitzie.

Damian.

Rachel.

Almost as if propelled forward by a force not his own, Nox walked quickly toward the Flamingo. Damian finished his conversations and hurried down the pink marble stairs toward the street.

The urge to call out was strong, but Nox bit his tongue. He doubled his pace, trying to look as nonthreatening as possible in his body language lest the security guards look over and decide to get involved.

Fifty feet. Twenty feet. Ten.

Close enough now, Nox let out an angry hiss of Damian's name.

The man jerked as if shot and skidded to a stop as he realized who was calling him.

Nox waited for Damian to run, to shout for help, but he did neither. Instead, his face broke into a relieved smile.

"Oh shit, it's good to see you."

# CHAPTER TWENTY

SAM GAVE himself a few minutes of grief and rage after Agent Allard took the phone and left. He pressed his hands into his face until it hurt, until the pain somehow made the anguish at his helplessness bearable. All that work to keep the phone safe, and now... now....

Tears clogged his throat and leaked out of his eyes. The salt stung as he gave up.

Just. Gave up.

The phone was his link to his father, the only way to save Mason and the Creels. Now what? Locked in this room, alone, no clue what any of these people really wanted—because he wasn't stupid. He knew they were lying to him, knew they were using him.

What did the agent call him? Bait? A shameful burn pushed the tears out harder, faster. The guilt made him nauseous.

He let himself cry, a flood of pent-up emotion let loose.

Hopeless.

Helpless.

The word *bait* repeated in his mind until Sam was sure he would start yelling and not be able to stop.

His father—his real father—would do anything to save him. If these horrible people contacted him, if they told Nox Sam was in danger....

He wouldn't hesitate to come running.

Sam moaned and then let the anger compel him up and out of the chair. Through swollen eyes he regarded the room. His next step.

He gave himself another few seconds of tears, of feeling squashed and trapped. Then Sam thought about Nox, fighting through everything—floodwaters and people trying to kill him—when he was just a little younger than Sam.

In the middle of hell, alone, Nox became an adult. He rescued Sam, raised him, worked, and patrolled the streets as the Vigilante to keep them safe.

The very least Sam could do was not sit around crying, waiting to be saved.

Angrily, Sam lifted his T-shirt and swiped it over his face until it was dry enough. He sniffled back any lingering tears until he could breathe again.

First, he was going to look in every spare corner of this place.

SAM KEPT an ear out for anyone approaching as he darted around the apartment, opening drawers and cabinet doors. A bedroom nightstand full of medications gave him a name.

Mr. White.

He remembered exactly where he'd first heard the name—Cade's voice saying, "It's from a friend of mine. Mr. White?" Startled, Sam knocked over a few of the amber bottles, rattling the rest.

He was in the place where Mr. White lived, the man who had sent the fake notes. The man who had directed Cade into their lives.

The connection to his… Carson Boyet eluded him for the moment, but the connection made him uncomfortable. He experienced a flash of reluctance to go on, but no, no. He wouldn't let Nox down like that.

Drawers and closets of clothes—beautiful, well made, expensive. Old leather albums of photographs, which Sam gave a cursory glance to. People at fancy restaurants. Dressed up for balls, standing on the steps of some grand staircase. There were even black-and-white photographs of a young man playing tennis on the rolling hills of what Sam assumed was a college campus. There was something familiar about the man, the shape of his face, the tilt of his head. It nagged and poked at Sam.

"Nice life," Sam said, flipping faster. In the back of the last album, a loose picture tipped out and onto the floor.

Sam bent to pick up the small square, which looked like a computer printout on thick paper.

It was impossible to mistake the woman in the photo. Sam had seen her picture tucked into albums at his house, the ones Nox rarely pulled from their places on the shelf in his office.

Natalie Boyet.

She looked sick in the picture, her eyes half-closed as she lay curled up on a bed, wearing a flowing white nightgown. The bed, the walls—they didn't look like his and Nox's home. A prickle on the back of Sam's neck made him turn around.

The wallpaper matched. The blanket was different, but....

Natalie Boyet, the woman he now knew was his biological mother, had lain on this bed in Mr. White's apartment?

Sam, suddenly repulsed, let the album drop to the floor. Still clutching the picture, he turned to the door and ran out into the main space. His mother had been here, in this strange place that was part run-down institution and part posh, well-ordered apartment. Why did she look sick in the picture?

Trying to distract himself, Sam shoved the picture into the pocket of his pants. A sheen of sweat began to form on his forehead, his back, even as he felt chilled.

*The kitchen. Check the kitchen. Maybe there's a knife, something....*

Sam haphazardly searched the kitchen, but there was almost nothing beyond some silver spoons, old and tarnished, and an elaborate coffee machine. The unplugged refrigerator revealed nothing, as did the cabinets.

Disappointed—and still feeling uncomfortable about the picture—Sam returned to the living room.

A split second later, the doorknob rattled and Sam, in a panic, threw himself onto the couch facedown.

"Sam?" Agent Allard's voice called to him.

Slowly, Sam pulled himself up into a seated position and blinked at the agent as if he'd just woken up.

Agent Allard seemed to be unraveling, his suit a rumpled mess, his thick hair tossed about. A grayish pallor covered his face.

"What?" Sam asked, wary.

He started to say something, but noise behind him from the hall zipped his lips. "You've got company," he said softly, standing back.

Sam nearly began to cry again as first Mason, then Mrs. Creel, and finally Mr. Creel filed into the apartment.

They were equally disheveled and dirty but blessedly alive and well. Sam leaped off the couch and ran to them.

Mason caught him in a tight embrace, and Sam sagged against him, choking back a flood of happy tears.

"Thank God, you're okay," Mason whispered against his ear, his strong arms drawing Sam even closer.

Sam decided it was the best place to be—in Mason's arms.

"I'll have them bring you something to eat," Agent Allard said, but Sam ignored him. He reluctantly pulled from Mason's embrace to check on Mr. and Mrs. Creel, who'd headed for the couch.

"Are you okay?" Sam asked, hurrying to Amelia's side. She looked pale but all right, her hands fluttering in her lap.

"Fine, fine," she said faintly as she reached up to cup Sam's face. "Just glad to see you."

Sam didn't like how weak and frail Amelia seemed or how Mr. Creel leaned against the back of the sofa. Eyes narrowing, he turned on Agent Allard.

"What kind of monster are you, treating people like this?" he snapped.

Agent Allard glared at Sam, then glanced over his shoulder.

"Shut up. I'll have them bring some supplies," he whispered hotly. "Don't do anything, you hear me? Sit down, shut up, and play nice." Without waiting for an answer, the agent pushed himself out the door and locked it behind him.

Sam curled his hands into fists. God help him, he hoped Nox threw that piece of shit into the river.

"Come on, it's okay. We're together now," Mason said soothingly. He caught Sam by the arm and led him back to the chairs near the sofa. "Come on. Are you all right?"

The haze of red subsided enough for Sam to nod. He turned his attention back to Mason and the Creels. Mason's lip was swollen, and there was dried blood on the left side of his jaw. The bruises were faint but evident. Sam ground his teeth together in anger.

"What did they do to you?"

"Sam...." Mason sat in the overstuffed armchair and pulled Sam next to him. "They just... wanted information."

"About my dad?" Sam asked, directing the question to all three.

Mason shook his head. "No. They wanted information about the police station—shift changes, things like that."

"That's weird," Sam said as he leaned back against Mason, drawing strength just from being with him again.

"Nothing makes much sense right now," Amelia Creel said softly, her eyes filling with tears. Mr. Creel took her hand in his, and Sam's heart squeezed.

Maybe Sam was bait. But he was also Nox Boyet's son. These people didn't know who they were dealing with.

# CHAPTER TWENTY-ONE

NOX BLINKED in confusion, his anger knocked askance by Damian's palpable relief at seeing him. When Damian threw his arms around Nox's neck, he jerked and almost grabbed his gun out of reflex.

"The guards are watching," Damian whispered hotly against his neck. "Pretend you know me. I mean, pretend...."

Wary but needing a few minutes to process, Nox returned the embrace, squeezing Damian so tightly he made a protesting sound.

"Air," he muttered as he pulled back slightly.

"You finally got here! What took you so long?" Damian said loudly, slapping Nox on the shoulder. "We need to get inside...."

Nox forced himself to relax and let the angry tension fade from his form. "Got lost," he volleyed back, clapping Damian's back so hard he nearly went down. "Fuck, I need a drink...." He leaned in close. "Get me in there."

Grimacing, Damian looped his arm around Nox's shoulder. "I can arrange that."

The guard and front-of-house guys were waiting at the entrance, perched atop the dirty pink marble steps. Their expressions were tired, but their eyes were alert with hawk-like interest. Nox couldn't miss the way the three watched Damian and him approach.

"Everything okay, Mr. Oh?" the guard called, hands on his hips. "You were looking for your friend."

"She must've left," Damian said, affable to a fault. "But this friend...." He beamed at Nox. "This one finally made it!"

A split second later, Nox realized that Damian couldn't say his name—and that he had no clue what the identification in Nox's pocket said. In the middle of their climb up the stairs, Nox tripped, bringing Damian's ear to his mouth.

"Daniel Burke," he muttered before laughing loudly. "Whoops! Fuck, the stairs are slippery."

The guard came to the edge of the stairs and peered down.

"You need help?"

"No, no," Damian said smoothly, dragging Nox to the top of the stairs. "Maybe we'll start with some coffee."

The taller of the two front men joined the guard at the top of the stairs.

"You know the rules," he said, his accent heavy and the bulge under his jacket obvious. "He's too drunk."

"I'm going to take him to my room first." Damian didn't flinch outwardly, but Nox could feel the tremulous current of fear under the man's skin. "Promise. He won't go out on the floor like this."

The guard moved away first, as if bored with the conversation. The front man waited an uncomfortable amount of time but finally moved back to his post, where his silent associate waited.

"Keep him off the floor until he's sober," the guard said and waved them through.

Nox gave all three men a cheerful salute as Damian dragged him past them and into the enormous revolving door, which featured a flourish of pink feathers erupting from a diamond vase at its center.

"Gentlemen, have a great night!" he yelled over his shoulder before they were swallowed by the glass enclosure.

"Oh my God," Damian exhaled, sagging a little. "Oh my God."

"We got a lobby to get through," Nox said softly. "Hold it together."

"Okay, okay." Damian straightened but kept his arm around Nox. "At the point where the marble turns to carpet, we're going left. There's an elevator hidden behind the… feather things."

Nox nodded. They shuffled a bit more and then came out the other side of the revolving doors.

Into an explosion of pink—more pink marble, pink velvet walls, plush pink carpet. Feathers and diamond-encrusted anything-that-couldn't-move completed the picture. Time and wear had taken their toll, however, and the Flamingo seemed more a faded aging movie star then a vibrant starlet. The patrons who milled about the lobby—most in various stages of intoxication—didn't seem to notice. Far beyond where they stood, Nox could hear the chimes, bells, and cries of exaltation that signaled the casino floor.

A few women—all dark-haired with big doe eyes and too much lip gloss—sauntered about in tiny pink cocktail dresses, each seeming a lazy clone of the other. Two stopped to eye Nox. He winked and then let Damian direct him toward the hidden elevator.

"This place is hideous," he said under his breath as they dodged around a few round tables, currently unoccupied.

"You've never been here? I thought you spied on everyone." Damian shoved Nox behind an explosion of six-foot feathers, all seemingly trying to escape the blindingly shiny vase they were protruding from.

"I go to the Flamingo. Twenty-one. Or I went." Nox felt like those days were a thousand years ago. He slouched against the wall, his gaze tracking anyone who might get too close.

Damian inserted a little card into the slot and keyed in a code. "This place mostly flies under the radar," he said as the pink velvet walls parted to reveal a tiny silver elevator car. "Mitzie knows everyone. She's been here since before… everything."

Nox followed Damian into the elevator. When the doors closed behind them, he dipped his hand into his pocket and pulled out his gun.

Damian, his guard clearly down, jumped as Nox pointed the weapon in his direction.

"Oh shit."

"What? Did you think we were friends now?"

"I… I got you in here," Damian said, slowly lifting his hands. "I…."

"You tagged along with us and you disappeared." Nox gestured with the gun for Damian to move back against the wall. "And that thing you left behind…."

"I… I was talking to Mitzie." Damian pressed his back against the shiny silver surface, his voice shaking. "She was our contact…."

Something twisted in Nox's gut.

"Our?"

What color left in Damian's face quickly drained.

"Rachel and me."

Nox felt a thundering boom inside his head. He knew it was wrong to trust her—in his gut, in his heart. He knew he should have thrown her overboard before they ever left the city.

And Cade was with her.

"Where is she?" he managed to spit out. "Where's Cade and LJ?"

Damian inexplicably brightened. Hands still up, he gestured toward the two-button panel against the wall.

"I can take you to them."

"They're here?" Nox's suspicions flared. He could be walking into a trap set by Rachel… except there wasn't any way she could have known he was coming. Or would figure out where she was hiding.

"Uh, yeah. Upstairs." He gestured again. "Just hit the top button. Please. You'll see. We're, uh… we're working together."

Nox sucked in a breath. "If you're lying," he said calmly, "I'll kill you. Doesn't matter if I'm dead a second later. I'll kill you as my last act on this earth."

Damian nodded slowly. "Believe me, I know."

Nox hit the button with his elbow, his gun and gaze still directed at Damian. The car lurched and then began to climb with a laboriously loud sound that belied its shiny interior.

After an excruciatingly long time, the car slammed and rattled to a stop. It shuddered dangerously as it settled. The door opened as Nox changed position, and he grabbed Damian, placing him in front of him, and leveled the gun against the back of his neck.

"Where are they?"

Damian stumbled out of the elevator and into a darkened corridor. Ahead, a door was outlined in light. They passed stacks of chairs and boxes as Nox listened intently for anything beyond Damian's panicked, labored breathing.

At the door, Nox clamped his hand down on Damian's shoulder. "Stop," he whispered. "What's on the other side of this door?"

"Cade. And LJ," Damian whispered back.

Nox's heart began to pound triple time. He refused to have hope at this point, refused to believe he'd come here and ended up with Cade—alive and well—on the other side of a door. How easy to bait a trap with someone he'd do anything to save….

His mouth dry, Nox prodded the back of Damian's neck with the gun.

"Slowly open the door," he whispered. "Slowly."

Damian nodded, reaching for the doorknob at a glacial pace.

Nox held his breath. *Please. Please let this be the truth, for once.*

The door latch clicked, and the door eased open, spilling light into the corridor.

Eyes adjusting, Nox pushed Damian inside and took in the scene before him.

Ostentatious as everything he'd seen downstairs—pink and diamonds and excess. An enormous white wood table stacked with computers and two men hurriedly dashing around the room.

His gaze zeroed in on Cade like a homing beacon.

Who hadn't yet seen him and who was digging through the cabinet beneath an extensive bar area, his back to Nox.

He let himself soak up the reality—this was real, right?—of Cade, maybe fifty feet away, standing, then turning, then....

"Where have you...." A familiar voice broke the stillness as Nox's gaze locked with Cade's.

"Oh, holy shit." Nox registered the voice as LJ's, felt Damian pull away from him and scurry to his left.

Cade's expression went through a thousand things, most of which Nox could identify as what churned deep within himself.

Shock.

Joy.

Fear.

Relief.

Cade seemed to stagger for a moment, then gained his feet. He started to move, bumping into and around the endless clog of furniture in the room.

"Are you real?" he choked out as Nox dropped his arm to his side, the gun aimed at the floor about a second before Cade flung himself the last few inches between them.

As Cade's arms closed around Nox's neck, he started to shake, overwhelmed by the warmth and familiar slotting together of their bodies. For a terrifying, panicked moment he wondered if he was still in that room, still being pumped full of his father's poison. But the dampness against his cheek, the murmurs of Cade against his shoulder, brought him back into his body, into this moment.

He let himself wind his free arm around Cade's back and hold him close.

"I don't know if I want to punch you or kiss you," Cade muttered, lifting his head so Nox could feel his breath, see his beloved face up close.

Nox didn't trust his voice as a thing he finally recognized as joy rushed through him. He turned his head enough for Cade to get the idea. Their lips met in a gentle brush, as if to connect the circuits. Then Cade's eyes closed, and Nox felt their bodies melt into one trembling being.

The kiss didn't explode. Nox didn't push his tongue into Cade's mouth or even feel a rush of sexual desire. He just felt contentment and peace as their bodies lined up from lips to legs slotted together.

Nox never wanted to let go.

But as warm and alive and reviving as it felt to hold Cade, Nox's lizard brain still rattled around on high alert, reminding him that Damian and Rachel were traitors and that they weren't anywhere safe.

Reluctantly he pulled back, disengaging Cade enough so he could look past him to the rest of the room.

LJ—jaw dropped but seemingly delighted—watched from across the room. Damian had skittered away as far as possible into the corner farthest from where Nox stood.

Rachel was nowhere to be seen.

Arm still tightly around Cade's waist, he gave their surroundings another careful look.

"Are you all right?" he asked, his voice hoarse with emotion. His heartbeat pounded in his ears as Cade pressed against him, arms locked around his chest.

"Yeah, yeah. We're fine," Cade said quickly. His face got splotchy red, eyes widening. "Rachel...."

"I got the gist." Nox pressed a ghost of a kiss to Cade's jaw. "Where is she?"

"She left." Cade's expression was pure misery. "She was helping us try to find you and we narrowed things down to the sanitarium, and then she... left."

Nox reluctantly released his hold on Cade, who followed suit. "We have to get out of here."

Cade gestured to his brother. "You almost missed us."

A flare of panic rose; then Nox shoved it down as he took Cade's hand—the one not holding his gun, which he aimed in Damian's direction.

"Where is she?"

"I don't know," Damian said, as far in the corner as he could put himself. "She didn't tell me, I swear."

"Can you get us out of here without me having to kill anyone?" Nox asked as Cade led him across the room. "Including you?"

Damian trembled as he pointed back the way they came.

"The lobby?"

"No," Cade said urgently, squeezing his hand tightly. "We need to be able to get this stuff out." The table was filled with laptops, some of them stacked together. "LJ's been in touch with his friends." He stopped, his breathing heavy and bordering on panicked. "We have so much to tell you."

The glassy eyes and pale complexion indicated a bit of shock. Nox wanted them out of here and somewhere safe, somewhere Rachel might not know about.

"You got another way out?" he called over to Damian, who appeared to be thinking hard.

"Back elevator. If you take it down to the sub-basement, you might only run into the janitors. I can tell them—"

Nox gave a sharp shake of his head. "No. You're not coming with us."

Next to the table, LJ stood, his smile wide. He offered his hand to Nox, then seemed to register both were full—Cade's hand in one and his gun in the other.

"Good to see you, man," he said, winking at Nox. "Glad you found us, 'cause I wasn't lookin' forward to chargin' into some villain's lair to save your ass."

"I can save my own ass," Nox replied, eyes on the table. "Can you narrow it down to one machine?"

LJ indicated the military laptop closest to him.

"I know I don't have to tell you this—but make sure they can't trace what you've been doing." With reluctance, he released his grip on Cade's hand and pushed back the shiver he got as their hands disconnected. Later. Not now. When they were safe, he assured himself.

"Anything else you want to take?" Nox asked gently while Cade stared at him as if he were a mirage. "Anything else you need?"

Cade shook his head, still seemingly unfocused.

"Then I'm gonna deal with our friend Damian and we'll get the hell out of here. Five minutes, okay?"

Cade nodded and then turned to help his brother. LJ was already disassembling the laptops, cracking them against the corner of the table.

Nox directed his attention toward Damian, who looked miserably resigned.

"You and me are going to have a little chat." Nox crossed the room to Damian in a few strides.

# INTERLUDE

*DAMIAN OH has lived on the Lower East Side for his entire life. Three generations living in one of the few remaining townhouses in the neighborhood. He's never wanted for anything, not really. He loves New York.*

*Even after his parents and grandparents retire to North Carolina, Damian stays behind.*

*He's tried, on visits to see them and then for the various funerals that seemed to follow one after the other, to get accustomed to being outside the city, but it's just too alien.*

*He lives in the same house, big and empty. He works long hours as an accountant for the city. He goes to the gym when he can. He takes in a ballgame or two with co-workers, old college friends who haven't made a mad dash for the suburbs. He gets promoted when his boss, Mr. Guthrie, steps down suddenly for "health reasons."*

*The storm cloud depositing more and more rain on the northeast corridor seems parked over Manhattan, and Damian sits at Mr. Guthrie's desk in mute horror.*

*Mr. Guthrie, it seems, never quite got the trick of covering his tracks.*

*It also seems he has retired with quite a windfall of kickbacks at his disposal.*

*Damian panics as he goes through the numbers. He calls an old college buddy with contacts in the construction industry to try to make sense of what he's seeing. He panics a bit more.*

*His cousin calls him from San Francisco and tells him to quit his job, come stay with her and her husband.*

*He puts her off.*

*He waits.*

*Half his department goes home and never comes back. He half pays attention to the news, the increasing catastrophic conditions.*

*Damian stops going home to sleep.*

*Soon, he's the last person in his department.*

*"You should leave," the head of security tells him as he packs up whatever's collected in the little desk he's used for twenty years. "Pretty soon, you'll be stuck."*

*Deprived of sleep and sitting on a powder keg of terrible information, Damian nods. At his desk, he sifts through the mountain of evidence that bribes have corrupted the building of the affordable housing that graces the southern tip of the island. Does the mayor's office know? Does the financer know? Does the real estate developer know?*

*Who can he trust?*

*In the end, nature makes a decision on his behalf.*

*Damian finally leaves one night. It takes him six hours to get home because all public transportation has ceased running and many streets are too flooded to use. He stands under a hot shower spray and resolves to gather all his findings, get the hell out of the city, and then turn it all over to a government agency once he's safely far away.*

*He finally sleeps.*

*In the morning the National Guard wakes him with a bang on his front door, alerting him that he has to leave the city immediately. Mandatory evacuation. Panicked, he packs a bag and then begins the long trek back to his office.*

*Which is a wet, smoldering pile of nothing.*

*He stands in the rain, jaw dropped. Everything is gone. All the evidence....*

*A man taps him on the shoulder.*

*"Excuse me, are you Damian Oh?"*

*This man is not familiar. Damian has never seen him before. But something deep inside him, some protective spark that seems almost supernatural warns him. Later, he will get on his knees and thank the ghosts of his grandparents and parents for this intercession.*

*"No," Damian says, offering a faint smile. "He left a few days ago."*

*Damian doesn't wait for an answer. He walks away as quickly as the ankle-deep water will allow him.*

*Heading to his house seems like a terrible idea.*

*Heading toward the pickup point is his only choice.*

*He gets about five blocks.*

*He goes down suddenly, his fall to the pavement blocked by his suitcase. On his back, Damian blinks up at the gray sky, the pounding rain. The barrel of a gun.*

*"Damian Oh," the man who approached him before says, this time not a question.*

*"Please," Damian manages to say.*

*"Hey!" Someone shouts. "Hey!"*

*The man with the gun looks up, startled.*

*A shot rings out. Damian closes his eyes and waits for death.*

*Another shot and then the splash of footsteps.*

*"You okay?" a woman's voice asks. Damian opens his eyes and finds a young woman standing over him, shielding them both with an enormous umbrella. There's a gun in her hand.*

*"I...." He doesn't know how to answer that. Someone is after him, he realizes in sharp terror. He's the only person who knows about all the laws broken, the codes violated....*

*She looks at him appraisingly. Her long hair is unnaturally black, her fur coat slick from the rain.*

*"You need a place to stay?"*

*Damian considers his options. If he heads for the pickup point, it's the most obvious place to be grabbed.*

*"Just... just for a little while," he says, struggling to his feet. The woman gives him a hand up. She's surprisingly strong.*

*"What is your name?" she asks. He can hear a faint accent in her voice.*

*"Damian."*

*"I am Ursula. You come with me. My girlfriend and I have a place."*

*Dazed and soaked to the bone, Damian follows Ursula to a strip club, the kind his college buddies wouldn't be caught dead in. The first floor has a few inches of water, so she leads him upstairs to her apartment. He meets the girlfriend, Mitzie. He has coffee and brandy.*

*He thinks he'll just be here until he figures out his next move.*

*But his next move isn't getting off the island. He works for Mitzie and Ursula as they provide hookers and liquor to the National Guardsman left behind to try to control the chaos. His accounting degree didn't prepare him for this, but it's a job, a place to live. He meets Jenny, who was Galina, who becomes Rachel, who pushes Ursula out and takes over.*

*Ursula might have saved his life, but Rachel is a force to be reckoned with. The fact that she lets him see parts of her the rest of the world doesn't know is almost an... honor. He knows things no one else knows—more secrets to pack away in his ever-chirping brain. She is the alpha and he is the agreeable beta. She is a survivor, and Damian very much wants to live.*

*Eventually hookers become dancers, and the horrible club becomes the Flamingo. Damian watches the city rise... into something dirty and sinful. It kills a little bit of his spirit.*

*Rachel meets Zed at Mitzie's now semi-respectable establishment. She brings Damian with her when she becomes manager at the Iron Butterfly, and Damian's standard of living rises exponentially. One day he wakes up and can't recognize himself.*

*He works for a foul-mouthed gangster who he admires. Sometimes. He loves his job. He loves the Butterfly. He wants it to succeed. He loves watching the numbers go up. He takes pride in the way he makes money for Zed and the employees.*

*No beloved house. No baseball games or college friends.*

*He carries around the truth about the ruined housing, the dead people who thought they were safe. He sees a corrupt city that didn't care, that doesn't care.*

*And he thinks... whatever. Maybe he doesn't care either.*

# CHAPTER TWENTY-TWO

CADE MOVED in a dreamlike state, body moving independently of his lurching brain.

Nox was there. Nox just… walked through the damn door, whole and… disheveled. He had a slight limp, and his well-tailored clothes looked like they had been run through the wringer. Cade had no idea where he'd been, what had happened after the shootout at the abandoned school across the river, how he'd found them. The brace of questions ran through his head on a loop as he watched his hands smash laptop after laptop against the table. Little cuts from the broken plastic and metal dotted his fingers and palms, but they didn't register pain at all.

LJ kept him moving, urging him to hurry, hurry, as the last piece of broken technology fell to the floor. Across the room, Damian sat in a chair with Nox leaning over him. He couldn't hear what they were saying, but Damian's head kept shaking no.

"Five minutes," LJ called over, picking up the military laptop and tucking it under his arm. "We goin'?"

Nox straightened up, gaze still locked on Damian.

"Yeah," he said.

"We understand each other?"

"Yes. Do you believe me?" Damian asked.

Nox didn't say anything, but Cade noticed he didn't tie Damian up or gag him.

"Don't follow us."

Nox pocketed his gun and gestured Cade and LJ toward the door they'd entered through.

LJ opened his mouth to say something, but Nox held up his hand to silence him.

Through the fog, Cade realized he didn't want Damian to know which elevator they took.

Silently, they waited for Nox to join them, then moved—with him in the lead—to the side door. Cade stilled the desire to take his hand, to keep their bodies close as they entered the dark hallway.

The danger wasn't over just because they were together.

"I know where we can hide for a while," Nox whispered.

"We need electricity, and I need to be able to get a signal," LJ muttered. "Or else this is just a heavy-ass doorstop."

"Don't worry, I got that covered." They reached the elevator, which sat, door open and empty.

"We're going through the lobby?" Cade finally managed to ask, his tongue swollen and dry.

"Yeah, I got an idea." Nox reached for Cade's hand and pulled him into the car while LJ followed behind. "Do what I do and we should be okay."

"Should be?" LJ leaned against the wall as Nox pushed the lower of the two buttons. "Not too reassurin'."

Nox threaded his fingers through Cade's and squeezed gently. It eased some of the panic thudding through Cade's body. "Sorry. That's about all I can give you right now."

Another potential near-death experience—Cade barely registered it.

The tiny elevator was providing another one at the moment. From the second the doors closed, the lurch and sway and sound of grinding enveloped them in a cloud of danger. LJ's complexion went vaguely green, and Cade shut his eyes tightly to fight against the urge to shout the place down.

When it finally ended its ride with a violent thump, Cade had to swallow his stomach back down. He opened his eyes to a world of dots... and a spray of pink feathers.

"You're both tipsy, not drunk. And you're looking for company," Nox intoned as he led them from the death trap. When he released Cade's hand, the sense of loss was physically painful, and Cade had to force himself to fall a few steps behind. "LJ, you stay in the back. Try to keep the case down low, like you're carrying a briefcase."

"Right." LJ dropped his hand and slotted himself in the V made as Nox and Cade walked in front of him.

A pink nightmare spread out in front of Cade, and the sights and smells of a low-rent establishment pulled him out of his dazed demeanor. The Flamingo was almost a parody of the Iron Butterfly, where an air of desperation replaced the secure knowledge that a losing hand wouldn't ruin your life. These people were not high rollers, not people visiting Las Vegas's sluttier cousin for recreational sinning. These were the desperate and the tapped out, many who were born here and never had a chance to leave.

In their disheveled states, Cade, Nox, and LJ didn't stand out. No tuxes here, no elegant suits or designer dresses. When a clatter of "entertainers" slunk in from the casino floor, Cade wanted to call out, correct them for their slouches, their disinterested looks.

He jumped when Nox called out, his voice loose and friendly.

"Ladies! Just who I was looking for!"

Three broke off from the group of six, as if a predetermined precision move. They were wearing identical pink minidresses, tubes of strapless vinyl that showed off large bustlines and long legs, their glossy dark brown curls falling over their shoulders.

Cade blinked twice. "You see three girls, right?" he muttered a second before the two groups met in a cloud of heavy perfume and cigarette smoke at the break between marble and carpet.

"Looking for us?" The tallest of the three, Cade could see the lines around her eyes and lips, her weary glare telling him she'd been at this for a long time. "You want to party?"

No warming up here, no charming the customer.

Nox looked her up and down and then turned his attention to the other two. Smaller and younger, they nonetheless signaled jaded to Cade, who practiced his best leer on the one hanging back.

"How much?"

The woman looked around, over her shoulder toward the front desk, then over to where a huge man in a tracksuit leaned against the wall. He didn't seem to be paying attention to anything but his phone.

"One thousand."

Nox rocked back on his heels and cast a look at Cade, so carefree and relaxed, it was all he could do to keep a straight face.

"You guarantee a good time?" he asked, slightly disbelieving in tone. "'Cause we, uh… we got some interests that maybe some of your other clients don't."

Almost as if they'd coordinated it, LJ tapped on the laptop case with his knuckles. The woman peered between Nox and Cade, toward LJ, her eyes lighting up.

"You got some party favors?"

The other two girls leaned forward.

"Oh hell yeah." Nox chuckled. "You got a room? We're not staying here."

There was a brief conversation in a dialect Cade didn't recognize before their head negotiator turned back to them. "Where you have room?"

Nox didn't hesitate. "The Standard."

The women wrinkled their noses in unison, an urge Cade resisted. The Standard was basically a fuck-by-the-hour motel, hastily constructed in the early days of the District to house workers brought in from off the island. In the subsequent years, it had become such a hole even people from this part of town thought it was an eyesore.

"Two thousand," the lead woman said, giving Nox a withering look. "All night. No one says no to nothing."

Nox clapped his hands together as if in delight. "Perfect."

Another quiet discussion in their native tongue, then the woman took Nox's arm in hers. "Let's go."

"Don't you have to ask if you can leave?" Cade blurted out before he could stop himself. A picture of Rachel—tiny, incredulous, and in an incendiary fury—flashed in front of his eyes. It made his stomach turn. How long had he followed her, sure that his gut was right and she was… not a terrible person. Not really.

The two other women exchanged looks.

"No. We can come and go as we please." The woman on Nox's arm tugged him toward the front door. "Let us go."

Cade felt one of the remaining women sidle up to him. He registered her choking perfume and soft hand on his arm, then followed Nox and his "date" into an enormous glass revolving door.

Every breath felt labored. He heard his brother chatting up the woman on his arm with an "aw shucks" accent that felt like a caricature. By the sounds of tittering laughter, it seemed his "date" was charmed.

"You look like the boy from the Iron Butterfly." A whisper from the woman at his side caught Cade's attention as Nox and the woman stepped onto the top of the steps. Cade felt a whoosh of cold air that matched his outside with his inside.

"Don't know who that is," Cade said in response, dropping in his own long-ignored accent. "That a show or something?"

Top of the steps. The wind and cold darkness.

An exchange of Russian between the woman in the lead and a mountain of a man sitting on a stool near the entrance. From behind, Cade felt a push as LJ bumped into him.

"Come on, man," he said with a laugh. "It's cold!"

The laptop case pressed against Cade's back as they hurried down the steps in a six-person pack.

No one yelled. No one began shooting. They walked away from the front of the Flamingo and into the shadows.

Cade held his breath. The woman on his arm didn't say anything else. Ahead, Nox led them down a side street and then another, loud and chatty. They were two blocks away from the Flamingo when he abruptly stopped.

Lost in his head, Cade nearly ran into his back.

"Ladies, thanks for your help." Nox pulled away from the woman next to him, and the gun made an appearance, unmistakable in the shaft of moonlight above them. "But we have to get going."

Beside him, Cade's date let out a little cry.

"No, no, you're fine. No one is going to hurt you," Cade said quickly as she pulled away and grabbed her friend in fear. He looked back to Nox for confirmation.

"I scream, you get shot." The woman Nox had negotiated with didn't even bat an eyelash. She stood, hands on hips, in front of him, as if the gun weren't even there.

"Or I give you a card worth a few thousand dollars, and you and your girls have a nice quiet evening." Nox's voice was back, his controlled stance. Cade watched the two face off, eyes darting back and forth.

"That's all?"

"That's all. You don't go back until morning." Nox reached into his pocket, then paused. "On second thought, you know a place outside the District you can hide?"

That seemed to break the cool stalemate. The woman dropped her hands. "Yes."

"Go there. And don't come out for a few days." Nox handed over a small plastic disk. "Password is written on the back."

The woman took it, her expression wary. "How do I know this is not a trick?"

"You don't. But you also don't have a second choice. If you scream, I'll tell the guards you tried to rob me." Nox shrugged. "I'm a pretty good actor, right? I can convince them."

She pocketed the card, a sneer building. "Fuck you."

"No time. You need to go. Now." Cade watched as Nox punctuated his words with a wave of the gun. "Right now."

Another nasty glare and the woman snapped her fingers. She started walking down the street, backward, as the other two scurried after her. The two groups watched each other warily until the women disappeared around the corner.

"Wow," LJ said, and Cade just nodded.

"What now?" Cade asked as Nox checked the street.

"We're going to take the long way around."


THEY WALKED at least twenty minutes through a weird zigzag of side streets, keeping to the shadows as Cade tried to swallow the chatter of his teeth. It was dark and late, and Cade realized as they looped around another block, that he didn't know what day it was anymore.

Finally, just when Cade couldn't feel his feet or hands, Nox led them over a half-destroyed fence, through a tiny lot, to a pile of what appeared to be garbage.

"It's a tight fit," Nox said quietly, slipping around the stack of old household appliances into pitch black. Cade went next, fighting his way into the narrow space, the overwhelming stench of mold and mildew filling his nose. He pushed forward until air and space became free once again. LJ followed, grunting as he shoved the case through.

"Up the stairs, come on." Nox moved in the shadows almost silently. Cade squinted to keep him in sight and checked back on his brother to make sure he followed. Up the stairs and Cade realized this dilapidated house was where they were going.

Once inside, the smell of disuse seemed to all but disappear. The house was old, yes, and in bad shape, but not the nearly falling-down wreck it appeared to be from outside. Nox moved like he knew the place, and Cade and LJ followed at his heels.

When they reached the main living space, Cade's jaw dropped. "What the hell is all this?"

LJ whistled behind him. Cade assumed this was his version of paradise.

Nox flicked a few switches, and low light appeared, bringing the room into clearer focus. The quiet hum of computers and monitors filled the air.

"A, uh... friend of mine. No longer in residence," Nox said briskly as he moved around the room to turn more switches. "He won't be back, and the security system is a paranoid's wet dream. We should be okay for a while."

Cade's jaw remained on the floor.

The reality of the last time he saw Nox and this moment—the disconnect, the fear, the not knowing where he was and what was happening—reared up, and suddenly Cade was mad.

Red hot furious, a wave that choked words as they tried to leave his throat.

"Living quarters are upstairs. Shower," Nox continued as LJ, clearly not rooted to the spot like his brother, continued into the room, laptop case banging at his side.

"Later. I need to get back online." LJ swung past Nox and settled down at a rickety desk piled high with equipment on every side.

"Right." Nox checked a bank of monitors and then turned to Cade. "You hungry? I think there's some food."

He looked so calm, so together. So... fucking in charge. The kiss, his touch, the trembling clutch of their hands seemed long gone as Cade's voice came roaring back.

"Where the fuck have you been?"

He felt better after he said it, after it sprung loose and Nox's expression of surprise morphed into an apologetic one.

"It's a long story," Nox started. "There's a lot, and I'm sure you two have shit to tell me," he added, putting his gun on the first open surface he came to. "And I know we need to keep our wits about us, but I really fucking want a drink."

Cade nodded sharply and set off on a mission to find liquor in the endless maze of wires and stacks of computer equipment and monitors. Dust kicked up at every turn, and he tripped over more than one bundle of cables. In a side room off the living area—perhaps once a dining room—he located a trove of extra components lining every wall. Another short hallway, another tiny room, this one clearly where the former occupant spent his downtime. A garbage can overflowed with trash, a stack of ancient porn magazines molded off to one side, and the stink of marijuana permeated the air. Nose wrinkling, Cade poked through the mess around the haphazardly placed futon until he located two half-full bottles of Russian vodka—the good stuff.

He pretended the stickiness on the bottles was dried liquor and nothing else.

Back in the main room, LJ had returned to his happy place—leaning over the laptop, which was now plugged into the main system.

"We're in business," he called as Cade walked in.

"Same. We have vodka." Cade looked around for Nox and followed the sound of things clinking together to an adjoining room.

In a kitchen slash computer-storage area, Nox was rooting through an open cabinet.

"Found some refreshments," Cade said as lightly as he could manage. He wasn't sure how to act. He was angry and scared and so fucking happy to see Nox at this moment. Mostly he didn't know what to expect.

Nox closed the cabinet, waving three dusty, mismatched glasses. "Let me clean these and we'll, uh… have a drink."

"You're okay, right?" Cade blurted out when Nox moved with a slight limp to the rusted sink. "There was blood, and we thought you might be hurt."

Nox averted his eyes, put the glasses in the sink, and then wrestled with the taps, struggling to get them to move.

A gurgle and hiss was followed by a stream of brackish water.

"I got shot, but, uh… they patched me up." Nox used his hands to rub the glasses under the growing stream of water as it slowly got clearer.

"They?"

Nox's shoulders hunched. "Like I said, long story."

"Hey," Cade broke in, his grip tightening around the bottles. "I've been looking for you. I've been scared out of my fucking mind," Cade said, his words gushing out, bumping into one another. "We came here to find you…."

"You should have stayed in New Jersey," Nox said, shutting off the water with a hard flick of his wrist. "It was safer."

"The Feds grabbed us." Cade's voice began to rise. "We got away, and we hid, and we came to the District to find you." Memories of Francis, following Rachel to the Flamingo, the distinct fear they would never see each other again crowded into Cade's mind. "And you're so fucking casual? Where were you?"

Nox leaned his elbows against the edge of the sink and was quiet for a moment. Then he took a deep breath and straightened up. "With my father."

# CHAPTER TWENTY-THREE

BEFORE CADE could sputter out a response, Nox held up his hand. "Let's sit down with LJ. I only want to tell this story once."

He dried his hands on his pants, then reached out for Cade, who didn't hesitate. Fingers linked, they walked back to the main space, where LJ was hunched over the laptop, typing away madly.

"Hey, can we get you for a second?" Cade asked as Nox tried to figure where the hell they could sit down. Releasing Cade's hand, he made do, moving a few unplugged components off a dusty ottoman and pulling it over close to where LJ sat.

LJ continued to type, even as he nodded. Nox sat down on one edge of the ottoman, Cade on the other, their knees touching. Somehow just that tiny contact gave Nox a chance to focus.

With a few quick clicks, LJ finished what he was doing. He turned slightly to face them, but Nox could see he was still monitoring what popped up on his stream.

"I got someone close to getting the details about the raid," LJ said. "And that money in your account...." He trailed off, nervously tapping his knee. "It's been steady for years. I think...."

"Laundered money," Nox broke in. "I'm 99 percent sure it's my father. It's where he's been hiding his getaway fund."

Nox watched as LJ and Cade exchanged looks. Neither of them seemed surprised, and the hairs on the back of his neck stood up.

"You knew my father was alive," he said slowly.

"We, uh... just found out," Cade murmured next to him. He put his hand on Nox's thigh, and Nox could feel the trembling. "Rachel told us."

Fireworks exploded behind Nox's eyes.

He'd been right all along.

Rachel... his father. Trusting her had been his greatest failure... he nearly choked on the bile bubbling up to his throat.

"She...," he managed, but Cade squeezed his leg.

"She didn't know… not until… not until Zed found out. Right before he was murdered," Cade said in a rush. "She… she was the one who sent the notes to Sam," he finished in a whisper.

Nox closed his eyes tightly and held his breath in an effort to control his blinding rage. His hours—days—locked up in his father's cell, going through the crazed cycles of Dead Bolt, barely touched the fury he was feeling.

"Fuck," he spat, pressing one hand to his forehead. He was going to kill her. Finally. Seventeen years later he was going to kill her just like she deserved.

Cade was talking, but the words didn't entirely register.

"What?"

"I'm sorry. I'm sorry I made you take her along. And trust her," Cade choked out. "I'm so sorry."

"Hey, not your fault," LJ interjected. "We got fooled." There was a note in his voice that registered with Nox. He opened his eyes and set his gaze directly on LJ's face.

"What?"

LJ swiveled his chair back around, staring at the screens, avoiding Nox's probing.

"LJ."

Scowling, LJ didn't turn back to face them. "I said we got fooled. All of us."

Awkward silence descended.

"So, your father is alive and Rachel is a confirmed bad guy," Cade murmured, clearly trying to break the stalemate. "What the hell do we do next?"

"Rachel left?" Nox reluctantly moved his attention from LJ.

"Like I said, we found an address…." Cade waved his free hand. "Long story, but we got down to three addresses that were pulling a ton of power outside the District for no discernible reason. One of the addresses… I don't know. Rachel made us repeat it and seemed freaked out. Then she left." Cade paused. The grip on Nox's leg tightened again. "It was Morningside."

Nox let that sink in, his brain rapidly moving pieces on the chessboard—so much information, the ticking tock of their rapidly decreasing time. Nox let everything sit on a blank wall, like back in South Carolina.

His father—alive and well and making money being a fucking drug dealer.

His father—alive and well and scamming people, creating a false narrative so he could gather his ill-gotten gains and disappear.

Rachel—manipulating him into getting involved with stopping his father....

The latter didn't make enough sense for him to deal with at the moment. He would just mark that "Jenny would do anything to survive" and move on.

Except.

"Do you think Rachel went to my father?" Nox asked aloud, the anger coming back in a wave. "To tell him you were here? And why you were here?"

He remembered his father's threat. Clearly he hadn't a clue where they were when he made it. Why hadn't Rachel told him?

"No." Cade shook his head. "I don't know. We just knew we had to get out of there as quickly as possible."

Nox tried to clear his mind of the red haze. Focus. "So that casino, the owner, Mitzie? Was working with Rachel?"

"Seems like she was an old friend," LJ said, low and nasty on the word. "Damian and her were workin' together too."

Made sense. "So why didn't Damian tell my father where we were back in South Carolina? They could have grabbed us any time between there and New Jersey without the Feds being involved."

"Alec is a Fed. Undercover," Cade said suddenly, as if he just remembered. "Jesus Christ, we have so much to tell you."


THEY TALKED until their voices began to grow hoarse. Cade retrieved the glasses from the kitchen, and they drank vodka between rounds of facts and gleaned information. At some point Cade got up to perch next to his brother, using a second keyboard to write everything down on one of the screens.

Rachel sent the notes to get him to bring down his father. Supposedly.

His father was a criminal mastermind. Clearly.

Alec was an undercover agent, which of everything he was told, felt screamingly obvious.

"So, the raid is coming down, my father is leaving, and there might be bombs." Nox refilled his glass with the last of the vodka. How long had they been at this?

"What's our next move?" Cade had dropped to the floor, onto a tiny nest of space surrounded by bundled wires and precarious equipment.

Nox considered the urge to end his father's reign with his bare hands against the survival part of his lizard brain that screamed, "Go. Now."

"The raid's comin'. Looking like three in the mornin', so we got about twenty-eight hours before this place is a shit show of the first order," LJ said. He looked them both over. "No way you can get everyone out in time," he added grimly.

"They have to stop the raid. Maybe… maybe we can give them your father's location. Send a message." Cade's voice grew hopeful. "Like, here's your big bad. You don't have to trigger a disaster."

"Another disaster," Nox said absently. He rubbed the glass between his palms. The city going up in flames after drowning so many years ago felt like a cruel metaphor. "So, we… leave?"

That didn't feel right.

"Warn people?" Cade didn't sound too sure of himself. "Like you did with that woman? Tell people to get out of the District?"

Nox was already shaking his head no. "As soon as a mass exodus starts, the radar will go up. And I don't think that the curfew, the cops, and the security presence on the street is an accident. They won't *let* people leave."

"Fuck," LJ said with a sigh.

"Basically." Cade struggled to stand up, his empty glass tipping over as he did. "So we send a message to the Feds. Tell them what's going on, what they're walking into. Then we find a way to get the hell out of here." He looked between Nox and his brother. "Yes?"

"Yeah," Nox said reluctantly. "LJ? How do we get them a message they'll take seriously?"

The frown on LJ's face didn't bolster Nox's spirits.

"Lemme see what I can do. Maybe I'll send them the specs of the buildings, the information about the places pulling so much power...." More tapping and typing, and the frown sank deeper into his face. "Maybe I can find a way to get to Alec directly...."

"We tried to kill him after he tried to kill Rachel," Cade said, running his hands through his hair. "Did I forget to mention that?"

Out of nowhere conscious, Nox's heart swelled with affection. They were so far from tuxedos and fancy clothes, flirting and touching at the Iron Butterfly, each trying to outcharm the other. Cade's hair stood on end, ill-fitting clothes alternatively tight and sagging on his body. Dirty, exhausted, in the middle of this chaos.... Nox had always skirted around the *L* word, but damn if that wasn't exactly what it was.

If he had to go through this cyclone of insanity, there was no one else he wanted by his side.

"Wonder if there's a working shower upstairs," Nox responded, prompting Cade to tilt his head and squint.

"Weird change of subject."

"Why don't we go up and find out?" Was that invitation clear enough? Nox watched Cade blink through it and then nod.

"Yeah. Let's go find out."

LJ didn't say anything as Nox stood, as Cade joined him. They headed for the rickety staircase in the narrow hallway, and Nox could feel Cade's body heat, feel the way their bodies shifted together for comfort as they navigated the stairs up to the darkened second floor.

Nox checked each door on either side of the small landing. A weak motion-sensor light gave them just enough to see. Four of the doors yielded nothing but empty rooms. The fifth, tucked at the far end of the landing, next to the stairs leading to the third floor, was the jackpot.

A dusty but clearly lived-in bedroom—queen-size bed haphazardly made, a dresser pushed up against the window, blocking the view, and a nightstand holding a single lamp.

"Let's hope Brownigan changes his light bulbs frequently," Cade murmured, brushing past Nox to turn it on. When he straightened up, the weak puddle of light barely spilled past him, and Nox was already moving.

Cade made a small sound of surprise as their lips met.

The silence of the room was filled with the sucks and licks of their mouths exploring. Nox felt his control slipping as he fumbled for the button and zipper of Cade's jeans. He tore away to catch his breath.

"Everything off," he whispered, his voice a low growl.

Cade breathed heavily as he took a half step back and reached for his waistband as he toed off his shoes. Everything was fast and slow at once—Cade watching Nox watching him, drawing out each second of anticipation. And then he was naked, completely stripped in Nox's space.

Every inch of skin—dirty, bruised, golden, and perfect—sent a wave of desire through Nox's body.

"I never thought I'd see you again," Nox blurted out, his heart banging in his chest.

Something in Cade's expression broke.

But he didn't say anything pithy or sarcastic or even soothing. He closed the space between them and pressed his naked body against Nox's fully clothed one. Eyes lowered, his hands were quick and effective—gentle and worshipful—in stripping Nox down to just his skin.

Nox held a breath, trembling under the tender ministrations. He knew he was staring, but he couldn't even blink, gaze locked on Cade, who tore away everything protecting Nox… and despite a lifetime of hiding, Nox did nothing to stop him.

# CHAPTER TWENTY-FOUR

CADE HAD officially forgotten how to breathe properly.

His chest felt bruised, like his ribs had been broken and his lungs were trying to function in wreckage. His hands shook as he pulled the clothing from Nox's body, the puckered and scarred flesh revealing itself in methodical precision.

They weren't the same men, dressed to the nines and being charming and deceptive in the Iron Butterfly those months before.

They weren't the same men, sharing a moment of naked intimacy and challenge in Nox's kitchen.

This wasn't Cade's apartment.

This wasn't a dark, angry moment on the farm.

This was naked need, relief. Cade's head swam as the thoughts that had kept him going all this time became reality. He loved this man in a terrifying and dangerous way. He hadn't known it that first day, in the alley, angry and defiant as Nox pressed his body against the brick wall, but now he knew he was never going to be free from these feelings.

Even if it meant another host of stupid-ass decisions that got him brushing up against danger. And death.

If that was his fate, so be it. Choices had been made. This was his decision.

"Stay with me," Cade murmured, running sure hands over Nox's muscular chest. "Just... don't leave me." The naked need in his voice triggered something in Nox, because in the next second, Cade was flat on his back on the bed.

Nox was fast, and Cade was unprepared, but God, wasn't that always the case, he thought, arching under the heavy press of Nox's body. Cade moaned wantonly as Nox moved down, pinning his hips to the bed and taking Cade's cock in his mouth in one smooth, well-practiced move.

"Uhgod," Cade choked out as his entire body shook under the warm aggressive mouth on his cock, the forceful press of Nox's hands, the absolutely perfect and frantic suction that conveyed the desperation of the moment.

The ceiling was pockmarked, and water stains spread across like a badly rendered Sistine Chapel. Cade gripped rough covers beneath him with tight fists and smelled the cheap fabric softener that wafted up.

He didn't want to be anywhere else.

Nox sprawled across Cade's legs, restraining him, and oh right, right, Cade arched up against the pressure until he saw stars. Through every second of it, Nox laved dirty affection on his dick, working up and down like there was a clock ticking somewhere over their shoulders.

And maybe there was.

Cade moaned and unhitched his fingers until he was free to reach down, to touch Nox's hair—grab, pull, hold in place—before he trailed down to those broad shoulders currently preventing him from moving his hips.

Nox swallowed a few times, throat working around Cade's cock, then lifted off with a smirk that sent Cade careening into space. He teased, mouth close but not close enough, hovering over Cade, fingers digging welcome bruises into his hips, and Cade thought, "I might not need him to touch my dick again to come," right before he began to shake.

"Oh," Nox murmured as he sank down on Cade's cock with tight suction.

He didn't get it all down his throat before Cade came with a helpless moan.

The orgasm rolled on and on. Cade's body arched as far as he could move with the pleasure of the release, Nox's mouth—Jesus—and his hands on Cade's hips. His hands fluttered and stuttered against Nox's shoulder, his teeth cutting into the soft flesh of his bottom lip.

He choked out Nox's name and shivered when the pressure became too much on his sensitive dick.

Nox pulled off so slowly that Cade jerked against the covers one last time before sprawling bonelessly. He shivered as Nox licked his way down, then up, until he rested his cheek against Cade's trembling thigh.

"Missed you," Nox breathed against Cade's skin, sending a cascade of goose bumps in every direction.

"Understatement," Cade whispered, stroking his fingers through Nox's hair. He wanted to bronze this moment, record it on an eternal loop.

Just in case.

CADE WOKE with a start, sprawled across an unfamiliar bed, blinking rapidly as he attempted to clear his head. For a terrible split second, he thought he'd dreamed the entire encounter with Nox—the fire, the sex—but the distant spray of a shower brought him back to reality.

He sat up, suddenly aware he was naked, and a pile of clothes at the foot of the bed was not only his borrowed duds, but Nox's as well.

A shaky breath escaped as he settled into the moment and the rabbit-fast beat of his heart slowly subsided.

With a rub to his eyes, Cade slipped off the bed and headed for the bathroom. Maybe it was weird to just want to make sure—to see Nox in the flesh, just as confirmation. Or maybe it was entirely normal to want to crawl into the shower behind him and hold on for dear life.

Either way, Cade opened the bathroom door and inhaled a lungful of steamy air.

Behind the frosted glass door, Cade made out Nox's long, lean body. Neither one of them had an ounce of fat to spare, living on adrenaline and fear and not much appetite. Maybe there was a future business in here—trouble losing weight? Let us send you on a journey fueled by danger, paranoia, and fear. Your body fat will be 2 percent.

"It's me," Cade called out, feeling stupid, but he knew he'd want *just to be sure*.

Nox stopped moving and slid the door open a few inches. Water spritzed out, hitting the wall and toilet.

"I didn't want to disturb you," he said, apologetic as he peeked out, suds decorating his hair and chest.

"No. Thanks for that. I haven't gotten a lot of sleep lately." Cade laughed hollowly. "You, uh… want company?"

"The answer when it comes to you is always yes."

Hastily, Cade stripped out of his briefs and socks and tossed them into one damp corner of the tiny bathroom. Two steps and he was sliding the door to the side so he could slip in behind Nox.

The shower wasn't built for two men of above-average size, recently suffering from a lack of food and burning an abundance of energy, but Cade made do and crowded up against Nox's wet, soapy body. He wrapped his arms around Nox's trim waist and buried his face between his muscular shoulder blades.

Heaven.

"I believe I owe you something," he murmured. Then he licked a stripe of clean skin and tasted the faint bitterness of leftover body wash. Didn't matter; he let his tongue follow the same path again.

Nox's entire body rippled with a low laugh as he leaned forward, simultaneously rinsing the soap out of his hair and seemingly making an invitation to Cade.

"Really?" Cade asked as Nox shook his head, droplets flying everywhere.

"I don't think so." Nox readjusted the showerhead so it wasn't directly on them. "But, uh… we can discuss it later."

The quiet response surprised Cade. He hummed a noncommittal answer as he slowly rubbed his palms over Nox's impressive torso.

"I mean, I realize we've been running for our lives, but your abs are amazing," he deadpanned. Then he bit the back of Nox's neck.

"That's very shallow of you."

"Thank you."

"Clearly you're starting to feel better."

Cade sighed and let his hands drift lower and lower, teasing against Nox's hips, stomach, ribs. "You're alive and here, and nice people are giving us food and running water. I'm so fucking happy right now I can't stand it."

And that was hyperbole, because things weren't settled and he didn't know where he'd be in a week, let alone a month. LJ and

Rachel weren't speaking, and his parents were somewhere out there, keeping Sam and Mason safe. But on the scale of "I hope we don't die" to "Happily Ever After," Cade felt a very solid four point five out of five.

At least three points of that was Nox, under his hands, breathing growing heavy as Cade mapped out his body with his fingers.

He touched him everywhere but there, the unmistakable hard-on that brushed against his wrist as he did figure eights in the crease of where Nox's legs met his hip bones.

"That for me?" he asked casually as Nox grabbed his wrist and drew his hand to exactly where he wanted it.

"Hmmm." Cade let his mouth wander then, tracing muscle and skin across Nox's shoulders as he gripped his dick tightly. "Show me," he whispered into his lover's ear, "how you want it."

Nox folded his hand over Cade's and began to move in a slow but intent rhythm. Up and down, a squeezing pause at the head and then down to the root before making the trip back. Cade kept his other arm around Nox's chest, rubbing against his back in a full-body concert of movement.

The water pattered against them, making the strokes easy. Nox breathed in and out, noisier with each passing second, shifting his body against Cade's in a restless twitch.

Cade felt his own arousal growing, transferring each buzzy spark under his skin to a kiss, a bite, and a flick of his wrist until Nox smacked his free hand against the tiled wall in an effort to keep them both upright.

# CHAPTER TWENTY-FIVE

NOX FELT his entire body racing for the orgasm. It had been so long since he felt desire or a need for completion, and it didn't escape him that only in Cade's arms did that feeling return. He pressed his palm against the cold tile, pushing back into Cade's arms and then forward into the joined hands that jerked him off in a near-perfect grip. He let out a long, low moan, stuttering for a moment as Cade rubbed off against his ass, and oh God yes, maybe they would talk about that later.

But for now, Nox sucked in a breath and let it out as his body seized and his brain sizzled out, coming against the now cool spray of the shower.

The tiny bathroom got quiet.

"You're welcome," Cade said, kissing the top of Nox's spine as he slowly let him go.

"Me? You came twice." Nox straightened up, washed his hands in the cool spray, then turned around to wash his back again.

Cade smiled brightly—a real smile—and Nox's heart did a thing.

"Thank you?" He reached around to grab some water and wash his hands. "I think we both need another shower."

"Wherever we end up, I want a hot-water tank the size of a hotel's." Nox grabbed the body wash again and squirted some into Cade's outstretched hands.

"You looking at real estate here on the island?" Cade joked, but Nox knew him well enough to know it wasn't a joke.

It was a test.

Nox filled his hand with the lemon-scented body wash and put the bottle down on the corner, biding time before he answered.

"We're not done," he murmured, rubbing his hands together. "But at least we'll move from here... together."

Cade gave him an inscrutable look and then ducked his head to soap up his body. "I might have heard that before."

"What happened at the school wasn't—"

"I know, I know. But this lone-wolf thing…. If you think I'm going to wait and pine for you and hope you're not dead, then…." He didn't finish the threat. Or look up.

Nox wanted to say "Please stay in the car and wait so I don't have to spend a second worrying you're not okay." But he knew that wasn't fair. And as frightened as he was to lose Cade physically, the thought of losing… everything else… filled him with dread.

"You came after me," was what Nox said instead.

Cade huffed and shoved Nox just enough to readjust the spray of water, kicking up the hot-water lever.

"Of course I did." He rinsed off and then aimed the warm stream toward Nox. "What else could I do?"

"I'd be an idiot to leave you behind again," Nox whispered, closing the short distance between them to gently kiss Cade on the temple.

"Excellent point." When Cade finally faced him again, the anxiety and pain of the past few months were etched into the brightness of his eyes. "I can handle being afraid. I can handle fighting back. But I can't stand around and not *do* anything. I can't."

"Then we do this together. You and me. And LJ."

A faint grin teased Cade's mouth.

"My brother, the third wheel." Cade shut the water off then as a shiver rippled over his body.

Nox drew Cade into his arms, and their bodies snicked together like puzzle pieces. Cade met the strength of his embrace and tightened his grip.

"We'll do this," Nox said, pressing his lips against Cade's ear. "Together."


Nox toweled his hair as Cade shook out his clothes and put them back on.

"I miss my closet," Cade muttered, staring woefully at the crumpled, sweat-stained clothing. "I miss shopping."

"I'm starting to miss underwear that fits." Nox tossed the towel onto the bed.

Cade buttoned up his shirt, one eyebrow raised.

"There's a solution to that."

"Saving the world commando…." They shared a smile over the bed, a moment's respite before Nox took a deep breath and Cade's expression told him he knew it was time to rejoin the real world.

The pounding on the door startled them both. Nox cursed leaving his gun downstairs as he stepped in front of Cade.

"It's me!"

"LJ," Cade said, already pushing past Nox to the door. "Shit, shit…."

He flung open the door to reveal a panting and flustered LJ, his eyes wide with panic.

Nox thought someone had found them. Maybe the raid was coming sooner than expected….

But LJ's words brought all of that crashing down.

"Alec has our parents. And Sam."

# CHAPTER TWENTY-SIX

MUCH TO Sam's relief, Mason convinced the Creels to go lie down on the bed in the other room. It was musty but quiet and gave them a chance to recharge, even if no one was relaxed enough to sleep.

The door clicked shut behind them, and Mason—who never seemed to falter or look worried—sagged a bit.

"I'm worried about them," he whispered as he joined Sam on the couch. Their arms went around each other in a way that felt natural, automatic to Sam. He leaned his head against Mason's shoulder and rubbed comforting circles on his back.

"I know. Maybe… maybe when the agent comes back, we can convince him to let them go," he said, trying to sound hopeful when he didn't have much faith at all that Agent Allard would do the right thing. "They don't know anything."

Mason nodded. Sam felt him sigh and slot himself a little closer in Sam's embrace. It felt strangely good to be doing the comforting.

"We barely know anything. Maybe they'll let us go too," Mason said, making a weak joke. "I just wish we could get word to… someone."

Sam's cheeks grew warm with shame and anger. He could kick himself for letting the phone get out of his hands. Now Agent Allard had it. If only he knew for sure his father or LJ had received the messages….

He twisted in Mason's embrace.

"What?"

"Mmmm… nothing. Just trying to get comfortable." Sam shifted until he was half lying down on the sofa and pulled Mason on top of him.

"Sam." Mason's voice was low and rough, and a shot of heat—entirely unrelated to anger—went right through Sam.

"I'm not...." Sam gave a weak laugh. "Just close your eyes and try to rest," he added, running his fingers through Mason's grow-out buzz cut. "Pervert."

Mason gradually let himself relax. Sam felt the tension ebb enough for Mason to begin breathing evenly.

For most of Sam's life, Nox had instilled a healthy sense of distrust in him. Don't assume people have your best interest in mind. Don't think anyone is helping you out of the goodness of their heart, because there was no altruism, not really, only people trying to get what they want.

Intellectually, Sam knew this to be a reality of life. The city was a hotbed of selfishness. Even his co-workers, back when he was a messenger, were always looking for a scam or hustle to get them more money, more hours, more favor with the boss. They were kind to Sam, but Sam didn't trust them.

So Sam had no intention of trusting Agent Allard or Carson Boyet. They were both clearly bad people and trying to capture his father.

Agent Allard had told him his intentions. He was bait to catch Nox. He took the phone....

He should have had me call.

Sam's thoughts jumbled and then righted themselves into more orderly lines. Didn't that make more sense? How easy to trap Nox—have Sam call him on the phone they were supposed to use to communicate?

Maybe he was pretending to *be* Sam....

"We'd have a code word, jeez," he muttered. Above him, Mason took a sharp inhale.

"Hmmm?"

"Nothing, sorry," Sam whispered as he moved his head slightly to press a kiss to Mason's jaw. "Talking to myself."

Sam lay perfectly still until Mason's breathing grew even again.

Something about Agent Allard's behavior didn't make sense.


THE CLICK of a door woke Sam with a start. He didn't remember falling asleep or even closing his eyes. Just thinking about Agent Allard, and then....

Mason was gone, Sam realized a second later, and he sat up with a jolt of fear.

"It's fine. They gave us some food." Mason's voice registered as being near the door. Sam turned to see him pushing a small utility cart to the couch. "Sandwiches and water bottles. Nothing we can use as a weapon. I checked," Mason said dryly.

"Who brought it?"

Mason shrugged. The little cart held a paper plate filled with sandwiches—some with meat, some tuna fish—piled on top of each other. The second shelf was crowded with plastic water bottles.

"Just some guy. He wasn't interested in conversation." Mason glanced at the door. "I'll see if the Creels are hungry."

Sam nodded, stretching his arms over his head to work the kinks out of his back and neck. Everything felt tight and cramped. When he moved his head side to side, his vision swam a bit.

It had been awhile since he'd eaten.

MR. AND Mrs. Creel—looking slightly better after their nap—joined them in the living room. A look under the plate revealed a stack of semi-crushed napkins. Sandwiches and water distributed, the only sounds for a while were chewing and swallowing.

"These are terrible. I want to eat ten more," Sam said, eyeing another tuna sandwich.

That made Amelia laugh. Quietly, weakly… but still. A laugh. Sam would take it.

"Clearly there are no good cooks in the area," she said, as if they were giving a restaurant review and not judging "this is what you serve hostages."

"Forget good cooks. I'd settle for some pepper," Mason said, nonetheless finishing his third ham and cheese. "And a beer."

"Amen," muttered Mr. Creel, ignoring the side-eye from his wife.

Their stomachs full and the mood slightly less tense, Sam felt like their little group was better equipped to handle whatever came next. Now, if he could just talk to someone….

Mr. Creel and Mason got into a conversation about where exactly they were in the building, in the city, which Sam vaguely registered as "trying to come up with a plan." It wouldn't work, of course—they had no weapons, no transportation—but Sam kept his mouth shut, let them work through their own frustration at not being in control.

Sam thought and thought.

If they were bait for Nox to come here, that left Cade, LJ, and Rachel. No way his father would just come here without a plan—that wasn't in his nature. His distrust of everything and everyone would lead him to expect a double-cross.

Calm settled into Sam's bones. Okay. They needed to be prepared for whatever happened next. Food and water, check. Rest, check.

"There's some clothes in the other room," Sam said suddenly, breaking into the conversation. "Maybe we should use them, you know, make sure we're warm and protected."

All gazes were directed at him now. Sam's skin prickled with sweat.

"I mean, we don't know where they'll take us next."

Mr. Creel nodded. "Good idea, son."


MR. CREEL sent Sam and Amelia into the bedroom to look through the clothing, something that smacked as misogynistic—not to mention treating Sam like a kid. Or the other lady in the room. Either way, he bit his tongue as he and Amelia went back to the bedroom.

She opened the closet, then the drawers, picked through each and tossed things onto the bed. It gave her something to do, Sam realized, and that set her a bit more at ease.

"I looked at the guy's stuff," Sam said, breaking the quiet. "He's the person who sent me the notes... the lies about who my parents were."

Amelia stopped what she was doing and focused on Sam.

"And you don't know why he did that?" she asked gently.

Sam shook his head. He wasn't sure why, but he pulled out one of the photo albums, still peeking out from where he put it away. He laid it out on the bed and flipped open the pages. "He knew my mom, though. He had a picture of her," he blurted out.

Amelia joined him, one hand on his shoulder as she glanced down.

She didn't comment on any of the pictures, but Sam felt her stiffen slightly at one of the photos of Mr. White as a teenager. He'd missed this page on the first look-through—Mr. White, in swim trunks, standing beside two dark-haired girls whose features suggested sisters or perhaps cousins.

"Maybe your dad knows. You can ask him when you see him," Amelia murmured. She squeezed Sam's shoulder and went back to her task. Sam watched her—the tension seemed to be back.

"You okay?" he asked, feeling uneasy.

"As well I can be," she responded, not letting him see her face.

A PILE of clothes in hand, Sam opened the door for Amelia, who carried a few jackets she'd found in the back of the closet.

"We'll be a bit warmer at least," she announced, placing the items on the couch.

Sam eased his load next to hers—a tweed jacket that would be too big on him and a black sweater were calling his name. He figured if he layered them....

The lock on the door clicked to open.

Carson Boyet appeared, looking far less together than he had before. Sam eased the sweater over his head as he walked to put himself between Carson and the rest of his group.

"You need to come with me," he said with a combination of strain and forced politeness. "Right now."

"I'd rather stay with my family." Sam put his shoulders back and lifted his chin. He was defiant—until a weary-looking Carson pulled a nine-millimeter from his suit-jacket pocket.

"Right. Now."

Carson was alone and looking a little ragged, a little wild. The gun said desperation.

Sam's defiance morphed into something else.

"Where are we going?" Sam asked, not moving from his spot.

"For a quick ride." Carson indicated the door with a tip of his head. "Don't worry, son. I won't hurt you."

"Ah, see, the gun confused me." Sam turned his head and winked at Mason, who seemed poised to rush their "host."

He took a few steps. "Let's go. Dad."

Carson faltered a bit at that as he walked backward toward the door. His gaze stayed directed at Mason, as if he could sense the young cop's desire to punch his lights out.

"He'll be back," he said, directing the comment behind Sam's back. To Mason, most likely. Perhaps Mr. Creel was giving him an evil eye as well. Sam walked through the doorway, remaining as outwardly calm and collected as he could.

The hallway was empty.

Oh God, if only he could let Mason and the others know. They could escape, get the hell out of here. But Carson didn't let him linger. He gave a gentle shove with his free hand, down the hall toward a far-off open door.

"A half hour, okay? Maybe a little longer," Carson was saying as Sam headed down the hall. "I'm sorry about the gun," he added, though out of the corner of his eye, Sam knew he hadn't put it away. "That guy with the blond hair...."

"Mason. He's my boyfriend," Sam said breezily.

Carson muttered something under his breath.

They came to the end of the hallway. Sam stepped through and blinked at the bright floodlight shining in his face. A metal staircase, rusted and shaky, swayed under his feet.

"Down, toward the car," Carson said as he joined Sam on the top of the stairs.

It creaked loudly, protesting the double weight.

A gun or falling to his death—Sam made a quick decision, nimbly flew down the steps, and jumped the last five feet or so to the ground. He wobbled a bit but stuck the landing.

Behind him, Carson clattered down, cursing the entire way.

The absurdity struck Sam, and he couldn't contain the smile on his face. Were they alone? Truly? He looked around and peered into the darkness. There were some trucks crowding the paved area, perhaps once a parking lot but now ripped up and overgrown. Beyond, there were trees and even deeper darkness, barely penetrated by the moonlight.

Maybe he could make a run for it?

But they weren't alone, he realized, as Carson thumped behind him, panting loudly.

"What the hell was that?" he wheezed, but Sam didn't turn around.

Someone was behind the corner of the truck farthest from their position.

His father? No, too small a figure. Sam squinted behind his glasses, wishing for perfect vision, wishing for a light.

The figure stepped out, arm up. Gun evident.

Carson pushed him from behind, lightly, like playground retaliation. "I said...."

He noticed the person approaching a split second later.

Sam felt Carson's hand at his back. He gathered up a fistful of sweater and yanked him back, the gun visible just beyond his right ear.

Sam held his breath.

"Who's there?" Carson called. "I said no guards."

The floodlight's glare captured Rachel as she stepped into their field of view.

She was dressed all in black, her hair tucked under a cap. The gun she had aimed in their direction was big—and equipped with a silencer. Her Cheshire Cat smile gave him a momentary hope until he realized she wasn't looking at him.

"Hello, Carson," she said, sounding sweet and young.

Behind him, Sam felt Carson's terror, like a live wire connected to his hand and transmitting into Sam's skin. The tremble as he raised the gun—Carson sputtered in the quiet.

"Hello, Jenny," he whispered.

Sam watched him lift the gun higher.

Rachel laughed.

"Aren't you glad to see me? Raised from the dead?"

Sam tried to get her attention, blinking his eyes, mouth gritted in a tight line. Should he duck? Knock his father off balance so she could shoot him?

"Jenny... I didn't... I thought...."

"Ah, you're right. No time to catch up. We can do that later. Right now, we're going to talk about what you owe me. And how I can help you clean up all your little messes."

Sam's frantic planning of how to distract Carson so Rachel could save him died a quick death at her words.

His heart sank. This was no rescue. This was a betrayal.

# CHAPTER TWENTY-SEVEN

NOX PUSHED past LJ and took the stairs two at a time to get to the computers.

"When? How?" he snapped as LJ and Cade clattered down the steps behind him. He registered he was shirtless, no shoes, as the cool air of the first floor hit him. Nox didn't care—all he could see was a red haze at the thought of Sam being in danger.

"Do they know we've been poking around online?" Cade asked as LJ pushed his way around where Nox was standing. He sat down at the array of computer monitors, and Nox couldn't help but notice the way his hands shook.

"I set it up so I could get messages from our phones, in case anything happened to mine," LJ said, tilting the screen a bit so they could see. "Sam, or someone in that group, sent us texts. Took forever to get to me, gotta figure out why...."

Nox's tone was sharp. "LJ...."

"Right, sorry." Flustered, LJ indicated the black text on a white background.

Two were from Sam, giving them updates on what was going on. The third was from Alec, dated today.

*Mr. Creel,*

*We have your parents, Mason Todd, and Sam Boyet.*

*Come to the Lennox Hill Hospital loading ramp at 1 a.m.*

*In exchange for the Vigilante, they will be released unharmed. No backup please.*

*Agent A.*

"Might as well be letters cut out of a magazine," LJ bitched, fingers plucking at the wireless mouse. "Sounds like a trap."

Nox breathed through the panic. At least he knew Sam and the others were all right. At least for now.

"Definitely a trap." Nox straightened up and turned to find Cade, eyes wide and panicky. "What are the chances your friend Alec isn't entirely trustworthy?"

Cade seemed surprised. "Besides the fact that he slept with me, pretended to be my friend, and turned out to be an undercover Fed?"

Nox squashed a flicker of jealousy. "You said you got away from him," he said encouragingly.

"He showed back up, followed up to where we were hiding. Tried to convince us to stay away. Not try to find you," Cade said, his expression one of concentration.

"That time, when you talked to him. Was he saying that in an official capacity?"

"No," LJ threw in. "He also didn't report his identification stolen." LJ stopped.

The sudden fall off the cliff into silence made Nox turn around. The questioning frown on LJ's face caught his attention.

"What?"

"Francis was waitin' for someone. His partner," LJ said slowly.

Cade cut his brother off. "No. No."

"Cade...."

"No." Cade stepped away, arms folded across his chest. "It was probably Rachel anyway. And none of this matters now. We have to figure out how we're going to save Momma and Daddy and Sam and Mason. That's it."

Nox followed Cade as he walked in nervous circles around the stacked equipment.

"We're going to meet them as requested," Nox said softly, shrugging off the cold air on his bare skin. "I'll turn myself in...."

Cade was already shaking his head. "No."

"Turn myself in. Volunteer to tell him everything, so long as he gets everyone out of the city before the raid," Nox finished. "It's the only way."

"You believe that text?" Cade's expression was incredulous as he whirled around. "Are you kidding me? It could be Rachel. It could be your father. It could be whatever low-level mobster tried to kill us on the boat. Who the hell knows? A Fed would not make an exchange like that."

"LJ, you can track the phone, right?" Nox knew Cade was right; there was no proof. "Contact them. Tell them we want proof of life. For everyone."

"Yeah." The clatter of LJ's fingers against the keyboard began a second later. "Got it."

"Do you trust Alec?" Nox asked gently. "Truly trust that he wouldn't harm Sam or your parents?"

Cade pushed his damp hair off his forehead. "He... hurt Rachel. It was a tense situation, but he... he really hurt her."

Nox let that sink in. A rogue federal agent. His father and his father's sinister plans. Rachel in the wind.

If someone were setting a trap, which one would it be?

"Traces back to...." LJ made a humming noise. "The phone traces back to the address in Inwood. Morningside Sanitarium."

The red haze returned behind Nox's eyes.

"My father."

"Rachel," Cade murmured. "She... she knew that's where he might be."

"If she wasn't working with him this whole time, she's a fool to go up there. My father would kill her in a heartbeat," Nox ground out, teeth pressed together as he tried to keep his anger under wraps. He needed to think straight.

He turned back to where LJ sat frozen at the keyboard. "She's either swimming back to New Jersey or...."

No one completed his sentence.

"You can't turn yourself back in to your father," Cade said, reaching for Nox's hand.

"He needs me." Nox squeezed their palms together, fingers entwining. "To pull off this smokescreen so he can escape. You get Sam and your parents, you get the hell off the island...." A plan began to form in Nox's mind, a feverish synthesis of circumstance and need. "I can stop him from planting bombs. I can kill him."

Cade watched him with growing horror. "He'll kill you."

Nox didn't discount that possibility, but he shook his head in denial. "He needs me. That's the bottom line. From the inside...."

"So we get off the island. I call the Feds and say what, exactly, Nox? Hey, go and kill this guy and his fucking henchman but not you? During the raid, watch where you shoot?" Cade squeezed Nox's hand. "We have to think of something else."

"What if Alec is involved?" LJ joined them in a small circle, hands jammed in his pockets. "With… this whole mess. Your father, the bombs…."

Nox held on to Cade's hand and watched as Cade's face crumpled a bit from rage to grief.

"You confirmed the raid is happening," Cade said, a note of halfhearted protest in his voice. "That's a real thing. He wasn't lying."

"My father told his business associates things were going down in a few days."

"He gets out early 'cause he knows it's comin' tomorrow. Leaves everyone else behind, sets the bombs. Alec comes in and pretends to save the day. Maybe even confirms he's dead."

Nox's brain clicked and clacked, shifting things together. "No. Confirms I'm dead," he murmured.

"The Feds in South Carolina…."

"Yeah, Cade, I know. But maybe that's just for show." LJ was getting louder with each passing second. Nox could feel his growing anger. "Get us to think we could come back to New York…."

Nox put up his free hand.

"Wait. Stop. Let me think."

His father controlling things behind the scenes.

Rachel forcing Nox to become involved—pushing him to find his father was alive.

The Vigilante and Nox Boyet were not the same people, according to the Feds. The Vigilante was dead in official circles. But so was Nox Boyet, for seventeen years.

"My father wanted me to come back. So did Rachel," he said slowly. "But for two different reasons. Why does Alec want me?"

Cade started to speak but stopped.

"You're valuable to him. Because he can… trade you for somethin' else he needs?" LJ offered.

"The only person I'm truly valuable to is to my father," Nox said, meeting Cade's anguished expression. "This isn't about Alec. I don't know if he's dirty or not, but this… this is my father."

"Even more reason to find another way." Cade started to pull away, but Nox held fast to his hand.

"Even more reason for me to go. I want you and your family and my family off this fucking island before everything rains down fire." A peace settled over him. To die in service of his family—the two people he honestly loved—was as close to a selfless act as he'd ever come.

The angry set of Cade's mouth told him that he knew exactly what he was thinking.

"You're insane."

"No, I'm being practical." A roil of sadness, a moment of "if only life were different" sent a spate of pictures through his mind—being with Cade, with Sam, somewhere that wasn't here, living a real life. What could have been. But he shook his head and they floated away like smoke. "LJ, send a text back. Tell them we'll be there."

LJ didn't move. Nox watched a wordless and angry conversation between the two brothers before LJ's head dropped in acquiescence.

"He's right, Caden. It's our only play right now," LJ said gently, resigned, as he walked away. "Momma and Daddy didn't ask for this."

Guilt ravaged Cade's expression. He crumpled a bit, and Nox had no choice but to pull him closer.

Cade fought the embrace, tense and stiff as Nox wrapped his free arm around him.

"I'm sorry I got your parents pulled into this," Nox whispered against his ear. "I'm sorry. But we'll get them out, you'll take them back home, they'll be safe."

In small increments, Cade melted into Nox's arms until they were fully embracing, Cade's head tucked against his shoulder.

"I don't want…." Cade muttered against his skin, and Nox just nodded, tightened his grip. He didn't really much want to die, but no one had a choice in the matter right then.

LJ cleared his throat. Nox didn't move. He kept on holding Cade, selfishly wanting as much time as they could manage before it all came to an end.

"Sent the response and, uh, Nox? I appreciate what you're doin', but I don't think we should trust they'll just let us go."

"You're right," Nox said. Cade shifted in his arms and slowly pulled away. Nox resisted, but Cade's stiff body language told him not to fight it.

"We can go back to the Flamingo. I don't doubt Mitzie has a shit-ton of guns somewhere in that pink nightmare," he murmured, turning away from Nox entirely.

"She's not just goin' to hand over anything we ask for," LJ argued.

Nox mourned the loss of Cade's nearness, the way he was already putting distance between them. Not meeting his eyes.

"No, probably not. But I'm guessing she can be bought." Nox crossed his arms over his chest. He needed to get dressed, get his gun. Build the wall between his desire for Cade—to be with him—and the reality of his world. His duty.

LJ scowled but went back to his keyboard. "Sendin' word to my contacts. What else we need?"

"I'll go and…."

LJ held up his hand. "We stay together. I am not spendin' another second wonderin' where you are."

His brother's word seemed to crack Cade's façade. A ghost of a smile played at the corners of his mouth, but when he looked directly at Nox, it quickly faded.

"I'm going to go finish getting dressed," he said flatly. Then he pushed past Nox to head upstairs.

Nox felt LJ's eyes on him as he briskly rubbed his arms. The cold was starting to make him go numb.

Maybe that was a good thing.

DRESSED WARMLY and armed with the military laptop and blueprints, the three men headed back out the way they came. It took forever, but Nox didn't want anyone finding their way back to Brownigan's before they were done with it. If Cade and the others couldn't get off the island before the raid, at least they could hide in the basement, stay safe until LJ could use his contacts to get them help.

It made Nox feel better about leaving them behind.

The area around the Flamingo belied the curfew. Drunks and their professional escorts mingled around the front steps, smoke from their breath and cigarettes creating a cloud in the night air. The raucousness gave them a bit of cover as Nox surveyed the scene.

He hated going into the lion's den again, back to where they were outnumbered and all but trapped. Mitzie coming to them....

The idea popped into his head unbidden.

"LJ, I need you to send a message to the Flamingo security office. Tell them there's a bomb in the building," he said quietly.

Ten minutes later, an alarm began to sound.

A stream of guests and staff began clogging the exit as the security guard tried to keep the giant revolving door from getting stuck. Shouting, people screaming and shoving—Nox felt a momentary pang of guilt for the chaos, remembering all too well the moments before the Iron Butterfly went up.

As the street filled, Nox indicated for Cade and LJ to follow him.

They skirted the growing crowd and aimed for the back entrance. A black limo—ten years out of date and with a rumbling muffler—began to inch its way toward the madness, honking at the people who were frantically running from the building.

Mitzie's ride.

Nox pushed Cade and LJ into the doorway of a closed shop and gave them a hand signal to stay put.

Through the throng of noise and humanity, Nox managed to stay on his feet and weave his way toward the back of the limo. With the cover of so many bodies, he was able to duck down and reach the back door.

The driver jammed on the brakes, unable to go forward. As the door opened, he was already shouting, screaming at the masses to move out of the way.

No one listened.

Nox held on to the bumper to keep from being knocked over as people ran past him. The wail of sirens in the distance made his pulse speed up. But then he spotted her, her fur coat obscuring all but the upper half of her face. Two men, each struggling under the weight of black suitcases, flanked her. They moved as an awkward unit, like salmon fighting the water to swim upstream, trying to get to the limo.

A shouted conversation between the driver and one of the men was the perfect distraction. They moved away from Mitzie, slamming into fleeing guests to clear a path. Nox stayed low, waiting until Mitzie got close, her boots in view, before he reached out and grabbed her hand.

She tripped in surprise, and they both nearly went down, but Nox struggled to keep them upright and moving. He got the door open enough to shove her in, then squeezed in behind her.

Mitzie screamed and kicked at him. He took the blows, locking both doors before moving toward the opening between the back and the driver's seat. Shouts from outside told him he'd been discovered.

Gun trained on Mitzie, Nox faced her.

"Shut up. We need to talk," he said, repeating it until she seemed to come out of her shock.

"Fucker, I will kill you," she snapped, the fear becoming fury. "Should have killed you before or turned you in, but Rachel would not let me."

"Shut up," Nox said. A commotion behind him meant the driver was trying to get into the limo. "You and I are going to make a deal. I want guns."

Mitzie stared at him, incredulous.

"Fuck you." She struggled to move under the weight of her coat. "We need to leave, need to go."

"There's no bomb," he said. "But there is a raid coming...."

The look of pure hatred would have set another man on fire.

"I know about that," she spat. "I know!"

"How about the bombs, Mitzie? How about half this island being blown to rubble?"

That stopped her. Nox watched her go still, her eyes piercing as she tried to work out if he was lying.

"Carson's gonna blow the island and get away," he said conversationally, even as he tried to keep alert to the driver, the guards getting into the limo. "There's not going to be anything left."

Mitzie's calculating stare was at odds with the way she shrugged. "Who the fuck cares? Let this rock sink into the water. I will be gone."

"With what? As much as you can carry?" Nox made a calculated decision. "Maybe I have a way for you to walk away with more than you've ever earned in this shithole. Or maybe… maybe you get to stay and make a move when all the other players have been cleared out by the Feds."

The doors began to rattle on both sides as Nox and Mitzie stared intently at each other.

"You give me proof," Mitzie said slowly, "and I will take both of those things."

# CHAPTER TWENTY-EIGHT

SAM FELT Carson's confusion—the way he twitched as he held Sam up as a shield, the way the gun shook just enough to be noticeable. Rachel, he knew, saw this as well. He could tell by her Cheshire Cat smile.

"Shall we go somewhere more comfortable?" Rachel asked.

Carson hesitated. "Sam and I were just on our way…."

"To?" Another question, but Sam got the impression Rachel already knew the answer.

"A meeting."

"With?"

Clearly irritated, Carson pulled Sam toward the car, his gun and gaze never leaving Rachel.

"Go away, Jenny."

Rachel laughed.

"We're going to talk, Carson. Right now. We're going to talk about what you owe me, about your little plan to reduce this island to rubble—all of it." Her tone was exactly how she sounded in South Carolina—a little sweet, a little salty. Sharp. Sam's stomach clenched. They were so foolish to trust her.

The long pause gave Carson away as Sam's brain registered what Rachel had said. *Reduce the island to rubble.*

"I have no idea what you're talking about." Carson cursed, then yanked at Sam's shirt. "Open the car door," he snapped.

"Carson, this is your last warning…."

"I'll… I'll shoot him."

Sam froze as the gun was now aimed in his direction, inches from his temple. A cold sweat began to trickle at his hairline, the small of his back.

"Your own son? I'm shocked." Rachel and her maddening smile moved closer, with a loose-hipped walk that suggested she didn't believe Carson for a second.

"Jenny, please. We have to go," Carson said, his voice pleading.

"He's going to kill you to get to the kid. You know that, right?" Rachel sighed as if disappointed. "If you don't have backup, Carson, you're not getting off the island."

Carson nearly wilted then, sagging as the gun redirected away from Sam's head. He leaned on the car, and Sam took the opportunity to pull away. For a brief moment, he considered running, but Rachel's gun was now trained on him.

"You think it was going to be that simple, Carson? No, no," Rachel said. She closed the distance between the three of them until she was a foot from where Sam stood nervously. "And we're going to end this bullshit once and for all."

"I can't believe you're doing this," Sam burst out, before he could contain himself. "I can't...." He shook his head, anger and disappointment flooding his feelings. Rachel didn't even blink, no discernible change to her demeanor.

"It's about survival, Sam." She turned away from him, almost like a dismissal, and redirected her attention to Carson. "Back inside, please. I don't like standing around in the dark."


CARSON, STILL silent, directed her up the stairs they'd come down. Sam went first, then Carson, with Rachel bringing up the rear.

"Let's keep this civil," Rachel warned. "No one has to get killed today, Carson."

He didn't answer.

Back inside Morningside, Carson shoved Sam a few yards down the hallway. Sam wondered if they were heading back to the apartment, but he doubted it. He stumbled along, nearly tripping when Carson grabbed and pushed him through a partially opened door.

The oppressive darkness lasted for a moment. Then an overhead light flickered on.

Sam blinked in surprise.

They were in an outer room, stark white and medical-looking. Beyond the glass wall he could see an expansive space, hidden in shadows but clearly a laboratory.

"This place is like Russian nesting dolls. Inside, another surprise." Sam turned around to find Rachel had put her gun away and was leaning against the door they just entered. "Nicely done, Carson. No one would ever guess what was going on in here, your little villainous lair."

Carson looked wan, almost ill. He watched Rachel warily, hands flexing. Sam suddenly realized Carson's gun was gone—and Rachel now had two tucked into her waistband.

"What do you want?" Carson asked finally, his eyes darting around the room as if seeking another weapon or a way out.

Rachel crossed her arms over her chest, a thoughtful look on her face. "That's an interesting question. You left me behind, Carson. Left me to do your dirty work, left me to die...."

"The cartel," Carson started, but Rachel shook her head.

"We both know that's a lie. There never was a cartel or big bads. Just you and Mr. Smith."

Carson's pallor went stark white.

"It took me a while to put it all together." Rachel's gaze flickered to Sam and away again. "And somehow, Carson, that makes it worse. You weren't running away from anything except responsibility."

"I thought... I thought you were dead," he said weakly. "On the ferry. If I had known you were alive...."

Rachel's lips pursed. "Ah yes. The ferry." She tilted her head. "And here, at the sanitarium. Who were you and Mr. White trying to get rid of?"

Sam was drawn to his father's face. He couldn't look away from the complex tangle of fear and anger. For a brief moment, he saw Nox in that mix, in those moments when his temper seemed so fierce that, if unleashed, it would destroy a city block.

He took a step back.

"You want money?" Carson rasped. "I'll give you money. As much as you want. And I'll get you off the island."

"That sounds wonderful. I accept." Rachel smiled. "But first, I need to know one thing. Absolute honesty—and I know that's an alien concept to you—but honesty is how you're going to come out of this alive and well, and with my help."

The moment of silence that followed plunged the room into oppressive tension. Sam felt it in his stomach. His hands tingled, and he took another step back to get farther away from the fallout.

"What do you want to know?" Carson asked finally. His hands curled into fists.

Rachel pushed off the door. She walked right up to Carson, so close they were nearly touching, her chin to his chest. She looked up, her face utterly serene.

"Did you have my parents killed?"

Carson immediately sprung to life. He let out a gasp, shaking his head no in a quick motion. "Jenny, Jesus Christ—no. They worked hard for me." He jabbed a finger at her. "They entrusted you to me! That has to say something."

Rachel stepped back, her expression unchanged.

"You're right, that means something," she said. "Maybe Mr. Smith had reason to...."

"Yes, exactly. He was... you don't understand. He was crazy. I had no idea what he was up to. I thought he was truly working for those... people."

She made a "hmmm" sound and turned to Sam.

"Your dad here turned out to be working for a con man, not a drug cartel," she said, amused. "That's his defense, by the way. I had no idea what was going on. I thought I was just laundering money for drug dealers."

With growing horror, Sam moved backward until he hit the wall.

"And now he's going to trade you and your boyfriend and those nice Creels for Nox and take off to parts unknown with an absolute shit-ton of money." She recited the story as if relating an episode of a television show. "What I'm wondering about is why he needs Nox so badly. Why not just kill him when he had him?" Rachel asked conversationally. "I'm just saying...."

"Jenny, I answered your question. I promised to pay you." Carson seemed to be resorting to begging. "I have a way off the island before the raids. We just have to get to an airfield in New Jersey. Then we'll be gone before the Feds know what happened—"

"I'm sure there'll be a lot of confusion when the bombs go off." Rachel turned her attention back to Carson. "Which is the point."

"I have no idea what you're talking about." Sam watched as Carson's rabbity gaze fell to the door. Rachel had moved away, almost as if she were daring him to try it.

"Carson, what did I do best, when I worked for you?" Rachel moved closer to Sam, who slid against the wall. He felt exposed, like a bug trying to find darkness before it got squashed.

"Scare the shit out of people," he muttered, which drew a hearty laugh from Rachel.

"Thank you." She gave a little bow in Sam's direction. "I was also the fucking master of getting information. The trick is to cultivate multiple sources, so what you have is a... three-hundred-and-sixty-degree view of a situation. For example, I aligned myself with Damian Oh, who had an excellent understanding of your scheme to get Dead Bolt exclusively into the casinos and hotels. But that didn't make sense from a business point of view, so I consulted my former... friend Mitzie, who owns the Flamingo and knows every dirty little secret of every businessman in the District."

Carson took a step toward the door, and something in Sam itched to stop him. To help Rachel. Disgusted with that impulse, Sam pressed his hands against the wall.

"So, for example, I know you promised a lot of people a cut in the worldwide distribution of Dead Bolt in exchange for a fuck ton of money." Rachel turned to Sam. "It's a scam. There is no worldwide distribution plan. He's going to take the money, blow up the District, and then run."

Rachel tapped her head with one finger. "Now, wait. Maybe that's why you need Nox. Someone has to take the blame for all of this."

"I had the police tell everyone he was dead," Carson snapped, but Rachel shook her head.

"No, you told them the Vigilante is dead."

"They already think Nox is dead!"

"So the most corrupt police department in America is lying. I'm sure that's the point. When the government cracks down—and nicely done, by the way. Blowing up the Iron Butterfly really forced their hand." Rachel began to take slow and steady steps toward Carson. "The Feds show up, gather just enough evidence that Nox is the mastermind, and then boom, the District is a battleground. Lots of rubble and dead bodies to keep everyone busy, just like last time."

Rachel's pitch changed ever so slightly. Sam heard it, but he doubted Carson did.

He thought about the boat, the storm. Rachel so terrified she wouldn't get off the floor of the cabin.

For a moment he wondered what happened after that ferry went down and how Rachel—Jenny—survived.

"And I will give you money and a chance to be gone," Carson pleaded. "Just let me finish these—"

"Loose ends," Rachel finished for him. "Like Natalie. And Nox." The last words were whispered. Sam barely caught them. He saw his father's face, but Rachel's back was to him.

"They'll be fine." Carson gestured toward him.

"Sam knows everything. He can tell the Feds," Rachel said, her voice back to full power. "He's young and sweet and innocent. One look at his baby face and the Feds will be mobilizing to track your ass down."

Paralyzing fear took Sam's breath away.

"I... I won't say anything," he managed, his voice hoarse. "I swear."

"I was going to let him and the others go," Carson said, and the shift was just... like... that. A blink and Carson's expression, his demeanor changed. "This is your fault, talking about everything in front of him." The victorious accusation in his voice was nauseating. "I was going to let them go," he added smugly.

Rachel nodded. "That's a good point. This is my fault." She winked at Sam. "Sorry about that."

Carson's eyes darted to Sam, who could feel every pore in his body dripping with sweat and fear.

"Should we, uh... take care of things now?" he said in a low voice to Rachel.

"No. We should make the exchange, and then, once you have Nox, we just...." She snapped her fingers. "Easier that way. Cade and LJ will most likely be there, backing him up, and they don't have anyone else to go to," Rachel said breezily. "We can get rid of everyone at the same time."

Bile choked Sam. He felt his legs give out, and he slid to the floor in horror. Sam covered his face with his hands, wishing he could tune out Rachel and Carson's voices. His mind worked frantically. Maybe he could call out a warning to Nox, give him time to stop the massacre.

Across the room, his biological father and Rachel discussed the best way to set up the ambush, like it was nothing to kill your own child. And about how much money she was going to get for all of this.

The nightmare continued.


THEY LEFT him in the room, in the lab, for the rest of the evening. He cried bitterly into the knees of his jeans, grieving the lost time with Mason, with the Creels. Why couldn't they let him say his good-byes, let him spend a few more stolen moments in Mason's arms? The betrayal, the senselessness, made him gag.

Somewhere in the middle of the sadness and tears, Sam made his decision. He would use his last breath to warn his father—his real father, his true father—of the trap. Let them shoot him; he didn't care. Sam would do everything he could to ensure Nox had at least a chance to save Mason and the others.

He steadied himself with deep breaths, fingers tight in his hair. In and out. In and out.

The door opened eventually, and a guard he'd seen before by the door of the apartment leaned in to beckon him over.

"Let's go."

In the hallway, Sam spotted Mason and the Creels huddled together a few yards away. He lifted his hand to wave, an acknowledgment Mason caught. The way Mason's face lit up at the sight of him sliced through Sam's heart. He managed a smile, a little thumbs-up to assure him he was all right.

Mr. Creel kept his arm around Amelia, placing his body between her and the guard closest to them. Sam prayed he'd be able to give them another chance to make things work.

The various guards directed the two groups back down the hall, and Sam brought up the rear. Agent Allard stood at the door wearing a black windbreaker, a sour expression on his face. There was an unmistakable palm print on his cheek.

Rachel, Sam thought automatically.

Mason and the Creels were tantalizingly near, but the guards formed enough of a barrier to keep them from getting too close or speaking. Sam watched as the three were herded down the rickety stairs and into a waiting black SUV. The door slammed shut, and Sam's heart broke. He wouldn't get a chance to say good-bye.

Another black SUV idled at the bottom of the stairs. Agent Allard led him to the car.

"Let's go," he said tightly as he opened the door for Sam.

Sam leaned in. "They're going to kill me. You know that. They're going to kill me and Mason and everyone else. Cade—who you said was your friend," he spit out. "How are you letting this happen?"

Even in the dark shadows, Sam could see the war going on in the agent's eyes. Could he stop this? Would he?

"Get in," he said finally and gave Sam a shove.

Inside the SUV, Sam's hopes fell again. Carson and Rachel waited for him in separate rows. Carson sat in the middle row and refused to look his way, but Rachel smiled—that same smile she gave him in South Carolina on the docks. The one he stupidly believed.

She patted the seat next to hers.

Without a word, Sam stepped up into the vehicle and dropped down where she indicated. The door slammed. A second later the passenger side opened. Agent Allard got in and signaled to the driver.

The vehicle rattled off as Sam stared out the window.

# INTERLUDE

*CARSON LOVES having Jenny as his right hand... girl.*

*Sometimes he forgets how young she is. Just a few years older than Nox, she runs his business—the legitimate one—and his household affairs. His other business, well, he's come to appreciate her brilliant mind and how quickly she synthesizes information from different sources.*

*She compiles blackmail information in efficient reports. She hires his freelance muscle. She is charming, but with an icy tinge so no one thinks they have a chance to get information or favors from her.*

*She's always armed, and she knows how to take care of herself. And protect Carson.*

*She's perfect.*

*Thankfully he never has to explain the "family business" to her. She is three generations of the same.*

*Morals, where Jenny is concerned, are malleable.*

*Carson likes that in a person.*

*He also likes her developing curves and long strawberry blond hair. It's a strange vanity for such a methodical person. At the office she wears skirts and sweaters, her hair plaited down her back. Some days he lets himself think about her in a schoolgirl's outfit, that tiny skirt and half-unbuttoned shirt. And a gun strapped to her thigh.*

*They are at the office late one night. Carson is signing papers, a neat stack Jenny has placed in his inbox. She won't let him leave until he's done.*

*Jenny sits at her desk in the outer office. The door is open between them.*

*When the elevator begins to groan, Carson thinks it's the cleaning crew. He's also thinking about how much his neck hurts and maybe Jenny can just learn how to forge his signature.*

*He laughs to himself. It's been two years. She probably perfected it the first week.*

*Distantly he registers the elevator doors opening and then... gunfire.*

*A spray of automatic weapons echoes through the office. Carson reacts instinctively and throws himself down and under the desk. Bullets hit the wall behind him, shattering the glass of a framed picture.*

*He thinks Jenny must be dead.*

*He thinks, I'm next.*

*Then two shots ring out, and the gunfire stops.*

*Silence.*

*Two more shots.*

*Silence.*

*"Carson? Are you all right?" Jenny calls, and he unfurls himself from the fetal position he waited for death in.*

*He peeks out, finds Jenny standing in the doorway of his office, smoking gun in hand.*

*"What the hell?" he rasps, crawling out from under the desk to stand on shaky legs.*

*Jenny is unhurt. She is... cool. Calm. She is eighteen, and she just shot a man who was trying to kill him.*

*Carson drinks a Scotch with shaky hands as Jenny calls "some people I know" to take care of the gunman and the mess.*

*In a panic, he sends a message to Mr. Smith—is this an enemy of their employers? A hit?*

*Mr. Smith has no information.*

*Paranoid now, Carson moves their office to a penthouse suite with a private elevator and an elaborate security system. He gives Jenny an enormous raise, a bonus. Trusts her with even more of his life.*

*"You saved my life," Carson tells her solemnly as they survey their fancy new office suite. "I won't forget that."*

*"It's my job," Jenny says demurely, drinking champagne from a delicate flute. Her hair is down, her simple black dress highlighting her lush body.*

*He is suddenly very aware of her, how young and beautiful she is. How sweet her perfume smells. He reaches out to stroke her hair and lets his fingers trail through the mass of waves, then tighten into a fist.*

*Jenny's breath becomes sharp. She goes stock-still under his hands. He tells himself she wants this as much as he does.*

*He keeps telling himself that as the flute falls to the floor and is crushed under the heel of his shoe.*

# CHAPTER TWENTY-NINE

THEY SAT in the limo until the street cleared enough for the driver to get in.

Mitzie spoke to him in clipped Russian. He threw Nox an evil look, then got in, backed down the street, and let the car idle when Mitzie called for him to stop.

"The cops and the fire department are going to be here for some time," she said, shrugging out of the enormous fur coat. Underneath, she wore jeans and a black sweater—under body armor, which was strapped with weapons and black fanny packs. It must've been fifty extra pounds. Nox was almost impressed. "I hope you are not in a hurry."

"Oh, I am. Is everything in the casino, or do you have a second location?" he asked conversationally as he leaned over and pressed the button so the window would go down.

"Second location. Where are your friends?"

Nox didn't have to answer. The sound of running feet and a slam into the side of the limo took care of that.

"What the fuck?" Cade snapped through the window. Nox slid over so Cade and then LJ could trundle into the back seat.

"Sorry," Nox said, seemingly indifferent in tone but reaching down to encircle Cade's wrist with his free hand.

"The guards just let us come over," LJ said suspiciously.

The driver barked something in Russian, and Mitzie opened her mouth, but Nox wiggled the gun back and forth.

"English, please."

Mitzie heaved a sigh. "Take us to the warehouse," she called back.

"So, she's helping?" Cade didn't look convinced.

"He will give me money. I will give you weapons and vehicles," Mitzie answered, bored. "Then you will all get the hell off my island." Clearly Nox's suggestion that she take over operations had settled into her brain, which could only work to his advantage.

"No arguments there," LJ muttered, shifting to keep the laptop secure.

Nox lowered his gun slightly. "Can I ask you a question?"

"You have the gun."

"Where's Rachel?"

Something flickered over Mitzie's face—irritation or wounded pride—and she turned her gaze and glanced out the window.

"She left. She did not say where she was going," she said finally. "Maybe she is already on a plane out of the country."

"Was she working with my father?" Nox felt the gnawing anger of Rachel's betrayal thick in his gut. Part of him never wanted to see her face again, and part of him wanted to kill her. It warred within him.

Mitzie looked surprised at his question. "Before, yes. Then... then Galina was free of him. Jenny, that girl, was dead. She thought *he* was dead." She regarded him with wise eyes, a tiny grin stretching her thin lips. "She used to talk about you... and that baby. In the beginning."

Nox stiffened. Beneath his fingers, Cade shifted his hand so he could be the one touching Nox.

"I don't care."

"She worried. Sometimes she would send someone up there to make sure the baby was all right. But then she stopped." Mitzie shrugged. "She did not tell me why."

For some irrational reason, that made Nox angrier.


THE WAREHOUSE sat as close as humanly possible to the shoreline on the Lower East Side. A row of well-constructed buildings lined the street. Nox recognized them as remnants of when the National Guard stayed there after the floodwaters receded. With so many buildings uninspected and potentially condemnable, the Army Corps of Engineers threw together living quarters—offices, medical buildings, and storage. The latter made up several blocks of the area.

As the limo pulled into the space in front of the largest building, Nox heard a vehicle drive past and then the beeping sound of a truck backing up.

"Your guards?" he asked Mitzie, who was pulling her coat back on.

"Yes. I do not trust you," she said.

"I don't trust you either."

Mitzie tipped her head back and let out a barking laugh. "Smart man."

The doors opened on either side. Outside, Mitzie's guards stood with their guns pointed at Nox and the others.

They didn't threaten violence, but Nox kept his gun on Mitzie, his finger on the trigger. If they shot him, there was an excellent chance his dying reflex would take her out as well.

He made sure to stay aimed at her head.

Beside him, Cade shivered as he slid out behind his brother and into the darkness. Nox smiled at Mitzie.

"After you."

It took both guards to help Mitzie out. She wobbled a little and then began to trek up the abandoned sidewalk. The wind whistled past them, and moon spilled just enough light to make their way.

Nox stayed on her heels, the gun at the back of her head. The guards flanked them, with Cade and LJ bringing up the rear. At the corrugated metal door, Mitzie flipped open a rusted-looking box, where a keypad lit up.

"We have about an hour," Cade whispered, coming up next to Nox.

The door creaked open as Nox nodded. A ticking clock replaced the steady thud of his heart as Mitzie entered the warehouse.

A flick of a switch and the structure was flooded with light. And holy hell, what it revealed.

Three military Hummers—painted black—were parked in a straight line down the center of the warehouse. On either side were towers of boxes, all bearing Cyrillic lettering. Long tables were set up, with a few long containers tucked nearby.

"You give me the money, I give you the guns," Mitzie said, looking expectant as everyone crowded into the warehouse.

"I give you some of the money, you give me guns, body armor, transmitters, and, uh… those Hummers," Nox replied, sauntering through an opening and into the main space. Mitzie could throw a little war if she wanted to—did the government know about this? Did they know about her? "Then, once we're safely on our way, you get the rest."

There was some grumbling on the part of the guards, who stood like blockheaded bookends behind Mitzie. Cade and LJ hurried to stand behind Nox—and his gun.

It was an old-fashioned standoff.

"I could kill you," Mitzie said casually.

"Then you wouldn't have the money." Nox shrugged. "And you could have killed us already."

Mitzie flashed him a devastating smile—a little bit charming, a whole lot evil. "You have no idea."

"I have things to do this evening." Nox gestured at the boxes around him. "Shall we get started?"

THE GUARDS threw Nox the nastiest looks they could manage as they tossed boxes of guns and ammunition into the back of the Hummer closest to the door.

"Same in the other one." Nox and his gun supervised as LJ set up the laptop on one of the tables. "Body armor, enough for us and four more people."

"I am being very generous." Mitzie lounged on a chair one of the guards found for her. She'd deposited her guns, packs, and that enormous coat on the second table and settled down to watch the parade of munitions.

"Yes, you are. LJ? Make sure Mitzie gets a hefty tip."

LJ clicked away as Cade leaned over his shoulder. A few of LJ's online friends helped him move a sizable chunk of money into one of Mitzie's dummy-corporation accounts, with a second, larger amount scheduled for twenty-four hours later.

For a dead man, Nox was racking up some serious debt.

When the two vehicles were loaded and the body armor laid out on the hood of the first one, Nox stopped pacing. LJ gave him a thumbs-up, and Cade tapped his wrist.

"Right. Let's wrap this up." Nox walked over and leaned on the boxes closest to Mitzie.

She was smiling as she scrolled through her phone, which was blinged out in pink diamonds.

"That is a very nice number," she said, looking up at Nox. "Very large."

"And more on its way." Nox crossed his arms over his chest. Out of the corner of his eye, he saw LJ packing up. Then he and Cade went to put on the armor. "We appreciate your help."

"I do for Galina." Mitzie winked. "And my bank account."

"She's probably going to screw you over, like she's done to everyone else," Nox said, his jaw tightening at the mention of Rachel. "I hope you kept some secrets from her."

Mitzie didn't say anything in answer to that, but her smile never wavered. She called out to her guards, who hurried over to her belongings and gathered them up.

"We are going now. Good luck to you." Mitzie stood, and one of the guards helped her into her coat. "I will be going to wait until things are a little more quiet." She brushed her hair out of her eyes. "A little more… available."

Nox gave her a two-finger salute. He watched as she departed with the guards in her wake.

Then they were alone.

"I have a more favorable opinion of lady Russian mobsters," Cade said, cracking a joke, but the tremor in his voice gave him away.

"We've got twenty minutes." LJ stowed the laptop in the second Hummer.

Nox put the gun on the hood and began to strap on the Kevlar, one piece at a time.

"I'll drive the first vehicle. You pull in behind me, but not all the way. Stay at the top of the ramp with the motor running. I'll send everyone up to you, and then you leave," Nox said brusquely. Cade started to say something, but Nox was already talking over him. "There's no alternative plan. You get everyone out of there. Head back to Brownigan's house and stay there. Get a message to the Feds."

"Hey. Great plan. What about you?" Cade forced his way into the monologue and pushed into Nox's personal space.

Nox watched the fire and fear in Cade's eyes. He longed to reach out and draw him close, apologize again for this mess, but he couldn't give himself that weakness right then.

He had to save Sam. Save all of them.

"I need to find out more information about the bombs, about Carson's escape plan. As soon as I get it, I'll let you know."

"And how exactly are you gonna do that?" LJ asked. He leaned on the Hummer's door, eyeing Nox with disbelief.

"My father needs me alive, at least for the next twenty-four hours. I'm going to use that to my advantage." Nox knew he was bullshitting, and from his expression, Cade knew that as well. "I already got away from him once...."

"And he'll be guarding against that now." Cade's anger grew as he leaned back and then slammed his fist down on the hood. "This is a trap! We know that!"

"There. Is. No. Alternative," Nox said slowly, his own emotions beginning to rise. "We are all there is. The three of us. We have to get Sam and your parents away from the immediate danger, somewhere safe, until we can get off the island. We know it's a trap, and we know what they're up to, so we can use that to our advantage."

Cade's eyes glittered, his jaw working hard against whatever he wanted to say next. Nox knew exactly how conflicted Cade was at that moment because he felt the exact same way.

Sam. Cade's parents. Mason. They didn't deserve to be caught up in this nightmare. As much as they wanted to be together, they both knew what they had to do.

"Cade, listen. We're going to save your parents. And you're going to get everyone to safety," Nox said gently. He reached out to touch Cade's face, but Nox pulled back as he flinched.

"But not you," Cade responded flatly.

"I'm going to do my best."

Cade shook his head. "No fucking platitudes. Promise me you'll come back in one piece." His voice was thick with emotion.

Nox swallowed hard.

"Cade."

"Promise me or...." Cade stopped as though searching for an ultimatum, but the confusion and frustration in his expression told Nox he couldn't come up with one.

Nox's face went hot. He felt the ticking clock, felt the fear that he couldn't save Sam and the others. And he felt the love for Cade, the warmth in his gut that began that first moment in the alley. This man was a fighter, fierce and kind-hearted at once, and Nox loved him.

In this warehouse, fifteen minutes from chaos and the unknown, Nox stepped close and pulled Cade into his arms.

"I promise," he whispered, bringing their lips close together. "I love you. And I promise."

# CHAPTER THIRTY

LENNOX HILL Hospital sat in the darkness, a hulking relic sagging in disuse and abandonment. Weeds grew tall around it, the protecting metal fence long fallen to time, weather, and vandalism. That section of the city hadn't enjoyed much revitalization money, and Nox realized why. It was a drug hub, and no one was going to mess with Carson's distribution access.

They didn't speak during the entire drive, each lost in their own thoughts. Adrenaline and fear pumped through Nox's body as he contemplated this large operation and having Sam in such immediate danger.

*Please let him be alive. Please.* The thought of a double-cross shook him to the core. They knew it was a trap, but Sam and the others dead was his worst fear.

Nox drove the Hummer down the parking garage ramp, as directed. The garage had the distinct smell of rot and decay, same as Morningside, and Nox choked in memory. Crumbling walls and slopes of mud, formed and reformed by water over the years, were evident in the sweep of the headlights.

But there was evidence it was all an act. The red emergency lights were lit up on the walls, a steady overhead blinking from all corners. It was disconcerting.

In the distance, the distinct outlines of two giant SUVs were unmistakable. On either side were ramps—one leading to the upper level of the parking garage, the other to the first floor and a secondary exit.

Behind him, he could see the headlights of the second Hummer, carrying Cade and LJ. He put the vehicle in Park and switched the lights to daytime—he wanted to be able to see. Hands sweaty, he rubbed his face. Then he slipped out of the front seat and slammed the door behind him. His gun sat at the small of his back, another—courtesy of Mitzie—strapped to his leg. The Kevlar sat heavy on his body as he walked out into the open. The transmitter—they each had one—he tucked into a pocket on his chest.

The headlights on the SUVs went on.

The light from the Hummer grew fainter and fainter behind him as Nox walked closer to the SUVs.

A voice called out, rough and strangled.

"That's far enough, Mr. Boyet."

Nox squinted into the darkness and glare, trying to make out who was speaking to him. "Who are you?"

A man stepped out, just to the edge of the shadows. "I'm the person who sent you the message," he said. "My name is Agent Alec Allard."

"Interesting setup for the Feds," Nox said. "Not your usual way of doing business."

Allard didn't say anything to that. Nox waited, aware that two more figures hovered behind the agent.

"Enough of this. I want to see my son," he called out. "You said they would all be released."

"Slide your gun—"

"Not until I see my son," Nox interrupted. "Show him to me." He kept both hands where they could see them, his gun snugly against his back, in his waistband.

A figure stumbled forward, but from the height and width of the shoulders, Nox knew it was Mason. The young cop stumbled into the light, handcuffed and sporting a bloody white T-shirt.

"Oh wait, not him," Agent Allard called. "Let me try again."

Mr. and Mrs. Creel were next, both handcuffed and shuffling as quickly as they could to catch up with Mason. Someone must have said something behind them, because they each grabbed hold of Mason and hurried their steps.

"Get out of here," Nox hissed as they passed him, headed for the exit. Mason's beaten face and anxious expression made Nox's jaw clench.

The footsteps grew faint as the three made their way up the ramp toward freedom. Nox trusted they'd be safe, because he couldn't think of anything else but getting Sam back.

"And here we are," someone else said, emerging from the shadows. Carson strode into the puddle of light, an imposing figure. "I'm a little irritated by your betrayal, Nox. We had a deal, I thought, and you broke it the first chance you got."

"Sorry about Antonio and that doctor," Nox said, trying to keep his voice casual. "To be honest, I didn't care for the accommodations."

"Ah yes, used to living in squalor." Carson turned his head and said something.

A second later, Rachel emerged. In front of her, Sam, handcuffed and a shield against Nox making any moves.

Red-hot fury boiled up. It took everything for Nox not to grab his gun. The only thing keeping him tethered to the moment—and not his rage—was Sam and the prospect of seeing him safe.

"Well, regardless, your little stunt has given me the chance to get to know young Sam. He's quite a good boy." Carson paused and crossed his arms over his chest. "I considered keeping him and letting you die in the street, but honestly, you deserve a better end."

"I'm here. Let him go," Nox managed to grind out.

Rachel gave Sam a little shove. Nox could see now she had a gun trained on his back. They moved slowly—a shove, a stumble, then a pause.

Nox raised his hands to shoulder height and calculated how long it would take to grab his gun if something went south.

"Or maybe I should keep you both." Carson turned to Rachel. "Jenny—oh, that's right. Nox? Did you know Jenny didn't die on the ferry? How lucky are we that she's here."

"Jesus Christ, let's just get this over with," Agent Allard snapped, just loud of enough for Nox to hear.

Rachel hadn't said a word yet. She walked Sam halfway between Carson and Nox, and Sam came into perfect view, his fear evident but his face thankfully unscarred. Their gazes locked, and Nox tried his best to convey calm.

Almost there. Almost.

Ten feet away. Five. Nox could see Rachel now, clearly. That smug look—the one he'd endured when she was Jenny, the face that haunted his dreams—threw him off for a second. He wanted to reach for his gun, blow her away, end her as much as he wanted to end his father. But Sam stood between them, and besides, he'd made a promise to Cade. And that promise meant not to be suicidal.

At least not yet.

"Nox, so nice to see you," Rachel purred, her voice pitched low. "I assume Cade and LJ are in the second Hummer." She smirked as she looked him over. "Mitzie helped you, did she?"

"I bribed her," Nox ground out, fingers flexing as he resisted the urge to reach over and strangle her. "I think she's going to kill you the next time she sees you."

"Somehow I doubt that," she murmured.

Rachel shoved Sam one last time, right into Nox's arms. He gave himself one incredible second to hug his son, to feel his warmth and the way he burrowed in close.

"Dad, Dad, I'm so sorry," he babbled against Nox's shoulder. "I'm sorry. I love you."

Nox's emotions swamped his reasoning. He wrapped his arms around Sam and squeezed him tightly.

"It's okay. I love you. Go up the ramp. Cade is waiting. Go ahead," Nox whispered back, cupping the back of Sam's head. "I love you."

"That's so sweet," Rachel said loudly. Nox's eyes snapped up. Rachel was pointing the gun directly at his face. "Now, Sam, be good and run along. Dad and I have some business."

Sam's anguished face broke Nox's soul into pieces, but he nodded. "Go on. Hurry," he said firmly, struggling against the urge to keep Sam close. "Go."

"I love you, Dad," Sam said again. Then he stumbled out of Nox's arms.

Nox listened to his footfalls, his gaze locked on Rachel and her gun.

But she wasn't looking at him—she was watching Sam go.

The expression on her face was unreadable.

A tickling feeling at the back of his neck gave Nox the early alert.

"Get low," Rachel murmured. "Move quickly."

Then she wheeled around, arm outstretched, and fired five shots point blank toward Carson Boyet.

The SUVs against the far wall gunned their motors as shots began to ring out from every direction.

In the crossing of blinding headlights, Nox threw himself to the ground and rolled back to where the Hummer sat, just as all hell broke loose.

# CHAPTER THIRTY-ONE

CADE SWALLOWED over and over as he leaned forward to try and get a glimpse of the Hummer and what was happening in the parking garage.

"Shit," a bruised Mason said beside him. He'd jumped into the Hummer when he emerged from the parking garage, urging Cade's parents to safety. The relief at seeing them crumbled something that Cade hadn't even been aware he was holding on to.

The idea that he wouldn't see them again.

"What's the plan?" Mason asked breathlessly, checking the gun he'd been handed as soon as the door slammed.

"Get Sam and get out of here. We have a place to hide out," Cade said automatically.

"You got anything that ain't a pistol?" his father grumbled as he rummaged around the boxes in the back. Cade heard his mother's breathless prayers and tore himself away from his vigilant watch long enough to turn around.

"Momma, you okay?" he asked, taking in her rumpled appearance and white face.

"Yes, yes, thank God." Amelia frantically wiped at her eyes. "Where's Sam?"

"I'll go…," Mason said, his hand on the door. But LJ cut him off.

"No. You stay here," he said sharply. "Momma, you need to get down on the floor, okay? Don't you get up until we tell you it's safe."

They waited in tense silence, the heavy breathing from each of them fogging up the windows. Cade wanted to scream out his frustration—this plan was foolish, and this plan was going to get Nox killed.

Cade didn't doubt Nox's love, but he also had no doubt that, if it came to Nox's life or Sam's—any of their lives—Nox was going to sacrifice himself.

"Mason and I can go…."

LJ shook his head, his lips a tight line. "We're stickin' to the plan."

A few seconds later, the headlights caught someone approaching. Cade tightened his hand on the gun in his lap but let out a relieved sigh.

Sam.

Mason opened the door before Cade even reached for his handle. He grabbed Sam by the shoulder and pulled him into the Hummer.

The door was barely shut when LJ shifted into reverse.

"They're shooting… Rachel shot Carson," Sam blurted out as he sprawled on the seat, halfway in Mason's lap. "I don't know what's happening with my dad!"

Cade didn't hesitate for a second.

Gun securely in hand, he opened the door.

"Go. Get to the safe house," Cade said to his brother, his tone brooking no argument.

"Caden, no!" Amelia's anguished cry didn't stop Cade. He slid out of the Hummer and slammed the door behind him.

He wasn't surprised when a second door slammed and Mason followed.

"Mason…."

"No offense, but you're not trained. I am." Mason had strapped on the Kevlar vest and held a rifle in one hand and a pistol in the other. He looked every inch the police officer he once was.

"I'll back you up." Cade's father came up behind Mason with a vest and rifle of his own.

Cade's vision swam.

From down below, the shots were unmistakable.

He didn't argue.

When they came down the ramp, chaos unfolded in front of them. Gunfire exploded from behind the Hummer and SUVs, two of which were T-boned in the center of it all.

Cade got low and desperately tried to identify someone in the darkness, but even the Hummer's headlights didn't illuminate the scene enough for him to locate Nox. Cade and Mason shared a quick look before Mason crawled his way to the opposite side of the ramp, and Cade held his breath as he threw himself to the ground and began to inch his way toward the shooting.

Behind a heavy concrete pylon, Cade tucked himself in and took a moment to survey the scene. The biggest concentration of fire was coming from between the SUVs, one of which was currently smoking from the engine and suffering from four blown tires. He counted one shooter from that angle, which meant Nox was alive.

Their directionality pointed beyond the T-boned SUVs, where at least seven shooters were unloading from behind their vehicles. Squealing tires caught his attention as a third SUV sped up the second parking-lot ramp, clearly in a hurry to get out of there.

They needed to get behind them, or at least closer, to take them out.

Two more guns joined the battle—Mason and his father, clearly, their aim brutally true. The SUVs began to take severe damage, pushing down the men who were firing on the Hummer.

A shadow emerged from the Hummer, ducking to a space between the T-boned vehicles.

Small, quick. Cade realized it was Rachel a split second later.

The gunfire went up another decibel. More shooters from the side of the Hummers gave Cade hope. He wriggled up the dark abyss of the unused ramp to his left to gain a vantage point. He could fire down, distract them for long enough....

Another figure darted in behind Rachel, and Cade would know that form in the dark or anywhere else in a heartbeat.

*Nox.*

Rachel began to fire on the bad guys with a semiautomatic, and Cade saw his moment.

Cade picked up his pace. He reached the highest vantage point he could, then eased himself up to peer over the concrete barrier. He drew his gun slowly, not wanting to attract any attention, and pressed his finger against the trigger.

Then he saw the glint of a gun, much bigger than the one in his hand, and he realized someone was mirroring his position across the parking garage and aiming toward where Nox and Rachel were semi-hidden but still open enough to potentially take a direct hit from above.

Panic took hold of Cade. He would never be able to pick off the gunman or warn Nox and Rachel.

He had nothing at his disposal but his Beretta and years of target practice with his father.

Cade took aim again, this time at the hood of the SUV rendered useless by the crash. One eye closed, he held his breath and let loose every bullet in the cylinder.

The SUV rocked as every one hit with precision. For a brief moment, the gunfire seemed to pause as both parties tried to figure out where the new shots were coming from. But Cade's distraction only lasted so long. The big gun across the way lowered toward the Hummer.

Frustration and fear overwhelmed Cade as his gun clicked empty. He groped in his pocket, feeling around for the second clip.

The boom of the big gun rattled the parking garage, and Cade flattened himself on the ground. Breath gone, he scrambled to his knees. They knew where he was.

The second boom sent dirt and debris onto his back. They were shooting at him now.

# CHAPTER THIRTY-TWO

IN THE spray of gunfire, Nox managed to get the Hummer door open as bullets zinged over him and intermittently hit the doors and hood. He tried to make sense of it—Rachel shot his father.

Rachel shot Carson.

Nox got his gun out and wriggled across the seat to grab the semiautomatic he'd dropped there.

He could leave—back the Hummer up, get the hell away from here, pray the SOB was dead.

He had to know for sure.

Taking a deep breath, Nox laid the barrel of the gun in the center of the slim opening between the driver's side and the door. He let loose in the direction of the greatest concentration of gunfire and sprayed the shadows with bullets. Headlights burst, and he could hear shouting and the sound of the SUVs being hit.

Two of them began to move, motors gunning and jerking into the crisscross of gunfire.

He aimed at the second SUV as it passed in front of the Hummer.

The screech of a vehicle above him coupled with the SUVs trying to escape, and he watched in what seemed to be slow motion as the one coming down the ramp and the one he was using as target practice collided in the darkness.

Garbled shouts and screams punctuated between rounds.

The drivers of the T-boned SUVs scrambled out of their respective vehicles, only to be felled by a spray of bullets from Nox's gun.

The fetid air of the parking garage became overwhelmed with smoke. He ducked back inside the Hummer to grab a second gun, but he had no time to reload. Through the windshield, now a spiderweb of cracks, he could see the third SUV trying to get around the collision. The wave of security still standing pushed closer, laying down fire so intense Nox couldn't poke his head out.

The SUV squealed and pushed at the SUV blocking its way until enough room allowed it to scrape past, and it sped up the ramp.

Cursing, Nox shimmied over to the passenger side door, semi in hand. Could he chase the escaping vehicle? The chances his father was in there, being spirited away....

Was he still alive?

Nox dropped out of the passenger side door, essentially sheltered by the T-boned SUVs. He tried to find a vantage point. More guns had joined the fight, but eventually he would get distracted or tired and they'd pick him off.

He sincerely fucking hoped Cade and LJ had followed the plan.

On his knees, Nox advanced, trying to find an opening to return fire. Maybe they'd think he was dead and move closer, make it easier.

But there was someone firing from his side of the battle.

Nox slid down, trying to look under the vehicles... and that's when he spotted her.

Rachel, covered in blood, returning fire from behind the pylon near the exit ramp.

Her left arm was pressed against her stomach, her right outstretched as she let off round after round. She was clearly injured, and the satisfied part of Nox warred with the fact that she had shot his father.

He refused to trust her again, but maybe he could use her.

Staying low, Nox dragged himself around the wreck. The gunshots from the other side didn't seem to be letting up, but they were clearly concentrating on Rachel's position.

Nox used the shadows and the angle of the smashed SUVs to get to the very edge, just a few feet from Rachel. She didn't see him at first, but when she lowered her gun, weary, she snapped it back in his direction.

Their eyes locked in a tense stare.

"Out of ammo," she mouthed, and Nox lifted the semi in her direction. She shrugged and pushed the gun away.

Every molecule in his body told him to shoot her and then get the hell out of there.

Nox found himself standing and laying down a wave of suppressing fire, which sent the security down into hiding, clearly taken off guard. He darted through the darkness and smoke and then threw himself down next to Rachel's bloody form.

"You kill him?" he asked, panting with an adrenaline rush.

"Hopefully. Otherwise it was a stupid plan," she muttered, her head lolling to one side. Up close, he could see blood across her lower half—stomach, thighs. "They shoved him in the SUV, got him out of here."

"Fuck."

Nox jumped up and returned more fire.

Back down at her side, Nox made a split-second decision. He handed her the handgun strapped to his leg.

"Don't worry, I won't kill you," Rachel said as their fingers touched. She heaved herself over and, as if she weren't badly hurt, began shooting over the concrete barrier.

His more pressing worry was running out of ammo as the exchange continued. They needed to get back to the Hummer, get more guns, or find a way to get the hell out.

He realized he was thinking *we*.

Gunfire began to erupt from behind their position. Nox wheeled around to cover them until he realized they were shooting at the guards.

Fuck. No one, apparently, listened to his plan.

But before Nox could figure out what to do next, Rachel's small form was wriggling forward.

Calling her name did zero good. Nox rose up as far as he could and laid down cover fire, the recoils hot in his hands. The barrage got her to the apex of the SUVs, and he saw her grab a semiautomatic from where it lay on one of the dead bodies.

Smart, he thought begrudgingly.

Her shots changed the dynamic enough for Nox to scramble to his feet and run to perch behind her. Bullets whizzed past his head, but he made it safely, breathing heavily as he rested against the metal of the vehicles.

"Alec," Rachel rasped, dropping back down, the weapon clutched in her hand. "Don't see him."

Nox inclined his head in the direction he last saw him, but Rachel shook her head.

She rose to lay down another spray of bullets.

In harmony came the sound of shots from above, each directed into the front of the SUV they hid behind.

"Shit!" Nox swore, tucking himself low.

When she came back down, Rachel—panting and wide-eyed, white except for the smears of blood—said, "Go."

Nox gave her the nastiest look he could muster up. "Self-sacrifice isn't your game, Jenny."

"Fuck off."

"Rachel…." Furious at his own need to get her out of there, Nox grabbed the material of her jacket and yanked at her arm. "Stay down. I'm going to get the Hummer. I'll distract them, and you make a run for it."

Fury and acquiescence warred on her face, but she nodded curtly, and Nox began moving backward as she stood one more time to keep the bad guys low.

Nox moved quickly, heading back for the shadows of the Hummer. "Let's go!" he shouted into the darkness, hoping whoever was out there would hear him—Mason, most likely, and Cade, godfuckingdammit.

A deafening explosion rocked Nox to the ground.

He regained his senses a second later, suddenly aware that most of the gunfire had stopped. He struggled to his knees, frantically looking in the direction of where he had left Rachel.

One SUV lay on its side, and through the haze, he could make out a body.

"Rachel!"

Out of the smoke, someone ran past him. Mason, he realized. He was running to Rachel, pulling her back behind the cover of the twisted vehicles.

The squeal of tires alerted him to the second Hummer, which bounced around the corner of the parking garage ramp and pulled within twenty feet of where Nox lay.

The passenger-side door opened, revealing LJ with a semiautomatic of his own. He sprayed the darkness overhead, enabling Nox to stumble to his hands and knees. Mason passed him with Rachel in a fireman's carry.

"Come on, come on," he yelled, heading low toward the second Hummer.

Doors opened and slammed. Through the smoke and darkness, Nox saw a terrified Amelia behind the wheel. Mr. Creel jumped out of the shadows and ran for the back door, and LJ kept firing until Mason and Rachel were in the Hummer.

Nox's heart was in his throat. Where was Cade?

# CHAPTER THIRTY-THREE

WITNESSING THE carnage from above, Cade barely kept his stomach contents in check. He saw Rachel go down, saw Mason and his father firing wildly as the second Hummer bumped down the ramp and skidded to a halt.

With a shake of his head—because God, he couldn't sit there and watch, and he couldn't be left behind—Cade began firing down toward the SUVs. The multiple fronts distracted the security forces. Divide and conquer.

In the confusion, Cade saw Mason scoop Rachel off the ground.

"What the fuck?" he muttered, spending the last of his ammo in concentrated fire toward the SUV. His gun empty, Cade ran down the way he came, staying low as the big gun let loose a wild blast that took out a chunk of the concrete barrier.

He saw the Hummer, saw the back door open....

Cade made it. Bent down to protect himself, he dove into the open driver's side back door and hunkered down on the floor.

In the back, trembling and crouched low, was Sam. On the seat, Rachel was slumped over, bleeding profusely.

"What is she doing here?" Cade snapped as LJ and his father crammed into the front seat and LJ climbed over to get behind the wheel—a post Amelia readily gave up.

"Dying," Mason said as he got in the back seat with Cade and Sam and slammed the door behind him.

LJ flipped the Hummer into reverse and gunned it backward up the ramp.

"Wait, wait, where's Nox?" Cade looked around frantically, then went for the door handle, determined to jump out of the vehicle.

"He told us to go." Mason was pulling Rachel's clothing aside, his face grim. Below him, Sam pulled off his jacket and handed it to Mason. Then he petted Rachel's head.

"She shot Carson," Sam said, clearly in a state of shock.

Cade tried to process it all, tried to understand why they were leaving without Nox.

"We can't leave...."

"Cade! We are goin'. Now," LJ shouted. He leaned over the seat to steer the Hummer expertly up the ramp in reverse, then bounced them into the street. "Everybody stay down."

Rachel slumped farther down in the seat, her head nearly in Cade's lap. He refused to look at her, refused to look at Mason as he directed Sam to "Press here, hard and steady. We have to stop the bleeding."

He didn't want to leave Nox behind.

Cade braced himself for gunshots—for fucking surface-to-air missiles at this point, but there was nothing—no one throwing themselves on the window or using a flamethrower to incinerate them.

That alone was slightly terrifying.

He attempted to catch his breath as they backed up, eyes darting everywhere to be on the lookout for someone attempting to stop them.

Two black-clad figures appeared at the top of the ramp, and Cade's throat closed on a panicked breath. But instead of aiming their guns at them, they waved them frantically through, pointing to the left.

"Go, go, go," Cade urged.

LJ slammed down on the gas, and the Hummer shot down the street, fishtailing as they fled. No one followed them out of the parking garage, and no one on the street pulled out after them.

"Who were those men?" Mr. Creel asked from the front seat, his voice gravelly and tense.

"Don't know." Cade kept watch out the back window. "Feds?"

"Doubt it." LJ continued to drive in a straight line—and Cade realized his brother had no idea where he was going.

"Can you pull over? Let me drive," Cade said, turning back around. "Let me drive."

"I ain't stoppin'," LJ said tightly.

"Come back here with Rachel. I know how to get us to the house," Cade tried again. The Hummer was bouncing over ripped-up streets. They were going to find themselves stuck if he didn't get his brother out of the driver's seat. "LJ, come on. You can stop. No one's following us."

LJ relented after another block. He eased the vehicle to a stop, put it in Park, and was out before Cade could move.

"Let's go, Caden," his father called, clearly nervous and clutching the semiautomatic in both hands.

Cade eased Rachel's head off his lap, trying not to notice how limp she was, how lifeless. He almost asked out loud if she was dead, but when he opened the door, he saw his brother and his expression of devastation.

"Careful," Cade said gently, jumping out and letting LJ take his seat.

He ignored the low, anguished sound his brother made.

Cade got behind the wheel, accepting a gentle squeeze from his tearful mother. His parents were sharing the seat, tightly wedged in. He assessed where in the city he was and put the Hummer in Drive.

"We need a doctor," Mason said from the back seat. "Right now."

"We can't go to the hospital." Cade gripped the steering wheel.

"Cade...."

"What, Mason? Where do we... goddammit." Cade navigated the roads, his heart in his throat. Nox said go to the safe house—but Rachel needed a doctor, and they needed to get back to Nox. The weight of decision pressed down on Cade's mind and body. He forced himself to ease off the gas. Getting pulled over right now would be the end of everything.

"The Flamingo?" Cade looked in the rearview mirror. LJ was bent over Rachel, whispering to her. "LJ. Someone there might be able to help."

"Yeah, yeah." LJ finally registered his brother was speaking to him. "Yeah."

As THEY left the old part of the city and entered the District, Cade checked the rearview mirror and his heart dropped. A black van had pulled out behind them and stayed close. Too close.

"Fuck me," he muttered under his breath, not wanting to frighten everyone.

"I see 'em." His father stared at the mirror on the passenger side, gun at the ready.

"If I try to lose them, it's going to get us noticed, and that's a bad idea right now." Cade's gaze rapidly flipped between the streets ahead of him and the rearview mirror.

They went two more blocks. Then the SUV sped up as the road widened, and it pulled next to the driver's side.

"LJ, get yourself ready," Mr. Creel called out. "They're on your side."

Cade heard the click of one gun and then a second.

The passenger side window of the other car rolled down and Cade darted a quick look.

It was Mitzie.

"Jesus Christ," Cade swore as he used his elbow to jam the button for the window. When it was halfway down, he yelled, "Rachel's hurt bad. We need a doctor right now."

Mitzie turned to the driver and motioned to Cade to follow them.

The black SUV shot ahead, and Cade prayed as he hit the accelerator and followed.

# CHAPTER THIRTY-FOUR

WITH RELIEF thudding through him, Nox watched as everyone he loved got into a Hummer to bug out of the parking garage. He remained behind, backing up the ramp to lay down a line of fire and keep them safe.

But there was no gunfire.

The remaining men were sprinting for the ramp to the next level up, where their getaway vehicle must be.

Which meant if Alec survived, Nox had a chance to grab him.

Keeping a safe distance and leading with his gun, Nox darted up the ramp.

He heard the shouting first and then a hail of gunfire. Nox dropped down lower to creep the last few feet. As he rounded the corner, he was startled at the scene before him.

The security men lay dead, scattered around a black sedan that idled loudly. In the center of it all stood the Fed, a literal smoking gun in his hand.

He climbed into the sedan and slammed the door behind him.

Nox watched him, mind working a thousand miles a minute. Clearly the jury was in—Agent Allard was an undercover Fed and a dirty one at that. But why bother killing his men?

Carson's men?

The sedan pulled out slowly, bypassed the lower level ramp, and went through an opening in the wall where concrete had crumbled and been washed away by floods. Nox waited until he was just out of sight and then took off at a run.

His trek wasn't difficult. Within five minutes, understanding dawned. The trail went toward the West Side, farther uptown. Inwood.

*Morningside.*

A disgraced Fed working with his father wasn't a surprise, and Alec being a double agent didn't make his top ten of shocking occurrences. No, it was the revelation of yet another person who could not be trusted with power. This city was soaked with them, cursed with an affliction to create monsters who thrived on other people's suffering.

When he was sure of where Alec was going, Nox slowed down to a trot. To catch his breath and give himself a moment to think, he hid behind a building overgrown with ivy.

The transmitter still gave him nothing but static. If he didn't get through to Cade and LJ, he was going in there alone.

"Alec is at Morningside," he said, pressing down on the button. "Going in. Meet me at Payson and Seaman, at the old park."

Static.

Nox took a deep breath. This was the moment of truth. Instinct told him to run forward, get back into the building, and find out what Alec was up to. Blow his father away just to finish things off forever.

Maybe he could find out where the bombs were set, save people the way he didn't have the chance to do at the Iron Butterfly.

He was in control. Element of surprise. He knew the building. He could do this.

Another spit of garbled noise from the transmitter.

But guilt stayed his hand. If he ran in now, without backup, without a real plan, Cade would never forgive him. He'd made a promise to the man he loved.

He swallowed, breathed. The Vigilante would be moving by now. Nox Boyet stood there, paralyzed.

"N…." The transmitter came to life. "Nox?"

Nox frantically pressed the button. "Cade?"

"Jesus Christ." Even weakly, over a hissing line, his anger was evident. "Are you all right?"

"Fine. Is everyone okay? Rachel?"

The silence was agonizing. "She's pretty bad. They're working on her."

He closed his eyes as a confusing swirl of emotions battered him. "She… shot my father."

"I know. Sam told me."

They shared a few seconds of confused silence.

"Sam? Your parents?" he asked finally.

"We're all okay. Why are… why aren't you here? You could have gotten away with us."

Static ate the line, giving Nox a moment to collect himself.

Why?

Because this had to end. Because they needed to take back some sort of momentum and stop hiding in the shadows. It was all well and good to plan, but this was the moment—he felt it in his bones.

He stepped out from behind the building and walked toward the sanitarium.

"Because this ends today," he said as the line cleared. "Where are you right now?"

"Mitzie and her guys showed up. They brought us to the Flamingo."

Nox's steps faltered. "Are you okay?"

"Yeah. I mean, we're not going to be best friends, but she's doing everything she can to save Rachel." Cade made a frustrated sound. "Rachel called her. Mitzie. Told her to give us backup."

*Goddammit, Rachel*, Nox thought. *Every time I'm ready to kill you….*

"Do you think she'll help us?"

"For more money? Yes."

"Fine. Get your brother to…." Nox thought of Rachel's bloody form. "Can he… I mean…."

Static rumbled.

"Yeah," Cade said flatly.

"Good. Send Mitzie up here as soon as you can. No guns blazing. They wait to rendezvous with me."

Cade made a frustrated sound, but he didn't protest. "Fine. If I tell you to wait for us, you're going to ignore me, right?"

"I love you."

Cade cursed, a string of violent, unhappy words. "Stay alive or I'll kill you." He paused as sounds of conversation bubbled up behind him. "I love you too."

Silence again, then a new voice.

"I say yes."

Mitzie.

The tone was far less cocky than before. He could hear her worry.

"What do you need?"

Nox walked slowly. "Everything you got. I figure we hit now, don't wait for the raid. Find out where he's putting the explosives. Kill everyone." He imagined Morningside in flames. He thought about Dead Bolt dying on this island... along with his father.

"I do not have an army." He could hear her grumbling through the static. "Your father will be well-prepared."

"He might be dead. And that leaves a bunch of stooges and some crooked agent. Now is the time to do this—before he can regroup." He sighed. "We can't wait."

"Fine." He heard a riot of voices in the background. "We will burn it to the ground."

"Yes," he said confidently as the gates of the institution came into view.

"I will need at least one hour."

He calculated the odds of surviving an hour inside Morningside and taking care of Alec and his father. Checked the ammo clip in his gun. Estimated the time between now and sunrise.

"Quicker if you can."

"This will cost you so much money."

The transmitter went dead for a moment, then a crackle.

"Dad?"

Nox's footsteps stalled.

"Sam? You all right?"

"Yeah."

"Not much of a reunion."

Sam cleared his throat. "Good point. I guess that means you have to come home safely."

Nox squinted at the brick monstrosity, his throat tight. Sam was born here, and this was where his mother died. This was the place that all the innocence of a sixteen-year-old crumbled into dust and an adult emerged. The Vigilante emerged. His home was a testament to mental illness and lies, his identity a scattershot of lies and violence.

But....

But now he had people waiting on the other end of this line for him to come back, alive and well. Allies. Answers.

The Vigilante was walking into Morningside, and who knew exactly what he would be when he walked out.

"I promise," he told his son. "I promise."

# CHAPTER THIRTY-FIVE

CADE'S ANGER and worry over Nox was tempered only by the crisis currently filling every corner of the most lavish suite he'd ever seen, high in the penthouse of the Flamingo.

He hugged his weary parents forever it seemed before reluctantly pulling away. When his father's mouth trembled and he said, "Son," Cade almost went down in a heap. He was grateful he hadn't known how much danger his parents were in before they were rescued. He would have gone out of his mind.

"Are you hurt? Do you need a doctor?" he asked, staring at his mother. They looked tired and a little worse for wear, but both demurred the need for medical attention. A maid brought them coffee and blankets, and Cade stationed them in a quiet corner.

Mason got a quick hug. Cade sensed the young cop had exactly the same agenda as he did—make sure their loved ones were okay and stayed that way. But he couldn't voice that right now because Sam was looking terrified.

Damian flitted around the suite, frantically chattering into the phone glued to his ear. After her conversation with Nox, Mitzie had gone into a whirlwind of sharply barked Russian with lapses into English as she ordered Damian to get her what she wanted.

In less than an hour, they would be heading up to Morningside with a bunch of mob muscle, an ex-cop, a hacker, and… Cade. Plus a shit-ton of guns.

"Do you have access to a tank?" Damian asked the person on the other end of the phone as he walked past Cade.

CADE WASHED Rachel's blood from his hands, got a black tracksuit from the store in the lobby, and grabbed a large bottle of ice-cold water. He collapsed on one of the pink velvet couches in the corner, unable to do anything for the moment but breathe through the panic and worry.

His brother wasn't back yet, and there was no word from where Rachel had been rushed to on a stretcher, trailed by people Mitzie identified as "her personal doctors."

Cade rubbed his face with both hands, the burn of his eyes and the buzz in his brain turning him into one throbbing mass of pain.

"Uh, is it okay if we sit with you?"

Sam and Mason—also clad in tracksuits from the store—stood over him. Cade assumed their pallor and shaky hands were mirrors of his own.

"Sure." The expanse of pink velvet seemed to go on forever.

The couple dropped down, sticking close together.

Cade was envious.

"We're just trying to figure out what we know that you don't," Sam said softly, his hand tight in Mason's. "Like... you knew my dad is alive."

It took Cade a second, but he nodded. "Yeah. He's, uh, a pretty fucking awful person."

"Not what I was expecting." Sam pushed his glasses up. "I mean, beyond the fact that we thought he was dead."

"Yeah." Cade itched to get up, grab a gun, and head up early. He knew Nox—no way was he waiting for them. No possible way could he sit there for an hour.

"Rachel acted like she was working with my... with Carson, but I don't think she was, not really." Sam's earnestness brought Cade back to the conversation.

"She sent Mitzie to help us," Cade said absently.

"She shot him. I think that was her plan all along." Cade could see Sam was pleading Rachel's case before even knowing if she was alive. "She acts scary but... you know."

"She is scary, but yeah, I know." Cade took a sip of his water. "She hates Carson as much as Nox does, I think."

Something seemed to pop into Sam's head. He leaned forward, his voice low. "She asked him if he killed her parents. Carson said no."

Mason scoffed from where he sat quietly, his arm around Sam's shoulders. "If he lied to her...."

"Yeah." Cade shook his head. "There's so much to...." Cade gestured toward the wider world. "All of it. I wish we had time to go over everything, but Nox needs us. We don't have time for anything else but getting up to Morningside." He tried to inject sympathy into his words. "Put everything aside."

As if the universe wanted to put that to the test, a door opened behind them. Cade turned to see his brother, splashed with Rachel's blood, stumble into the room.

Surgery, in a room that was not a hospital.

"They wouldn't let me stay," LJ said, anguish tingeing every word and breath. He sat down heavily in a chair that Damian got under him before he could collapse. "Shrapnel from the SUVs, a few bullets," he recited. "She needs blood."

Damian snapped his fingers, calling out a litany of names. "Find out her blood type. Line up anyone in the area who can donate." A rush of black-clad men hustled to attention and disappeared upstairs and out the door.

Cade felt horror and revulsion building. He never worried about Rachel making it out okay. She seemed invincible, forever bouncing back from whatever happened. The thought of her not making it never crossed his mind.

Nox, Cade thought. The clock was ticking to get him help. He and Damian shared a look, one that needed no explanation. They were at least two people down and running out of time.

"LJ," Cade whispered, hunching down to reach his brother's shocky line of sight. "Just... hold on, okay? Rachel is... badass doesn't even come close to describing her. She'll pull through just to prove us wrong," he said gently, rubbing a circle into LJ's leg.

LJ's blank stare turned heated, his eyes dark and angry as he turned to face his brother. "You need to go get those fuckers," he muttered. "You need to kill them all."

Cade threw his arms around his brother's neck. "That's the plan."


PEOPLE CAME and went for the next twenty minutes. Mitzie and Damian paced, phones attached to their ears, begging and cajoling person after person to come help, but it was clear they weren't getting far.

Cade sat next to his brother, one hand on his shoulder, a thrumming energy building into a nuclear blast under his skin. Nox was out there, handling this alone again, but this wasn't drug dealers in his neighborhood, this wasn't a few guys with a death wish.

No, these were people with plans. Guns and vehicles and buildings with reinforcements. If only they could trust the cops or the fucking Feds….

He jumped out of his chair and rushed to Mitzie, nearly knocking her down.

"Call the police."

Mitzie laughed in his face. "You are crazy insane. They will not do anything."

"The cops won't get involved because they think Carson has power. The mob jabs and retreats because they think he has a cartel at his disposal. Right now, we have the ability to let everyone know just how untrue that is."

The entire room ground to a halt. Mitzie's expression softened and then blossomed into a smile that bordered on evil.

"Tell them the truth. Send them to Morningside."

Cade threw his hands up. "Invite everyone to a party at Morningside."

"There's our manpower," Damian said, nodding along. "It's going to get messy, though. We can't trust anyone."

"Of course not. But if they all want to kill each other, that's fine by me." Cade clapped his hands together.

"Let Nox know," Damian said to Cade.

Cade went to the radio and whispered his message to Nox over and over into silence.

"Nox, come in," he repeated. "Nox. Please."

Nothing.

Panic began to rise. He glanced around the rapidly emptying suite. Things were mobilizing. They would soon head out to provide backup for Nox and an exit once things started getting… crowded. LJ was back with Rachel. His parents had followed to provide moral support. Sam and Mason remained, huddled together. They held hands, their heads close as they whispered.

Perfect. Because they were the only two people here who would understand why Cade was about to slip out the door.

# CHAPTER THIRTY-SIX

NOX FELT the weight of every moment he stood in the shadows and watched Morningside, watched the National Guard trucks being filled with plastic-wrapped white boxes.

The stencil on the side said "Medical Supplies," but Nox knew better.

Those goddamn white panel trucks he'd taken so much pleasure in destroying back when he was just the Vigilante, trying to stop the drugs in the street, were lined up on the driveway. Each received a pallet of their own boxes, these much more anonymous.

Everything else seemed more stable—like it would take a little more time to ignite. He assumed the trucks were all fitted with some sort of timer. They'd park near enough to the NYPD main headquarters in midtown, near the docks, and when the time came....

Chaos.

The National Guard trucks would glide through the panic, seemingly on a mission but actually moving product out of the city. It was fucking genius.

Nox itched to move. He bounced on his toes, flexed his fingers open and closed. Was it an hour yet?

Close enough to call?

Somewhere in that cursed building were his father and Alec... and the accumulation of years of lies and deceit and murder. Nox was done waiting. This ended now.

"Sorry, Cade," he muttered as he tucked the transmitter in his pocket. Then, gun in hand, he moved stealthily toward the Morningside grounds.

All the activity seemed to be on the north side. Nox took the long way, circling through the ruined neighborhood beyond the sanitarium's overgrown grounds. He came through on the south side, where most of the structure's damage lay. It was also the side most shielded by trees and landscaping—a smart way to hide what was going on beneath the canopy of green. Ruination displayed to anyone who happened by.

Nox rested behind a pile of smashed concrete, most likely once a garage. The sun would be up shortly, removing his cover of darkness and exposing him to whatever security his father had set up.

He needed a distraction.

He reached into his pocket and pulled out the turned-off transmitter. Could he ask Cade for one more favor? Sitting down on the sharp debris, he flicked it back on.

Cade's voice flooded the silence.

"Jesus fucking Christ," he swore as Nox cradled the little black box close to his chest.

"Shhh," he said, even as he doubted anyone was close enough to hear.

"Don't shush me. You shut off your transmitter," Cade snapped, now whispering himself. "We called the police."

Nox thought he couldn't have heard that correctly.

"What?"

"We called the police. And Mitzie's sending word out among the thieves and criminals of our fine city," Cade whispered hotly. "We're sending full battalions of crazy up your way."

This is why I work alone, Nox thought, legitimately speechless.

"Why would you do that?" he managed finally, his mind working frantically now on how to get into the building quickly.

"Because we need them to be overwhelmed, Nox. Me, LJ, Damian, and Mitzie's goon squad are dead meat as soon as we get close. But now everyone's showing up, and they don't give a fuck about anything but what's in those trucks."

"They want the explosives?"

Cade laughed, low and dirty. "Oh, baby, we didn't tell them that. We told them Mr. Smith is making a getaway with a shit-ton of Dead Bolt and stacks and stacks of cash and, oh right, there is no cartel. No one's showing up to help. They're just coming to take."

"That's a good idea," Nox admitted. Although it shrank his time to get in and take care of his father and Alec to… ten minutes ago.

"It was mine."

Nox heard street noise in the background—the rumble of a garbage truck—on Cade's end.

"Where are you?"

The transmitter gave him static but no answer.

"Cade, where are you?" Nox asked again, struggling to his feet.

"You need backup," Cade said finally. Reluctantly.

"Turn around. Go back into the fucking Flamingo and wait," Nox snapped. "Right now."

"You're not the boss of me."

Nox heard a door slam.

"Cade, what the fuck?"

"You're also not the only badass in the family."

Nox's transmitter went quiet, and he realized Cade had turned it off.

Goddammit. A taste of his own medicine sucked.


FURIOUS WITH Cade, furious with everything, Nox gritted his teeth and crept closer to the south entrance of Morningside. From across the street, he could make out a small pathway, probably forged by animals and scavengers. It was overgrown enough that he imagined it hadn't been used in a while.

Well, it was worth a try. Either he'd have the element of surprise or he'd be escorted to his father at gunpoint.

The sky was streaked with gray-blue. Nox only had a few minutes before sunlight outed him. He crouched and ran across the open space, into the tangle of trees and bushes.

Breathing heavily, he waited for shouts or alarms, anything to indicate he'd been seen. After a few minutes of silence, Nox resumed his forward motion through the bramble.

Tree branches snapped back into his face as he pushed through, their roots tripping him as he negotiated the choke of vegetation. With every step, Nox waited to be discovered.

Nothing.

At the edge of the tree cover, Nox paused. The disused wing of the sanitarium was overrun with thick swaths of ivy and weeds growing out of broken chunks of brick. Double metal doors—long kicked in and dented by people looking for anything they could carry out—hung off their frames. The distance between where he crouched and those doors….

A hundred feet at least.

Between them? Ripped up blacktop with vegetation growing through the cracks. Giant weeds, six, ten, fifteen feet high, happily taking up the space.

Nox stuck his head out as far as he could. The trees and bushes blocked his view of the north-side activity—which meant they couldn't see him either.

Now or never. The sun inched closer to breaking through, so Nox took a deep breath and ran like the devil was on his heels. He dodged the monster stalks of weed and piles of driveway being pushed aside by nature's renewed domination. He tripped once, then again, barely registering the pain in his recently injured leg. The metal stairs were home base. He dug in the last few feet and threw himself into the shelter of the building.

Panting, Nox ducked into the mildewed darkness of Morningside Sanitarium one more time.

One last time.


WHEN THE flooding receded—after Mr. White left the valves open to hasten the damage and kill the people left behind—the second floor collapsed, leaving a mess that Nox now found himself crawling through. He tried to breathe through the mold, the dust, the memories of his mother, and the torment he endured here under his father's hand.

His heart hammered, and he pulled his T-shirt up over his face to keep from choking and giving his position away.

Holes in the ceiling sent slim shafts of light the farther he went. Nox tried to estimate the ground he was covering—how close was he to the center of the building? The reception area?

He skidded down a particularly large pile of debris, narrowly missing a rusted water pipe sticking up in the middle. On the other side, he hit a whole new world—clearly excavated, shored up, and housing construction materials.

Nox dusted himself off, coughing as quietly as he could as he tucked himself behind a stack of drywall. He still couldn't hear anyone, and there was no artificial light to indicate that this part of the building was being used.

He moved slower in the semidarkness now; the floors were level, the walls repaired. No motion sensors or cameras that he could see, no alarms. Ahead, he saw a sliver of light from floor to ceiling.

A wall, neatly constructed, seemingly acted as the end of the line for the old space.

The light alerted Nox to the tiny white cameras at the top of the wall. He hung back and moved to the side as far as he could. As he weighed his options, a growing sound caught his attention.

Shouting, nothing he could make out. It grew louder and louder, seeming to pass by the wall and then grow fainter. He heard a loud slam, followed by a spray of gunfire.

Cade's plan was working, and apparently the mob got there first.

Nox decided to take advantage of the chaos. He sprinted to the wall and quickly pressed his free hand over every inch until he felt something give. The opening was barely a door, but Nox pushed until he could squeeze through.

And found himself in the once-grand foyer and reception area of Morningside. The doublewide front door had been boarded over, and everything not bolted down in the place had been shoved up against it. They were clearly waiting for an assault—prepared for whatever came their way.

But there were no guards here.

To his right, outside the entrance, the battle raged—gunshots, shouts, the revving of motors.

No one guarded the staircase. Where was everyone?

Trying to recall his time here as his father's prisoner, Nox took off for the stairs. At the top, he registered three dark-suited men, all heavily armed, conferring frantically in a circle. Each seemed to have a different opinion of what to do, voices rising louder and louder as Nox crept closer. They indicated a particular door and then the exit.

It seemed at least one of them wanted to get the hell out of there.

An explosion from outside rocked the first floor. The men grabbed their guns in unison—and the one angled in Nox's direction spotted him.

Three quick shots—Nox moving forward with absolute determination—eliminated the guards before one got a shot off.

He reached the bodies and took a quick moment to relieve two of them of their hardware. Now weighted down with guns, Nox maneuvered himself around the corner.

Police sirens wailed in the distance.

"What the fuck?" someone screamed from back where Nox had just come from. "Where the fuck is everyone? Holy shit!" Nox pressed against the wall and waited for the man to get closer.

He never came. Nox heard two shots, a heavy thump, and then silence.

Footsteps, then indistinguishable sounds, but close. He raised his gun. Nothing.

Refusing to wait any longer, Nox eased around and tried to get a look down the hallway. He could see a shadow. He could hear breathing.

Nox moved quickly and turned the corner just enough to let his gun take the lead. He swung, finger on the trigger....

And came face-to-face with Alec Allard, gun drawn, standing over the guards Nox had killed.

# CHAPTER THIRTY-SEVEN

BRAVADO, CADE discovered, didn't last all that long in times of great crisis.

He'd made a deal with Sam and Mason—give him a head start, then rouse the troops and get them the hell out the door and to the sanitarium.

There wasn't much rhyme or reason. Nox was capable of lone-wolfing the shit out of this. Mitzie and her goon squad were armed to the teeth and, as far as he could tell, both good at killing and enjoying the same. Cade and his lousy handgun were ill-equipped to walk into absolute madness—drug dealers, criminal masterminds, dirty cops, and gangsters, to name just a few of the current participants. And yet here he was, driving a delivery van full of rattling bottles of liquor through the streets to Morningside.

Love and madness seemed to ride a very thin line for him when it came to Nox. If a friend came to him and laid out the timeline in detail, Cade would only have to get to "and then the casino where I worked blew up" to urge said friend to get out while he still could.

And yet....

About ten blocks from Morningside, Cade started to see police activity. Vans, SWAT vehicles, patrol cars—some parked on the sidewalks, some forming barriers to further travel.

Cade swore, backed up, and headed across town. He'd go the other direction.

The transmitter he'd turned off burned a hole in his pocket. One-handed, he reached in and clicked it back on. Static filled the van and Cade's head as he turned left to go uptown and encountered more blocks. These, however, were not cop cars. No, they were Hummers like Mitzie's, each more armored and jacked up. Men in black leather jackets milled around, a few on their radios.

Cade kept driving. His brilliant plan began to make him a little nervous. Mitzie and her men were going to hit the same roadblocks he was finding.

"Hey, who's listening?" he asked, holding the transmitter in one hand as he drove.

"Me, it's Sam," came the immediate response.

"Did they leave yet?"

"Just about to. LJ's pretty mad at you."

"How's Rachel?"

There was a long pause. "Alive? That's all I know."

"Okay, I need you to tell Mitzie that the cops are blocking half the streets, and the entire District underworld is all over the other half. She probably wants to approach from the east side. Those are her, uh… people."

"Right, got it."

Cade heard a blitz of static that meant Sam was on the run.

Close to the waterfront now, Cade tried the last street before he drove off the island entirely. It was clear—at least clear enough for Cade to gingerly maneuver the van around potholes and wrecked pavement.

Sam, meanwhile, was relaying Cade's warning to Mitzie.

"We are coming," he heard her call out. "You are a fool, by the way."

"No disagreement there," Cade muttered. He checked every cross street with a quick glance—vehicles, more than this neighborhood had seen in seventeen years. Finally he saw the top of Morningside Sanitarium over the buildings.

And a pluming cloud of smoke.

His gut clenched. "Hurry up," he said tightly into the transmitter. Then he dropped it on the passenger seat.


CADE DROVE as far as he could past Morningside, then angled the van down a cross street made extra narrow by a toppled storefront. The van scraped and whined as he drove over the rubble, and when he reached the other side, a nasty grinding sound punctuated the press of his foot against the gas.

Fabulous.

He got another few blocks before he noticed flashing red lights ahead. Cade eased the van to a stop, then collected the transmitter and exited, leaving the keys in the ignition. Congratulations to anyone who found the thing—enjoy the liquor and the damaged transmission.

Cade pulled his collar up, and then, hands in his pockets, he walked toward Morningside Sanitarium.

He kept the cops on his left, alert to the din that seemed to be getting louder and louder. Black smoke continued to rise over the skyline, and Cade's growing panic about Nox reached a fever point.

How he was going to get into the middle of this… battle and find Nox seemed unnecessary details. What he knew intimately, clearly, was that his boyfriend wouldn't be waiting for the cavalry to arrive. He would run into the fire, determined to find his father, determined to end this. And fuck it, Cade was going to help him.

The road ended. Cade stopped, shocked as his way was blocked by a concrete wall. He tried to register its existence, so weirdly out of place. About ten feet tall, it filled the space between the buildings on either side.

NO ENTRY it said, in hand-painted black letters.

"Fuck," Cade muttered as he turned to backtrack around the block.

The rumble of a fleet of trucks startled him.

The ground nearly shook with the force of the trucks moving. Cade realized they were on the other side of the wall.

He looked toward the buildings on the right, then the left. Both looked abandoned, but only one had a front door.

Cade ran toward it and then stopped to peek inside. Dark, clearly unlived in for quite some time, at least on the ground floor. The original purpose seemed to be some sort of store with a big window—boarded up—and narrow expanse. He stepped in but then realized it was an illusion. About fifty feet back, the floor opened up.

Walking over the mess of debris and dust, Cade slowly approached the back of the building. He felt the wind before he saw the wall was missing.

Clever, he thought. Someone had cut through the building to the one next door, which was also missing part of its outer wall. Too precise to be an accident.

The grumble of the trucks got louder, and Cade walked until he reached the outside again. Through the doorway, he could see the cleverness of the work Carson had done. The derelict buildings and rough-hewn streets hid the extension of the parking lot beyond the one Morningside already had. It linked up through the side streets, connecting it all together and ending in this parking lot full of panel trucks.

He ducked back in before he could be seen.

A few men in blue jumpsuits were loading metal boxes, each the size of a large toolbox, into the back of the truck farthest from him. Carefully. They snapped at each other as each gingerly executed movement got them from the low wall of boxes to the inside of the truck.

From what he could see, they were loading four boxes into the back of each white panel truck. He counted the trucks idling before him and the ones parked in a row—twenty-five.

A sick feeling washed over Cade.

If the plan was executed with the trucks parked near the city limits, they could take out entire blocks with the force of the explosions. The fire, ripping through new buildings and old foundations....

He had to stop them.

# CHAPTER THIRTY-EIGHT

NOX TIGHTENED his grip on the gun. He didn't have time for Alec—time enough to kill him, maybe. The smell of smoke was beginning to creep up to where they were.

"Where's my father? Is he dead?" Nox asked, figuring he might as well get some information before he ended the crooked agent's life.

Alec regarded him warily. There was blood all over his clothing, a wild scratch down his cheek.

"You can't kill a cockroach," he said, his voice hoarse. "Rachel's going to be pissed." He cocked his head to one side. "Is she still alive?"

Nox shrugged. "Don't know, don't care," he said coolly. Alec's tone was conversational, but he hadn't lowered the gun. "Why did you kill all your men?"

The agent looked confused for a moment. Then he laughed, dark and nasty. "Not my men, not agents. They worked for Carson's little faux-cartel operation."

"You work for my father." Nox took a step closer, emboldened by Alec's calm demeanor. He felt a rush of satisfaction at confirmation that Carson's operation was a con. Whatever they ended on the island, ended the malignancy.

A strange look came over Alec's face. He lowered his gun to his side. "I work for the federal government. I was sent here to root out the dangerous drug cartel running the island," he said, his voice filled with venom. "Imagine my surprise when it turned out to be a fucking lie."

Nox scoffed. "Please. You're working with him, taking the money and running like the rest of the rats. Tell me where my father is. Then I can shoot you, and this will be done."

"I work," Alec repeated, "for the federal government." The weariness in his expression wasn't faked; Nox was sure of that much. "And after five fucking years of my life, this assignment is coming to an end, one way or another."

"You can say that again. Where's Carson?" Nox asked, his finger itchy against the trigger.

Alec pointed at a door, down the hallway behind them. "Two flights down. One guard behind the door. He's paranoid about too many people knowing where he is."

"Guns?"

"Of course. He's got the doctor in there with him, but the rest of the guards are outside fighting whatever the fuck is going on. All the way down the hall, last door. His little... bunker," Alec said calmly, turning to face Nox. "Those aren't my people out there, by the way."

"No." Nox approached him gingerly. "Cops. Every mobster who's pissed about how my father's done business over the years." He didn't mention Mitzie and the others. "He's not getting out of here alive."

Alec shrugged. "Fine. I don't give a fuck. He's got this building on a timer. Doesn't want anyone to get into his lab and steal the Dead Bolt formula."

That gave Nox pause. "The trucks outside. Some of them are full of product. And—"

"Explosives, I know. The product is a decoy. His associates have paid an exorbitant amount of money for it and the recipe. They'll take delivery, believing the raid is several days from now—"

"And get caught red-handed when the Feds swoop in."

Alec's smile was bitter and fake. "That's the plan."

"Then Carson and his money disappear as the city burns. He'll leave a body behind. Again." Nox ached with unreleased anger, a tightness from the back of his head to the soles of his feet.

"You know he's set you up to take the fall—faked evidence, a money trail."

Nox licked his lips as he lowered the gun a bit more. "He introduced me to his associates."

Scoffing, Alec wiped a hand across his brow. "The least of your worries."

The gun came up as the back of Nox's neck prickled with urgency.

"You can tell them the truth."

Nox's stance didn't seem to faze Alec one bit. He looked weary, as if he'd seen too much to ever have a moment's peace again.

"It's almost sweet how you think that's what they're interested in." Alec checked his watch for a painfully long time. "The triggering devices they're using to blow the trucks are duds. That was the best I could do. Doesn't stop them from blowing them individually. You need to take him out before it goes that far."

"What are you going to do?" Nox debated whether Alec got to walk up that staircase or if he was going to die down here with Carson. His answer would determine his decision.

"Contact my superiors and tell them the raid has to be executed early. Before those trucks turn the District into a graveyard."

The horror of it bloomed clearly in Nox's mind. The District would be a fireball, easily killing most of the people trapped there by the curfew.

Alec said bitterly, "Perfect plan, right? Pretend to be an agent on the take, spill everything he needs to destroy the city, and walk right out the door. While my bosses debate how much they can get out of this raid beyond a few dozen convictions."

"I'd be sympathetic, but you put my kid in danger, not to mention a bunch of innocent people who weren't a part of this," Nox snapped, his anger returning. "You could have brought your people in at any time. Ended this bullshit. Five fucking years?"

Alec stepped into Nox's personal space, nearly bumping into the gun. "I am not in charge of this operation. I am a fucking pawn. You have a problem with any of this? Go talk to my boss." His gun drawn again, Alec gave Nox one more venomous look, then ducked past him. "Fuck you. Kill your father. Then I suggest you make a run for it. You haven't got a lot of time."

"You can call from here. I don't trust you out of my sight."

"Someone has to stop those trucks before they get into position," Alec snapped, not looking back. "I'm not off the goddamned clock just yet."

Nox watched him disappear up the steps, back the way they came.

For a moment he considered following, but he couldn't leave with Carson Boyet still breathing.

# CHAPTER THIRTY-NINE

ONE MINUTE Cade was making a decision about what to do and the next minute the chaos that seemed to be far away erupted within sight of the vehicles. The men loading the trucks ducked down and scattered out of Cade's direct line of sight.

Cade flattened against the wall and held his breath as a spray of bullets got closer and closer to the trucks.

The wail of police sirens followed the volley, and Cade panicked for a moment. Getting arrested was the last thing he wanted to do, especially without knowing if the explosives had been neutralized.

Voices outside his hiding place. Cade fumbled for his pistol.

"We gotta send the trucks now!"

"They're not all loaded!"

"Send the trucks! I'm gettin' the fuck outta here."

Cade held his breath and waited for them to come closer, but they were running in the other direction.

"Take that one. Drive downtown and park it...."

"No fuckin' way."

The voices stopped moving.

"You gotta...."

"You do it. I'm outta here. No money is worth this shit."

"Hey!"

A shadow ran by the door while the other man remained, cursing up a storm until a voice came over a loudspeaker and cut him off.

"This is the police. Put down your weapons."

Shouting began, then a barrage of gunfire. Cade dropped down as bullets bounced off the bricks just beyond where he was hiding.

Then silence.

"Turn the ignitions off and get out of the trucks with your hands up."

The rumble of the fleet lessened. Cade heard doors open and men calling out, "Don't shoot, don't shoot."

He also heard the sound of trucks being put in gear and the squeal of tires as some tried to make a break for it.

Cade jumped up and ran to the doorway. He had to get them to stop shooting. If one stray bullet hit the boxes or a truck crashed when they were so close together....

This entire area would be a crater.

Bodies lay slumped around the remaining trucks. Cade jumped over them and ducked for cover.

He could hear the cops screaming at the trucks to stop. Someone fired a gun, and Cade held his breath. *Idiots.*

Options—he didn't have many. Surrender and tell the cops what he knew....

And end up in a cell.

Try to stop the trucks himself....

Cade fumbled for the transmitter as the loud crashes reached his ears. He inhaled sharply and waited for an explosion.

"Sam! Sam!" he whispered hotly. "Sam!"

"Yeah, I'm here. And they're on their way."

"Shit. Okay. Slight change of plans. Mitzie's gotta stop the trucks. There's like...." Cade risked life and limb to skulk around the front of the truck to catch a quick count. "Five, maybe six white panel trucks. They're loaded with explosives, headed for the District."

Sam audibly choked.

"Tell her her men have to stop the vehicles without firing on them or causing them to crash. Tell her that very clearly, because otherwise...."

"Yeah, okay. Got it."

The transmitter went dead, and Cade sagged against the tire. Now to get the hell out of here....

"Hey! Where the hell are the rest of the trucks?" came a familiar voice.

Alec.

A shower of voices responded, and Alec began screaming at the cops. "Send your patrol cars after them! Don't let them get to the District. And do not fucking fire on them!"

*Oh, thank God. What the fuck, Alec is a bad guy. Was it a trick of some kind?*

Conflicted, Cade eased over to the next truck, staying low and out of sight, feeling safer now the shooting had stopped. He ducked between two of the parked trucks and watched the proceedings through a narrow strip of daylight.

A phalanx of cops had the drivers down on the ground, handcuffed. Two squad cars were smashed up, pushed to the side by the mass exodus of the trucks. A truck lay on its side, and two men were poking around the contents.

"Get the fuck out of there. Where's the bomb squad?" Alec was yelling, waving his badge over his head. "Who's in charge?"

Some of the officers were listening intently, but a few more were standing to the side, hands on their guns. One was whispering into his radio, and Cade remembered quite suddenly that if Alec was a bad guy, so were potentially a number of the cops on the scene.

"Sir, I'm going to need you to settle down," one of the officers said. He was very tall, with broad shoulders and an oily voice. He walked toward Alec, fingers curled over his unholstered gun.

Cade scurried closer, finally ending up at the truck closest to the action. He could see all the cops were not focused on their commanding officer, but rather on Alec.

"I beg your pardon? I'm a federal agent, and I am ordering you…." Alec sounded furious. He lowered his arm and turned toward the officer.

"My supervisor has asked me to bring you down to the station." The man moved calmly, securely. He reached around for the handcuffs hanging off his belt, and Alec lost it.

He pulled his own gun in an instant, and everything went to shit.

# CHAPTER FORTY

NOX STOOD in place long after Alec walked away.

The Feds, he realized now, weren't coming to save anyone. They had their own agenda, and part of that agenda was pinning this on Nox. He needed leverage.

He fumbled for his transmitter, which began to squeal with static. It seemed to echo through the hallway.

"Cade?" he asked as he began to move, trying two locked doors before he found an open one. Nox ducked inside and found himself in a dark and empty room.

"No. Mason. We're outside." The sound of gunfire punctuated his words. Another explosion echoed through the transmitter, and Nox heard it, felt it in real time.

"What the hell did they blow up?" He thought about the rigged explosives and how the clock continued to tick over his head.

"Entrance." Mason was yelling now. "Where are you?"

"Second floor, back of the building, south side." Nox paced in a tight circle. "You got Cade?"

"No." The static went wild and blocked out everything else Mason said.

"Coming to you." Mason's voice came back in a loud burst. "Everyone's moving to the front."

The foundation of the building rocked, and the sound of gunfire was unmistakable. Nox shoved the transmitter in his pocket, headed out the door, and ran to the back of the building.

From the window, he saw Mitzie's black Hummer slide into the parking area, swimming against the tide as the other vehicles— and the trucks with the Dead Bolt—pulled away. When it came to a screeching stop, two of her men jumped out first, brandishing some heavy weaponry.

Nox ran to the security door and pushed it open as an alarm began to scream. Then another. Then another. The stench of smoke coming from the first floor was unmistakable.

From the back of the Hummer, LJ and Mason emerged. Mason spotted Nox at the top of the stairs and poked LJ. He called something to one of the men and ran toward the metal staircase.

"Cade's okay. He talked to Sam," Mason said breathlessly as they got close.

Nox pushed first Mason and then LJ through the door and slammed it behind them.

"They stole the drugs," LJ said, indicating the scene below. "Cops are grabbin' everyone they can, but not in equal numbers, if you get my drift."

"Where is he?" Nox began to walk down the far hallway.

"Not exactly sure. He said to send Mitzie and her guys after the trucks with explosives in them." Mason's expression hardened. "It's just me and LJ and those guys. And Damian's... somewhere," he pointed out. "Too many fronts to fight on."

Nox couldn't argue with that.

He steadied his thoughts as best he could, though the screaming alarms could too easily take him back to the night his mother died. "You need to find Cade and get the hell out of here. Carson set this place to blow up."

Mason and LJ exchanged looks.

"What about you?" LJ asked.

"I'm going after Carson." He hesitated for a moment. "Tell him I'm going to keep my promise best I can, okay? And Sam...."

Mason shook his head. "I'll take care of him."

"I didn't come all the way here to be a getaway driver," LJ said, hoisting his gun. "What do we need?"

Nox warred with himself. If his father had a bunker, the last stop before he escaped, there would be evidence—actual evidence to clear Nox from this madness.

Mason's eyes widened. "There is something."

"I'm going to deal with my father. You... you wait up here. If I'm not back in ten minutes, you go," he said finally.

Below them, the progress of whoever got the front doors opened was slowed by the sound of police sirens and men with bullhorns telling them to surrender.

The response was more gunfire.

"They get up here, you go," Nox said, beginning to walk backward.

"Right." LJ moved toward the emergency door.

The power cut out, leaving them shrouded in red light.

Nox gave them a salute and went to the door Alec had pointed out to him. He opened it cautiously and disappeared into the echoing darkness.

# CHAPTER FORTY-ONE

CADE LET out a panicked shout as gunfire erupted again. He flattened against the blacktop, gun in hand, and tried to catch his breath.

When the sounds stopped abruptly, he assumed he'd look back out and find Alec lying in a pool of blood.

Instead, he turned his head to find a scatter of blue-clad bodies and the men who had been cuffed on the ground gone.

"Oh shit," Cade muttered, hurrying to his feet. He debated quickly—back the way he came or....

"Come out, right now!" someone shouted. "I fuckin' see you. Come out. You got a gun? Slide the gun out."

Not a cop.

Running would get him a shot in the back. Cade knew that for sure. Better to try to talk himself out of this.

"Okay, here," Cade called, sliding the gun as far as he could. It came to rest near one of the truck tires.

"Come out. Hands over your head," Alec barked out.

"Right."

Cade tucked his hands on his head, skirted between the trucks, and emerged into the madness that was the parking lot. The cops were now the ones on the ground being manhandled into cuffs—at least some of them. Others were keeping watch, offering assurances into their radios, ignoring the curses of their fellow cops.

Thirty men, each seemingly drawn from central casting's idea of mob muscle, had taken control of the scene.

Alec wasn't on the ground, Cade quickly noted. He was leaning against a bullet-ridden police car, snapping angrily into his phone. He gestured with his free hand for Cade to drop his arms.

"I want a fucking helicopter. Do you hear me? I've got the money, Raymond. I have it, and I want out of here before the Feds show up."

Some of the men were whispering to each other. Two of the cops, a man and a woman, exchanged looks, took their badges off, and then jogged up the driveway.

Alec saw him.

"I'll meet you there." Alec disconnected the call, his gaze still locked to Cade's face, and yelled, "Go. The Feds are coming earlier than expected. You don't have much time."

No one questioned him. A sea of black leather jackets and blue uniforms dispersed in all directions, a few stopping to relieve dead, wounded, and cuffed compatriots of their wallets and guns on the way.

Cade stood in shock, hands still behind his head.

He started to say something, but Alec shook his head minutely.

When the last man disappeared around the corner, Alec went into a flurry of action. He ran to Cade, grabbed his arm, and then yanked him toward the building with the secret opening.

"No, no, I have to get inside Morningside. I have to help Nox."

"You can't help him now," Alec said grimly, his grip forceful against Cade's struggle. "That place is going to blow up in less than ten minutes."

He'd heard about women gaining superhuman strength to lift cars off babies. Cade imagined that was what this felt like as he dug his heels into the ground, pulled his fist back, and let it fly directly into Alec's face. The sting and shock went up his arm as Alec crumpled at Cade's feet.

He didn't stop to check to see if Alec was following him as he turned and ran up the driveway.


THE RATS were leaving the sinking ship.

Cade chugged up the incline as vehicles sped past him, bumper to bumper on their way down the connected blacktop. He ran until his lungs were tight and screaming, his eyes locked on the smoking brick monstrosity ahead of him. National Guard trucks rumbled past, nearly hitting him. More white panel trucks, he realized in a panicked rush. More explosives.

Because most of the players had left the area, Cade made it to the back of the sanitarium without being shot at or seeing a policeman. The sound of gunfire came from the front of the building.

Still breathing heavily but alert, Cade slowly climbed the metal stairs and cursed not retrieving his gun before he made a run for it. At the top, a heavy emergency door barred his way. No way of telling what was on the other side.

Cade gingerly turned the handle. The unmistakable shriek of emergency alarms grew louder as he opened the door.

Smoke stung his eyes as he cracked it open and went low, ducking through and dropping to all fours.

He was at a corner—the hallway straight ahead was filled with smoke, while the one careening off to the left seemed clearer. Cade could hear voices and distant gunfire, punctuated by the claxon call to get the hell out.

Cade went in.

Scurrying along the smokeless hallway, Cade stayed down until he reached another hallway, then stood up. Now to find Nox.

In this seemingly rebuilt section of the sanitarium, Cade followed yet another endless hallway—stark white and flashing with emergency alarms. The smoke, he realized, was hot on his heels. Around a blind corner and finally something tangible—automatic double doors with hazard signs and rules about entering and leaving.

But one of the doors was open, the mechanism stuck, as it jerked when it tried to close.

He broke into a run.

How his nerve had not run out—that was the actual mystery.

Through the broken door and into a darkened, cavernous room, Cade heard the roar of the flames before he saw anything. A long table filled with broken lab equipment and covered in pieces of glass was dotted with fire, like a science class experiment gone terribly wrong.

Three bodies lay on the floor, shot neatly through the forehead. Two women and a man, each wearing a lab coat. Small square boxes, wrapped like the larger ones he saw being loaded into the trucks, were scattered around them, as if they'd been headed toward the door with boxes in hand.

Stealing the merchandise, Cade thought.

Cade quickly scanned the rest of the hastily abandoned room and coughed into his fist as smoke began to creep into the room through the vents.

He pulled his shirt up over his nose and mouth and pulled his hood down enough to shield most of his face. Cade needed to get the hell out of here.

The cotton of his sweatshirt wasn't able to contain the flood of smoke, which was increasing by the second. Cade knew the flames were coming, knew the fire in this room would soon begin to feed on everything in it, and most of that was primed to blow.

Suddenly the emergency lights went off and the alarms went dead, leaving a pulsing silence behind. Cade froze. Glass and metal crunched under his feet, warning him of the danger around him.

A flicker of flames from behind some overturned tables his only illumination, Cade gingerly took a step toward what he hoped was the door. Then another, then another—every crunch and crackle biting at the soles of his boots. Hands outstretched, he knew that one trip meant damage, meant he might not make it out that door.

That thought—*don't fall, don't fall*—echoing in his head and controlling his movements, was the last thing rumbling through him as an explosion ripped through the lab. Cade felt his feet lift off the ground, and he was carried through the smoky darkness into a solid surface—the wall, maybe near the door, maybe not.

His teeth rattled, his brain protested, but Cade felt himself slipping into unconsciousness before he hit the ground.

# CHAPTER FORTY-TWO

NOX CREPT down the steps, alert to any deviations from Alec's warnings. He didn't trust the man.

At the bottom of the stairwell—clearly new and fortified, like a fucking fortress—Nox located the door, which looked as if it guarded a bank vault. No noise, though he doubted anything would penetrate all that steel.

He reached the door and tried the handle. Locked.

Gun up, he pounded twice. "Open up! The place is on fire!" he shouted and stepped back. "We gotta get out of here!"

Nothing. Then the door creaked as a lock was thrown. It opened slowly—Nox couldn't see what or who was on the other side.

He shot twice at the center of the shadow and heard a thump. A gurgle. Then nothing until he heard a shout—a man's name. Harry? Maybe? Nox moved in silence, aiming down the hallway and pulling the trigger until he heard the man fall.

In the hallway beyond, emergency lights were on, giving the darkness a red-tinged glow. Nox stepped over the dead guard and checked the right and then the left. The doorway Alec had directed him to was a few dozen feet away.

Nox crept down the hall, the silence suffocating. At the doorway—reinforced steel, made to withstand just about anything—Nox pushed aside the body of the second guard, drew a breath, and rapped twice.

Nothing. Nox banged on the door again.

"Hey! We got trouble!" he shouted, banging hard.

A scrape of metal against metal and the door slid open with a groan. Nox stayed out of sight until it was wide enough for him to wedge his body through, his gun pointed directly into the room.

"Move," he shouted.

The person on the other side fell back, and Nox charged into the room. It was bright white and contained only two people—Dr. Khanna and his father.

"On the floor, hands where I can see them," Nox said to the doctor, who complied quickly. Nox kept his eyes on Carson, who lay on a table, bloody bandages wrapped across his shoulder and one around his left eye.

The uncovered eye was filled with venomous rage as it tracked Nox's entry into the room.

Carson laughed nastily and weakly propped himself up on one arm. "Hello, son."

"Shut up." Nox kept his gun trained on his father as he bent down to do a quick pat down on Dr. Khanna with his free hand.

"I'm not armed," the man said, but Nox checked to make sure.

"Fine. Get up and get the hell out of here. I'd recommend you keep your hands in the air. It's a fucking free-for-all out there."

"You stay here!" Carson shouted, clutching his arm over his stomach. He struggled to get up. "You have to help me!"

Dr. Khanna's loyalties were clearly bought and sold easily— but saving his own hide was the biggest payoff. He scrambled up, slipping on the concrete floor. No backward glance or words for Nox. Dr. Khanna was gone before his father could stop screaming in rage. Nox's head turned for just a moment. When he looked back at his father, he was pointing a semiautomatic at Nox.

"I am not going to jail," Carson wheezed. "I am not—I have worked too hard...."

"You can blow your brains out if you're looking for other options."

It was a standoff.

"I am getting out of here and off this fucking island," Carson spit out, struggling to his feet.

Nox watched his father's entire body work to stay upright.

"Outside, right now, are every enemy you've made in the city," Nox said conversationally. "You rigged this place to blow first, right? Should have probably waited a bit...."

Carson's panic was evident. He glanced at the door behind Nox. "I have time. I have plans. You think you know everything...."

"About the explosives? About the setup with the Dead Bolt shipments?" Nox stayed perfectly calm. "Well aware, Dad. They're being dismantled right now. The Feds will arrive for their little raid, and you'll be the perfect prize."

"Alec...."

Nox smiled genuinely. "Set your ass up."

Carson wobbled, the gun dipping. "No, no."

"Yeah."

"They think I'm dead." With his empty hand, Carson clawed at his neck and face, the bandages shifting, blood smearing. "They already—"

Nox cut him off. "Not anymore. Carson Boyet, alive and well and about to spend the rest of his life in a little tiny cell." Nox gestured to the bunker where they stood. "Until they haul you out and strap you to a gurney. How many people do you think you killed, Dad? How many people are going to cheer when they shoot you full of poison?"

Carson wasn't listening. Nox could see his father devolving into panicked madness, spit bubbles at the corner of his mouth, blood seeping from the bandages.

"They'll think it's you. That's how I arranged it. They'll think it's you. They'll find your body...." Carson raged. A shift in the direction of his head—as if his other eye still worked—indicated the black duffel bag sitting in the corner.

Nox's real prize.

"It's over, *Dad*. They're either going to take you out in a body bag or handcuffs. The choice is yours."

"Shut *up*!" Shaking, Carson tripped forward, waving the gun in Nox's face. "I will tell them you did all this, that you were behind all of it. You think I won't kill you? You think I care about you?"

"No, I've never thought that," Nox said calmly.

Then he pulled the trigger.

A rose bloomed across Carson's chest as the force of the shot sent him careening backward. His arms flailed as he fell and hit the wall behind him with a thud. The gun flew out of his hand, bounced on the floor, then skidded away.

The silence that followed was deafening.

Nox automatically stumbled over to get to the gun. Carson was down, but Nox wouldn't take the chance he wasn't out. He kept his gun trained on his father, who panted and gasped, splayed out like a marionette whose strings had been cut. The dark wound gaping in the center of his chest whistled as he struggled for air.

Nox didn't feel anything for a moment—not remorse or sympathy. Not anger or fear. He didn't even feel satisfaction at ending Carson's reign of selfish terror. Every wet breath fell on deaf ears.

Carson's lips were moving—maybe begging for his life, maybe cursing Nox's birth.

Part of him wanted to know what his father's last thoughts were. But that part was too small to impact the rest of him, the part that was turning and leaving, grabbing the bag on his way out, the part that kept walking out of the panic room and down the hallway, the part that alerted him that this place was going to blow up very, very soon. He quickened his steps up the stairwell and back to the second floor, to where he'd met up with Alec.

He peered out into the hallway and got hit with a face full of smoke and heat.

"Mason!" Nox called out, choking at the toxic smell. It wasn't just building materials burning. The scent tickled his throat, coated his tongue.

And the sensation hit like a bolt of destructive lightning.

For a moment he was back in the cell, feeling his veins opening up to the Dead Bolt. Nox sagged against the doorjamb, inadvertently sucking in lungfuls of the deadly smoke. The bag seemed to weigh a thousand pounds, and his knees buckled as the hallway became flooded with water and people screamed to be let out.

"Nox, Nox." From a distance, Nox heard a voice, felt someone grab his arm. He dragged himself to his feet, propelled forward by the force of someone else's strength.

The light and air hit him like a fist, and fresh air filled his lungs.

"You okay?" Mason had him on one side, holding him up like he weighed nothing.

"He all right?"

LJ.

"Yeah, we gotta get out of here."

"Cade." Nox's mind tumbled and flashed through faces and places as he blinked against the sun. "Where's Cade?" he rasped, slowly coming back to himself.

"Cade? Cade? Come in." LJ was yelling into his transmitter as Mason tried to get Nox down the stairs.

Static responded.

Suddenly Mason drew his gun and pointed it into the parking lot. Another black Hummer arrived and skidded to a stop beside the one they'd driven in.

Damian's head popped out of the driver's-side door as soon as he got it open.

"The Feds are coming. A battalion," he yelled breathlessly. "We have to get out of here."

"Not leaving without Cade," Nox insisted. He pulled away from Mason and shoved the duffel bag into his hands. "Take this somewhere safe. I need to find him."

"You can't go back in there," Mason said flatly.

"Leave. That right there is the proof you need to get out from under the warrants against you." Nox prayed he was right. "That goes up, Sam and the rest are going to end up in jail."

Mason was clearly torn. Nox knew he'd hit on the right thing to say. "Go now."

Lips in a tight line, Mason ran down the stairs. LJ didn't follow.

"You too."

"That's my brother."

His tone brooked no argument. Nox took a deep breath as he watched Mason jump into Damian's Hummer. In seconds they were slamming into reverse and heading back down the hill.

"Stay close. We don't have much time," Nox said. He took as much fresh air as he could, then pushed back into the dark madness of the sanitarium.

# THEN

*IN THE chaos, in the darkness and rain, the driver doesn't notice that it's not Mr. Smith who climbs into the back seat of the limo—it's Carson.*

*He pulls into the mix of cars, city trucks, and National Guard vehicles clogging the street.*

*"Where are we going?" the man asks nervously.*

*Carson, still trembling, struggles to catch his breath.*

*"Back where we came from," he rasps into the intercom.*

*They inch along for a while, then cut down a side street. The water splashes up against the windows as Carson holds the gun in his lap.*

*They drive south and then east, fighting traffic the entire way.*

*Carson isn't sure what his plan is. He assumes Mr. Smith had a way off the island—a private and secure way—and he's going to use it to save his ass.*

*How, is the question.*

*The driver pulls the limo up to a security checkpoint, and Carson, distracted, glances out the window.*

*Gracie Mansion.*

*The mayor's residence.*

*Panic overwhelms him. Everyone from the mayor's family and staff knows him. He doesn't trust his disguise to keep him safe, so he contemplates leaping from the limo, making his way....*

*The decision is taken from his hands as the vehicle is waved through to the front of the mansion.*

*Gracie Mansion's expansive porch is lined with dark figures. Carson hides his gun under his coat as the door opens and he steps into the torrential rain.*

*Head down, he hurries toward the steps, splashing through the rising water.*

*Men with automatic weapons flank either side of the double doors. Carson's mind races. Was Mr. Smith working with the mayor? Still hidden in the folds of Mr. Smith's coat, Carson puts his hand on the doorknob, takes a deep breath, and pushes.*

*He expects chaos, but the house is eerily silent. No one follows him inside.*

*Distantly he hears voices. Gun drawn, he follows the sound to a side parlor where two young men in suits are standing over a small antique table covered with papers.*

*They look up when Carson reaches the doorway. The larger of the two, muscles threatening to rip through the seams of his jacket, angles his hand to go for what Carson assumes is a gun but stops when Carson shows him his.*

*And then he takes a calculated risk.*

*"Mr. Smith has met with an unfortunate accident," he says, adopting the man's aristocratic tone. "I will be taking over operations."*

*He means for it to buy him time, but a silent conference between the two men changes that very, very quickly.*

*"Okay." The large man shrugs. "What do we call you?"*

*"You can call me... Mr. Smith."*

*HIS NAME is Antonio. His smaller and more attractive compatriot is Louis Freck. They are recent hires of the deceased Mr. Smith's, due to their respective connections in New York City, both legal and illegal.*

*They are also ambitious, a fact Carson quickly homes in on.*

*Mr. Smith—the former—has created a new synthetic drug he wants to manufacture and distribute. Antonio's uncle runs heroin up and down the East Coast. Louis's family is in pharmaceuticals, respectable in every way, except for their connection to Antonio's family "business."*

*"Does anyone know about this yet?" Carson asks.*

*"No. It's just plans for now," Louis says.*

*"Why Gracie Mansion?"*

*Antonio and Louis exchange looks—more silent communication.*

*"Thomas Gerrity and, uh... Mr. Smith the former were tight,"* Antonio says, unaware of the bomb he's dropped in Carson's lap. *"They had something going on. After the mayor was evacuated, he told us to come here."*

*Sirens wail dramatically from outside.*

*For now Carson is safe. In control.*

*"Where is Mr. Gerrity now?" he asks calmly.*

*Carson still has enemies. People who know too many of his secrets.*

*"He's evacuating on the ferry."*

*Louis makes him coffee. Antonio asks if he needs anything taken care of.*

*Outside is chaos. The city is flooded with death and desperate acts of survival.*

*No one will notice a few more bodies. Carson gives Antonio a list.*

# CHAPTER FORTY-THREE

THE FLICKERING flames licked at his feet as he opened his eyes. Cade didn't register the pain for a few seconds—the weight against his legs, the heat, the bleeding from the cuts on his hands and any bit of exposed skin. His first thought was *move! Now!* But when Cade tried to sit up, a cloud of smoke tendrilled around his throat and squeezed.

He couldn't breathe.

Coughing, Cade leaned back with a moan. His body jerked under the weight of sucking in air—and failing—as a tiny voice reminded him that the air could be found closer to the floor.

That worked. He could fall over very easily.

A few strong kicks and his legs were free. Now he could roll over onto his stomach, into the mess, and contemplate his belly crawl across the glass to safety.

To air.

Goddammit, Cade thought, coughing as he dragged his body a few inches. I am not going out like this, no fucking way.

The thickening smell of chemicals made the smoke almost palpable, and a lack of oxygen was rapidly becoming an issue as Cade frog-crawled over the destruction left by the explosion. Liquid seeped into this clothing, and he shielded his face as much as he could against his arm, mouth tightly closed. Who knew what concentrated poison—the root of Dead Bolt—was in the puddle underneath him?

Some of the liquid might be blood... his. The thought was almost abstract. How much damage had the explosion done? His lungs ached with a lack of fresh air, but the rest of his body seemed fine. Was he fine? Was he moving? A distant voice patiently reminded Cade that he was currently marinating in chemicals designed to disrupt people's minds.

*Goddammit.*

Another drag of his body and he realized he couldn't tell if he was going in the right direction. What if he was wrong? What if he was heading for the wall or the fire itself or....

# CHAPTER FORTY-FOUR

NOX STRUGGLED to stay focused on the search for Cade and not the way his brain was begging him to take a huge sucking breath of the toxic smoke.

It was dark and loud and terrifying. He felt LJ at his side, coughing and cursing. It kept him anchored.

Another explosion rocked the building, this time in the direction opposite the bunker. Then a whoosh of air and a screaming yawn of noise. Nox's eyes watered as he watched a section of the roof collapse through the smoke and onto the second-floor hallway.

The floor under their feet trembled violently.

LJ grabbed Nox and pulled him down the opposite hall.

"Cade! Cade!" Nox choked out, desperate to believe he was still alive.

# CHAPTER FORTY-FIVE

"CADE! CADE!"

Distantly, Cade heard his name being shouted over the still-shrieking alarm. He opened his mouth to answer, but the only thing he could manage was a wet and vicious-sounding cough that burned like he was gargling glass.

"Cade!"

Blinking, Cade raised his hand—in the dark! It was too dark!—in a last-ditch attempt to get the voice's attention. The siren screamed back at him in response, and he felt the strength ebbing out of his body the longer he stayed still.

The poison was seeping into his clothes, into his lungs, into his bones....

Suddenly Cade's body left the floor. For a second he believed he was flying, but his feet hit the ground—knees buckling, arms flailing, and out of the dark and smoke he heard his name again.

"Cade!"

"Cade! I got you. Let's go!"

It was his brother. LJ fisted his hands in Cade's shirt and dragged him through the hellfire and out into the hallway. Another set of hands pushed him along from behind. He could feel his back against a chest, arms going around him....

Nox.

The farther they got from the lab, the quicker Cade's senses came online. He blinked through streaming tears and coughed out the blackness in his lungs as he stumbled to keep up.

"This place is comin' down. We gotta get out," LJ rasped.

They stumbled down a long hallway as the creaking moans of a building minutes away from collapse grew louder.

"The door," Nox rumbled against his ear. "See the door?"

Cade's throat burned. He heard his brother cry out for a second. Then blessedly, the door swung up.

Daylight. Stairs. Cade began to feel currents of fresh air replacing the smoke and dust.

Until another explosion brought them down to their knees. The staircase beneath them swayed dangerously.

Cade and LJ clung to each other, shielding their heads and faces from the falling debris. Goddammit, another building trying to kill him. Cade was starting to take it personally.

Nox moved, one hand on LJ's arm and the other on Cade's. Cade felt himself being pulled down, and he resisted automatically—no solid purchase, just the swing of a metal staircase coming free of the brick wall that was rapidly shaking itself to rubble.

"Jump! Now!" Nox screamed, and Cade gave himself over to the moment and let gravity take over for his fear.

He was more thrown than anything, flying through the air, losing contact with Nox and LJ as he careened down. It seemed to last forever, until he slammed into the blacktop, the clattering crash of a ladder landing a few inches from his head.

Everything hurt. Everything. He couldn't seem to get air into his struggling lungs as Cade felt himself sprawled out, cheek against the ground.

"Get up, get up," someone said. He felt hands pulling at his shoulders, forcing him to his feet. Cade groaned as he swayed hazily, black spots flooding his vision.

"Take him." That was Nox.

Cade reached out blindly. "No, no, stay," he said, his hand connecting with something solid. "Not leaving you."

After a second's hesitation, Nox pulled Cade into his arms.

The embrace almost made Cade dizzier. He wrapped his arms around Nox in return, ignoring the piercing pain from his left hip to his right arm.

"I love you. I'm right behind you," Nox whispered, hoarse and weak against Cade's ear. "I promised, didn't I?"

Unable to speak, Cade just nodded.

"And you were right, not the only badass in the family."

Cade blinked hard as he pulled away. The light was starting to register, the sound of destruction behind them. Nox's face was bloodied. A track of dried blood went from his hairline to his neck.

Cade went to wipe it away, but the movement made him cry out in pain.

"Take him back to the Flamingo," Nox said. Then he brushed a kiss against Cade's protesting lips. "I'll be there as soon as I can."

Pulled gently from Nox's arms, Cade leaned heavily on his brother as they moved, slowly, toward the remaining Hummer. Debris, some of it on fire, sat on the roof and hood.

"Hurry up," LJ called back. Cade tried to open the door, but his hands weren't working properly. "Or he's gonna come get you."

LJ bitched under his breath as he held Cade up against his side while he opened the door.

"I need to make sure we're safe."

Cade heard Nox's voice in the distance. He heard approaching sirens as he flopped down in the back seat of the Hummer. Everything else happened in flashes—a door slam, another, LJ muttering to himself as the vehicle backed up and then did a quick turn.

Not safe until we're all together, Cade thought. Then he closed his eyes.

# CHAPTER FORTY-SIX

MORNINGSTAR SANITARIUM burned.

Nox—bruised, bloody, exhausted—stood a distance away and watched.

He watched his nightmare turn to dust, a clutch of pain twisting in his chest. Of everything he could possibly regret, freeing his mother from that hellhole was the one he would take to his grave. Natalie didn't deserve her life, or the suffering.

All the demons.

# INTERLUDE

*Nox is five.*

*He loves his trucks and his dinosaurs and his dragon-slayer sword.*

*When it's nap time, he takes his cat and curls up on the sofa.*

*When he's hungry, he eats from the tin of crackers on the bottom shelf.*

*His mommy has been crying for three days, hiding in her room. At first he thought it was a game, but it wasn't like hide and seek. She was sad and afraid and made him stay in the room, but when she fell asleep, he got bored and went downstairs.*

*Now she won't let him back in there with her.*

*He's bored. And lonely.*

*"They're coming! They're almost here!" Mommy screams from the top of the stairs. "We have to get out of here!" She's running now, running down the stairs, and Nox is afraid. He takes his cat and his sword and hides under the dining-room table.*

*He doesn't know who is coming, and he isn't sure what he is more afraid of—the unknown things or his mommy.*

*"Oh my God, Nox, come on, hurry, hurry." Mommy pulls away the chairs, and Nox starts to cry, his little heart pounding in his chest.*

*She grabs his arm. He drops his dragon-slaying sword and his cat in the struggle because Mommy is strong. She drags him to the front door, shrieking the entire way, words he can no longer understand.*

*Outside, it's early. People are walking down the street, and Mrs. Gonzalez has Cabo, her dog, peeing on the little patch of grass surrounding the tree in front of their house.*

*"Run! Run!" Mommy screams as she yanks Nox onto the top step. "Run!"*

*Mrs. Gonzalez looks up, and Nox sees her afraid face.*

*"Natalie, what's wrong?" she calls. "Are you all right?"*

*Nox gulps back tears. His arm hurts, and his knees hurt where they're scraping against the stairs. Everything is so scary, and he wants someone to help him.*

*"You!" Mommy shrieks. "You're with them!"*

*More people are stopping and staring. Nox cries harder. Why are they watching? Why doesn't someone help him?*

*Mrs. Gonzalez has taken out her phone, her scared face getting more and more serious.*

*The police come. So does Daddy.*

*Mommy is still screaming on the top of the stairs, still holding Nox by the arm. Everything hurts—his arm, his wrist, his back, his stomach. He can't stop crying. He needs to use the bathroom.*

*Mommy gets angry when she sees Daddy. Her words spit out, curse words that he isn't supposed to hear. She calls him terrible names, says she knows he's poisoning her food and sending demons to spy on her. She knows he's a monster.*

*The police come up the stairs. They grab Mommy. Daddy is shouting. Nox falls to the ground. Someone steps on his hand, and he cries so much it makes him sick.*

*Nox goes to the hospital in an ambulance.*

*A nice lady named Jasmine with pink-tipped braids comes to sit with him. She explains Mommy is sick and needs to go away for a while, and Jasmine will be taking care of him. When he asks for his father, she smiles without showing her teeth and offers to get him ice cream.*

*It's his first memory of his mother's illness. It's his first memory of his father's abandonment.*

*Mommy comes home right before Nox turns six. He and Jasmine have planned a birthday party with a chocolate cake shaped like a dinosaur egg and so many fun games. When Daddy brings Mommy home, she looks smaller, like she shrunk in the washing machine. She kneels down, smiling—with her teeth showing—and says his name.*

*Nox doesn't go to her. He still remembers hiding and her hurting his arm. He remembers how afraid he was and how the man stepped on his hand. He's afraid of her.*

*"Go ahead," Jasmine says gently.*

*"Nox," his father says sharply. "For Christ's sake."*

*Feet dragging, Nox goes to his mother, staring at the shoulder of her pale pink coat. She pulls him into her arms and hugs him until his middle hurts.*

*"I'm sorry," she cries in his ear. "I'm sorry I scared you. I love you."*

*Mommy lets him sleep with her in the big bed for a long time after that, even though he's six and not a baby. He likes this mommy, soft and gentle and sweet, who reads him his favorite books and lets him watch cartoons during dinner. She says, "I love you, Nox, my sweet boy," all the time.*

*He wants her to stay forever.*

# CHAPTER FORTY-SEVEN

MEN AND women in windbreakers swarmed through the grounds of Morningside Sanitarium, and a helicopter bearing the seal of the DEA circled overhead, looking for a place to land. The smoldering ruins of what was once Nox's nightmare sent plumes of smoke into the morning air as the fire department continued to spray water and foam into the mess.

He'd sat there for almost three hours, watching the operation roll out. He could have left, could have headed back to the Flamingo where everyone was waiting, but he wanted to know he wouldn't be followed. Wouldn't have someone knocking at his door with a gun and a warrant.

It was over.

Blinking through the exhaustion, he approached the edge of the crime scene, a twitch in his hands as he tried his best to look casual. Dirty, bloody, and barely standing—but casual.

"Sir, I'm going to need you to step behind the tape," an earnest young officer said, coming up on Nox's right.

Before he could speak, Alec approached, clad in a black windbreaker, waving the kid away.

"He's fine," the agent said sharply. "He's with me."

One brow raised, Nox followed Alec as he gestured around the far side of the rubble.

"How'd you explain everything to your bosses?" Nox asked, his voice low as they walked through a maze of hoses and black SUVs, fire trucks, and agents.

"Carson got paranoid, tried to speed up his getaway. Some of his associates betrayed him…." Alec gestured the mess.

"You got all the trucks? No explosives in the District?"

Alec rubbed his face, which sported a serious bloom of a bruise. "Funny thing. A few of the trucks are unaccounted for." He gave Nox a withering side-eye. "Not to mention zero sign of the trucks with Dead Bolt."

Nox kept his expression neutral. "No explosions, though, so that's good. I assume you have bomb squads thoroughly examining the District."

"Nox...."

They stopped walking under a canopy of trees, away from eager ears.

"You'll probably find everything when you finish your little...." Nox gestured toward the fleet of SUVs. "Raid of the city."

"Or it took off for parts unknown, since news of our raid seemed to have been a popular topic of discussion on the organized crime network."

Mitzie.

Nox shrugged. "You have enough to deal with here." He looked Alec in the eye and took in the glint that seemed to have been missing the last time they talked. "You're done. Five years, wasn't it?"

"Five fucking years of a nightmare that's over." Alec's anger seemed to cool down quickly. "Caught a criminal, broke his stranglehold on the city." There was a hint of pride in his voice.

"His maybe, but not a corrupt police force, crooks in city hall," Nox said dryly. He watched as people in hazmat suits poked around the steaming rubble. "You also let a bunch of mobsters and trucks of drugs get away."

Alec threw him a withering glare. "One thing at a time."

"Which brings me to...." Nox crossed his arms over his chest. "I took some things from the bunker."

Alec perked up. "Where are they?"

"Safe." He cleared his throat. "Not here."

"My superiors are going to want those," Alec said slowly.

"I'm sure they are."

Nox clamped his mouth shut, let Alec stew for a few minutes.

"What do you want?"

"No charges. No warrants. Nobody looking at me or my people. You've got seventeen years' worth of criminals to round up and prosecute, so you don't need to be bothering us. Clean records for everyone. And you and your bosses stay out of my accounts and my business. We haven't done anything wrong."

Alec let out an irritated sigh and rubbed at his chin again. "Debatable, but all right. Anything else?"

Nox thought quickly, imagining his father's penthouse apartment and then zeroing in on the room with all those black hard drives.

"I want my father's apartment." He gave him the address. "And you're going to come up with some incredibly true-sounding story about Nox Boyet hiding from his father's evil empire for all these years."

Eyebrows went up as Alec realized what Nox was saying. "So now you're not dead."

"No. I'm alive."

The silence ticked between them.

"Did you assist Carson Boyet in the act of manufacturing and distributing illegal drugs, committing acts of murder, blackmail, money laundering, and racketeering?" Alec asked finally, taking a few steps back.

Nox stepped over a hunk of concrete that had been blown out of the foundation.

"No."

"You'll give me the bag?"

"Yes."

Around the back of the sanitarium, another crew of firemen were dragging hoses back to their truck. This side of the action had more people in dark suits and bulletproof vests talking into phones as a few took pictures of the mess.

"Then we're fine. I'll need statements eventually. Maybe you and the gang can work on those before we sit down," Alec said casually as he was waved down by a gaggle of Feds.

"You find some bodies for us to look at?" Alec called out, making Nox's stomach squeeze with trepidation.

"Where you told us to look." An older woman with a phone in both hands looked warily at Alec. "Three of them. All were shot."

Alec motioned for them to lead them to the bodies. Under a tree, far from the action, Nox saw three body bags—all with a federal logo on them.

"Identify him and then go," Alec said under his breath.

Alec motioned to one of the agents. A tall woman wearing dark sunglasses and carrying an assault rifle slung over her shoulder knelt down, as if they were concerned this corpse would rise again.

Well, his father had a habit of that.

She unzipped the bag and peeled back the corner.

Carson Boyet, white-faced and stained with his own blood, lay silent and dead at last. The bandages were all but ripped off, exposing the damage of Rachel's shots. Farther down, he could see his own.

"Far as I can tell, wounded and alive when the building came down," Alec said as Nox nodded along with the lie and squatted to look into his father's face one last time. "Didn't get a chance to escape."

Rest in hell, please and thank you.

It was over, at least this part of it. At least this corner where Nox's father was nothing he'd ever imagined, where he was strangely mourning yet another version of the man whose blood ran in his veins.

"Yeah, it's him," Nox said finally, getting the message loud and clear. He stood up and dusted his hands off on the sides of his jeans. "Carson Boyet."

The second two bags were opened quickly—the guards he killed on his way to his father. "No clue," Nox said with a shrug. "Never seen them before."

"We'll check prints. I'm going to assume lengthy records," Alec said dryly. "Thank you for your help."

The sun shone brightly on them, the sky an infinite blue. Nox tipped his head back for a moment, let the heat burn at his closed eyes, and then nodded.

"Do you want the body to be released to you?"

Nox almost jumped in surprise. He leveled Alec with a look he hoped answered the question.

"Of course." Alec glanced at the agent. "If you need a ride somewhere, Agent Bellecosta can drive you."

"I'm fine. I know my way from here." He stuck out his hand, an unexpected gesture, judging from the surprise on Alec's face. "Thank you for everything."

Alec met Nox's hand with a firm shake of his own. "I'll be in touch tomorrow so we can get some statements," he said, loading the words with a meaningful glance. "Give Caden my best." Alec touched his jaw lightly, and Nox suppressed the urge to smile.

"Will do."

Well aware of the people around them—and loyalties that couldn't be determined—Nox stayed neutral. He ended the handshake and stepped away with a purposeful stride.

He didn't look back, didn't acknowledge the agents or the firemen. He stuck his hands in his pockets and strode toward the last remaining part of this godforsaken place still standing.

The front gates.

Foolhardy maybe, but Nox walked past everything—the emergency services, the District cops, the burly DEA team currently disembarking the landed helicopter—and kept going, his body moving like metal being pulled toward a giant magnet.

So much from that night was gone, shoved into rubble by bulldozers or just fallen from neglect. He wandered through the neighborhood where he'd escaped Jenny, fought the rising water to save his infant brother, and decided in that moment that he wasn't going to let anything happen to Sam.

And if they wanted to kill him? They'd have to work much harder than that.

The courthouse in Harlem was a beautiful piece of architecture long abandoned, but now Nox saw people through the windows, hanging laundry over the sills and watering plants.

A small community growing.

His steps took him thirty more blocks, through grass and slender trees growing from uprooted concrete and more and more buildings that showed signs of life.

The city was still there, despite the destruction and death and disregard of the people who'd been entrusted to keep it safe.

The city wasn't entirely gone.

It just needed some time to be reborn.

When he reached Ninety-Second Street, Nox paused at the corner. Sweat clung to his skin, and his breath came heavy as he blinked his home into view.

It would never be brought back to full glory—that life was gone, and more importantly, that life was a lie. He had no illusions anymore, about who his father was or where that money came from. His mother's life hadn't been worth much to his father; even Nox was an afterthought, a loose end his father never cared about.

The kindest thing his father ever did for him was leave him to his own devices.

Nox took the last few steps of his journey to what had been his home for so long—his prison and his safe haven. He went through the back door, giving himself a few moments to absorb the memories— good, bad, worst—as he went from room to room.

He took a few things—photos of his mother, a few maternal family heirlooms, and the stuffed cat both he and Sam carried around as toddlers—loaded into an old backpack he found in the hall closet. Nothing else seemed to matter at this moment, standing in the house's shadow. It was just things, objects, a cellar still holding the last remnants of his mother's insane intuition.

Maybe Sam would want to come back and collect his belongings, but Nox knew he'd never come back to this place.

His mother gave him Sam, and she gave him the means for survival. He would never stop being grateful for that.

Backpack over his shoulder, Nox exited and locked the back door out of habit. He walked around to the front of the house for one last look. The wind picked up around him, nudging Nox from his spot.

He took the hint and kept walking.

# CHAPTER FORTY-EIGHT

"CONCUSSION," PRONOUNCED Mitzie's live-in doctor. The Flamingo had been abandoned entirely by its management and security, and Mitzie hadn't returned with her men.

Guests wandered the lobby, confused and on phones, frantically calling for a way off the island, while more junior staff tried to keep the place going, unsure of what to do next. Sirens could be heard in the distance, emergency vehicles screaming past now and again, helicopters overhead.

In the penthouse, their merry little band huddled together and waited for Nox to return.

Cade was relegated to one section of the endless pink velvet sofa, enduring the aches and pains of the abuse he'd put his body through and the throbbing in his head. From his vantage point, he could see Sam and Mason at the other end, seemingly unable to keep their hands off each other. LJ had disappeared as soon as they arrived back at the suite. No one had mentioned Rachel's name for good or for bad, but LJ's absence signaled to Cade's tired brain that she was most likely still alive.

"Doctor said you can rest your eyes," his mother said as she sat down beside him. Her gentle hands and soft voice made—almost—everything better. She touched his forehead and brushed his hair from his eyes.

"But I can't fall asleep, right?" Cade had some vague medical knowledge from movies and television.

"Old wives' tale." Amelia traced the scrapes and bruises on Cade's face. She'd already washed him clean and helped him into a soft tracksuit. He really missed having his own clothes.

"Is he back yet?" He cracked his eyes open, stifling a sound of pain.

"No," Amelia said briskly, fussing with his hair a bit more. "I expect him any time now, though."

In the back of his jumbled mind, Cade wondered if they should move. Maybe to Brownigan's. Maybe… who the hell knew.

At least they had some insurance. Before losing himself in Sam's arms, Mason had opened the duffel bag and narrated the contents while Cade lay on the bed trying to keep his skull from cracking open.

Money. Like, a shit-ton of cash.

Black hard drives that Cade recognized from Brownigan's.

Flash drives that, once Damian plugged them into a laptop, revealed a cornucopia of information about the lines of corruption in the city.

Carson Boyet's blackmail file.

The identification was for a Mr. Andrew Carroll, of Los Angeles. The tickets to Moscow were also in that name.

"We can use this," Damian said, almost excited at the prospect. "Trade it for—"

"No, no. We give it to the Feds, get ourselves clear," Mason said firmly. "That's what Nox would want us to do." He coughed. "Wants us to do."

The tense silence didn't quite dissipate, even as they all drifted to points elsewhere.


CADE WOKE up with a start. His mother was gone. Instead his father sat in a chair beside him, a gun across his knees. The incongruity of the oval pink leather chair and his father's "salt of the earth" scowl made Cade laugh.

Then regretted it when it ignited all his pain centers at once.

"You all right there?" Lee Creel leaned forward, "Want me to call your momma?"

"No, sir." Cade shifted, and the aches and pains reignited. "Is he…?"

"Not yet," his father answered quickly, patting Cade's shoulder gently.

Cade sighed and closed his eyes again.


NOISE WOKE him up a second time—a babble of voices that made him tense up for a moment. But when he realized it wasn't anger, Cade let himself relax.

Happy sounds.

He struggled to sit up, eyes still closed to fight against the swoop and spin of the room. He was rewarded with a gentle touch to his face and then a kiss.

Cade opened his eyes and saw Nox, smiling.

Smiling.

"Hey," he said, but Cade only wanted one thing. He ignored the pain and drew their lips together one more time.

At some point they separated because they needed air.

Cade lay on the pink sofa, his hand tightly clasped with Nox's as he regaled them with what happened after they escaped.

"Can we trust Alec?" Mason asked.

Nox shrugged as he indicated the black bag. "I don't trust anyone who isn't in this room. But that's our insurance for the moment. We have a deal in place."

"The bag for our freedom," Mason said, looking serious. He would clearly argue anything less.

"Yes. And a few more things." Nox waved off Mason's questions past that. "We'll talk to him tomorrow. After we get our stories straight."

The babble of voices began again.

"First things first. We need to move somewhere else. Mitzie's disappearing act, along with the explosives and drugs, doesn't make me feel all that safe here."

Cade frowned. He didn't disagree—but moving from this ugly but palatial space to Brownigan's safe house…. His mother would need cleaning supplies just to relax enough to sit down.

"I have a place for us to go, but we need to wait a few days."

"Rachel can't be moved yet." LJ cut coolly through the conversation.

All the talking ceased.

Cade felt Nox's hand squeeze his. "Rachel isn't coming with us."

A sharp intake of breath—Amelia's—broke the silence.

"Then neither am I." LJ turned and left the little grouping of people fanned out around the couch.

"Dad." Sam, all wide-eyed and tenderhearted, dropped down to sit next to Nox. "She helped us."

"She lied," Nox said plainly. "She betrayed us."

Damian nervously cleared his throat. "Not... not really."

Nox's head swung in his direction. "Seriously? I'm not sure why I haven't thrown your ass out the window yet."

"Dad." Sam's voice was a little more forceful. "Maybe she didn't tell us the whole truth, but she tried to kill...." Sam stumbled over the word. "She tried to kill him. She put herself in that situation so we could get away, and then she could kill... him." It clearly made sense to Sam—and really, it made sense to Cade, although maybe that was his scrambled brain.

"We should probably wait and ask her," Mason threw in. "Before making decisions."

Cade felt Nox's temperature rising, the storm clouds descending over his face. "We? *We're* making decisions?" he asked, incredulous.

"Yes... sir," Mason added the second word hastily, as if remembering who he was talking to. "We're all adults here. We should all have a say."

Before Nox could roar out a response—and Cade could see it, right at the tip of his tongue—Sam stood up and walked over to stand next to Mason.

"He's right. We can discuss it as a group," Sam said defiantly, his chin up.

"Agreed," Cade threw in. Nox gave him a lethal stare.

"I'm hurt. You can't yell at me," Cade murmured.


WISELY, MASON and Sam disappeared after that, as did Damian. At least out of Nox's firing range. He sat ramrod straight next to Cade, allowing him to touch his hand and not much else.

"I love you," Cade said softly, trying to pierce that armor.

Nox rolled his eyes. "Not going to work."

"It's all I got right now. Everything hurts too much." Cade tugged at Nox's hand until he reluctantly leaned down and they were nose to nose.

"I'm not taking Rachel with us. Your brother is going to have to realize that," Nox said while Cade gingerly nodded his head.

"We'll talk to her, make a decision," Cade said sweetly, wrapping one arm around Nox's neck to keep him close.

"No." But Nox didn't fight, and Cade rewarded him with a long, drawn-out kiss.

"She can't do anything right now."

"No."

"My brother is as stubborn as I am. As you are."

"No."

"Sam's really grown up, hasn't he? In such a short time...."

Nox sighed as he dropped his forehead to Cade's shoulder. Cade petted his hair gently.

"It's okay. Like I told you, you're not the only badass in the family."

# CHAPTER FORTY-NINE

ALEC TOOK their statements. By himself.

They'd found the missing trucks with the explosives, parked in a garage in West New York. The Dead Bolt, however, had eluded capture, as had Mitzie. Nox gave him the location of her "enough arms for a coup" warehouse as a consolation prize.

Nox gave the black bag to Alec, whose eyes lit up with delight. "Everything's in there," Nox said, not mentioning the information copied from the flash drive and the cash that sat in his old backpack near the door.

"As we discussed, the charges and warrants attached to all of you are vacated. I explained how Carson Boyet manipulated information to terrorize you." He zipped the bag and put it over his shoulder. His hair was cut and styled, his suit high quality. The bruise on his jaw was lighter. There was even a jaunty skip to his step; the broken man from the sanitarium seemed to be long gone.

Nox tried not to be too curious.

"Makeup," Cade whispered in Nox's ear, and from his pleased expression, Nox could tell Cade was definitely the origin of the injury.

"And?" Nox sat patiently at the enormous dining-room table, his hand proprietarily on Cade's knee.

Alec's eyebrows did a little dance.

"The residence was searched and, uh… cleaned up." He gave Nox a disapproving look. "The lease is attached to a von Zandt Corporation, which is…."

Nox's heart squeezed. "My late mother's family company."

"Ah, that makes sense. As Nox Boyet is alive and well, that would make you the new owner." He paused as he turned to leave. "Of course, I had to remove some… questionable items."

"Sorry about that." Nox thought about the bodies in the bedroom.

"It's quite all right. My compensation was… worth the cleanup effort."

Nox thought of the hard drives, now property of the US Government. Or Alec. Who the hell knew, at this point?

"Your official documents will be delivered later on today. Some things you have to sign, etc." Alec walked toward the penthouse elevator. "You can move over to your new place in a day or so. If you need anything, call. I'm off to Albany to meet with Senator Freck to discuss how to assist the city in regaining its former glory."

"Alec, thank you," Cade called. Nox tamped down on his flicker of jealousy.

Alec threw Cade a wink and a charming quirk of a smile.

"You're welcome." Something came over his face—a slight drop in the façade. "I'm sorry I couldn't tell you the truth, Cade. It just wasn't possible."

Cade nodded, twisting in his seat. Nox's flicker became a flame.

"You were undercover, in a dangerous situation," Cade said. "You were playing a part. I get it."

There was a long and terrible silence, during which Nox's blood pressure went up a few hundred points. Cade and Alec were staring at each other in a way that reminded him of just what their previous relationship was.

He hated it.

He wasn't too proud of his reaction either.

"Not all of it was an act," Alec said finally. Softly. Like Nox wasn't in the room.

And then he was gone.

Nox let out a long sigh.

The others were huddled in one of the bedrooms, told to stay out of sight until Nox was sure everything had been worked out.

"Hopefully the last we'll see of him," Nox grumbled as Cade gave him a little shove in the arm.

"You're lucky I find your caveman act appealing," he murmured, pressing their bodies closer together. "Forget about him. That's the past. This is our future."

"Well, I'm not dead anymore, but…." Nox squeezed Cade's thigh. "I need to figure out what our next step is."

"South Carolina?" Cade asked, but he didn't sound convinced. Or even hopeful.

"Maybe. Alec isn't there, at least." Nox offered him a wan smile at the joke. He couldn't blame Cade for wanting to get the hell out of here. His parents would be leaving soon, and if LJ stayed with Rachel…. "Let's go tell everyone what's going on. They're probably all pressed against the door."

LJ REFUSED to speak to him, and Sam kept giving him reproachful looks until Nox thought he was going to pop an artery. Even Amelia Creel seemed to be judging him.

Over Rachel—a liar and a fucking murderer!

Damian took the hint, however. He moved into his regular suite at the Flamingo, leaving Cade the extension to his room. One less thing for Nox to be annoyed about.

But he knew he had to give in and speak to Rachel, if only for his own edification.

WITH A handful of paperwork that Alec had sent over, Nox walked to the far bedroom, which had been Rachel's pseudo hospital room since she'd been brought in. Cade stayed on his heels, quiet but approving as Nox knocked gently on the door.

LJ answered, his face a hard mask.

"I have some papers I want you to look at," Nox said, cool and disinterested. "Make sure they're on the up and up."

"Not now." The door started to close.

Nox blew out an irritated sound. "Is she awake?"

The door reopened.

"You upset her, and I'll shoot you."

It was dark and smelled like disinfectant. Rachel's small form was dwarfed in the king-size bed, medical equipment flanking either side, an IV line strung on each.

"Rachel?" LJ whispered. "Honey?"

Rachel made a raspy sound, as if clearing her throat.

"Nox and Cade want to talk to you," LJ said, the warning clear in his voice. His words were for Rachel—but the tone was for them.

"Mmmm, 'kay," Rachel murmured sleepily.

A small light on the bed stand was the only illumination. Nox clutched at the papers like a lifeline and moved to her side.

Big eyes flickered open at him; her face, in the dim light, was clearly marked by a bandage on her forehead and a pale complexion. From her neck down, and seemingly down under the covers, she was wrapped in white gauze and tape.

"Here to kill me?" she whispered. "Make it quick."

"Stop it. They're not going to hurt you," LJ said. Nox didn't turn around, but he heard Cade pulling LJ to the corner, talking to him calmly.

"Why?" It was the only word Nox could think of.

Rachel swallowed, her eyelids drooping. "Had to flush him out. Had to get rid of him."

Nox's jaw clenched. "You lied to me."

"Had to see for yourself. Wouldn't believe me."

"I started to trust you."

Her nose wrinkled, and she made a choking sound. At first he thought she was having trouble breathing—then he realized she was laughing.

"Idiot."

"If you lie to me again…," Nox muttered as Rachel continued to laugh at him.

"Done," she said, eyes fully closed. An expression of grief sank over her. "He killed my parents. He made me… he took so much…. Now we're done."

Nox's breath wavered as he stared down at her.

"Were you coming to kill her? Tell me the truth," Nox whispered. Rachel's head shook minutely.

"No." Rachel's lips moved, but he had to lean down to hear her. "Couldn't. She didn't do anything wrong. She just wanted to protect her babies."

Nox stared at her. In all the states he'd known her—Galina, Jenny, Rachel—he'd never seen her this vulnerable. Never seen her emotions this close to the surface. A tiny tear tracked down her cheek.

He straightened up, pulled himself together.

Nox strode past the end of the bed and shot LJ a long look. "You sure about this?"

LJ puffed out his chest, defiant. "Yeah."

"She so much as cheats at checkers and both of you are gone," Nox snapped. Then he walked out the door without a backward glance.

# CHAPTER FIFTY

A FEW days later, they used Mitzie's Hummer and a delivery truck from the Flamingo's loading dock to move everyone to the penthouse space.

No guards in the lobby, and barely any cars in the garage. It seemed the residents and long-term vacationers in the District had hightailed it out of there as soon as they could.

Or they'd been arrested. Cade assumed some of each.

He was feeling better, the headache mostly gone, though he couldn't look at a string of words for very long. Which was fine. His days and nights were filled with Nox and shadowing him like he was going to disappear in a puff of smoke.

They hadn't discussed what was next, and Cade was loath to bring it up. His parents were making noises about going home, and about how much room there was at their house.

LJ guarded Rachel like she was a princess and he was a dragon. If she wasn't relocating south, he wasn't going anywhere.

Mason and Sam could often be found huddled together in discussion. Should they go to Boston as originally planned? South Carolina for a new start?

Was Cade crazy to not want to let any of them out of his sight?

THE PENTHOUSE was a bad guy's lair that rivaled Mitzie's dystopian pink nightmare in its lack of appeal for actual humans to live there—cold, sterile, with appalling wallpaper most likely purchased from a home décor catalog for dictators.

"Maybe a few cheerful throw pillows would chase the supervillain vibe away," Cade said lightly as he wandered through the enormous space. Every hallway produced another set of rooms. The kitchen alone was the size of his old apartment. His mother discovered the space, and they rarely saw her after that unless she was serving something delicious in the dining room.

Cade counted six bedrooms and seven bathrooms, each more garishly gold than the rest, while Nox stood in the doorway of a small office, frowning.

"What?" Cade asked, coming up behind him. The room was just some standard furniture and empty shelves.

"Your friend Alec might have made himself a very wealthy man," he said, leaning against the doorjamb.

"He probably turned it all over to the government," Cade said, trying to sound positive.

"Uh-huh." Nox turned around and gave Cade a lazy look. "You believe that? After everything?"

Cade threw his hands in the air. "My suspension of disbelief died a cruel death a long time ago, Nox."


MASON AND LJ left on an important mission—fetch whatever LJ felt was important in Brownigan's lair and bring it back. It took three trips, and with Sam's help, the formal living room became their central hub.

Nox made only two rooms off-limits—one of the bedroom suites and his father's office.

"Get what you need out of there, then lock the door," was all he would say, and no amount of charm from Cade's lips could get more out of him.

"We have enough space, we don't need it," was his only answer.


TWO WEEKS after the tides turned, Rachel could sit up for longer periods of time. Occasionally she left the room she shared with LJ and shuffled slowly to the living room wrapped in a blanket. Amelia restrained herself as much as possible but couldn't quite quit the urge to fuss over her. There was so much soup and homemade bread that everyone benefited.

Rachel bore the attention stoically, a knit beanie covering her hair and a scarf around her neck. The snap and sizzle of her sharp wit returned in tiny snatches. Cade found himself poking her gently with his words, trying to get a rise.

"We need to find you a job you can do from the couch," he muttered as he walked through the living room, happily ordering a new wardrobe off a high-end men's clothing site on his tablet. "Because I assume you can't cook."

"Fuck you." Rachel threw him a killer glare; he could feel it boring into his skull. "If you put me in the kitchen, you'll be dead before you swallow the first bite."

"That bad, huh?"

When he got closer, a pillow sailed into his back. Cade could barely hide his grin.

He didn't fear for his life yet, but it was a start.

His parents stuck around another week. When Rachel's bandages came off—courtesy of Mitzie's doctor, who was now, apparently, Damian's doctor, making a house call—Lee Sr. began making noises about getting off the island and back to the house. And Cade's refusal to deal with "what comes next" came to a head.

# CHAPTER FIFTY-ONE

AFTER SLEEPING in one of the smaller spare bedrooms for a few weeks, Cade commandeered the master bedroom suite as his and Nox's. This room was huge, with a real view. Unlike in the spare room, when he opened one of the three bureaus, he didn't hit the edge of the bed. He was halfway through stripping out the linens—to be replaced with extras he found in a closet roughly the size of his old apartment—when he realized he hadn't asked Nox.

Hadn't asked him if he wanted to move to better, more permanent-feeling digs.

He assumed, which, he thought nervously as he sat on the naked bed, seemed to be his main problem. They loved each other, they had been through this nightmarish ordeal for months, and now....

Now.

Once they'd moved to the penthouse, any rumblings about going to South Carolina with his parents disappeared. Cade didn't even consider it.

They settled in. Cade settled in—into the penthouse, into this bedroom, into a life with Nox, and at no point were words spoken.

"I love you" went a long way, but it wasn't practical on its own.

Cade dragged the discarded linens to the laundry room and then reconsidered and stuffed them down the garbage chute. Carson had slept on those sheets, and they should be decaying in a landfill somewhere, not touching human beings. Anything else that seemed "personal" to that dead motherfucker—as Cade referred to him in his thoughts—was long gone, and furniture from other rooms brought in to make it less... touched by evil. Paint and décor sites were bookmarked on the laptop he'd commandeered.

He was setting down roots here. Was Nox doing the same?

His parents were drinking coffee together in the kitchen. Cade bypassed that hallway, not wanting to face another round of "so what are you goin' to do?" and headed for the living room, where the rest of the crew was working.

It was almost strange to see everyone clean, fed, and cheerful.

Mason and Sam were on the couch, organizing piles of paper by date while LJ manned his ever-growing control center of laptops and monitors. Nearby, half reclining, half sitting up, Rachel had a laptop of her own and was staring intently at the screen. Every few seconds she scribbled something down on a legal pad.

"Hey," he called out casually. "Anyone need anything?"

LJ peeked out from the side of mission control. "Momma fed us, and we got snacks to last until lunch." He gave Cade a wide smile. "You here to work?"

"God no." Cade kept walking, lest he be pulled into a monotonous task of LJ's, like reconciling receipts or whatever the hell Rachel was doing.

"Dad's on the roof." Sam bit his lip as he attempted to insert a piece of paper into a stack precariously balanced on the coffee table.

"Thanks," he said casually, as if that weren't the reason he came in here anyway.

Without looking up, Rachel gave him the finger as he walked by.

He was glad she was feeling better.


THE ROOFTOP garden was a surprise. They didn't discover the access through the back hallway until a week after they moved in. It was clearly neglected, clearly not anything the previous tenant had cared about. Dead trees and empty planters had been knocked over during various storms, the trellis smashed to bits by wind. It was the last thing anyone worried about—except for Nox, who had taken to disappearing for a few hours every day to come up and set it to rights.

Cade found him sitting on a wooden crate, surrounded by a neat and tidy expanse. The view was incredible if you ignored the endless drone of helicopters.

"Wow, you've worked miracles up here," Cade said quietly, coming to sit next to Nox and knocking their hips together until Nox took the hint and scooted over.

"Needs furniture, plants. A privacy screen." Nox rubbed his hands against his jeans. Cade wouldn't admit it out loud, but he thoroughly enjoyed ordering clothing for Nox and watching him walk around looking gorgeous in his choices. "Maybe we can put potted trees along most of the edge." Nox swept his arm around the perimeter. "Definitely a new trellis."

Putting down roots, literally, Cade thought, and a fissure of delight worked through him.

"That's going to take some time to grow in." He leaned his shoulder against Nox's.

"Yeah, but I think it'll be worth it."

Cade held his breath.

"So you're staying here," Cade said finally. He stared straight ahead, taking in the District, the water, and the world beyond their little corner of it.

"Yeah. I mean…." Nox laughed, a short bark of amusement. "I don't know how to be anywhere else. This is… it's my city. And it's been to hell and back…."

"Part of the way back." Cade smiled when Nox turned his head. "It still has a ways to go."

"It does." Nox relieved of burdens, Nox relieved of questions—this man wasn't the same one who pushed him against the wall and teased him all those months ago. No. This was a version of that man who had some peace.

And clearly some goals.

"And you want to help it along."

Nox looked at him, and Cade almost swooned at the earnest sincerity.

"I really do."

Unable to keep himself from playing cool, Cade closed the gap between them and pressed a kiss to Nox's mouth. He tried to pour as much as he could into the kiss—his appreciation, his respect, his love.

Him signing on.

When they broke apart, Nox was smiling.

"I am aware we've had an unconventional start to things," he said. "And I'll understand if you want to go back home…."

Cade smacked him lightly on the back of the head, then stroked his fingers through Nox's hair.

"This is my home."

This time Nox was the one who brought their lips together. "Our home," he murmured.

# CHAPTER FIFTY-TWO

A FEW days later, Nox found Cade in their bedroom, bouncing a tennis ball against the wall.

"They're leaving," he said when Nox sat down on the edge of the bed. "Damian's getting them a ferry to the airport and tickets back to South Carolina. First class, even. Momma's pretending not to be excited."

"They'll be safe." *Safer.* A city in quiet simmering chaos—as the criminals hid in dark corners—would only stay that way so long. Cockroaches eventually felt safe enough to venture back out. "No one has any reason to go after them."

"I know. And I know they hate being locked up in this building. They're not city people." The ball thunked against the same section of wall with unerring accuracy. Cade's voice sounded as dull as the thuds.

"LJ is gonna make sure their accounts are full. The farm'll be paid off slowly so as not to arouse any suspicion."

"Putting all those ill-gotten gains to use. All good."

Thunk.

Thunk.

"It's okay to miss them," Nox said quietly, folding his hands between his knees.

"Less missing and more... I don't know. I want to believe that things are settled between me and my dad." Cade threw the ball one more time and let it roll away. He turned to face Nox, a half smile on his lips.

"You could ask him before he leaves."

"Ew. Gross." Cade sighed, then flopped down in Nox's lap. "Can't we just pretend that all the not-fighting was out of love and not a heightened sense of fear and panic?"

Nox tightened his arms around Cade's waist, keeping him close. "Sure. But then they'll leave, and you'll feel guilty."

"Maybe he'll feel guilty."

"Maybe he will."

Cade laid his head on Nox's shoulder. "And maybe he's getting older and one of us should be slightly less pigheaded."

"Not saying a word."


Nox was not invited to the Creel-family meeting.

He tried not to show his relief.

They used the spare apartment across the hall, the one occupied by Mason—and Sam, which Nox pretended not to notice. Nox sat in the living room with Rachel, who managed to read a book without turning a page.

There was a door slam about an hour in, but no one walked back into the penthouse, and the private elevator didn't sound the alarm, so no one left. Nox suspected Cade was the slammer.

Sam, hovering in the kitchen, served them crudités and a cheese plate like they were in a fancy restaurant. He brought Rachel tea on an actual silver platter.

Nox got a beer.

No one said a word.

After hour two, Rachel mumbled something about a nap. She ignored Nox's offer to help her to her room but sweetly accepted Sam's thick red wool blanket that he draped over her lower half.

"Thank you, honey," she said, slowly lifting her legs so she could curl into a slender *S* on the huge sectional.

"Do you need anything else?"

"Yes. Tell your father to stop scowling at me."

Sam gave him a disapproving look.

"I'm *not* scowling," Nox snapped. Then he picked up the cheese plate and pretended to be interested in the individual cuts.

"Be nice," Sam mouthed before he headed in the direction of the kitchen.

Rachel pretended to be asleep, her nose twitching as she tried to suppress her smile.

"He's gone. You can stop pretending you're a human being."

She snickered, but she didn't open her eyes.

"We've come so far, Nox. Remember how we used to want to kill each other?"

"Yesterday?" He stuck a hunk of swiss cheese into his mouth and chewed loudly.

"Ten seconds ago." Rachel shifted, her movements slow and deliberate. He wondered how much pain she was really in, because a normal person would probably still have a morphine drip stuck in their arm.

Not Rachel.

Probably not him either, so he understood. Begrudgingly, as always. He understood Rachel.

He understood Jenny and Galina too, but he didn't have to like it.

"Why don't you go out and punch some criminals. Young Caden and his family will work out their dramas, and then you can bang in celebration," she grumbled, pulling the blanket up to her neck.

He resisted the urge to help.

"Big talk for someone whose boyfriend is in there."

That got him a death glare.

"He's not my boyfriend."

"Don't make me say lover. He threatened me on your behalf. If that's not love…."

Rachel made a gagging face and then closed her eyes again. "Shut up. I'm sleeping."

Nox finished the cheese and the sticks of carrot and celery. He got down on the floor and did a hundred push-ups until he heard the rattle of the front door.

All the Creels were alive and kicking, so Nox assumed it had gone well. Amelia's beaming smile was telling, as were her red-rimmed eyes.

"I'm going to make some chicken and biscuits," she said, sniffling as she marched toward the kitchen. "One last dinner before we head out," she added, Sam at her heels.

LJ gathered up a sleeping Rachel and carried her into the bedroom without saying much. He seemed less jolly than usual, but Nox thought that had more to do with Rachel's ordeal.

Finally it was just Lee Sr., Cade, and Nox in the living room for a long and awkward pause before Cade looked heavenward, a sigh on his lips.

"Have we had enough togetherness yet, Dad?"

Lee Sr. made a face that offered Nox a glimpse of his future—sarcasm and a barely contained eye roll of exasperation.

"Is that a hint for me to get out?"

"Not out out, more like go help Momma so I can stick my tongue in my boyfriend's mouth."

"I swear to God, you hit fifteen and stopped growing."

When Cade opened his mouth to retort, Lee Sr. held up one hand. "Do. Not."

Lee Sr.—perhaps as a mark of defiance—didn't go into the kitchen. He took his time sauntering into the library down the hall, much to Cade's amusement.

"So," Nox said when they were finally alone. "Things went okay?"

"Everyone's alive and my momma is happy, so that's all the important stuff." He pushed Nox back onto the couch and climbed into his lap. "Thank God you have no neighbors or else they'd have called the cops."

"Airing of grievances?" Nox pulled Cade closer, slotting their bodies together in a weird mix of lap dance and cuddle.

"So many." Cade smirked, linking his arms loosely over Nox's shoulders. "Some went pretty far back, and I'm going to be honest—I might have started making up shit just to get a rise, but like I said, everyone's alive, and you saw my mother's expression."

"All that matters," Nox said in response, though it was mostly fake. He didn't have any experience—normal experience—with mothers.

Cade gave him a long assessing look, head tilted to one side as if he were studying him. Nox tried to look neutral, school his face.

"I think I promised you my tongue in your mouth," Cade said sweetly. "Maybe my dad will come back in and be scandalized."

Their mouths came together like hungry magnets, and Nox slid his hands down Cade's back to his ass.

Might as well make it a big scandal.

DAMIAN MET them in the lobby with a limo idling outside. He would get them on the ferry with an escort—with Mitzie MIA, her employees were looking to Damian for work—and that escort would make sure Lee Sr. and Amelia got on the plane. There would even be a car waiting for them in South Carolina to take them home.

Sam, Mason, and Rachel said their good-byes upstairs.

There were a few tears—Sam and Amelia had grown quite close. Many thank-yous and promises to keep in contact, to visit. Amelia and Rachel spoke quietly for a long enough period to make LJ restless.

Then they headed down in the elevator.

As Amelia cried and hugged both her boys close, Lee Sr. and Nox regarded each other a few feet away.

"So," Lee Sr. said, "What are you plannin'?"

"In general? Or was that a more specific question?" Nox stuck his hands in the pockets of his jeans and rocked back and forth on his heels.

"Cade says you're stayin' here. Working in the city." Lee Sr. glanced around as if crazed ninjas were waiting to attack. "That a good idea?"

"We haven't really discussed the particulars yet," Nox hedged, glancing over to where Amelia and the boys were still clinging together. "But we know we want to do something."

"Dangerous place."

"True. But I've lived here my whole life. Not sure I know how to be anywhere else."

Lee Sr. nodded slowly. "I can appreciate that. You know where we are if things don't work out." He extended his hand.

Nox blinked a few times in surprise and then reached out to shake.

"Thank you, sir."

It seemed like Cade's father had more to say, but the hugs were winding down, and clearly it was time to get going before Amelia brought her suitcases back upstairs.

The parents switched places—Lee Sr. regarding the boys as they stared back, Amelia wrapping Nox in a warm and vanilla-scented hug.

"Take care of yourself and my boy," she murmured. "And that sweet son of yours and…."

"I'll take care of all of them," Nox whispered back and pressed a quick kiss to her cheek. "Although I might just let Cade think he's in charge."

Amelia pulled back, beaming. "He'll like that."

She gently patted his face and regarded him with a steady and loving gaze. "You're a good man. Dangerous… but good."

Nox shrugged and hoped he wasn't actually blushing, because that would just be embarrassing.

It took another few minutes, but after an exchange of hearty backslaps with Cade and LJ, Lee Sr. gathered up Amelia and their bags.

Damian, who'd been waiting unobtrusively by the door, beckoned Nox over with a wave as the good-byes wound down.

"Thanks for taking care of this," he said gruffly.

"The least I could do," Damian said nervously. "Alec was at the Flamingo. He took some computers, but otherwise he told me I could stay in business."

Nox's eyebrows went up. "Seriously?"

"He clearly meant in, uh, a legal sense." Damian shrugged. "He's putting some of his people up in my empty rooms."

"What happens when Mitzie comes back and discovers you're running her hotel?"

Nox imagined Damian being very, very dead.

"Why would she come back? If she was the one who took the Dead Bolt…."

He sighed. *Fuck.* Sometimes he forgot that shit was out in the wide world. And given how much money he'd paid her—yeah, there was no reason for Mitzie to come back.

"So, you going legit?"

Damian stuck his chin out. "I was always doing my job in a legal manner," he said loftily.

"He just worked for a gangster," Cade added, surreptitiously wiping at his eyes.

"As did you," Damian pointed out. "Regardless of the path, the Flamingo will be a legitimate establishment once I figure out how to clean the books." Damian sighed. "I mean, I'm good, but this isn't something they teach you in accounting class."

"LJ's becoming an expert at that sort of thing. Hire him to help you," Nox said. It would be good for the Flamingo to stay afloat— keep people employed, at least. Maybe Damian could repaint the nightmare....

It took another five minutes to get Cade's parents out the door. The boys both kept it together, even as Amelia's tears began again in earnest. Nox racked his brain for things to say, like "We'll visit" and "They can come here," but the truth was, getting on and off the island wasn't going to be easy.

An idea bloomed, and he pulled LJ to his side to whisper in his ear.

"Why didn't I think of that?" LJ muttered. Then he went to his parents with a big smile slapped on his face.

"When you get settled, my friend Danny will stop by and fix up a computer for you. Then you can chat with us whenever you want." He put his arm around Amelia's shoulders.

Lee Sr. looked uncertain.

"Secure line, our server. It'll be fine, Daddy," LJ said, "Government won't be able to listen in." His grin was charming. "I can guarantee that."

# CHAPTER FIFTY-THREE

FROM THE penthouse apartment and wrapped in an expensive black duvet, Cade watched the sun come up on another exciting day of watching the District fall like a boxer with a glass chin.

The casinos were shuttered, at least until "investigations were completed," which meant people were out of work. A lot of people. Without tourists, most people were without a source of income. Cade worried.

Some of the workers would try to get off the island, to ply their trades in other places, but still more were in the familiar bind of having nowhere to go and no way to get there even if they did.

It wasn't a place you could invite people to come back to—their lives had been uprooted but replanted in other places. Not many would have the desire to homestead in a hellhole.

What the hell was the draw?

Cade sighed and pressed his hand against the thick glass. How idealistic to believe if you took down the people at the top the rest would sort itself out. The casinos and the people behind them were at least temporarily out of the business, the Dead Bolt operation destroyed, but that meant addicts without a fix.

Taking down Carson and his evil empire had unleashed a Pandora's Box of problems.

Everywhere in the city, federal agents swarmed, sticking their noses and guns into anything that looked even vaguely suspicious. In Albany, Senator Louis Freck was on the news every night, calling for hearings on how the problem in New York City got so bad. Public support was on his side—most people forgot he was the one who had called for legalized gambling and prostitution to "save" the city in the first place.

Short memories, Cade thought.

"The National Guard knocked on the door downstairs, wanted to know if we needed transportation off the island."

Cade turned to find Nox a few feet away, still dressed for bed in just a pair of boxer briefs, quiet as a cat burglar.

"Bet that brought back some memories," Cade said, offering a smile.

Nox shrugged one shoulder, his blue gaze locked on the scene outside their palatial new home. "I'm a little bit better off this time around."

"We could still leave." Cade turned completely and leaned his back on the cool glass, the blanket wrapped around his shoulders. "Travel. Relocate to a city slightly less corrupt. Buy a cabin in the woods and hide from people for a few dozen years or until my PTSD evens out." He said it jokingly but only meant it about 10 percent that way. "We could do it."

"We could." Nox avoided Cade's eyes by glancing down at his feet.

"Or we stay here and… you know I want to say something ridiculous like 'right the wrongs committed against this city and let it shine again,' but I'm afraid I'll sound like an asshole."

The ducked head couldn't hide the smile Cade knew Nox was sporting.

"That sounds like quite a lofty goal."

Nox tipped his head so Cade could see him grinning.

"It might take a lot of money."

"Good thing you're disgustingly rich."

"And a lot of hard work."

Cade shrugged and stepped forward as the blanket fell to the rug. "I'm unemployed."

"We'd need a team…." Nox tucked his hands behind his back and furrowed his brows.

"We know the city's last honest cop, a hit woman, and a hacker. The legal business owners want to clean this place up. If we got a cute kid and a dog, we might have a hit television series."

Nox made a face. "And what's your role in all of this, exactly?"

Cade took great pleasure in the sultry roll of his hips as he met Nox halfway across the living room. That hungry glance was unmistakable, so it was no surprise when Nox moved lightning fast to grab him, bring him into a tight embrace.

"Every hero needs a hot love interest," Cade murmured, tilting his head for a kiss.

A FEW hours later, Nox was dressed and sitting at the antique writing desk they had dragged into the formal living room, where they conducted their "business." LJ worked at his setup of monitors, Rachel at his side as they combed through the inner workings of a criminal empire.

Nox didn't want to touch any of it.

A silver laptop opened in front of him, Nox played with what was important to him—the money.

While the Feds concentrated on Dead Bolt, money laundering, and racketeering, Nox dove into the rows and rows of blackmail and protection numbers that filled Carson's many hidden accounts. LJ—moving quickly before the government stooges could get into everything—directed a major portion into the old trust funds, where the one and only—very alive—Nox Boyet could access it.

*And oh, thank you, piece-of-shit Father. Thank you for hiding all that money in my trust fund and Mom's old accounts so it would look like I was the bad guy. Except you died before you could finish the frame, and now... now I'm just stinking filthy rich.*

At some point they might come knocking. The myriad trails might lead them to his door. He had every expectation they—whoever *they* might be—would get to him, because paranoia didn't disappear overnight. But he had LJ and Rachel and time.

The Vigilante was dead, and Nox Boyet was just a victim of his father's murderous greed. The government and the gangsters had more pressing things to worry about.

Because the corrupt police department and city officials—currently quaking in their boots and cooperating with the federal government with one hand while shredding documents with the other—had skeletons in their closets and blood on their hands. The innocent victims in those collapsed buildings, the people who drowned or froze or starved....

Let the government start at the top. Nox was starting at the beginning. His father hadn't been working alone.

"Hey, Sam made lunch." Cade stuck his head through the open door. His smile and open expression made Nox's heart do stupid pattery things. It was like the light had been turned back on inside him.

"Was that an invitation?" Nox began to shut down the windows, tucking away some things to share in the future.

"He's a nervous wreck, and there's, like, eighteen serving dishes, so yes, please. Come and help us manage it." In his untucked silk button-down, loose jeans, and bare feet, Cade looked like an advertisement for—well, he could sell anything with that face, and Nox would be buying forever.

"Mason'll be fine."

Nox got up and shut the laptop as he went.

"Uh-huh. I reassured him. He made a pie." Cade shrugged. "Honestly, I didn't try too hard after that, because I had a craving for red velvet cupcakes, and he promised me some tonight."

Hand in hand, they walked through the living room and into the formal dining room, where seating for twelve meant plenty of room for what looked like every serving dish from the kitchen.

LJ already had a full plate in front of him as Rachel poured herself a giant brandy snifter of wine. Raiding the ill-gotten gains of Carson Boyet was still an incredible pleasure.

"You could just drink out of the bottle at that rate." Cade fake-tutted as he grabbed an empty plate and set to work on the spread.

"Yours is over there," she said, settling down into the chair next to LJ. Her hair fell in silver-flecked red waves down past her ears. It was as though the serious injuries she sustained had finally broken Rachel's agelessness. The scars could barely be seen—just a few puckered pink corners from the neckline of her oversized white sweater. She moved a little slower, slept a little longer—all overseen by LJ, who divided his time between the endless laptops and monitors and hard drives in the office and making sure Rachel was okay.

Nox would never trust her 100 percent, but he realized he didn't have to.

"You're practically a redneck. My brother is rubbing off on you," Cade said, taking a seat across from her.

A snort from LJ got Rachel's attention.

"Wellll, truth be told, every chance I—"

Her gaze narrowed. "Whatever you're thinking of saying next, please don't."

Cade dug his fork into a mound of macaroni and cheese and made a face.

"Yes, please don't."

LJ snickered, wiped his mouth on a dove gray damask napkin, and leaned over to kiss Rachel's cheek as she flushed with embarrassment or maybe delight.

Nox walked into the kitchen, following the sounds of classical music and the clash of pots and pans. The enormous gourmet kitchen looked like a cooking cyclone had blown through, dirtying everything and laying it haphazardly in the sink and the open dishwasher.

In the middle of the chaos? Sam, in a red-stained T-shirt and flour-coated jeans, struggling to take a giant lasagna from the oven.

"You got that?" Nox asked, hurrying to grab a stray oven mitt from the counter.

"Yeah," Sam huffed out as he dropped the tray on a precious bit of free counter space.

Nox closed the oven door.

"Are we expecting an army or two?" He tried to sound lighthearted. "I thought Mason was just having a chat with Alec at One Police Plaza, not inviting the entire force back for lunch."

Sam turned around, his mouth drawn into a frown. "Don't joke."

"It'll be fine."

"They're corrupt! You know that. And Mason...."

"Mason was cleared of all charges. He's walking in there with the Feds having his back," Nox said gently. "He'll get his job back, particularly now that the federal government is overseeing the force."

Sam's lower lip quivered. "That's what I'm afraid of."

"Listen, I know you're worried, but Mason is a good man and a great cop. He's exactly the kind of person they're going to need."

Nox heard the smooth patter of his voice, the con-man sell—and so did Sam, because his eyebrows did a little dance above his new black-rimmed glasses.

"Seriously?"

"It's true. And maybe we can use him for intel...."

Sam threw a potholder at his head.

They stayed in the kitchen, eating the lasagna right out of the pan with their forks and splitting a bottle of beer. It felt like old times, but they weren't rationing beans out of a can, and Nox had finally accepted that his little boy was all grown up.

Sam talked about what to do next. He had a brand new and official birth certificate and social security number, thanks to Alec. That meant school or a job, though Nox tried to downplay the latter.

"You can work for me," Nox said. "I'll pay you good money to keep us in pasta and cheese."

"Gee, that doesn't sound like you keeping an eye on me or anything," Sam groused.

"I let you have your own apartment," Nox pointed out and then took the last swig of beer in the bottle.

"I'm across the hall."

"And I pretend not to notice Mason lives there too."

Sam blushed and hopped off the counter to avoid his father's gaze. "It's safer. He's like… a roommate."

"Uh-huh," Nox teased gently. He tossed the empty bottle into the bin.

The doorbell rang across the apartment, pausing the lighthearted mood. Nox walked quickly out of the kitchen, through the dining room, and into the living room, Cade at his heels.

A quick double knock had them standing down before they reached the door.

"Someone get Mason a key," Nox yelled over his shoulder as he reholstered his gun and Cade bypassed him to open the front door.

Mason Todd—back in dress blues—had a stern look on his face.

"You need to check who's on the other side before you open the door," he began.

Cade steered Nox back into the dining room so Mason and Sam could kiss in peace in the foyer.

One easily made out a "You look so hot" and a lot of sucking noises, so Cade shoved Nox into a chair and handed him a bowl of roast chicken and potatoes.

"Eat your feelings," he said. Then he settled down on Nox's lap.

It didn't take long for the young lovers to join the party, which seemed to unhitch Nox's jaw. They sat down, chairs touching, as Mason complimented Sam on each dish without even taking a taste. Cade caught Rachel's eye—she made a gag face right before she accepted a forkful of pot roast from his brother.

This penthouse of sin and corruption now looked like a honeymoon hotel.

"So," Nox said loudly, cutting through the chatter. "Mason seems to have his old job back—congratulations." Everyone raised a glass—water, beer, Rachel a second snifter of wine—as the young cop ducked his head, clearly pleased with the attention. Cade watched Sam force a smile and pat Mason's knee.

He clearly wasn't pleased, but the high road was a good choice.

"Mason's working. Rachel and LJ are at your beck and call." Cade sighed and leaned against Nox's strong body. "That just leaves me and Sam."

"Besides feeding all you people, I'm going to take some classes online," Sam said. "Maybe you can do that too."

Cade made a face, lulled by the gentle circles Nox was rubbing into his back. "No thanks. To both cooking and studying."

"And whoring is out, I assume," Rachel piped up.

"Yes, whoring is out." Cade resisted the urge to stick his tongue out at her. "Though...." He stopped himself. It was a thought kicking around in his head, one he hadn't voiced just yet.

"Though?" Nox asked in full growl.

"There's a lot of people out of work with the casinos closing down. Tourism is all this place has." Cade looked at Rachel and then Nox. "Damian wants to make the Flamingo legitimate and... maybe we can help him."

Silence filled the dining room. Everyone looked thoughtful—although Nox remained unreadable as ever. At least his face; his gentle touches didn't abate, and Cade took comfort in that.

"That might be a good idea, actually," Nox said finally, startling everyone, including Cade.

"We have the money," LJ chimed in. "I mean, you have the money."

"*We* have the money," Nox repeated, a faint smile dawning. "Alec's cleared the Flamingo and Damian, so he's pretty much the only person operating without an investigation hanging over his head."

"As the casinos are cleared out of the undesirable element, buyers are going to show up." Rachel put her glass down and leaned her elbows on the table. "They're not all going to be good guys like us," she said dryly. "It's just a matter of time before bad actors with a lot of capital make offers no one can refuse."

Cade plucked at Nox's sleeve, and their eyes finally met in a direct gaze. He saw a sudden willingness, like Nox had opened a door or a window. He saw approval of the idea.

He saw a keen mind finding potential in the offering.

"Put people to work," Cade said. "Start the ball rolling on legit businesses." He gave Nox a wink. "Keep an eye on things. Wait to see who walks through the door and tries to offer protection. Or anything else… unseemly."

LJ cackled with delight. "A giant shiny sting operation."

A little thrill ran through Cade's body. Nox's grin was gorgeous. The idea was fucking genius, and the room suddenly hummed with potential. Only Sam had a furrow between his brows as he contemplated the lot of them.

"Adrenaline junkies," he muttered as Mason dropped a kiss on his cheek. "You're all actually crazy. So we have this money now and resources and… power. What happens if it makes *us* corrupt? That seems to be what this place does to people!"

"Rachel is our canary in the evil coal mine," Cade said, leaning back in his chair. "If she starts looking too happy, we'll renounce the money and move back to South Carolina." He winked at Sam. "Become farmers. Find Jesus."

Sam didn't look convinced. "It was an actual question."

"You're right. It's easy to take what we have right now, the position we're in, and get some revenge," Nox said eventually. His gaze snapped to Rachel. "I'm not going to lie, Sam. That's a powerful urge."

The good humor of the room, the smiles, muted.

"But I don't think it's a good enough reason to run away. We have the resources to fix some of what's wrong in this city," he went on. "We have the desire to. I think that's worth taking a little risk."

Cade had honestly never loved him more.

"Plus, we have Rachel as our barometer of evil," Nox deadpanned.

"I've turned over a new leaf," she said, demure as she sipped some of her wine.

"Not too far over," Cade whispered as he leaned down to kiss Nox. "We're going to need her devious mind."

# CHAPTER FIFTY-FOUR

NOX SLIPPED into his leathers, a swath of moonlight guiding him from the bed to the closet to the door. After an evening of planning that left them all hyped up—and an excited conference call with Damian—the couples had split off into their bedrooms—Nox and Cade in the master, LJ and Rachel in the guest room three doors down, and Mason and Sam to the maid's apartment across the hall.

He wouldn't admit it out loud, but Nox liked his little team close by.

His family.

In the center of the king-size bed, Cade lay on his stomach, watching Nox with keen eyes. Silent, he laid his head on folded arms and didn't speak until Nox pulled the hood up.

"Be careful," he murmured.

"Of course." Nox walked to the edge of the bed and knelt so he could lean over. "Pretty boy."

"You better not use that line on anyone else." Cade lifted his head for a kiss.

Their mouths met, slanted and perfectly fitting together like two puzzle pieces clicking. Nox let the taste of Cade's tongue, the mint of his mouthwash, carry him away for a delicious second before he reluctantly pulled away.

"I'll be back in about two hours. Maybe three," Nox promised, even as Cade smirked.

"Right. I'm not waiting up." Cade dropped his head back down, and Nox took in the perfection that was this man—this cocky kid with the beautiful face who had his back and his heart safely tucked in his hand. "Maybe I'll make you pancakes in the morning. Maybe."

"Maybe I'll bring you breakfast in bed." Nox took the Sig from the top drawer of his nightstand, leaving behind the matching one for Cade.

"This fantasy is lovely, but we both know that means you'll just make coffee." Cade stretched and snuggled back under the sheet. "Go. Patrol the city. Scare people shitless. Save the innocent. Don't get caught."

Gun tucked under his hoodie in his waistband, gloves on, Nox turned to go, but something made him pause at the doorway.

Cade's adoring gaze hadn't wavered.

"I love you," Cade said matter-of-factly.

"I love you too," Nox responded, still quiet and shy in volume but heartfelt. And the way Cade smiled reinforced that.

He took the back stairs down twenty-five floors to the freight elevator, then to the parking garage below the building. Out the side door and into the alley, where darkness swallowed him up.

The Vigilante had work to do.

# EPILOGUE

SENATOR LOUIS Freck sat in his office long after his staff had gone home for the weekend. He'd kept a smile on his face for the past week as everyone in the state capitol back-slapped themselves over the "successful raid" in New York City. He gave interviews to the press, serious and solemn as he talked about his beloved city, his outrage over the neglect shown, and how healing could begin.

Now he was free of attention and scrutiny and could be fucking furious.

Resting his head in his hands, Louis stared at his blotter, red spots flickering in his gaze. Millicent would tell him his blood pressure was too high, to breathe, to relax, but really, what he wanted to do was bring Carson Boyet back from the dead and strangle him.

A perfectly articulated plan, with benefits for everyone involved, giving Carson a chance to disappear into the ether with his money, blown to hell.

Louis felt the outrage in his throat, cutting off his oxygen. His face burned, temples throbbing to a wild beat.

Now he had to clean up Carson's mess, salvage what he could.

The Dead Bolt lab was destroyed.

His inside person was dead.

Two truckloads of the stuff were in the wind.

He'd sent some people to track Mitzie down, but she had a head start and enough money to have him chasing his tail for months.

Right now, New York was an exposed wound—exposed to the world, the top story on every cable news show. *How could we let it get this bad?* How had corruption destroyed a city as violently as the weather that victimized it years before?

Louis saw his picture, clips of him running for mayor more than a decade ago, in every one of those stories. At one point he'd capitalized upon saving the city, and now he was going to do it again, all the way to the White House.

Once upon a time, Louis worked for the mayor. Once upon a time, Louis worked for Mr. Smith. And Carson Boyet. Now he sat, respectable and respected, in Albany, working his ass off to make friends on both sides of the aisle. Keep his public persona squeaky clean. Beautiful Millicent, Veronica and Louis Jr. earnest-faced elementary school students. Any evidence of his past deeds swept away with bribes and destruction of private property.

Carson was supposed to finish the job, wipe the slate entirely clean. Reduce the city to rubble while Louis pocketed Dead Bolt's chemical recipe. The final players in this little melodrama would be dead—real or otherwise—and Senator Freck would sweep back into the city its hero once again. Rebuild, rebrand, bring the city back from the dead, truly.

See what he could do? He could do that for the whole county.

His people were already on it, imagining the ads, the walk-throughs of Louis surveying the smoking ruins in a hardhat, nodding earnestly, vowing to bring the city back better than ever.

Once upon a time, Louis's backers were thieves and racketeers. Now they were a political party, corporations and household names.

This time, Louis didn't work for anyone.

The phone rang on Louis's desk, startling him. He imagined it was Millicent, wondering where he was, but the number set him straight.

He answered with a snarl.

"What?"

"A greeting that I don't appreciate," the voice said on the other side of the line. A thread of smugness set Louis's teeth on edge.

"Do you have news I want to hear?"

"Nothing's changed here. The police and the mayor's office are smiling to the Feds' faces but shredding paper and deleting hard drives as we speak."

"I don't care. Have you found her?"

"No." The voice gave a chuckle. "And I don't imagine I will."

"I want those drugs."

"I know, I know." There was a long pause, and Louis fought the urge to hang up. "But I found a surprise for you, sent it to your apartment. Not the one with lovely Millicent, of course...."

Louis sat up straight. "What are you talking about?"

"A package, an… act of good faith. I will continue my work for you, and you'll be endlessly grateful for what I sent you."

Louis's heart beat faster. "You found some?"

"Before the cops destroyed it. You're welcome."

Everything turned upside down, and Louis stood up, his body vibrating with excitement. He'd pick up the package from Victoria's, get it to the lab at his family's pharmaceutical company….

"Louis? My generosity is not free."

Back to reality. "Fine, whatever you want." Louis was going to be richer than a king, and president—what did he care?

"Well, how accommodating, Louis, thank you. I'll be in touch." The phone line disconnected.

Louis let out a whoop, an actual sound of joy, because God, yes. Yes. Reverse engineering would take longer, but Dead Bolt would be his and his alone—at least once he ran down Mitzie and relieved her of her drugs. And her heart.

The pharmaceutical market had no idea the miracle he was going to unleash.

And once he was the savior of not just New York City but the entire country, Louis would step into the highest seat of power in the land.

Whistling, Louis made two calls. One to Millicent, letting her know he'd be a little bit later and not to hold dinner.

The second was quick and simple.

"Keep an eye on them, especially Nox Boyet. I don't want any more surprises."

The Vigilante and his team will return.

Read how the series started

THE VIGILANTE:
WHO KNOWS
THE
STORM

TERE MICHAELS

The Vigilante: Book One

In a dystopian near future, New York City has become the epicenter of decadence—gambling, the flesh trade, a playground for the wealthy. And underneath? Crime, fueled by "Dead Bolt," a destructive designer drug. This New City is where Nox Boyet leads a double life. At night, he is the Vigilante, struggling to keep the streets safe for citizens abandoned by the corrupt government and police. During the day, he works in construction and does his best to raise his adopted teenaged son, Sam.

A mysterious letter addressed to Sam brings Nox in direct contact with "model" Cade Creel, a high-end prostitute working at the Iron Butterfly Casino. Suspicion gives way to an intense attraction as dark figures from Nox's past and the mysterious peddlers of Dead Bolt begin to descend—and put all their lives in danger. When things spin out of control, Cade is the only person Nox can trust to help him save Sam.

www.dreamspinnerpress.com

# PROLOGUE

New York City
*Before*

## SEPTEMBER

*NOX BOYET is fifteen and his only problems in the world are his upcoming physics test and the tiny shorts Patrick Mullens insists on wearing to lacrosse practice every damn day.*

*His father is traveling to parts unknown—again. He talks to the man's assistant more than he talks to his father, by a ratio of about ten to one. His mother has been at the hospital for four months due to "exhaustion"—again. Exhaustion means relapse and hospital means sanitarium, and he stopped needing codes when he was ten. Mrs. Grimes from across the street checks in on him every day, brings leftovers from the family dinners, and Nox uses the emergency credit card to eat a lot of pizza.*

*Then it starts raining.*

## OCTOBER

*NOX BOYET is a few weeks away from turning sixteen. He desperately wants two things: for Patrick Mullens to stop being a cock tease (five minutes into a mutual hand job in the shower stall after practice and suddenly he remembered a piano lesson? Bullshit.) and for his father to let him have the old Beemer they leave at the house upstate.*

*He's getting A's in everything at Trinity, and the headmaster referred to him as a "fine young man, like your father" after assembly. He'd tell his parents this in another attempt to get the Beemer, but his father hasn't been home in over a month. His mother? Five.*

*Mrs. Grimes said the LaMontes are leaving Manhattan because of the weather. She's staying to "watch the house," and Nox is secretly glad.*

*And it hasn't stopped raining for almost three weeks.*

## NOVEMBER

*NOX BOYET is in hell.*

*Most of the neighborhood is deserted. Residents have fled for drier climes—some have moved temporarily to winter bungalows and summer residences outside the city. Every day there's another solemn story of people drowning and residents of the city and outlying areas being rescued by boaters. The subways and trains aren't running due to flooding. The tunnels in and out of the city are closed. Buildings have collapsed under the strain of the torrential downpours and ministorms sweeping in from the ocean. Nowhere on the island seems safe—and no one is making ark jokes anymore.*

*Mrs. Grimes has her nephew Roy staying with her at the house "for protection." She still comes across the street, splashing through the muddy river that is Ninety-Second Street, to check on him. He wants to tell her it's okay and he's fine, but honestly—he's not.*

*Trinity, like all the other schools in Manhattan, has cancelled classes. Most of his friends have left the city with their families. Patrick called him twenty minutes ago to say they're going to stay with his grandmother in Chicago. There are rumors the bridges will be shut down, like the tunnels already have. He's trying to be brave, but his father's assistant says she can't reach him and the lady who answers the phone at his mother's hospital says she isn't taking calls. She's in "isolation."*

*So is he.*

*He stays in his room, trying not to jump at every little sound. The power has been going on and off for almost two weeks, and if it weren't for all the crazy survivalist stuff his mother has hoarded in the basement, things would be way worse. He's never been so grateful for her paranoia and his father's black AmEx.*

*He's only a kid and he's not ready for this much responsibility.*

*On his sixteenth birthday, a policeman comes to the door as National Guardsmen roll down the street in jeeps, using a loudspeaker to tell people to be prepared to evacuate. He asks if Nox's mother is home, or another adult, but no, Nox is alone.*

*Very alone.*

*The policeman tells him he's very sorry, but Nox's father is dead. His body was found at his office building near the stock exchange—a mugging, most likely. His assistant identified the body.*

*So sorry for his loss.*

*Nox doesn't cry. He walks around the house in a fog, the loudspeaker announcements of urgency fading to background noise. His father is dead. His mother is lost in a land of her own.*

*There are no grandparents, no aunts or uncles. All of the people considered "family friends" have fled, and really, it was mostly social, the connection from the Boyets to the movers and shakers of old money on the Upper West Side. They were hidden away in this house, shamed by his mother's illness and his father's workaholic ways.*

*He has no one.*

*A DAY later, the National Guard goes door to door telling people they have to evacuate in twelve hours. The ferries will be departing from the Seventy-Ninth Street Boat Basin. Nox, curled up on his bed, looking at pictures of his mother on the wall, makes a decision.*

*He fills his waterproof backpack with some food and water and all the money he can find in the house. He layers on the ski clothes he got last Christmas and prints out a map that will direct him all the way up to Inwood, where his mother's sanitarium, Morningside, is.*

*He's going to get her, and then they're getting the hell out of Manhattan.*

HE HAD no idea what he was walking into—and no idea he wasn't coming back.

*Now*

SOMETIMES PATROL took Nox down past what used to be the Seventy-Ninth Street Boat Basin on the West Side. There was a memorial to the people who died when the ferries sank on Evacuation Day—a block of stone engraved with 1,957 names, the date. "Unknowns" tacked on the bottom for those who were never identified brought the number well over 2000. No bother of sentiment, no solemn saying emblazoned on a bronze plaque.

Only two names on that list mattered—he knew the location by touch, knew the curve of each hammered-out vowel. They were the reason he couldn't ever leave this place—they were the reason he walked fifty blocks a night to make sure the neighborhood was safe.

There were other memorials, other tributes to those who died during the storms. The floods downtown and on the Island, the fires in the Bronx and Queens, the building collapses on the East Side. But Mayor Freck's legacy was an administration that liked to remind the survivors their loved ones would want them to move on—they would have wanted the city to rise again.

Plaques said, *We remember*. The enormous hotels and casinos that cluttered inhabitable parts of the island said, *We've moved on*.

THE DISTRICT—blocks and blocks of Central Park West, Times Square, and Midtown real estate converted into casinos and hotels, built up and beautifully maintained, with a thriving clientele of wealthy jet-setters and a well-staffed security force that kept it as calm and orderly as a debutante ball. The New City.

After the storms, the city was left a hollow shell. So many uninhabitable buildings, so many residents forced into shelters in New Jersey, Connecticut, even Pennsylvania. Wait for the water to recede, wait for inspectors to check the buildings, wait for insurance companies. Real estate prices went from millions to pennies as abandoned buildings continued to sit dark and empty, molding as months passed with no one to tend to the mess. People, museums, and businesses relocated, with vague talks of "going back" when things got fixed.

When the federal money was slow to trickle in, the "going back" became "moving away permanently." With no commuters and no tourists, New York was a ghost town within five years of the evacuation. The wealthy business owners and their boards collected insurance checks and moved elsewhere—other states offered incentives to relocating businesses and the bottom line was simple. Cheaper to be elsewhere, cheaper than trying to rebuild. Cheaper to take tax breaks and move the headquarters of your company to Chicago or Dallas. Even better, most of your employees followed, because there wasn't anything to tie them to a rapidly declining city.

The middle and lower classes just couldn't survive. Many stayed as long as they could but in the end, six years after the storms, the population of New York dwindled to the lowest numbers since the turn of the century.

Three years later, as the remaining citizens complained of war-zone-like conditions and the rest of the country wondered why nothing was being done besides organized looting—Broadway in Las Vegas, museums around the world dividing up the great works of art, pro sports teams lured to nearby cities—a mayoral candidate named Louis Freck swept in like Hannibal on the elephant's back.

He demanded more aid from the federal government while at the same time preaching the resiliency of New Yorkers. He called for a radical plan to save the city: bring money in by lining the streets with gold and hookers.

Oh, he put it in a much nicer way. Playgrounds for the rich and richer. There were dioramas and beautifully rendered sketches for presentations, followed by minimovies and simulations as Freck's popularity grew. Worthless real estate revitalized by investment—all from the pockets of developers, not the citizens. The desperate New Yorkers attended rallies, cheering at the chance to have some hope. Rebuild the industry and the rest of the city would grow around it.

Freck won. No one even remembered who ran against him.

Things happened quickly after that. Dump trucks and backhoes from private companies cleared away the rubble; construction cranes once against dotted the streets. After two years, the skyline began to rise again.

Freck made an impassioned plea, and legalized gambling came to Manhattan Island.

Casinos.

Luxury hotels.

Boutiques.

Five-star restaurants.

The people in the outer neighborhoods waited for the trickle-down effect as time ticked by. One year, two years. Three years—so many promises, but the District needed time to grow, to make back their investments. It would happen—just be patient. Surely all of the money being poured into the District by visitors—surely it would reach their desperately empty pockets. Jobs would be plentiful.

Freck kept a few promises. He left some neighborhoods alone, zoned for residential rather than commercial use. They had power, fresh water. Crews removed debris from roadways, sometimes even repaved. A newly visible police force—as in, people actually saw black-and-whites cruising the streets.

It was a start, so no one questioned the curfew in the Old City. And now? Seventeen years since the Evacuation? No one bothered to complain about it. They'd grown used to the restrictions, the "doing without"—grown accustomed to the division of the city and abandoned their hopes that one day the largesse of the District would visit them as well.

Nox walked through Old Riverside Park, crossing up toward Ninety-First Street as he headed home. It was quiet. Curfew kept citizens inside after dark; the police didn't bother to patrol this far north, and the dealers generally stayed downtown near the underground clubs.

Generally.

These days they were growing bolder. Money was finally trickling out of the District, as whores and gambling bored the tourists after a while, and the "classy" joints couldn't keep patrons entirely satisfied. Visitors wanted something else, something thrilling and dangerous. Something they couldn't get anywhere else.

The secret of Dead Bolt: You could only get it here. A few hits of the pool-blue powder and the euphoria beat anything sold in those shiny casinos.

The movement of crime into residential areas worried him. For years he'd taken care of the stray criminal that ventured into his territory. He kept an eye on the street trade—he knew who had which neighborhood in their sights, which of the street gangs that had popped up over the years were an actual threat and which were just overgrown clubs for the bored and underemployed. The visitors could take care of themselves—he didn't care what they stuck into their veins or how many of them kicked it in alleys downtown. They were part of the problem, bankrolling the festering wound of corruption strangling his city.

Nothing would change so long as more money could be made on strangers with itches to scratch than on those carving out livings amongst the ruins.

THE COLD October air smelled like more snow—winter seemed to start earlier and earlier with each passing year, a double-edged sword of less crime and less food mixing together in five months of desperation. Junkies and dealers, workers and citizens, all trapped inside and trying to survive until spring.

It was crazy to stay—he knew that. It was just… still home to the ones who couldn't force themselves to leave. They'd survived the hell of the Storms; they'd made it when so many others perished. Maybe it was a badge of honor to scrape out an existence here.

He was a different story.

Where would he go? There were no fresh starts in the world for him. If he left the city, he'd leave behind all the tricks and lies he used to stay hidden. Here, money talked and laws were loose—he could play the system on the island. Off it? He'd be just another penniless drifter with no education, no plan, no real identity.

So he stayed. And he wondered if one day this city would be anything like the one he remembered.

A few blocks from home, movement caught his eye: two dark shadows hovering in the doorway of a long-abandoned store near the corner. A sliver of moonlight illuminated only their general shapes—men, most likely, darting together and pulling away but too tense, too sharp for it to be a romantic encounter.

A deal.

He blended with the darkness, stealthy and slow as he gained ground on the spot of transaction. The crisp, cold air was still, the icy sting pulling into his lungs with every breath. His clothes kept him warm; the black color let him blend into the shadows. The breathable fabric across the lower half of his face left him anonymous. A blackjack in his hand kept him safe.

Murmurings of the conversation caught his ears. He paused, listened.

*How much can you get me tomorrow?*

*A pound.*

He ducked and dodged the piles of bricks—buildings had come down on this street, destroyed by storms and fire, ignored by the city—until he reached the doorway one away from theirs.

Black-gloved hand tight on the weapon, breath held, eyes steady.

He exhaled and stepped out into the open.

They were unprepared for him. One lethargic and drunk on his own smug power—no police, people hidden away, no one to challenge him. The other's brain a mess from Dead Bolt and neglect, no idea how to defend himself.

It was over in a few seconds; the dealer lay unconscious, the junkie cowering in the corner.

"Stay out of my neighborhood," he said simply. He took the bag of poison and dumped it out into the dirty, slushy snow that lingered from the last storm. With the heel of his boot, he crushed it down to unusable dust. "If I see you here again, I'll kill you," he said, quieter now.

The man nodded, frantic and jerky in his movements.

He searched the dealer, taking his gun, credit cards, and identification pass before rolling him onto his back. A check of his pulse—alive and well—reassured him that his work was almost done.

His gaze on the wide-eyed junkie, he tugged the dealer's right arm away from his body until it was straight. Unfurled the fingers. A perfect target.

This was his signature, how they knew he meant business. He raised his foot, then brought it down onto the man's palm with his full weight behind it.

The dealer jolted awake, then passed out again from the pain.

Practice meant he knew exactly where to connect to break bones.

The junkie swallowed a scream; he scrambled away, tripping and falling in his haste.

Spoils in his pocket—and no backward glance—he continued his journey home.

At the corner of his block, he paused. Once upon a time it had been prime real estate—million-dollar brownstones, homes of the old moneyed elite who sent their children to Trinity, Dalton, or Spence. Pure class.

His mother's family had roots in the city that went back to when it was New Amsterdam. His father's people came later but in time to fight in the Revolutionary War.

He was a child of this city, generations of architects and bankers who believed this to be their legacy to the world.

They would hate it now.

The shadows cloaked his path to the doorway. Inside lay the world of another man, a man who worked a job and was responsible for another life, who paid his bills and lent a hand when his neighbors asked. He kept a low profile because he—more than anyone—knew that danger lay everywhere. And in everyone.

Nox dropped the gun down into an open grate; below, he could hear the rush of water that flowed under the city. Sewers, long-abandoned subway tunnels—the water lapped at the shores of Manhattan Island and crept up underneath them, a few more inches every year. The water would sweep the gun out to the Hudson. The credit cards followed, disappearing into the darkness.

The identification pass might get him into places he needed to be—that he kept.

When his knees finally creaked under the pressure, he stood up slowly, working out the kinks in his back as he twisted side to side. He had three hours before the alarm would sound on his other life—the Vigilante's night was over, and it was time to go home.

TERE MICHAELS unofficially began her writing career at the age of four when she learned that people got paid to write stories. It seemed the most perfect and logical job in the world, and after that, her path was never in question.

(The romance writer part was written in the stars—she was born on Valentine's Day.)

She writes happily ever afters in the big city—with heaps of snark, angst, and humor. Her focus is on characters and all the ridiculous ways they trip through life and love. She has written fifteen books including her popular Faith, Love & Devotion series and the multilayered dystopian saga The Vigilante.

Nothing makes her happier than knowing she made a reader laugh or smile or cry. It's her reason for sharing her work with people. She loves hearing from fans and fellow writers and is always available for speaking engagements, visits, and workshops.

Find her at:
Website: www.teremichaels.com
Facebook: www.facebook.com/tere.michaels.9
Instagram: https://www.instagram.com/teremichaels

# THE VIGILANTE:
# WHO KNOWS
# THE
# DARK

## TERE MICHAELS

The Vigilante: Book Two

A wanted man after the destruction of the Iron Butterfly Casino, Nox Boyet must flee the island of Manhattan—the only home he's ever known. Together with Cade, Sam, and the rest of their ragtag group, Nox must find a place to hide from the District Police and the violent group of unknown drug dealers on his tail.

The solution—the Creel family farm in South Carolina.

But home isn't quite sweet for Cade, the prodigal son. As Cade struggles with his own secrets, shadows of the past threaten not only Nox's life, but his relationship with his son, Sam.

Nox knows there will never be peace unless he finds the answers to all his questions—and the answers lie back on the island. Cade and the others must choose their paths—find safety or follow the Vigilante into the darkness of the city? The city where Nox will come face-to-face with the past.

# www.dreamspinnerpress.com

# TERE MICHAELS

# Faith & Fidelity

Faith, Love, & Devotion: Book One

Reeling from the recent death of his wife, police officer Evan Cerelli looks at his four children and can only see how he fails them. His loving wife was the caretaker and nurturer, and now the single father feels himself being crushed by the pain of loss and the heavy responsibility of raising his kids.

At the urging of his partner, Evan celebrates a coworker's retirement and meets disgraced former cop turned security consultant Matt Haight. A friendship born out of loneliness and the solace of the bottle turns out to be exactly what they both need.

The past year has been a slow death for Matt Haight. Ostracized from his beloved police force, facing middle age and perpetual loneliness, Matt sees only a black hole where his future should be. When he discovers another lost soul in Evan, some of the pieces he thought he lost start to fall back in place. Their friendship turns into something deeper, but love is the last thing either man expected, and both of them struggle to reconcile their new and overwhelming feelin

# www.dreamspinnerpress.com

# TERE MICHAELS

# Love &
# Loyalty

FAITH, LOVE, & DEVOTION: BOOK TWO

Faith, Love, & Devotion: Book Two

Seattle Homicide Detective Jim Shea never takes work home with him—until now. A judge banged his gavel, declared a defendant not guilty, and laid waste to a family. The emotional fallout of the trial leaves Jim vulnerable and duty-bound to the victim's dying father.

It's that man's story that screenwriter Griffin Drake and his best friend, actress Daisy Baylor, see as their ticket out of action blockbusters and into more serious fare. But to get the juicy details, Griffin needs to win over the stoic and protective Detective Shea. Their attraction is immediate, and Daisy encourages Griffin to use it to their advantage: secure the man, secure the story. Neither man has had much luck when it comes to love, and when their one night together evolves into a long weekend of rapidly intensifying feelings, both Griffin's fierce loyalty to Daisy and his very career is put to the test.

Because the more Griffin is drawn into a new life with Jim, the more his Hollywood life falls apart. Secrets and broken trust threaten Griffin's relationships, and he'll have to choose between telling the truth or writing a Hollywood ending.

# www.dreamspinnerpress.com

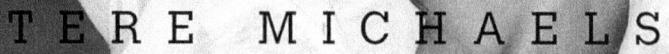

# TERE MICHAELS

# Duty
# Devotion

## FAITH, LOVE, & DEVOTION: BOOK THREE

Faith, Love, & Devotion: Book Three

A year after deciding to share their lives, Matt and Evan are working on their happily ever after—which isn't as easy as it looks. As life settles down into a routine, Matt finds happiness in his role as the ideal househusband of Queens, New York, but he worries about Evan's continued workaholic—and emotionally avoidant—ways. Trying to juggle his evolving relationship with Evan and his children, Matt turns to his friend, former Seattle Homicide Detective Jim Shea.

The continued friendship between Matt and Jim is a thorn in Evan's side. Jealous and uncomfortable with imagining their brief affair, Evan struggles to come to terms with what being in a committed relationship with a man means, and the implications about his love for his deceased wife, the impact on his children, and how other people will view him. His turmoil threatens his relationship with Matt, who worries that Evan will once again chose a life without him. But now, the stakes are much higher.

# www.dreamspinnerpress.com

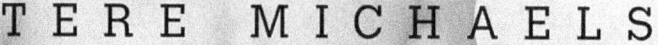

# TERE MICHAELS

# Cherish & Blessed

**FAITH, LOVE, & DEVOTION: BOOKS FOUR & FIVE**

Faith, Love, & Devotion: Books Four and Five

*Cherish*

After several years of happy coupledom, Matt and Evan can relax in the knowledge that their little family has survived the worst of it. The two older girls are away at college, the twins have yet to fully hit teen angst, Matt is doing well with his part time security consulting, and Evan is about to be promoted to captain—it seems like things are calm and bright.

Until they aren't.

As the holidays approach, Evan and Matt get a shock no parent is ever prepared for: feisty Miranda, Evan's eldest, has a new boyfriend, Kent, and they are talking marriage after just three months together. In fact, Miranda wants to bring him to Thanksgiving dinner—along with his parents, Blake and Cornelia.

*Blessed*

Lives are in transition as everyone gathers at the stunning Hamptons beach home of Daisy and Bennett to celebrate the christening of their new baby. Griffin and Jim—secretly growing tired of their rootless lifestyle—are in a rocky spot in their relationship. And as the godfather, Griffin finds himself yearning for something he's sure Jim won't be interested in.

Fatherhood.

Matt and Evan are looking to reconnect during the long weekend, as their respective careers pull them in separate directions. With less time spent together, Evan grows concerned about what will happen when the last two kids leave the nest.

# www.dreamspinnerpress.com